BLACKSHIRT MASQUERADE

BLACKSHIRT MASQUERADE

AN
AGENTS OF ROOM Z
NOVEL

JASON MONAGHAN

First published by Level Best Books/Historia 2022

Author Photo Credit: Alice Turian

First edition

ISBN: 978-1-68512-096-2

This book was professionally typeset on Reedsy.
Find out more at reedsy.com

To Dea

Prologue

Action

Expect trouble, they said. Within the hour I could be facing a mob armed with bricks, broken bottles, and any weapon they could find, all fired up with the zeal to grind my face into the tarmac of London's streets.

Observe, listen and report had been the brief. I told my newly made comrades that I was a writer, but what I aimed to write was the epitaph of the British Union of Fascists. Donning one of their collarless black shirts had seemed a shortcut to my objective, but on that sunny Saturday morning, it felt more like a shortcut to losing an eye.

One of the men seated opposite me in the furniture van wore an eyepatch, just to emphasize my fears. Facing down trouble was routine for a Blackshirt, and this man had already paid a price for his support for fascism. Twenty of us bumped across London in the back of the old windowless van, hanging onto strops or sitting on crates. I did not say much to the other men as this was all new to me and I did not share their excitement at the prospect of going boot-to-boot with a horde of socialists.

The rally was in the north of Kensington, at the interface of middle-class and working-class London, where shopkeepers, publicans, and small business owners struggled against the lack of money in their customers' pockets. We dismounted on Kensington High Street some way short of the growing anti-fascist demonstration and a police sergeant directed us to take a back-street route on foot to reach our destination. The council had suddenly reversed its permission for the BUF to meet in the Town Hall, so the organizers had hurriedly erected a makeshift podium where a street market normally stood.

I was unsettled how good it felt to be back in uniform, even this all-black outfit, marching the streets of the capital. Other men in the squad were ex-army and clearly enjoyed having a sense of purpose once more, replacing loyalty for King and Country with devotion to Leader and Party. Our squad marched smartly into position at the far end of the street and formed up facing a line of policemen. The copper straight opposite me shook his head and muttered to a colleague.

Defence Force Blackshirts almost outnumbered the civilians we'd come to protect. Perhaps moving the venue at the last minute had simply confused people, or perhaps the critics were right and Sir Oswald Mosley's movement was on the decline. My mission could quickly be over.

A scattering of anti-fascists beyond the police cordon jeered at our arrival. At the command we stood 'at ease', not at ease at all, waiting for a fight that surely would come. My pulse rose. A hundred yards back down towards the High Street stood a second line of Blackshirts, then a heavier police cordon of perhaps fifty officers. Beyond them, a trade union flag waved like a battle ensign rallying socialist demonstrators hell-bent on denying the Leader his right to speak.

The Leader had not yet arrived.

'Where's Mosley?' hissed Julian. Boy-faced Julian Thring was the squad leader, and a young man of interest to me as his father was a man of particular interest to the Security Service.

'He should be here by now,' Julian continued. 'I hope the reds haven't managed to stop him.'

The reds would surely try. It was only a matter of time before the missiles would start to sail over the police cordon and men would burst through to bring battle to London's streets yet again. The crowd was finally building in numbers as people found ways to slip past the demonstrators or simply brave their way through. A parade of women in uniform marched in via the side street opposite the podium, led by a banner and a little band. I spotted one figure in the lead group, tall and straight-backed as she marched closer. Did I imagine she glanced my way? At least there was one person in this whole pantomime worth caring about, and I filled the tense waiting time by using my rusty officer training to assess where the biggest threats lay.

At our end of the market street, at least, the demonstrators were few in number, and I couldn't see anything to suggest they were organizing an assault on the police line. Just two dozen policemen and a parked police Wolseley blocked the road before us, but the danger did not come from that direction.

Only a thin screen of Blackshirts and a handful of coppers covered the side street that came in at right angles. It looked like an open door, and I could almost feel the draught.

What puzzled me was that demonstrators in their hundreds should have been here by now – trade unionists, Labour party members, communists, intellectuals, and maybe even some of those militant Jews I'd heard so much about but never seen. Even the group down the High Street end was not the bubbling mass of outrage that it should be. It was almost as if the mob had been ordered to stay back, stay away. By an unsettling coincidence, the policemen also acted as if they knew this would be so, looking far less nervous than they should be on the cusp of a riot. A pair of them even shared a joke.

Some would say that this is how democracy should work; a peaceful assembly of citizens asserting their political views. Knowing what I did about the BUF and their opponents, I would say that was rot.

In India, my company had a veteran sergeant who claimed to have a sixth sense for danger. Right now he'd be growling, 'It's too quiet.' The high rooftops could be the lips of a canyon on the North-West Frontier, a hundred dark windows could be caves hiding enemies, while alleys the world over can spew a howling mob with clubs and knives at a moment's notice. I'd never found dwelling on the past profitable, but dark memories could not easily be pushed aside.

It's too quiet, the ghost of that sergeant whispered.

Two men dressed as civilians might be detectives, judging by the attention they gave to small details on the ground. I watched them move from one doorway to another, checking, nodding, conferring. It wasn't a riot they feared but something else.

Another man, hook-nosed, stood just beyond the police cordon at our end of the street. He was wearing the flat cap that was close to uniform issue for the working man and sporting what looked like a knitted tie of reddish hue. I'd seen him before, at another rally, before the bricks had started to fly. Hook-nose was standing a little back from his comrades, less restless, *doing nothing.* He wasn't directing the action, he wasn't talking nervously to the next man to bolster his own courage; he was simply standing around with his hands in his jacket pockets. If he was another detective, he was well buried within the socialists.

'I say,' Julian nudged me.

A tramp of feet announced the arrival of the I Squad marching from the side road, menacing in their breeches and high boots with hair cropped short. Normally they provided a bodyguard to the Leader, but his tall, smart frame was still nowhere to be seen. At their head was borne the Union Flag and the fascist standard of rods and axes. Barely visible between their ranks was a woman of matronly build.

'It's just Amelia Symes,' Julian said, clearly disappointed.

We'd had dinner with the prospective BUF candidate for Kensington North the night before. I still felt a little rough. She ascended the platform.

'Attention!'

Every Blackshirt faced the podium and shot his right arm skywards at forty-five degrees. Gathered in front of the speaker, the Women's Section showed far too much enthusiasm, rising almost on tiptoes to thrust up their hands. Civilian members copied the fascist salute raggedly. I clicked my heels and stiffened my arm with the rest, blending in.

I felt idiotic. Then, I experienced a strange sensation of pride. I was no longer the outcast, the coward, the dilettante, the friendless nobody; I was a Blackshirt. When the salute relaxed, whatever stimulant was coursing my veins subsided, common sense returned, and I fell back from broad-chested superman to plain Hugh Clifton once more. I turned my back on the speaker.

'She's on,' Julian urged.

'We're keeping guard.'

'There won't be trouble. We've scared the reds off today.'

'Are you sure? Are you totally sure? We need to be facing the threat, not the cabaret.'

Julian turned reluctantly around and then ordered his squad of a dozen men to turn with him.

'There's nothing happening,' he grumbled. 'We'll miss the speech.'

'We know what she's going to say, we heard it over dinner last night. Peace through a Europe united by fascism.'

We were too far away to stand much chance of hearing what was said, as the council had banned the use of an amplifier. Mrs Symes launched into her speech as loudly as her ample lungs could achieve. Several windows along the street were open, but no heads hung out, no faces showed. Perhaps the neighbours were listening but chose to remain invisible within the shadow of their homes.

'No, you're right.' I turned back so I could watch the audience. Infiltrators could be the main threat, aiming to distract the police just long enough for an attack to be launched by that bigger crowd down the High Street end. The sun shone directly into my eyes and served to make the alleys and windows darker. On the Frontier, high terrain up-sun was where the danger would lie. British soldiers wouldn't look into that glare for more than a moment and so kept their heads down, not spotting the sniper waiting to kill them.

Another sash window slid upwards. The building was deep in shadow against the bright sky, but Mrs Symes was bathed in sunshine.

I almost expected the shot. It cut apart the morning, echoing round and round the buildings until drowned by the screams. First came the shock and the instinct to freeze, then the urge to run. Amid the yells of confusion, I snapped out of the trance.

'There! Up in the window.'

'It missed her, it missed her!' Julian chanted, almost hysterically. The other Blackshirts were fixed to the spot, frightened, undecided, but the Women's Section swarmed to protect the speaker as the rest of the crowd broke up in all directions.

If the sniper fired again, it would be straight into the backs of the women. My response came automatically. 'Come on, you lot!' I broke into a run through the scattering civilians. British officers led from the front and that training was burned into my soul.

The police line remained immobile, constables pointing and shouting, but that police Wolseley roared into motion with bells jangling. A sergeant riding in the passenger seat waved and yelled at Blackshirts to get out of the way. The black car tore past, then screeched around the right-hand corner into the side street opposite the podium. I led the chase after the car, just spotting it taking a wide left turn before vanishing behind the shops where the shots had come from.

Glancing back, I was not alone. A gaggle of Blackshirts followed my lead, and policemen on foot were running behind them. Another shot came from ahead, muffled as if from around that next corner. I began to cough – my injured lung would not permit this pace for long. For a moment I wondered what I was trying to prove but the time to reflect was gone. One of the bolder Blackshirts overtook me to reach that turn first. We rushed around the corner into a dead-end street with the back doors of shops on the left, and a little cobbler's at the far end. The Wolseley was halted, slewed at an angle with its motor still running, its bell still clanging and doors thrown open.

The police sergeant was out of his car, shouting a challenge. Then came another shot and he spun back against the Wolseley, slid down its wing, and fell sideways onto the cobbles. The other Blackshirt skidded to a halt, but I hurtled past him. That car offered the only cover. Staring up at me wide-eyed, the sergeant pressed his left hand against the stain seeping through his uniform, but his right still clasped a revolver.

I ducked down beside the dying man and seized the gun from his limp hand. Two men broke from a doorway to my left, heading for a passage at the end of the back street. One saw me bob up and our eyes met. He stopped and lifted a rifle from beneath his coat, fumbling with its bolt. I levelled the revolver on reflex. One shot straight to the chest threw my target against the brickwork, hat flying and arms splayed. The second man, head down and raincoat flapping, dashed into the passageway.

As the bleeding rifleman slipped to the floor, he let his weapon drop. Coming to rest half-propped against the wall, the man rolled his eyes, panting, gripping his chest. I sprinted across to threaten him with the revolver.

'Don't move or I'll fire again!'

I glanced towards the passageway where a silhouette in hat and raincoat had stopped running. Up came an arm and a pistol aimed my way. Only a lead drainpipe offered cover and I shrank behind it. Another shot cut through the London morning, then another. The passage funnelled the noise forward and the back street's high walls served as an echo chamber as one report mixed with the next, almost masking the sickening *whup* of bullet against flesh and the crack of bone.

I was still alive. I swept the revolver up to fire back, but the killer was gone. Raincoat Man had paused just long enough to shoot his erstwhile colleague twice in the head. The body at my feet would be telling no tales. I could also see the police driver now, lying crumpled and motionless beside his door.

Half a dozen more Blackshirts ran up, shouting angrily after their vanished quarry. Two knelt by the dying police sergeant offering him words of comfort little better than lies, while Julian found the police driver and pronounced him dead. Shocked, scared faces looked for leadership.

'Keep back!' I motioned the unarmed men to stay behind, then cautiously moved into the passageway, revolver first. Somewhere ahead and out of sight, a car door slammed, an engine surged and Raincoat Man made his escape.

It had all been a rush and a blur, noise and terror, but the reality of the past two minutes now struck home. Just three months ago my father had rebuked me as a wastrel, my few remaining friends pitied me, and my sometime wife dismissed me as a coward who would amount to naught. I had no political views, cared nothing for the Leader and his dream of a fascist Britain, yet this is where I found myself.

Returning to the blood-spattered back street, a dozen men stood waiting for me in their fencing-style black shirts, tight belts, black trousers, and boots. As a man they came to attention, clicking heels, saluting stiff-armed, fingers pointing above my head, gleams of admiration in their eyes. An organization priding itself on *Action* had found a new hero.

It had not been part of the plan.

Chapter One

March 1935

'Mr Hugh, your father is looking for you.'

A library is for reading in, preferably undisturbed. I barely glanced towards Hopkins.

'If you found me, he can find me.'

Hopkins showed no reaction. Butlers possess a skill to meet rebukes, irony, sarcasm, and slights with the same expression of polite disinterest. He turned sharply as a voice bellowed his name.

'Hopkins! Is he in there?'

'He is sir.'

A heavy tread approached, and Hopkins discreetly vanished.

'Hugh!'

Dorothy L Sayers and *Murder Must Advertise* would have to wait. I laid the book gently to one side, but my father snatched it up.

'Another detective novel?'

'Elementary, dear Father.'

'You need something to do, my lad. Something more than just wait for me to die.'

'Given that we Cliftons are notoriously long-lived, that isn't my ambition.' At twenty-eight I was half my father's age and born in a different century.

'So, what is your ambition? To sit here and read cheap novels? Drink my whisky—'

Hopkins reappeared at the door. 'Excuse me, sir, but Viscount Wickersley is here.'

'Damn, he's early. Show him to the orangery, Hopkins, and we'll be there in a minute.'

'We?' This was news and deserved proper attention.

'God knows why he wants to see you, but he does.'

I smelt a rat. A whole sewer full of them. 'This isn't something you've arranged? Another family friend taking pity on the black sheep, stray dog, or whatever I've become?'

'Don't get all sorry for yourself. There's plenty of men out there who'd rather be sitting here in the warm reading books instead of breaking their backs with honest work. If you're not going to get off your arse and help with my business, you can at least give Wickersley the time of day. No, it wasn't my idea to bring him up here, if you must know. He telephoned and said he had something to offer you. Honest work, if you can remember what that is.'

As I extracted myself from the leather chair it squeaked to proclaim its own luxury. So now I was off my arse. On better days I knew my father was right about needing to find new purpose, and if nothing else it would be good to see Charles again. I made my way through the house in his wake. My father had bought Moat Hall a decade before when the aristocratic heirs to the ancestral seat had been struck by a double dose of death duties in quick succession. Old money made way for the new.

Freshly repainted, refurnished, and stocked with numerous potted plants, the orangery lent an exotic feel to this corner of Yorkshire. Mines owned by RT Clifton Limited ensured there was no shortage of coal to maintain a temperature more suited to the Mediterranean than northern England in March.

'Charles!' My father greeted Viscount Wickersley, who was well turned out in tweeds. I was conscious that I was informally dressed, even sloppily so, in open-necked shirt, sleeveless sweater, and flannels.

'Reginald.' They shook hands. 'And good to see you again, Hugh.'

I greeted my former comrade. 'Good to see you again. I heard you made major.' Charles had still been a captain when we were in India and had yet to inherit his title. Rank seemed to have added years to him, and inches of height. It was always an odd experience to meet taller men than myself. Clean-cut and Viking blond, Charles must have been six feet four inches tall in his socks.

'Will the viscount be staying overnight?' asked Hopkins.

'Sadly, no, there's a train I must catch at four.'

'Drinks, Hopkins. And hurry those sandwiches along. We don't want our guest to have to eat and run. And we'll have that French white; what's the year, Hugh?'

I shrugged. Labels were unimportant if the wine worked.

'The white, that special one.'

Hopkins recalled the vintage and year precisely, and Father agreed he should fetch that.

'Apologies for being early,' Charles said. 'I managed to catch an earlier train and got ahead of myself.'

'So, choose a chair. Just got them this month, threw out those dreadful old ones we had. Had this whole place done. There's plenty of slack tradesmen to be had when you need them, and I nailed them down to what I was prepared to pay and not a penny more.'

'Actually, Reginald, I'd like to speak to Hugh alone.'

'Oh. I thought you were coming to offer him an honest job.'

'Something like that.'

Father hovered for a few moments more.

'But it is rather private.' It was clear that Charles was not going to expand on the reason for his visit in committee.

Intriguing.

'I'll leave you, then. There should be sandwiches shortly – I'll join you for those, at least. I'll be in my study.'

I waited for my father to leave. 'Take a seat, do.'

Charles chose one of the rattan chairs and ran one hand down the smooth finish of the arms. Hopkins brought in two whiskies, glasses, and a carafe of water with an 'as requested, sir.'

I didn't bother with the water. 'Thank you, Hopkins.'

'Bit early … but it is late afternoon in Rawalpindi,' Charles joked, raising his glass.

'What, it must be over two years now?'

For a few minutes, we filled in the years and talked a little of times past – the good times, ignoring the bad. Charles had been attached to headquarters in Rawalpindi, senior to me in both age and rank, but we shared an interest in books and in the culture of the land we went out to rule. He let his eyes fall on the parkland where spring had not yet arrived this far north and remarked on how remarkably fine the weather had been for his journey. Signaling an end to the casual chat, Charles set down his glass with obvious purpose.

'So, what brings you up here? Was it my father?'

'Indirectly, I bumped into him in London earlier this year – I won't pretend it was by chance. Naturally, we got to talking about you, and how unfairly things have turned out. He wants to see you gainfully employed, and from what he says he has no role for you running his mines and his businesses.'

'He's tried, but I'm not a businessman. And…' It was difficult to explain the distance between us. Success of the father was matched by disappointing failure of the son, and we both missed my mother in ways neither of us could express.

'I know you don't see eye to eye, but your father has worked very hard to get where he is.'

'Fifteen hundred miners have worked very hard to get my father where he is.'

'Do I detect a touch of the socialist about you?'

'Politics don't interest me.'

Charles was eyeing the silver-bound cigarette box on the table.

'Oh, please help yourself.'

He did. 'And you?'

'I've only a lung and a half left. I need all the pure oxygen I can get.'

That thing which was difficult to mention had been mentioned and

Charles exhaled heavily. 'I am sorry, it was rough what happened out in India. A chap would normally get a medal—'

'But I was cashiered. And nobody stood by me, not even you.'

Charles glanced out at the garden again, as if to check that the weather was still fine. 'Hmm, not your regiment's proudest moment. And honestly, the doctors said you were done for. I'm afraid the choice was between a dead man or the son of an earl to carry the can.'

'Except I didn't die, inconveniently for all concerned.'

A moment's pause followed the barb, but Viscount Wickersley had come almost two hundred miles to hold this conversation and was not to be deterred.

'Would you say you still have a love of country, after all you went through? The King, the Empire?'

I weighed this up for a moment. 'It wasn't the King who shot me. And cruel as it was, I perfectly understand the logic of what happened. It's the world we live in. It's the world we were defending.'

'Are defending.'

I shuffled in the rattan chair. 'Do you remember that day we went to dinner with the nawab of wherever? We just ate and ate until we nearly burst. On the way back to the post my horse shied away from something in the road. It was a man, dead; starved to death or diseased. His little dried-up corpse was still there the next day when I led a patrol out. And I could taste that banquet back in my mouth, bitter, acid...'

Charles simply listened, perhaps observing my manner and noting my words. He'd worked in military intelligence on the frontier, keeping eyes on subversives who wanted to see a free India. I'd been seconded for a few months to give me a little experience.

'Another day I was in the bazaar and a woman who can't have been more than a child herself tried to give me her baby son. She said she couldn't feed him anymore, asked me if I would take him and raise him as an Englishman. It seemed comic at the time – we even laughed about it in the mess that night when I was telling the other chaps. "Raise him as an Englishman".' I shook my head. 'As if one day he'd be sipping scotch and looking out contented at his garden.'

'You don't sound like a man with no interest in politics.'

'I've an interest in fairness, in justice. Sorry if that sounds like pompous rot, but I was treated unfairly by the army. It made me see what an unequal world we live in.'

'Do you have any contact with communists?'

'Not unless they work in our pits. And if they do, they keep their politics secret, or my father would have them out on the streets as quick as blinking.'

Charles nodded. 'What do you think of Sir Oswald Mosley?'

'Not a lot. The *Daily Mail* likes him, but I don't often read the *Mail*. Some of my father's friends say he's the answer to the country's woes, but he sounds like just a rabble-rouser. He's not even in Parliament anymore, is he?'

'No, but he's got a following. He's still young for a politician and he could have gone far if he'd stuck with the Tories, or even Labour.'

'But I've been reading that he's finished.'

'Yes, yes, his star has fallen since that riot at Olympia last year. Branches closing, members leaving, and the BBC won't have him on the air. But he's still lunching with the Prince of Wales, popping off to Italy to see Signor Mussolini and sending his mistress to Berlin to meet Herr Hitler. Curious people are asking what he's up to.'

'Curious people such as who?'

He raised his eyebrows and opened his free palm by way of reply.

My glass was already empty, so I reached across to the drinks tray. 'Top-up?'

Charles waved the decanter away.

'I'll just have a small one.' I poured what I told myself was a small one, fast becoming that person my father and wife accused me of being.

'What do you think about the Jews?'

'I knew one or two at University, decent chaps, kept to themselves mostly. And that shoemaker near the college, Manny Crystal. I've bumped into a few antisemites who tell me that Jews are conspiring to take over the world, but I don't believe a word of it. Poor Manny couldn't even control his apprentice, let alone take over the government.'

He was attentive, not commenting.

'You're not by any chance trying to get me into politics? Is there a seat going somewhere that needs a disreputable young candidate to throw the pomposity of the others into sharp relief?' An uncomfortable thought struck me. 'Surely you don't want me to stand for bloody Mosley's tin-pot party?'

'No.' Charles smiled. 'Not exactly. But what are you going to do, now you're fully recovered?'

'You mean after the separation, and no longer with my wife's estate to enjoy, so begging at my father's door again? I've got friends exploring exotic places, digging holes in Palestine, Egypt and so on. I thought about joining them, but it's taken longer than it should have to get my strength back and I catch every germ that's going round, so God knows how I'd fare out in Mesopotamia. I'm out of breath after a fifty-yard sprint.'

'We build monuments to the fallen, but we let ourselves forget the crippled.'

'Crippled is pushing it a bit.'

Charles finished his own glass. 'So, you're ready for a bit of an adventure? When I was last talking to your father, he mentioned you consumed those modern detective books as if they were opiates.'

'I still read the classics, but Agatha Christie has more pace than Plato if not as many deaths as Homer.'

Now my visitor's expression changed from affable to shrewd. 'Everyone deserves a second chance. I have a contact in London who is looking for a man with your background and skills.'

'What skills?'

'You're brave—to a fault, as it happens. You're well read, you're born inquisitive. You're used to having money, but you don't flaunt it. You're not from London, you're not part of one high society set or another and you still have that charming coalfields accent. And you're not political, barring a little social conscience which never hurts when you're dealing with the common man. I couldn't do this particular job; discounted on all fronts.'

'So I'm a misfit, and they want a misfit?'

'If you don't mind my asking, what happened to your marriage?'

'Those rioters shot that too. Leonora wanted a hero, not a cashiered invalid.'

'In a curious way, that also helps. No wife, no children.'

'It sounds like selection criteria for sending a soldier on a suicide mission.'

'No, no, but you have flexibility to go here, to go there. You can smile at a pretty society hostess and she won't see a happily married man chancing his arm.'

'Well, if society hostesses are part of the deal, I'm in.'

'Honestly?'

'I'm reading three books a week, every newspaper or magazine I can find, and going for long walks through a land that was green and pleasant before my family covered it in mines and slag heaps. I've shot as many birds and rabbits as I ever wish to, and I'm being lectured on a daily basis by my father and his well-meaning but very dull friends about how to mend my life. I don't exactly have a full diary.'

'Let's take a stroll around those gardens.'

I called for our coats, and we were soon walking the gravel path towards where the original moated manor once stood, its site now shrouded by trees.

'That's a very fine house your father owns,' Charles said.

'And he's threatening to leave it to my sister,' I admitted. 'She married well and already has two sons to further the dynasty.'

'So you truly have nothing to lose. Conquer or die.'

'Conquer or…come on, Charles, you're being very mysterious. Who exactly do you work for? More importantly, who will I work for?'

'You'll be…independent. You won't legally work for anyone.'

'You dodged my question.'

'I don't work for anyone either, I've left the regulars so I'm a private person now. Although I have the interests of His Majesty's Government at heart, Defence of the Realm and all that.'

'So, you're what the newspapers would quaintly call a spy?'

'No, no, dear chap, far from it. However, that is what they would call you, if they were to ever find out what you're up to. Which for everyone's sakes they never will.'

The thrill could not be suppressed. I discarded any worry that some mundane office job would lie at the end of this particular rainbow.

'Bluntly, we need someone inside the British Union of Fascists. Communism is the biggest threat our country faces, but the Security Services have no difficulty penetrating socialist groups. We know who they are, and we know what they want. Russian spies are on our streets and the British Communist Party is being directed by Moscow, but the fact that we know that gives us comfort.

'Our fascist compatriots are another matter. They don't cling to any particular region or industry. They cut across classes, which means they have friends in high places. The Home Secretary thinks that Mosley presents no threat, that he's a model patriot. It's difficult to obtain warrants or do anything to curtail his activities.' He paused. 'Most of the curtailing is being done by the communists, with bricks and cudgels.'

'Does your contact encourage that?' I asked.

'One could propose that the communists will keep the fascists in check, and the fascists will keep the communists in check and the rest of us can continue our happy lives. Except that was not the outcome in Germany, or Italy, or Russia for that matter. There are close to three million unemployed men in this country, and I can't see any of them voting Conservative at the next election.'

'Are we due an election?'

'Yes, soon, and Mosley will make his bid for power. Once he has it, you can call full time on British democracy, so we need to know what the fascists are up to. No heroics, just simple, straightforward intelligence gathering. They're not all society hostesses, so it could get rough. You need to be aware of that.'

'Of course.'

'And I should warn you that the pay is terrible, which is another reason you fit the bill. All our best officers have money behind them.'

'I don't like living off my father's money.'

'Well, keep on his right side, for the good of the Empire. Turn over a new leaf, make him think it's all of his doing if you must, but however much you are tempted you can't tell him what you are really up to. And don't try to impress your wife as a way of winning her back. Being an agent is not as glamorous as your paperbacks make out—stick with the bitter, disillusioned officer in disgrace.'

'Is that me?'

'Every inch.' He stopped walking and let the criticism sink in. 'Come up to London as soon as you can. We'll find you a flat and a cover story.'

'How about bitter officer in disgrace...'

Charles smiled. 'That will only carry so far. Have you ever thought of becoming a writer? London is full of writers, or young men who want to be writers.'

'What am I going to write about? I'm rubbish at poems.'

'How about trying your hand at one of those detective books you're always reading? Write one of those, it can't be hard.'

The idea appealed. Indeed, it was a long-held but closely guarded fantasy.

'You don't even have to complete it. Just about all the so-called writers I know never finish a thing. It will be useful to have an occupation that allows you to work on your own, to hours of your choosing.'

'I'll give it a go.' I certainly would. 'But my father thinks you're finding me honest employment.'

'Oh, I'll put you on the board of an old soldier's hospital out in Woolwich. You won't have to do anything beyond turn up once a quarter and vote for whatever seems sensible, but your father can convince himself you're running the show and boast about you over dinner.' Charles smiled. 'Maybe he won't cut you off just yet.'

A gong sounded from back towards the house; Hopkins summoning us to tea. We turned back.

'How soon can you come up to town?'

'As soon as I can pack. I don't own much, and it's all out of fashion.'

'Excellent. I'll set up a meeting with the man you'll not be working for and find an occasion where I can launch you on the social scene. Join the

BUF up here if you can, so you're a ready-made supporter when you arrive in London. It will provoke fewer questions.'

Two years of frustration simply melted away. Here was a chance to make a mark, and it might even be stimulating. 'There's a branch in Halifax, I've seen the posters. I could drive over tomorrow.'

We drew close to the house. 'Sandwiches, Mr Hugh.' Hopkins waited by the orangery door.

Charles paused before entering. 'So you're on the team?'

'Just promise me this is not a suicide mission.'

Chapter Two

She chose the north end of Hammersmith Bridge as the rendezvous. It offered a clear view in all directions, was a public place with plenty of passing traffic, yet was not busy with pedestrians who might witness the exchange. A quirk of the bridge design meant the footway was separated from the road by a thick green girder which protected her from being simply run over or hustled into a motor car.

The exchange would be after that busy time when workers stream home, but the sky would still be light. At least it should have been, but the Blackshirt clerk was late and the lamps were already lit. A mist rose off the river, and she had already emptied her cigarette packet and tossed it over the railing.

Shopping bag in hand, she was determined to wait. This was her one chance and her last chance, as now she'd seized the opportunity to obtain the fascists' precious report her treachery would be quickly exposed. After tonight she must vanish, whatever happened. If the exchange went wrong, her ally waited in his anonymous Austin just off the north ramp of the bridge. At least she gambled he was an ally. His name was made up, obviously, and she suspected that he faked his accent for the same reason she suppressed her own, but if everything went to plan she wouldn't even need him.

As a final resort, she could run to the safe house in only four minutes, and anyone who tried to follow her would regret it. For a moment she slid her right hand into her coat pocket and touched the cold metal.

A man approached from the landward end, and as the mist shifted it was clear he was the clerk who worked at the fascists' Curzon Street office.

Despite posing as a typist when she volunteered for the fascists, she'd not found a way to get herself posted to that building and couldn't afford to wait. Intelligence was slow work, but Oswald Mosely's movement was growing and changing too rapidly for a cautious approach. When that bloody desk-warrior Calhoun had urged her to be careful, he only half meant it.

The clerk was carrying a brown paper package the size of a large book. Mosely's creatures were often young, impressionable, and poor. Two hundred pounds clearly appealed to this one's baser nature and she'd thrown in the deepest purrs of thanks, with a flash of her eyes encouraging his hope for a reward beyond money.

Excited at the prospect of success, wary of betrayal, she slipped her right hand back into her coat pocket.

'Hello,' he said nervously.

'That it?'

'Er, yes.'

She proffered the shopping bag and he took it in his free hand, then reluctantly passed the package across.

'I'm not going to check it. I know your address,' she said.

'Sorry,' he said.

A car screeched to a halt. The clerk made an attempt to grab her with his free hand, failed, but managed to block her escape to shore. As she pulled out her knife, she shoved the youth away. He heard the click and saw the blade and saw sense too. The package fell to the floor and she let it fall. It would be worthless.

A man vaulted over the girder at the road edge, pulling a pistol from his coat.

'Stop, traitor!' He wasted time shouting his order and before he could shoot, she grabbed his pistol arm and lunged for his eye with the knife. As she struggled for control of that gun it went off in an explosion of sound, and pain lanced through her leg. Her blade slashed in a wide circle and the man fell back, holding his face. Both screamed in agony. She grabbed the bridge rail for support and the pistol vanished into the water, but a new attacker came in with a knife of his own held high in a reverse grip. He had no idea how to use it. Even without the power of her legs she thrust at him and snagged his coat low on one side, but the fool came on, jabbing down with his little blade. Searing pain bit into her left shoulder, the one she was relying on for support and she stumbled, barely registering the third stab – the one that should be fatal.

Cheek-down on the pavement she heard the shouts, the car departing and another arriving as if at the same instant. Through a bloody mist, she saw her red knight come to the rescue.

'Are you hurt?'

Stupid question, stupid question!

'I've got to get you into the car.'

More shrieks split the London evening as he dragged her across the pavement, over the bridge girder, and into the front seat of the Austin. At last other Londoners took notice, but it was all too late. Fascists were murdering their way to power on the continent, but not in Britain. Not until now.

Chapter Three

I was assigned a handler, rather as if I was a music hall artiste or a prizefighter. Commander Marcus Calhoun was stocky, dark eyed, and dark haired where he wasn't balding. He might be ten years my senior, so must have served in the War. Calhoun came to my new flat just once and spent much of his brief visit looking out of the sitting room window towards the narrow communal garden that ran alongside the side street opposite.

Sixty-four Havelock Mansions was a first-floor apartment in a seven-storey, turn-of-the-century building, its butterscotch brickwork now soiled by London's sooty nights and growing traffic.

'Happy with the apartment, Clifton?'

'Yes, I always liked Bayswater,' I said.

'Museums, art galleries...I hear you like books and that sort of thing. We need a man who can listen and learn rather than just barge in—too many army officers think with their swagger-sticks. How are your languages?'

'Schoolboy German, French, and Latin of course. I did a lot of reading at university in all three, but I've not had much opportunity to speak them beyond the odd European tour. I have fragments of ancient languages, and some colloquial Punjabi, but I sense none of that will be of use in London.'

Calhoun chuckled. 'No. Brush up your German though and read Herr Hitler's awful book. We don't know who is pulling Mosley's strings. He could be making it up as he goes along, or he could be in bed with both Mussolini and Hitler for all we know.'

'He certainly shares their dress code.'

'Quite. Get along to one of his rallies as soon as you can but take anything you hear with a pinch of salt. Mosley's the best orator in the country and he knows how to tell a crowd what they want to believe. And get to as many of their little local meetings as you can, there's one most days somewhere in town.'

'I've been to a few already.'

'Good. Learn their creed, learn to blend in. That unfortunate India nonsense will seep out sooner or later, but it could even work to your advantage. Mosley picks up a lot of strays, men who have failed in this or that, discredited, disappointed…'

I nodded, reluctantly. Intelligence was his game and Calhoun had me firmly categorized.

'So tell me how this spy game works. What am I looking for?'

'Money, in a nutshell. We don't know how much the BUF has or where it's coming from. Without money Mosley can't stage a revolution and can't even fight an election, so stop the funding and we stop the fascists. Observe, listen and report, that's all. Don't pull in your friend Wickersley any deeper than he needs to go; he's valuable floating out there in society and we don't want him compromised. I'll be your contact, but if we ever meet in company, we will be strangers. I will deny your existence as surely as I deny the Devil.'

I'd be on my own, clearly.

'I hear you're a crack shot? Not that it will be needed, but a man needs to be able to handle himself. We're not sending you to Moscow, but a knife in the back hurts just as much here as it does there.'

'Do I get a gun?'

'No. You're not that kind of agent.'

'Well Charles has invited me to a soiree at Baroness Rockwell's as my baptism of fire, so I guess I can risk venturing there unarmed.'

Calhoun's frown showed he did not appreciate my attempt at levity. 'Be careful with the women…' he warned, but his pause was longer than it should have been. Perhaps he'd been unhappy in love. 'Mosley has a strong female following, everything from seamstresses to duchesses. The prettier they are, the more dangerous they are.'

'Well, as you said. I can handle myself.'

Chapter Four

Armed only with a smile, my first mission was to attend a party that 'all the right people' were attending. 'And some of the wrong people,' Charles added as his chauffeur carried us towards Belgravia.

From the outside, Society parties looked like sheer frivolity, where wealth was squandered in the most lavish manner possible. The rich and the famous and the titled enjoyed themselves at their townhouses or country retreats while one man in five struggled to support his family on dole payments of under a pound a week.

'There's a purpose to all this,' Charles said. Society hostesses chose their mix of guests carefully, he explained; someone from the government, aspiring politicians, an actress or two, military types, ex-debutantes, a scholar perhaps, philosophers and artists. 'Oh, and social climbers,' he added with a smile. The unlikely mingled with the highly influential. Society parties oiled the machinery of empire. It sounded like him justifying the ostentatious behaviour of his class, but I knew he had a point.

'This will not be Mosley's inner circle,' Charles warned once the chauffeur had deposited us on the kerb. 'For all his man-of-the-people act, he's a snob and keeps to a close group of well-placed friends. And indeed, their wives. Baroness Rockwell attracts hungry people who want to get deeper into the movement.'

It was a fine townhouse, well-staffed by servants including a butler to greet guests. Many great houses reduced their staff during the War and afterwards employed far fewer than was once the norm. Charles gave a nod towards a grand lady in tiers of pearls, tall and finely dressed and making the utmost effort to fight off the years.

'Baroness Rockwell. May I present Hugh Clifton.'

'Ah, you're the dashing young man Wickersley has been so keen for me to meet. I'm delighted you could make my little soirée at such short notice. And you're new to London? It's always exciting to have fresh blood. And I hear you've just joined the Party too? Now who do you know here?' She rattled off a list of names. 'Come, you must meet some *people*.'

I was introduced to Earl Obscure, Sir Almost Famous, and Mrs Formerly Suffragette and made polite conversation with each. The King's Jubilee was a favourite subject for small talk – who had been invited to what social occasion. I decided to catch the big parade in May, if for nothing else than to provide anecdotes for future conversations of no consequence.

My usual party priorities were as follows: first, secure a drink; second, identify the most interesting young woman in the room. Sheer prettiness only carried so much currency; I needed company with something to say beyond chatter repeated verbatim from her last conversation. Spy mission or not, as a minimum I would enjoy myself. There were dirtier jobs in the world.

A quiet blonde girl, not long a debutante, stood half alone and half feigning interest in the cut of a young man's suit. She needed to be saved from the extended monologue about which tailor was the finest in Savile Row. After a minute or two of my futile intervention, it was clear that she really *was* interested in that young man, and the suit conversation had been a simple diversion. She'd been startled by my accent and the man almost mocked it. This was clearly not the place to play Northern Boy Made Good, however much it might be my father's favourite game. I needed to blend in.

Polite hello, offer name, pleased to meet you. Repeat several times. Take a second glass of champagne. Dilute the accent. Don't act like a spy, however spies acted.

Charles came back, his hands empty, and I whisked a glass of champagne off a passing waiter's tray to offer him. 'Thank you, no. I've shown my face and played my part, You're on your own now.' Charles lowered his voice so

I could barely hear him. 'Keep your eye out for a man called Thring. He's an accountant of no particular wealth or status, so he's a bit of a curiosity moving in these circles.'

'Could he be involved in their fundraising?'

'If he is, that makes him of particular interest to us. Say hello if you can.'

With a drink in both hands, I looked around for anyone who looked as if he should be an accountant. Along opposite walls of the ballroom was a succession of tall gilt mirrors that magnified the space and helped identify who to talk to now Charles had left me alone. Demanding attention over the far side of the room was a vivacious brunette, who tossed back her head in a laugh. Her dress was deep blue, sleeveless, gathered at the waist by a large square gold buckle. As she was beside one of the mirrors, an equally stunning twin stood by her shoulder. She pushed an empty glass onto a man old enough to be her father, who nodded to obey her request and turned to find a replacement.

No doubt she was one of those dangerous women I had to look out for. I was up to the task. Swiftly, I dodged through the party and presented my offering.

'Good evening.'

'And good evening to you.' She spoke quickly, her accent well-crafted but not top-of-the-tree aristocratic. Her eyes widened to betray interest.

We touched glasses. 'Hugh Clifton.'

'And you can call me Sissy.'

'That's an interesting buckle – is it, what, Chinese?'

She glanced down. 'Why yes. Fancy a man noticing something like that.' Clearly, attention to detail pleased her.

'Ah, Sissy.' Baroness Rockwell appeared from the blind side. 'I see you've met Viscount Wickersley's protégé.'

'We were in the army together.'

'Oh, army,' Sissy said. 'Yawn. I hope you're not still army? Soldiers can be so dull.'

'No, I'm done with my soldiering.'

'You're a trifle young to have fought in the War,' said Baroness Rockwell.

'The Great War, yes; I was too young to even lie about my age. But there's no shortage of wars. I saw my action in India.'

'My, India; is it terribly exotic?' asked Sissy.

'Exotically terrible. There are splendid palaces, magnificent princes, jungles, and high mountains. Tigers, elephants...and millions of people just aching to kill Englishmen.'

'Hugh has recently joined the Party, so we should be seeing lots more of him,' Baroness Rockwell said.

'Oh super.'

Sissy's previous admirer returned, but Baroness Rockwell drew him away. 'No, Desmond, she has a drink now and I'm sure Sissy doesn't want to hear any more about salmon fishing. Let's leave the young people to get to know one another.'

Sissy lowered her brow. 'You're not obsessed with salmon fishing, I hope?'

'Not as conversation.'

'Mmm.' She took a sip of her champagne. 'You're from the north?'

'Well observed. So, I need a little help down here, a frontier guide.'

'Very well, I shall be your guide.' With exaggerated formality, she took my arm. 'Who do you know?'

'Just Wickersley...and now you.'

Women provided the colour, as the men were all formally dressed. One by one Sissy picked out Lady Splendid, the Junior Minister for Something Unimportant, Colonel Paunch, Loud Posh Boy and Sad Bored Girl. A father-and-son combination stood slightly apart from the gaiety, as if not comfortable in such company.

'And them?'

'Oh, that's my friend Julian and his father, Howard Thring.'

Thring was an upright and thin man, hair only clinging on above his ears, his jaw firmly locking out the idea he would ever laugh.

'He's very close to Sir Oswald, he's a rising star in the Party.'

'Rising star?' My chest thumped a little faster. Alluring as Sissy might be and tempting as it was to spend the rest of the evening in her company, my first legitimate target was in sight. This is where the spying started – if it had not started already.

'He's just an accountant, really,' Sissy said, half in a whisper of conspiracy. 'Oh sorry, you're not in trade or anything?'

'No, nothing like that.' I judged that young Thring must be only a few years younger than I was, perhaps Sissy's age. 'Is his son a rising star too?'

'Oh, Julian's an enthusiastic follower, but you wouldn't think it, from his demeanour. His new fiancée is the keenest of the lot though, more Mosley than Mosley. I haven't seen her tonight.'

Boyish, with dark, slicked hair pretty much like my own, Julian Thring employed all the bodily expressions his father had no time for. He glanced to left and right, grimaced when he took a gulp of champagne, and then gave almost a sigh of satisfaction. His father said something which may have been amusing by barely moving his lips, but young Thring's eyebrows shot up and he gave a nervous guffaw. Perhaps he was being held on a short leash and simply wanted to enjoy himself. He needed a friend.

'Are you in the Party too, Sissy?' I asked, almost casually. My, she had a fine neck and her lips seemed to spread from ear to pearl-draped ear each time she smiled.

'Mother drew me in. Yes, that was my mother who introduced us, Baroness R. Our Women's Section is very strong.'

Any ideas that female fascists would be steely-eyed, frumpy, frustrated Tory guildswomen simply evaporated. Motives for holding Sissy in conversation moved from seduction to subversion, even if seduction might creep back later.

'Defeating the communists is one thing, but in between we do have some super fun,' she said.

'My father is a Conservative and they never have fun.' It felt good to mix a little truth into the masquerade.

'I thought you were all card-carrying socialists up north?'

'Well, Father employs plenty of them, but he owns a pair of coal mines, a coke factory, and a brickworks. He's about as far from the common man as you'll find in that part of the world.'

She cocked her head. 'Would I be right in guessing that you don't get along with your father?'

'He doesn't approve of my lifestyle.' Now was the opportunity to lay on an accent as thick as a pit-prop. 'Get thyself a proper job, lad! When I was thy age I worked twelve hours a day, seven days a week for thruppence...' Oh her smile was so appealing. Whatever Calhoun and his crew wanted out of that evening, I already rated it a roaring success. 'His friends are the same, all claim to have worked their way up from nothing and never tire of boring you about how they did it.'

'So if you don't work twelve hours a day, what do you do?'

'A gentleman should do as little as possible.'

'But I can tell you're not a gentleman, Hugh Clifton.'

After a moment's self-doubt came the faux admission. 'I'm a writer.'

She slapped my arm. 'My God, and I suppose you live in a garret and drink absinthe and smoke French cigarettes?'

'I rent a modest flat in Bayswater but go lightly on the absinthe. I can only carry the struggling author game so far.'

'Should I have heard of you? What do you write?'

'Detective fiction.'

'Oh.' Her face fell, but on the positive side, it meant she was not one who devoured that particular form of literature and would insist on reading everything I'd written. Which would not take long.

'And what's your latest story called?'

'It's bad form to bore people with my plots.'

'Bore me.'

Fiction only took a moment to concoct. '*Blackshirt Detective*. My hero is a Blackshirt who solves mysteries.'

'Oh my, that's topical. It should get people talking.'

'I hope for the right reasons.'

'And I say, I saw Bertie Bertram here. He's a publisher, I'll introduce you.'

Damn. If this charade continued, I'd have to write a bloody book. 'I'm not quite at that stage yet.'

'Don't tell me; you're one of those writers who hasn't *actually* had anything published.'

'Not as such.'

'Oh what a pity, your *oeuvre* was going to be my afternoon reading for the next month.'

'I don't have much of an *oeuvre*, I'm afraid.'

She clinked her glass against mine again. 'To the success of *Blackshirt Detective*.'

'To success.'

After another sip, she adopted a quizzical pose. 'Is that why you joined the Party? To become a Blackshirt and get colour for your book?'

Damn again; that guess was too close. I needed to create as much truth as possible to pad out my lies or I'd be caught out in pretty short order. 'More the other way around. My detective was a depressed ex-soldier struggling with ghosts from the War. Then I read Mosley's *The Way Ahead* and it changed my thinking, and it changed my character's thinking too.' Escape was needed from this shaky ground. 'Introduce me to those *rising stars*, would you?'

Sissy led across to where Thring Senior appeared to be briefing his son on who should be spoken to and in what order. Handshakes accompanied introductions.

'Hugh has just joined the Party.'

'Well, earlier this year,' I admitted.

'Good man,' said Thring.

'Splendid,' echoed the son.

'Clifton, ha? What brings you to our side?'

'Mosley's economic policies offer the best way to steer this country out of the mess the National Government has created.' My script had been rehearsed, but I hoped it didn't sound rehearsed. 'The crisis hit us hard in the north, and I've seen how the communists are infiltrating our cities and heavy industry. We don't want a revolution in England.'

'It's happening already,' Thring said. 'Communists and Jews trying to silence us with violence. Are you ready for that, Clifton? Are you ready to stand up for your economic policy, stand up for England?'

'I am, sir.' I drew up to my full six-foot-one. I glanced to see whether

Sissy approved, but she was already out of reach; throwing back her hair and laughing at another man's joke. She and her mother might amount to no more than camp followers in the fascist movement, but Howard Thring was in the vanguard. Colourless, unsmiling, he was the real target.

'We're polishing our machine for the election,' Thring said. 'There's a rally next Saturday, Camden, a big one, The Leader is speaking.'

'I'll be there.'

'Will you?' Thring prodded my chest. 'Be aware there's no room in this movement for passengers, Mr Clifton.' His stare was hard, icy. He prodded again. 'There's no room for spectators or the half-hearted. You're either with us or you're against us.'

'I'm with you. All the way.'

'Good.' The finger drew back. 'The reds know where we're meeting, and they'll stop at nothing to silence us. Expect trouble.'

Chapter Five

Having committed in public to being a writer, even if quickly exposed as an *aspiring writer,* I had to write a book. Or at least, start writing a book. I'd bought an almost-new Olympia Elite typewriter which now sat on the table in front of the trio of windows that made up the room's curving corner. A pile of virgin paper by its side gave the lie to my life as a novelist. As a minimum, I needed to hammer out twelve pages of *Blackshirt Detective,* drop a few screwed-up draft pages into the wicker wastebasket and leave one sheet half-finished sticking out of the machine to maintain the charade. If anyone were to come around, whether invited or otherwise, at least my alibi was intact.

Although I'd have to write more before their next visit.

Perhaps a genuine struggling writer lived nearby who would type a hundred pages of unpublishable dross for a few pounds. The worse it was, the more embarrassed Sissy would be to show it to her publisher friend.

A hero had come easily to mind, but Howard Thring now provided the model for a humourless villain with ice blue eyes. I held no fear of libel because the damn thing would never be published.

I rolled the paper into the machine and typed the title in capitals, banging those tabs to position it near the centre of the page. I was half-way through adding my name underneath before a thought stopped me. *A serious writer would have a pen name.* Out came the sheet, which became the first crumpled ball of paper in the basket. A second sheet was soon covered in a list of hand-written pen names, each pulpier than the next, crossed out one by one. After a coffee and a squashed fly biscuit and a little more crossing out, I reached a conclusion. A fresh piece of paper was rolled into the machine and using just one finger of each hand the arduous task of typing a novel began in earnest.

BLACKSHIRT DETECTIVE
by Vincent Hammer

That would do nicely.

Mrs Ainsworth came around in the late afternoon. Perhaps in her early thirties and dressed for the office, she sat primly cross-legged in the armchair while I lounged on the little sofa after making her a cup of tea. It was unclear where in the intelligence hierarchy she rested, whether she was just a humble typist, a trusted secretary or was an actual agent posing in the kind of role most men would expect a woman to be given.

'You have a typewriter,' she observed.

'I'm a novelist, of a kind. I learned to type up action reports in the army, so I could type my own notes.'

'That won't be necessary, Mr Clifton.'

'Leave it to the professionals, eh?'

'Exactly.'

I dutifully dictated a report of my meetings. Every observation had to be carefully phrased and correctly balanced, not being sensationalist nor downplaying detail that could turn out to be important in the right hands. Mrs Ainsworth took notes in shorthand as names and facts tumbled out. The report made a far better story than that I'd planned for the as yet nameless Blackshirt Detective, and Mrs Ainsworth would be a much more competent typist than Vincent Hammer. She'd return to that office somewhere in Mayfair without a plate on its door, create a host of notes on all my contacts, index them and then file them in what I imagined was a vast room lined with head-high oak filing cabinets. It was likely the Security Service already had files on the people I named, and all I was doing was adding to their bulk even if not simply duplicating what they already knew.

Dictating notes had never been so exciting.

On the North-West Frontier, I had learned to sense when I was being watched—from up among the rocks, from the shadows of a *gallie* in a tight-packed town or from within the depths of an otherwise innocent crowd. As I joined the queue outside the hall in Camden, everyone was wary of everyone else. Working people checked that their friends were still with them, solid in the face of the common threat of poverty. Better-dressed middle-class men and women were nervous about being *seen*, and by whom.

I made sure I was seen, especially by the hard-faced men in black guarding the hall up ahead. Avoiding being self-conscious, I willed myself into believing that I was a believer. I *wanted* a BUF victory, I *wanted* to chant for Mosley. Above all I *wanted* to be one of those chosen Blackshirts, back in uniform, defending the empire, the King and Christian decency.

Perhaps fifty policemen stood well back, blocking the streets to the growing crowd of anti-fascist demonstrators. North-east London was tough territory for the BUF and their Camden club had been attacked more than once.

Yes, someone had paid me more than a moment's attention. A man, mid-thirties, well back behind the police, lost in the crowd now. There, again, checking that he'd not been noticed. Oh, but he had. Hook-nosed, flat cap, and russet knitted tie. A line of police concealed Hook-nose once more.

Not forgetting a face had become a matter of pride. Soon after arriving in the Punjab the company sergeant-major had told me with authority that all Sikhs looked the same with their beards and their turbans, unwittingly laying down a challenge to prove this opinion wrong. Quickly I learned to tell Gill from Dewana, the younger Josan from the older Josan, and remember their names too.

A dozen Blackshirts stood 'at ease' in front of the hall. Their eponymous shirts were in fact collarless fencing jackets of black silk, buttoned over on the left. A small metal badge featured the fasces symbol of rods and axes, while a mix of styles of civilian trousers, boots, and shoes completed the mostly black outfits.

Men and women slipped through the police cordon, to heckles and boos from beyond, and then joined the queue that filtered into the hall. A pair of Blackshirt stewards controlled access through the door and I gave one my ticket.

'Are you a member, sir?'

'I am, I am.' I proudly showed my card to the young man.

'There could be trouble,' the Blackshirt warned. 'But you look like you can handle it.'

My grin suggested that I could indeed handle it and would relish the chance to slug a few communists. A flash of bravado might fool the stewards, but it was a sobering thought that I could shortly be expected to fight for a cause I did not believe in. As I was nodded through, a hand brushed against my jacket feeling for weapons.

The hall was already three-quarters full, with perhaps two hundred people seated in twenty rows of chairs, plus a few choosing to stand at the back. At the front, a little stage had been set up.

Choosing a seat in the very back row allowed me to study the attendees as well as whatever was going to happen on the stage. Blackshirts formed a perimeter guard around the room and one noticed me noticing them. *I must learn to look without looking.* This is how it would be now, for weeks, possibly months; the imposter, the spy, the enemy.

The audience on those uncomfortable mismatched chairs would not have looked out of place at any parish meeting across the land. Most would be tagged as working class, ironically for the many that were not working at all. Young men and a surprising number of women waited expectantly, hungry for a job and probably actually hungry too. Desperate people sought desperate measures. It was a far cry from Baroness Rockwell's soirée and broke any illusion I had that the BUF was just a hobby for self-opinionated toffs and their bored children. This was a street movement as surely as the communists were – no wonder the two hated each other so much.

Making her way to a seat a few to my left was a young woman with her skirt bulging over her belly. She gave a nervous smile. Some would say it was not fitting for her to be here, but here she was. A flat-capped man grasped her hand and laid an arm on her shoulder – her husband or the one responsible for the baby bump at least. She crooked her back to ease the weight she carried and sat down with relief. The hook-nosed man in a russet tie who had taken such interest in me outside was nowhere to be seen.

The hall was full. An older man in a medal-decked but shabby suit with an empty sleeve stood up to face the audience in front of the little stage at the head of the room. A Blackshirt ushered him away from the centre and he took up a new station off to one side. A pair of drummers came to the front and began to beat out a rhythm I should remember, then four black-clad praetorians strode onto the stage. One carried the Union flag, another the fascist flag with its fasces symbol copied directly from Mussolini's Italian Blackshirts, who had copied it in turn from the ancient Romans.

Some of the crowd cheered, others remained restless. One boo from the back had the Blackshirts immediately craning their necks to identify the culprit.

More Blackshirts marched in, immaculately and identically uniformed and wearing shiny knee-high boots. I'd been warned about them, the I Squad, Mosley's bodyguard. A man strode from the shadows and reached the lectern in a couple of strides. Tall, matinee-idol handsome and not yet forty years old, the Leader gave a straight-armed fascist salute and half the audience responded. I kept my arm still, not sure of the form. A man glanced my way as he held his own salute firm, noticing my inaction.

Next time I must do the salute.

'Men and women of London!' Mosley launched straight into his monologue, soon pointing to the old sailor at the front who had lost an arm at Jutland back in '16. He had been abandoned by a government that did not care. 'The National Government cut the wages of the heroic British Jack Tar to save money!'

Cries of 'shame!'

The Navy had mutinied at Invergordon in '31, but the government had hushed it up. It was much worse than the newspapers said. 'It's come to this. *Mutiny* in the Royal Navy!'

Patriotism was offended, passions stirred, pity invoked, and the speaker paused for applause every few sentences. Yes, it was theatre, but even I could see that Mosley had a point. What *had* happened to the 'land fit for heroes'?

The audience shuffled but stayed attentive in hope of hearing something they had not heard before as Mosley switched to talking about jobs, the scandal of three million unemployed. 'Where's the slum clearance programme we were promised? This is no National Government, it's a Tory government and the Tories do not care about you...' he pointed to a random member of the audience. 'Or you...'

Cheers and jeers came in equal measure.

'...and there's no answers from Labour, supposed guardians of the working man.'

'And working woman!' One of the audience shouted.

'The rich stay rich and the poor stay poor.'

It was heady stuff and the audience loved it. To be exact, not all the audience loved it.

'The People's flag is the Red Flag!' Suddenly the standing part of the audience heaved and surged. 'Say no to the fascists!'

On both sides of the hall, Blackshirts moved swiftly towards the back.

'Down with Mosley!'

'Bye Bye Blackshirt!' someone sang, loudly and off-key.

People started to stand up and chairs clattered to the floor. Staying seated in a fight was a bad idea. The pregnant woman ducked into a low crouch. She could be giving birth, right here, right now. As the clamour rose all around, here at least was a cause worth fighting for, a person worthy of protection. The woman dropped something, and her escort and his flat-capped friends stooped to her aid, pushing back their chairs to make room. I was almost by her side when she stood up and screamed 'For the people!' and hurled a fist-sized cobble straight at the speaker. It went wild and thumped into the Union Flag, but her partner threw true and hit a Blackshirt. Mosley's bodyguard immediately formed a screen around him.

Another stone struck the old sailor just above his eye, then all was mayhem. Two more stones flew, then fists flew and chairs tumbled in all directions. The woman grasped another cobble to enhance the punch of her little fists. One of her friends was brought down by a chair crashing onto his head from behind. Mosley had abandoned trying to speak and was nowhere to be seen. A Blackshirt officer in a peaked cap took over the lectern and began directing his men to counter-attack.

Now was the moment to act. I used my weight to bruise through the press of bodies, kicking loose chairs out of the way. I grabbed the no longer pregnant woman, forcing her to drop the stone then pulling both arms easily behind her back. 'Best get out of here, girl!'

'Fucking fascist bastard!'

'Now, now, fascist is a rude word.'

Gutter-level abuse continued as I propelled her forward towards daylight and safety. Stewards were bundling protestors out into the street but letting the innocent pass swiftly.

'I've got one!' I yelled cheerily, and they let me pass. Outside, perhaps thirty Blackshirts and a few men without uniforms punished those thrown out, kicking victims already on the ground. Men reeled under punches in a growing brawl around the door. The line of police stood impassively, more concerned by the angry crowd in the street beyond. Anti-fascists outnumbered fascists heavily and only that police line prevented a bigger and much more one-sided battle.

Maintaining a firm grip, I steered my struggling charge well clear of the fighting. 'Keep moving if you want to keep your teeth.'

With no gratitude at all, she kept up a machine-gun rattle of swearing and kicked back at my ankles. After quickly releasing her arms, I gave the woman a final push towards the police line. She turned and spat, but her aim with spittle was no better than with a cobble. 'Bastard!'

'My pleasure, love. Now bugger off and find a safer pastime.'

She straightened her dress that no longer concealed a sack of stones. 'You'll never win!' Spinning on her heels she marched straight past the policemen, nose held high.

Two constables rushed forward now, truncheons in hand. I half raised both hands in submission. 'Bit late, chaps!' I feigned my best Sandhurst officer accent, knowing that the police respected rank, and they ran straight past. As whistles blew, protesters vanished from the scene, back beyond the safety of the police cordon.

Now came the coughing, the punishment for that burst of action, robbing me of breath. Clutching my chest, I willed it to end. Adding to my discomfort, a stinging from my right shin suggested that woman had taken the skin off with one of her heels. It was little thanks for saving her hide.

Calm returned obstinately to the London street. Dust was knocked off black shirts and trousers. Bloody noses were dabbed. Three injured men were carried out and laid on the ground, and the old sailor received help with a cut on his forehead. The Leader had presumably been whisked away to safety. Violence had spoiled the mood of hope and the crowd dispersed as quickly as it could.

From behind me, an educated voice cut through the hubbub. 'Hugh Clifton, isn't it?'

On reflex, I turned and shook the hand offered by the Blackshirt.

'Julian Thring; we met at Baroness Rockwell's.' He was in full fascist garb and looked taller, more confident than when under his father's eye. 'This always happens, we can never meet in peace. And we're not allowed to carry weapons, which is unfair in my book. I saw you doing your bit, though.'

'I ejected one young woman, it's hardly Victoria Cross territory.'

'But she was a right little vixen, I saw how she fought you.'

'To be honest I wanted her out of there before she really got hurt. But it's a start. I'll work up to tattooed dockers in due course.'

'I'm glad to see you're up for a fight.' For his own part, Julian the junior accountant with his public-school accent and baby-face looks was not an obvious candidate for a street-brawler.

'I'll defend what I believe in.' It was an easy half-truth. The communists had hardly won my vote with that volley of rocks.

The BUF commander who had directed the fight back now emerged, waving his peaked cap to organize the clear-up. A purple scar began above his left eyebrow, pulling it out of shape, and continued past a dull eye vertically down his cheek. From his free hand dangled a piratical eyepatch that had been torn away in the fighting. It was not an encouraging advert for recruiting new Blackshirts.

'How do I get one of these natty uniforms?'

Julian stepped back a pace and spread his arms to allow me to admire his own outfit.

'Blackshirts are selected. It's not who you know, or who your father is in our party, it's what you do and what you can do. We're all about action. Did I hear you were in the army?'

'Lieutenant, first South Yorkshires, and then I commanded a platoon of Sikhs out in the Punjab. Saw a little action, even caught a bullet.'

'Jolly good, you'd be perfect for the Defence Force. That's us—the Blackshirts—I'll propose you if you're game.'

'Super,' I said on reflex. It was in for a penny, in for a pound now.

Julian paused. 'I hope you don't mind buying your own uniform.'

Chapter Six

Calhoun arranged to meet in a small cafe in a side street off Cambridge Circus. He seemed pleased with the initial reports.

'Your first street fight.'

'My first street fight on British soil,' I corrected.

'Of course.' Calhoun talked over the names Mrs Ainsworth had typed up. 'They're all familiar. We already know something about each one of them.'

'I thought you might.' It would be handy to hear what Calhoun already had on Sissy, but probably prudent to keep any personal interest well hidden. 'So is any of that information useful?'

'Vital. People keep drifting into this movement and drifting out again. Or we think they're out, but we don't know for sure. Communists are the real threat, as you've seen for yourself.'

My shin still throbbed. The bruise was impressive.

'But while Mosley is still at the crease, we can't take our eyes off the ball.' He took a sip of tea. 'I'm glad you've met Howard Thring, he could be the key to unlocking the secret of how the BUF is funded. Their popular base is tiny, so money is the only thing keeping them going. Mosley's rich, but he's not that rich, even with his paws on his late wife's estate. She was the daughter of Lord Curzon, you know. Since Lord Rothermere pulled out their bathplug last year, their cash supply should have dried to a trickle.'

Hence, Blackshirts had to buy their own uniforms.

'But they're still going. We don't know where their money is coming from, we don't know where they bank or how the cash gets there. Howard Thring is the senior partner of a medium-sized accountancy firm, Thring and Winter, with offices off Fenchurch Street. A lot of their clients are in shipping, international trade, that kind of thing. If anyone is finding the Blackshirts more money, it's likely to be him.'

'Sissy Rockwell described him as a rising star.'

'Ah, the honourable Cecilia Maude Elizabeth Poe-Maundy, only child of the Dowager Baroness Rockwell. Some cousin has inherited the title but not the estate.' Calhoun as good as confirmed that the Security Service held a file on Sissy. 'I gather she's very attractive. Fascism has some kind of allure for giddy young women. Perhaps it's the uniforms.'

'Well, giddy or not, Sissy introduced me to Thring. He was far more serious than anyone else I met at that shindig, and his son looked out of place.'

Calhoun gave this a moment's thought. 'Tell me more about his son.'

'Julian Thring. New money, public school, and I think I heard Edinburgh University. I'd guess he's twenty-five, twenty-six or so, but looks younger, newly engaged—'

'To who?' This was clearly news.

'Melissa someone, I've not met her.'

'Meet her.'

'I will, no doubt. Apparently, she's a diehard fascist. Julian seems pretty fresh on the London scene too, so I'm working at being his very best chum. He's invited me to become a Blackshirt.'

'Well done,' said Calhoun. 'First run for the home team.'

* * *

Black House on the King's Road, Chelsea, was once a teacher training college, but now served as headquarters-cum-barracks for the Party and trained young men for a very different purpose. Calhoun passed on rumours it was about to be let go to save money, but it was clearly still in operation. I attended to be fitted for my uniform 'shirt' and pay my seven shillings and sixpence.

I cast a critical eye over the cut of my uniform in the fitting room's long mirror once the tailor had finished his work. 'Why choose black shirts?'

'It's practical,' Julian said.

'We look like Italians.' It did indeed have a very tight fit, suiting young, muscular men.

'The communists have grabbed good old British scarlet. The police and the navy have blue, and we don't want to pretend we're the army and turn out in greens and browns.'

'And I suppose that a gentle shade of saffron doesn't convey the right message.' My attempt at satire escaped Julian. Perhaps it was unwise to show anything less than single-minded commitment. 'Although isn't there an American organization that clowns around in white cloaks and hoods?'

'I don't know about America,' Julian said, 'but black it has to be. It sets us apart, shows who we are. We can tell our friends from the red scum who try to break up our meetings.'

Puffing out my chest made that man in the mirror an imposing figure. Black was the colour of power, echoing mediaeval princes, clerics, and government ministers in their top hats. But it had a sinister edge too; true darkness was blackest black. An evil twin brother lurked behind the glass.

'You look the part,' Julian said, oblivious to the irony in what he was saying.

'Excellent.' One thing was sure, I was not going to adopt that shaved-neck Teutonic hairstyle. Julian also retained a fashionable sweep of hair, liberally slicked by Brylcreem.

'There's going to be a parade for the King's Jubilee,' he said. 'I hope you'll be free?'

'I wouldn't miss it for the world.'

'You'll be in my squad,' Julian indicated a pair of stripes on his sleeve.

'Splendid.' It would be good to be simply infantry after my disastrous experience of command in India. 'Who was the chap in charge at the Camden riot? Impressive scar.'

'Ah,' he said, 'that was Captain Parker. He's in Department Z.'

'Are you talking about me, by any chance?' Another man in black stepped out from behind a run of clothes lockers. Julian flinched, but I tried not to. At a guess, Parker was originally from the Midlands from his accent. The most dedicated fascist couldn't have designed a more intimidating look than the black eye patch straddling a jagged purple scar that ran from his forehead almost to his mouth. Parker put a hand on each hip and nodded approval at my appearance. 'Very smart. You're the one thrown out of the army for shooting down an unarmed crowd in India?'

I tensed, ready to defend my reputation on reflex, then played the part of that evil twin. 'They got what they deserved. We didn't win an empire by being soft.'

Parker nodded, possibly even approving. I had to shift the topic.

'Department Z? That sounds very mysterious.'

'Intelligence section,' Parker said. 'We identify threats and hunt down traitors.'

'Traitors? And what happens to them?'

'Oh, you know.' He gazed straight at me, as if he not only knew who I was but also what I intended. 'They get what they deserve.'

Chapter Seven

LONG MAY HE REIGN

Huge letters made of flowers had been strung across the façade of Black House. King George V's Silver Jubilee provided a superb distraction for a country out of love with itself, with waves of parades and fetes and speeches across the country. In contrast, for the forces of law and order, it provided a source of worry and work they did not need.

The sun was out for the King's drive-past, as were the people of west London in their thousands. Marcus Calhoun came up quietly beside Inspector Renton of Special Branch; tall, gaunt, with his unbuttoned raincoat hanging from his shoulders.

'You're out early. Are there stormy waters ahead?'

Renton barely glanced his way. 'The fact they let you out in the daylight suggests there might be.'

'A little bird tells me you've got some explosives to worry about.'

'Half a ton of commercial blasting explosives have been stolen from a Cornish quarry, together with wire and detonators. Of course, you know that already.'

'I didn't know it was half a ton. You've kept it out of the newspapers well.'

'They'll cotton on soon enough. Then we'll have panicking ministers to humour.'

'Someone can do a lot of mischief with half a ton,' Calhoun said. 'Any leads?'

'We'll communicate through the appropriate channels if we have any information we need to share.'

'Oh, but these are appropriate channels,' said Calhoun. 'In my trade at least.'

Renton gave a dismissive noise, as if he had little time for intelligence men. 'So if this is an appropriate channel you can tell me if you've heard anything about a plot to blow up the King?'

'Not a whisper; you?'

Renton shook his head. 'But why else nick it now? They've missed the big procession already, so what's left worth blowing up?'

'Well, there's going to be an election sooner or later. The smart money is on the autumn.'

'Meaning we have to be on our toes at every parade between now and then, and every miserable little political rally. We've got to watch the Irish, the communists, and every lunatic group going.' He nodded towards the rank of Blackshirts lining the road in front of Black House. 'Could it be that gang?'

'It's not their style, is it?'

'You tell me. Or is MI5 still blind to what Mosley's up to?'

Calhoun smiled, noticing a certain tall Blackshirt standing 'at ease', hands linked in the small of his back. 'We're not blind. Are you?'

Renton gave merely a harrumph. Across the road at Black House, Union Flags and fascist flags dangled from poles, and crusader-style shields hung from window ledges. 'Whispers are that the King has got a lot of sympathy for Mosley and the Prince of Wales is halfway to buying a black shirt himself.'

'Friends in high places,' Calhoun said.

'So, if it's the communists who nicked the explosives, wouldn't this be a good spot to set them off? Two for the price of one?'

'Speaking of which, I've spotted one of your men.'

The man was clearly a detective in civilian clothes, paying more attention to the crowd than the king's approaching car, checking for any discarded suitcase, box, or barrel where there should be none.

'And I'm looking for yours.'

Blackshirts were spaced at intervals in front of their headquarters, with Party members crowding the pavement behind them. Renton and Calhoun mixed with less politically committed patriots opposite, where policemen were posted to mirror the Blackshirts.

'On days like this, it almost feels like you're co-operating with them. Them over there, your men over here...'

'We are not co-operating with that rabble,' growled Renton.

The Blackshirts snapped to attention. Mounted police trotted past, then came the King's Rolls Royce. It was approaching at a stately pace from the left, preceded by a cheering that rippled closer. As the cheers grew, so did the tension. In front of Black House the crowd was solidly fascist, but some of those opposite would despise Mosley and even the King himself. Renton and Calhoun studied each face for expressions of hate, checked each body for that tension that precedes action, watched each arm as it started to wave a hat or simply wave.

As the Rolls came close, an order was barked and the Blackshirts clicked their heels and saluted in unison. Calhoun smiled to see Clifton playing his part, his right arm pointing skyward. Civilians to either side followed suit.

'To think we have to stand and watch this,' Renton muttered. 'On the streets of London.'

'It's just not British,' Calhoun said, with more than a touch of irony.

Worrying numbers of ordinary men and women were making that salute and cheering intensified as the black car with the big glass windows cruised past.

Renton let out a heavy 'whew,' of relief as the King's car receded and was followed by those of lesser men. 'That's that, then.'

'We live to fight another day,' said Calhoun.

Chapter Eight

'And I swear, I swear, the King saluted back!' I delivered my Jubilee anecdote with pride and panache.

After the big parade, Julian mentioned that the squad would be guarding the prospective candidate for Kensington North that Saturday, and the candidate, Mrs Symes, would be coming up to town the day before. Halfway through his explanation as to why his father was too busy to dine with her, I leaped in with the suggestion we invite her to dinner. My treat. My father's treat, to be honest. He continued to feed my bank account with money, ensuring that even if his son were disreputable, I would not be *poor and disreputable.* Choosing a modest restaurant quite close to Harrods, I entertained Mrs Amelia Symes and her husband Hubert, Julian Thring and his fiancée Melissa, plus Sissy to 'make up the numbers.'

As host, I sat at the head of the table, with the two couples ranged on either side and Sissy placed at the distant end. She looked particularly stunning tonight with shoulders exposed by a jade green dress that appeared to be held up only by a few strings of pearls. I could admire her from afar.

Mrs Symes filled an enormous floral evening gown. She was vocal and self-assured. 'I once fire-bombed a police station,' she said when I asked to hear more about her part in the Suffragette movement. 'I went to prison for it, and the police starved me and tortured me. We were political radicals, and we still are.'

'When will there be an election?' Sissy asked, a little distant from the conversation since we sat down.

'Soon, perhaps too soon for us. MacDonald is gone, good riddance, but

Baldwin? He'll do nothing. The people should elect the Prime Minister, not a few dozen Tories sozzled by brandy and cigars.'

Hubert Symes sat to her left, red-faced and jolly and sporting a huge walrus moustache. He'd flown with the Royal Flying Corps and defied the odds to survive the Great War. His passion project was the BUF Flying Club and he talked as if it were an air force in the making. 'We have the greatest navy in the world, so now we need to build the RAF into the greatest air force in the world. Britannia must rule the skies as well as the waves.'

Judging by his prodigious name-dropping, plenty of aviators and racing car drivers were keen for the bright, mechanized future that the fascists offered. Sissy's eyes started to wander the room as the old pilot chattered about horsepower and speed records. When he paused to accept a refill of his wineglass, I took the chance to steer the conversation away from machinery.

'You said an election could come too soon?' I asked Amelia.

'We need time to implement the Fuller Report.'

Julian nodded, as if he knew all about this. What was the *Fuller Report?* I mentally added it to my required reading list. Perhaps Calhoun had a copy.

'...Europe united by fascism.' Mrs Symes was rehearsing the next day's speech on us. 'Fascist countries each working for the good of their own people – all their people, not just the landed gentry or the church or union leaders.'

'Or Jews,' Melissa said. She was plainer than I'd expected Julian's fiancée to be. Rather shorter than Sissy, chubby faced and with blonde curls. She had the look of a farmer's daughter.

'I don't care about the so-called *Jewish Problem*,' Mrs Symes said with a tic of her head. 'It's a distraction. What we need is a central council for Europe that will prevent war and encourage trade. And cultural exchanges – their opera stars come here, our choirs go there. And it will be culture for everyone, not just the rich. We raise up the working man to aspire to more than just drudgery.'

'Or brown ale and football,' threw in Mr Symes. A smile crumpled his chin and his moustache twitched as he chuckled.

'Democracy is failing industry, failing the workers, and the women of Britain are left to pick up the pieces and feed their starving children. We won the vote, but you can't eat votes. Too much is made of the British love of democracy, don't tell me you think the workers love democracy—'

'They love brown ale and football,' Mr Symes added another tuppence's worth of political insight.

Mrs Symes gripped her wineglass and started to jerk it back and forth as she forced her point home. 'What they love most is not getting sent off to get killed at the whim of politicians. I lost both my brothers in the War. Hubert was lucky to come back without a scratch, or I'd be one of those half a million women without a husband. Without peace, we have nothing, nothing.' A little red wine slopped onto the tablecloth, leaving a blood-spatter stain.

'So we'll compete in the election?' I asked. 'But why, if democracy is the problem?'

'We have to take power democratically because that's the system we have. See what Herr Hitler has done for Germany. He didn't come to power by force, he was elected.'

I'd read the tedious, angry book Hitler wrote in prison. There was little chance that *Der Führer* would be so easily voted out of power.

'After we win, we can correct the system.'

'Hitler's certainly doing the right thing about the Jews,' Melissa added.

'Sorry for sounding stupid, but what is it with the Jews?' Sissy asked. Perhaps she was playing dumb or perhaps was simply winding Melissa up so she could run at full pelt.

'They control the money,' Melissa said, as if any idiot should know that.

'All of it?'

'The big banks, the newspapers, they're everywhere.'

Julian waded in to support his fiancée. 'The Jews try to stop us at every turn. At Olympia last year we had our biggest rally ever, and they ruined it. Jewish advertisers forced the newspapers to turn against us and membership has been falling ever since. We have to fight back.'

'Surely you knew that, Sissy,' Melissa said. 'Where have you been the past year?'

'It's just conversation!' Sissy snapped.

'But the Jews are not the problem,' Amelia asserted.

'But they're filling our cities,' Melissa insisted. 'They don't speak English, they take our jobs, run sweatshops at a pittance that men can't feed their families on…'

'In the East End, just perhaps,' said Amelia, shaking her head.

'Yes, there's a quarter of a million of them, pushing real East Enders out of their homes.'

I thought it unlikely that Melissa had met many real East Enders, and even less likely that she would invite any of them round for tea.

'We're building a lot of strength in the East End,' Julian added, 'but the Jews are fighting us for every ward.'

'Yes, yes, but most of the country doesn't care about the Jews,' Amelia insisted. 'There aren't any out in Norfolk, or Somerset, and that's where our bedrock support comes from, the countryside. What about Yorkshire, Hugh? Do you have this *Jewish Problem*?'

'Not at all. Not out in the pit villages at least.'

'You will one day, just wait,' said Melissa with extra conviction, glaring at me, daring me to contradict her.

Perhaps as host I'd been too liberal with the wine and opinions were starting to win out over manners. Amelia thumped the table. 'We follow the plan put forward by General Fuller,' she insisted. 'We stop this marching around dressed up like little Mussolinis and start organizing for an election.'

'I enjoy the marching,' Julian objected. 'It builds solidarity.'

'It's not winning votes!' Mrs Symes insisted. 'You must have read your father's Plan Blue!'

The table fell silent.

'No, actually I haven't,' Julian said. He glanced sharply my way, then at Sissy, and then lowered his voice in what came close to a rebuke. 'Those papers are restricted.'

'Oh,' Amelia said, settling back. 'Yes, of course. Well, it will sort out the mess our party is in. We'll win that election. We'll take power and we'll keep it.'

Sissy stood close by my side on the pavement in Knightsbridge as I tried to hail a cab to take her home.

'Sorry, it was my fault things got a bit fractious,' she said. 'I didn't mean to sound dim, with that question about the Jews, I just...'

'Never mind, it livened the evening up.'

'Julian used to be quite charming before his father poisoned his mind.'

'That's an interesting choice of phrase.'

'Amelia is right, why are we picking on the Jews all of a sudden?' She stopped herself. 'Sorry if you're in that camp...'

'I'm not.' Clearly the British Union of Fascists was not as united as they pretended.

'Get Melissa talking about horses or choral music and she's fine, but I'm sorry I pushed the Jewish question now. The Party can be great fun, our camps in the country, the dinners...'

'But? There's a *but* hanging there.'

'Oh, Mosley is utterly charming, and his wife Clemmie was too. And I've met some wonderful people, but there's this hate...the fighting in the streets...I hardly ever go to a meeting, there's always a brawl. Amelia is right about the marching and the uniforms—sorry when you've just bought yours. It's jolly exciting in a Girl Guides sort of way, but are we really going to fight communists in the streets with machine guns?'

I could not recall anyone talking about machine guns.

'And—' she waved her cigarette hand in the air—'well, it would be very scary if that's the way things turn. I'm going to come and hear Amelia tomorrow but I'm worried that thousands of reds will turn up and one of my friends will be hurt.' She touched my arm. 'It just takes one communist with a knife.'

'I've been up against worse,' I boasted, in the way a brash young fascist should. An attempt to flag down a black cab failed but bought me another minute in her company. 'This Plan Blue is nothing to do with stocking up on machine guns, is it?'

'No, no, it can't be, Amelia was talking like it was something she approved of. It sounds like something Julian's father has concocted and is keeping to the grown-ups.'

'You mean Mrs Symes may have let a rabbit out of the hutch without meaning to?'

'Maybe she did. Is that important?' She looked sharply at me, as if she'd seen straight through the charade. 'Why did you really join the Party? You like to talk, but you don't rant on about the Jews and the unions and a new European order like so many of the others do.'

'Must try harder, then. Death to the Communists!' I raised a half-hearted fascist salute and this time a cab driver mistook it for a hail and pulled up beside the kerb.

'That wasn't criticism, by the way,' she said as I opened the door of the taxi for her. 'You're a good man, thoughtful. If the Party needs anything, it needs thinkers.'

She was right; there was no fascist Karl Marx, no global vision. Each fascist was scrabbling around for ideas on what they wanted or what they stood for.

'Let's forget all that nonsense at the table,' Sissy continued. it's late and we have an exciting morning tomorrow.'

'Can we perhaps have lunch after the parade? The Dorchester, perhaps?'

'That would be lovely. Good night, Hugh.'

'Good night.'

'Take care tomorrow.'

Chapter Nine

Take care, Sissy had said. No heroics had been Charles' instruction. Forgetting both pieces of advice I rushed towards danger as the 'Kensington shooting' unfolded, my head still full of the guff rammed into me at Sandhurst. A British officer never flees; he laughs at danger. The sniper's bullet missed Amelia Symes but over the course of two minutes, I saw three men die on the cobbles of a London back street. Laughing was the last thing I felt like doing.

Just seconds after Julian's Blackshirts saluted me as the hero of the hour, a scrum of police officers piled in, pushed me against the brickwork, snatched away the smoking revolver and punched me in the gut.

'Bastard...scum...get your fucking face to the wall...fascist bastard...don't you say nothing!'

Pulled upright, spun around, handcuffed I was arrested amid a barrage of abuse. With one officer gripping me by each arm, I was frog-marched a couple of hundred yards to Church Court Police Station past a jeering crowd of socialists keen to see me strung up from the nearest lamp post.

A sergeant confiscated my watch, along with my wide black belt, tough army boots, and little fascist badge with its potentially dangerous pin. Putting on my posh officer voice paid no dividends at all as I was shoved into a cell with little formality. I was of course coughing like a consumptive by this point and repeatedly told to shut up.

Discoloured white paint peeled from the brickwork around the room, revealing earlier layers of dirtier white paint beneath. In contrast, the door was a nauseating shade of chlorine green. It stank of sweat and stale tobacco.

Parade...shots...run to back street...grab gun...more shots.

Over and again I ran through the events of that morning in my head, then ran through it repeatedly with police officers of increasing seniority until it sounded pat and I barely believed it myself. A solicitor named Newburn arrived, a legal stormtrooper appointed by the Party. We were allowed twenty minutes alone. Newburn frequently had to argue the case of Blackshirts detained for brawling, but this case was exceptional, he said. By now the police would have spoken to witnesses and corroborated my story. Nobody had a shred of evidence that I was a police killer; the Party would take the case to the House of Lords if it had to.

'Were any of the women hit?' I asked.

'No. The bullet missed Amelia Symes by a hair's breadth.'

Renton was the name of the Inspector who ended up conducting the final and most exacting interview. I assumed the lack of a uniform meant he was from Scotland Yard, or Special Branch, or some tentacle of the security services. He owned the haggard look of a man who had committed a couple of decades to police work; long days, late nights, endless cigarettes and strong tea, grim discoveries, distraught victims and villains he nailed in the end. Given his age, a world war and an IRA terror campaign probably featured in his life story too. Those detectives probing the streets immediately before the shooting could well have been his men.

Inspector Renton prowled through the facts yet again. 'Did you kill the man you said was holding a rifle?'

'No, I wounded him.'

'How many shots did you fire?'

'One.'

'And you can prove that by checking the gun,' Newburn intervened.

'We can count bullets, Mr Newburn.'

'My client could not kill three men with one bullet.'

'And that's stating the obvious. So, Mr Clifton, the man you say was pointing a rifle at you. Did you intend to kill him?'

'Any shot is an intent to kill and surviving a bullet wound is down to luck.'

'So you admit you intended to kill him?'

'I only had a moment to react and fire. The important thing was to bring him down, which I did. Then he was shot by the man in the raincoat—his accomplice. He shot to kill.'

'Why would he do that?'

'I'd only be guessing.'

'Guess.'

A pause was required before putting the shooting into context as I now understood it. 'I'd say he wanted to silence the rifleman. He could just as easily have shot me, but there were more Blackshirts behind me and coppers running up too, so he couldn't kill us all. Presumably, the man on the ground knew the identity of Raincoat Man and was killed to stop him revealing it.'

'That's a lot of speculation. I hear you're a writer of detective stories.'

'I can assure you this is not a story.'

Renton glanced at the notes on the table before him, probably more for effect than to jog his memory. 'According to your statement this so-called Raincoat Man shot at you, but you didn't get a chance to shoot back?'

'I was too late. He was gone down the snicket. The Alley. Sorry, we call them snickets up north. It had a bend in it, towards the main road.'

The Inspector huffed to show he had no time to discuss regional dialects. 'Which one of them shot the police officers?'

'I don't know.' At least the idea that I had shot the policemen had been set aside.

'Other than saying he wore a raincoat, what else can you tell me about the second man?'

'Not a lot beyond saying he was a man, white, neither young nor old. Short, maybe, or he ran with his head down. He wore a trilby, homburg, a hat with a brim. And a belted raincoat, tan I think. It was a sunny day, he didn't need that coat. He had the turned collar up. I only saw him for a moment before he went into the dark of the alley, then started shooting at me.'

'You said he was shooting at the man on the ground.'

'As it happens, but I wasn't to know that. I thought I was the target.'

Renton nodded, possibly acknowledging that he'd think the same in that position. 'Where did you get the revolver?'

'I took it from the police sergeant just after he was hit, as I've said. Why was he armed? Do you routinely arm your sergeants? I saw detectives there, too. What were they looking for? On the ground, in the doorways?'

The Inspector became stony-faced and ignored the cross-questioning. 'Your shooting skills came from the army? From which you were dishonourably discharged?'

This was pure rhetoric. Newburn laid his hand on my arm. 'I think my client has answered all your *pertinent* questions, Inspector.'

Renton ignored him. 'Do you keep up your weapons practice?'

'Gentlemen shoot, as you well know,' Newburn said. 'My client holds a valid Firearms Certificate, which I will happily procure for your perusal. His hobbies are completely legal.'

The inspector looked down at his papers for longer than he needed to, turning one over, then another.

'Now, can we agree that my client has answered all your questions Inspector?'

'For now.'

'It was fortuitous that former Lieutenant Clifton had the requisite skill and courage to rise to the occasion,' Newburn stated. 'His action undoubtedly saved lives, and he prevented one of the assassins from escaping justice. Britain should be grateful.'

Renton glanced away at the conclusion of the speech, framed almost as a rehearsal for what would be said in court. If any of this came to court.

'The Party wishes to convey its sympathy to the Force and to both officers' families for your sad loss. Sir Oswald will be writing to each of the families personally.'

The Inspector nodded and growled, maybe in appreciation. 'You're free to go, Mr Clifton.'

The stone face fell away, to be replaced by tiredness or perhaps relief.

Outside the chlorine door, the uniformed station commander conferred with Renton, who grunted some agreement. The officer approached and offered his hand. 'And now we're off the record, I have to say that me and my men are very appreciative for what you did Lieutenant Clifton. It took a lot of courage. I'd known Sergeant MacNamara for ten years; he had five children. And Constable Hughes was only married in the spring.'

'I wish I could have done more.'

'At least you got one of the bastards.'

Suddenly I was no longer scum who could be punched and abused by his officers. I just smiled; I'd fought enough battles that day. Property restored, relieved by a welcome trip to the washroom, and fully dressed once more, I made my way through the station. A policeman started to clap, then another, then all joined in—with the exception of Inspector Renton. Hot, sweaty, tired, hungry, I expected to walk out into a cool evening, not flashbulbs. Reporters and photographers huddled in ambush by the main door, yelling out, demanding to know my name and my story.

'The Director of Propaganda will brief you before you speak to any reporters,' Newburn hissed. 'Don't hide your face like a criminal, just get into the car.'

I ducked inside, Newburn darting around to the other side. '*Blackshirt* will run a whole feature on your exploits in the next edition, and the *Daily Mail* want your story, so prepare to be famous. Shame about your history, being cashiered and all. Can we turn that to an advantage? Your good name restored?'

That bitter disillusioned officer would have said no, but the spy said, 'Why not?'

'We just need to call at Black House first,' said Newburn, as casually as if proposing to stop at a corner sweet shop for a quarter of humbugs.

At that moment, nothing appealed more than a bath, a sandwich, a cup of tea, and a stiff drink or two but another twenty minutes' delay would be no more than a minor inconvenience at the end of an exhausting day. I pinned the fascist badge back on my uniform as London streets passed by.

A reception party was waiting in the lobby of Black House. I straightened up and began a modest grin for the expected applause and handshakes. The man known as FH, Neil Francis-Hawkins an ex-army officer who ran Black House, stood in the centre of the group, a look of glee in his eye but Major Taylor who led the Department Z intelligence section was not grinning at all. His little moustache was as stiff as his upper lip. Two unsmiling Blackshirts either side oozed brutality. Both their faces were familiar—these were members of the I Squad, the biff boys. Sliding from behind them came Captain Parker, whose scarred face might no longer be able to frame a smile even if he was capable of one.

'This way Clifton,' said Parker curtly, with no warmth and no hint of congratulation. He led towards the rear of the building, with the two biff boys falling in behind me, close enough to kick my heels if I slowed down. Newburn, my legal protector, had vanished from sight. I was prepared to be clapped on the back and celebrated as a top-notch fascist but something different awaited me in the cellars of Black House. Led down a staircase, I had a growing urge to escape, barge past those guards, and have done with this whole affair. Even attempting it would betray me as a spy, but by the time I'd planned my move the moment to act had gone. Parker stood outside a black door and I was ushered into his lair.

No windows allowed light or air into this room. Its walls and ceiling were painted black and a single bulb hung by its cord, off-centre. I was urged towards a bare wooden chair at the far end that faced two more behind what looked like an old school desk.

The two black-clad guards took station each side of the black door, their backs to the black wall. Two officers in black sat down with funereal faces, adding to the sense of doom. It was nothing if not dramatic. At least I wasn't handcuffed or tied up; I'm not sure how I would have coped with that degree of helplessness. Taylor took out a notebook. The colour of its cover was predictable.

Escape was impossible, cries would go unheard. I imagined beatings, torture, more beatings, then extended torture terminated by a blubbering death or a merciful bullet in the head when my usefulness ended. My hands started to shake. But this was England, Land of Hope and Glory, home of *habeas corpus*, cricket, and fair play. I dearly hoped that these men still knew that.

'What. Happened?' Parker asked, bluntly, with as much menace as he could muster. Then the questions rattled out, rapid as machine-gun fire, unrelenting and unforgiving.

Are you a member of the Communist Party?

What have you told the police?

Who did you tell about the rally?

Why was it you were there just at the right time?

I could stand the dank air no more and lapsed into a bout of coughing, then another. Finally, in a fit of exasperation, Taylor ordered one of the thugs to bring me water. It came in an enamelled tin mug, not a glass I might turn into a weapon, and it was quickly snatched away.

Are you a member of the Communist Party?

Did you know this shooting was planned?

Did you shoot that man just to silence him?

Who did you see running away?

Why did you let the second man get away?

Are you a member of the Communist Party?

Reprise.

For two hours. Perhaps three. I'd done this already with the police and with Inspector Renton and I no longer believed half of what I was repeating. At least no one had tried to hit me, or with my hands still free I would have laid him flat out then taken the guards on too. They looked bored now, their reactions would be slow. Abruptly, the questions stopped. Taylor whispered to Parker, and without explanation, they left the room and took the guards with them. I heard the key turn in the lock.

Bastards. I was going to destroy this organization, root and branch. My bladder was bulging, but that was one urge that had to be fought. They would not have the satisfaction of seeing me piss my trousers. A fear came that they would turn off the light and leave me in pitch darkness for hours or days. I'd welcome the sleep, but when I woke the suffocating blackness would crush me.

I hoped to God they were not out there sorting the instruments of torture, sharpening the scalpels, testing the pliers, and deciding which body part would be snipped off first. To divert me I imagined them nibbling scones and discussing the score, much like the tea interval at a cricket match. The thought of tea simply renewed my thirst.

Two new guards came in, a Changing of the Thugs.

'Could I have a drink please?'

'No.'

Back they came, Tweedledum and Tweedledee in black. Yes, it was easily three hours by now. I denied the Devil and all his works – or at least being a member of the Communist Party for the umpteenth time.

Question followed question followed question. It became difficult to stick to the story, I missed things out as each repetition made it more incredible. The two officers became quiet, exchanging whispers. Taylor checked a pocket watch. 'Thank you, Clifton, that will be all,' he said suddenly, snapping his book shut, and offering a smile that went beyond his lips. 'You're a brave young man and a credit to the Defence Force.'

Taylor stood up and saluted, and both men by the door joined in, stiff armed in their respect. Parker looked sour as if disappointed he couldn't rip out any fingernails. He stood up slowly before matching the salute. Gingerly I stood and returned it.

'And if you ever think of joining Department Z, come and see me.' Taylor smiled in a genial, head masterly way. 'We need men like you.'

'Be back here at nine tomorrow,' Parker snapped. 'You have an appointment.'

Wearily I took the stairs back to the surface one step at a time, the officials up ahead chatting lightly as if this was just another day at the office. What a terrible place the world would be if the Black House inquisitors ever wielded real power.

Chapter Ten

Driven home in a cab, it was after midnight when I finally sank into that bath, eating a piece of bread and cheese as the tub filled and washing it down with the last of the whisky. At least there was a bottle of French wine handy, which I took into the bathroom with no thought of decanting or allowing it to breathe or any of that nonsense. I drank from the bottle and toasted my survival. 'A perfect gentleman, a perfect spy, a perfect Blackshirt hero.'

Damn, I'd missed lunch with Sissy.

After too little sleep, I was whisked off by car to the Sunday appointment. Julian collected me, and it was a relief to see a friend. Life had taken a perverse turn when a man whose attitudes were so alien, and who I intended to betray, amounted to my best friend in the city.

Black House adopted a welcoming face today. I donned that uniform again and was shown into the small meeting room, lined with leather-bound books from some distinguished member's library. An officer strode in, quite slight, with a prominent scar ticking up from the right side of his mouth that twitched as he spoke. Scars were almost standard issue around here.

'Joyce,' he said. 'Director of Propaganda.' He was no older than I was and looked younger.

A salute seemed in order, and Joyce returned it.

'First the photographs, then you have interviews for *Blackshirt* and the *Daily Mail*, then *The Saturday Review*. The *Mail* is important because it is owned by Lord Rothermere, an old friend of the Leader. You may not be aware that Lady Houston owns *Saturday Review* and she is very influential.'

I nodded. *Know thine enemy* had become a watchword and I had read as much pro-fascist literature as I could lay my hands on.

'Sit.' Joyce himself took a chair. 'You will tell how you thwarted the communist plot to disrupt our lawful democratic meeting…' he went on for several minutes laying down the dogmatic content that must underlie the stories the press printed. 'Propaganda is everything,' he concluded. 'It is how we bring mass support to our cause. It is how we persuade people to think as we do.'

I tried to ask a few questions but was rewarded only by a straight recital of Joyce's view of events. 'And as for your background, this rumour that you were dishonourably discharged is nothing but slander. You are the model of the army officer class who are flocking to join us.'

Joyce stood to admit the official BUF photographer Kay Fredericks and tried to direct her art, which control she chiefly ignored. The Director of Propaganda left the room and allowed her to get on with the job.

Setting my jaw straight, I posed for a photograph that was not me.

Former Lieutenant Clifton struck a pose looking just off the photographer's shoulder, gazing into some pure fascist future. His chest was puffed out in that pompous manner Benito Mussolini had mastered and his importance was emphasized by wearing a commander's peak cap borrowed for the shoot. His jaw was set firm, and the camera caught a twinkle in his eye.

Joyce was putting out a story of communist snipers attempting to kill a female politician with two decades of campaigning for peace and women's rights behind her. It would score hits all over the newspaper-buying population. With their agent on the front page of the *Daily Mail* as well as *Blackshirt* it must have been the least covert operation in the history of the Security Service.

'I hear Lord Rothermere is pleased,' Julian trilled as he drove me away from the morning of interviews only slightly less gruelling than those of the days before. 'He's talking about backing us again, now the commies have shown their cards.'

I'd changed out of my uniform and back into myself. 'I say, could you drop me at the Dorchester? I'm lunching with Sissy.'

'Certainly. Lunch for the hero, what? Shame I can't join you. Sissy's an amazing girl, isn't she?'

'She is.'

'I'm going on to see Father, he's so excited by what happened yesterday and what it means for us. He's going to talk to Lady Houston again; she's got millions just waiting to find the right cause. And we might snag Lord Nuffield too, the industrialist.'

'That's good. It's excellent, in fact.' I attempted to remain in character, scared of what I'd suddenly become, disorientated by the lurches in fortune of the past 24 hours. The baying faces of reporters outside the police station, pressing forward, merged with the image of a Punjabi crowd surging closer, my desperate attempts at authority being drowned out by the yells of anger, then by the volley fire. I'd put all this aside as the shots rang around the Kensington street, as bullets zipped from the alleyway, and as I'd fought back on the side of the law. In that moment, I'd forgotten myself, briefly becoming again the man I had ceased to be. Fascism could be my remaking. That would be the story, anyway.

'Hugh!' The martini was almost as welcome as her gentle hug hello and peck on my cheek. 'Darling, you could have been killed!'

'I wasn't.'

The Park Lane Hotel was new, and I'd heard was already attracting 'all the right people.' Walking those Persian rugs between polished classical columns, I appreciated the Old-World charm repackaged for a new age. Settling back into a chair it was impossible not to enjoy how Sissy bubbled with life. Thank goodness she had agreed to a hurried rescheduling of our lunch date, or that would have been another grudge to chalk up against the communists.

'Gosh when they started shooting, we didn't know where to run to,' Sissy said, 'everyone just ran around like headless chickens. Mrs Symes was in a total funk, I had to pull her off that stage. I did that, me. All the men had buggered off. Thank God she wasn't hit, or any of us. But you...' she took my hand across the table. 'You just ran straight towards the danger. You're such a hero.'

'When you're trained to do something, you just do it. Swimming, driving a car; think too much about what you're doing and you'll drown, or crash.'

'Oh stop it with the false modesty!' She lowered her brow theatrically. 'But did you really shoot that terrorist? Was it really terrible?'

'It's afterwards that it becomes terrible,' I said with total honesty.

'But you just drew your pistol and shot him dead. Gosh.'

'It wasn't my pistol, and I didn't kill him, for which I'm glad. I've never actually killed anyone and don't want to break my duck.'

'Oh.' She sounded disappointed, released my hand then took another sip of her martini. 'So who did kill him?'

'Bizarrely it was his team-mate who did for him. Perhaps they'd vowed not to be taken alive, honour amongst communists or something. I shot him, true, he was badly wounded but might have survived. I was going to hold him there until the police arrived.'

She sipped at her drink again. It was unclear if I had risen or fallen in her estimation now that I was revealed not to be a cold-blooded killer.

'I'm not a hero. Perhaps, for two days until the newspapers are rolled up as firelighters. And someone is bound to rake up my history in the meantime. You do know about my history, don't you? I was thrown out of the army.'

'I did hear something; one asks, but it was probably some horrible mistake.'

'No, it wasn't a mistake it was perfectly deliberate. I was leading a patrol through this godforsaken frontier town. Two local tribes had been having a ding-dong and chose that moment to kick off again. We calmed it down, separated them, pushed both groups back, but then half a company arrived on the far side of the square commanded by a major and he was having none of the softly-softly approach. Someone started shooting, and the crowd rushed our way trying to escape, as there were only twelve of us as opposed to fifty rifles on the far side of the square. I ordered my men to hold their fire, but then I was shot. It was probably one of our own bullets coming straight through the crowd but I never knew for certain.

'I just lay there in the dirt, and there's this man coming at me with sheer hatred in his eyes. Dark pits of eyes. He had this big curved dagger or meat cleaver or something.' A diner at the next table chose that moment to drop his own knife with a clatter and the anecdote paused. 'My Sikh corporal dragged me back, and my men stood over me with fixed bayonets else the mob would have cut my head off.'

'How horrid. But you were brave, so why…?'

'Because nine local civilians were killed, including four women and a child. Twenty or so injured, one blinded, a boy lost his leg. Three of my men were hurt. They called it the Swat Massacre. Someone had to carry the can for ordering the first shot, and I wasn't expected to survive, so it seemed like a jolly good plan to blame the dead northern nobody, bury him, shrug shoulders and move on. It was more convenient than blaming a very well-connected major who was still alive and lined up for the House of Lords.'

'But you did survive.'

'Inconveniently for everyone concerned. So there had to be a Court Martial, I was cashiered and only escaped worse punishment because they just wanted me gone from India without too many more questions. I was stretchered onto trains, a ship, more trains then dumped at my Father's house where everyone thought I would be forgotten. But nobody forgets, so I lug the shame around like the dead body of my old self slung over my shoulder.'

'But not anymore!' Sissy squeezed my hand again. 'You're a hero now.'

Glasses clinked together. 'Hero of the party,' she said.

'To the Party.' After those hours in the all-black cellar, I almost choked on my words.

'Oh, rot the Party,' she clinked glasses again. 'To life, to us!'

'To us.'

She laid down her glass with purpose. 'On Friday, before all this, you asked about machine guns. We've not got any yet, but we have rifles and pistols… We're having a camp next weekend and my girls would just love it if you could come out and teach us to shoot like you can.'

I nodded.

Sissy touched my hand again. 'And I'd love it too.'

Chapter Eleven

My next rendezvous with Calhoun was in a little coffee bar on the Euston Road on Monday morning. Calhoun seemed to have a knack for choosing places that were busy enough so that two men speaking quietly would not be noticed but were cursed with an awkward and unpopular corner that other customers would avoid.

'*Blackshirt Hero*.' Calhoun spoke with only a hint of irony. 'How better to hide my agents than have their face all over the front of the *Daily Mail*.'

I was certain that this meeting would mark the end of my short innings with the Security Service.

'Although the saving grace is that in real life you don't stick your chin out like that, with your nose up. And that bus conductor's hat isn't your everyday attire. You're hardly a *secret agent* anymore though, are you?'

'Sorry I muffed it.'

'Just tell me what happened, exactly. And then this afternoon you can go through it all again with Mrs Ainsworth for the record.'

The story had been repeated so often for the benefit of the police, Department Z, and the press it was hard to know where fact ended and propaganda began, but I went through it all again, using the sugar bowl, salt cellar, and cutlery arranged at angles to help build the scene. I answered all the obvious questions, tailoring them for my real role rather than the one I adopted for everyone else.

'Raincoat Man was ruthless,' I concluded. 'That rifleman was killed without any hesitation, clearly to preserve secrecy.'

'That takes discipline. The kind we might expect from a foreign agency.'

Calhoun posed the thought. 'The Russians haven't been this bold in England yet, but we know they have assassination teams on the continent. It's in their interests to see left and right fighting in the streets. For every recruit this shooting brings to the fascists, it will bring two anti-fascists to oppose them. They're two sides of a coin, one feeds off the fear of the other. Moscow knows that.'

'The Russians…' A shiver went through me, recognising the significance of what I had stopped, or what I may have unleashed. 'Whoever was behind the shooting, this is more complex than it looks. Beforehand there was no big demonstration, no attack like I saw in Camden the other week. The rally should have been indoors, not on a street corner. Someone pulled strings to have us moved to exactly where that sniper could shoot at Mrs Symes.' My assertions grew bolder. 'The police were relaxed, like they knew there would be no trouble either.'

'You can knit together coincidences and twists of fate and imagine there is more substance than there is,' Calhoun said. 'It's not only our side who can plant a spy in the fascist movement, anyone who can pay their shilling can join.'

'There was a man I saw at Camden I call Hook-nose. A little shorter than me, a little older, blondish hair, 'tache, seems to have a favourite red tie. He was there again in Kensington, mixed in with the socialists and there was something about his manner that just didn't seem right.'

Calhoun betrayed genuine interest. 'Go on.'

'He was acting like I would act if you'd planted me in the communists. And I saw detectives in plain clothes searching for something.'

'Go on,' Calhoun repeated.

'And there was an armed police sergeant in the Wolseley. England prides itself on not routinely arming policemen. I quizzed this copper about it—Inspector Renton.'

'You quizzed Renton?' Calhoun found this amusing.

'You know him?'

'He's made destroying the BUF a personal project, and he'll destroy you too if you give him half a chance. Did your cover hold?'

'You've seen the newspapers. Renton thinks I'm that fascist glove puppet on the front page. And if he's out to destroy the BUF, perhaps his men were in on the plot.'

'That's stretching the conspiracy a little far. Renton is Special Branch. They're working on identifying the dead rifleman and digging out the bullets. As soon as we have a name, and they've finished trampling on the evidence, I'll feed through what I can.'

'To me?'

'Who else?'

'But you can't want me to carry on? Not after all this? My cover is blown wide open, the whole country knows my face. I should just call it a day, slink back north…'

'No, you, you're right where we need you to be,' Calhoun said smoothly. 'And your cover is burnished to perfection. It's the best way to hide, right out in plain sight where you don't look as if you're even trying to hide.'

'I've started packing my trunk.'

'As you said yourself, the whole country knows your face. You'd be a prize trophy for any communist extremist with a grudge or any fascist offended by their hero suddenly deserting the cause.' He stopped talking, allowing me to imagine the legion of fanatics on left and right lining up to slit my throat. 'You are our entire operation inside the Blackshirts. It will take us six months to replace you and we don't have six months.'

On Sunday morning I'd been relieved to have got away with my life, but dammit I had no life before I became a spy. For a multitude of reasons, I couldn't run back north now; I couldn't fail again.

'So what now?'

He smiled. 'Carry on, find their money, as before. What did you learn from your dinner with Mrs Symes?'

I summarized her political views as I sipped tea and took bites from a digestive biscuit.

'Our last intelligence was that they're in too much of a mess to put up candidates if an election happens this year.'

'Mrs Symes mentioned a report by Fuller – that's the Great War general?'

Major-General Fuller's book *On Future Warfare* had been one of many books read whilst I was convalescing the previous winter. His ideas that modern warfare required the mass use of tanks, aircraft and trucks instead of horses had won him few friends in the army or the Treasury.

'Fuller joined the BUF last year, just as everyone else was leaving after the Olympia fracas.' Calhoun said. 'He's been to Nazi party events in Germany.'

'But you know about his report?'

'It's powerful medicine, all about cleaning up the BUF and making them more like a real political party than a boy scout troop. I'll have a copy dropped by, for your education. Your eyes only. If Mrs Symes is a fan of Fuller, that puts her on the more respectable side of the party, let's say even the electable side of the party.'

'I'm not so sure how respectable she'll be once she has our vote.' I was disappointed that I was teaching Calhoun nothing. 'There's talk of building an air force.' I tried to make what I could of Hubert Symes' ambitions.

This might indeed be news. 'It sounds like another one of their fantasies.'

Perhaps Sissy's rifle stockpile was also a fantasy not worth mentioning, and I shouldn't drop her in it before I had the full facts. By this time, I was becoming desperate to show my value as a spy, to tell Calhoun something he didn't already know.

The waitress came over and Calhoun pulled a handful of coins from his pocket. 'I need to go, I've another meeting.'

'There's something called Plan Blue,' I blurted out. 'Symes let it slip.'

Calhoun paused in the action of checking his change and waved the waitress away.

'Did she say what Plan Blue entailed?'

'She went mum straight away when she realized I wasn't party to it. I'm sure it's to do with preparing for an election. Howard Thring might be involved in it too.'

'Find out what you can about this Plan Blue—but take care.' He lifted his finger. 'And I mean that.'

* * *

Harry Bretton-Smythe looked every inch the former Guards officer. At once people knew he could be trusted

No, no, I couldn't have a lead character with a double-barrelled name. I'd be mis-typing Bretton-Smythe on every rotten page of the rotten book. I tore out the sheet from the typewriter and screwed it up. After a moment's thought, I slightly unscrewed it into a bulkier and more satisfying ball and added it to my credentials as a real writer within the wicker basket.

Harry Bretton could be trusted to get the job done. At six feet three, he was the model of a Guards

Vincent Hammer stopped typing. *Was the model* or *looked the model*? Perhaps *very model*. Damn, this was going to be hard. Better stick with *was* for now or that basket would fill up in no time.

Mrs Ainsworth interrupted my artistic flow. She insisted on coming up to my flat rather than standing in the hall, took a copy of the Fuller Report from the bottom of her shopping basket, and stated that I had until four o'clock to read it. Steely-eyed she told me I was to remain in the flat until she called to collect it again. I made a coffee, lounged on the sofa, and began to read. Fuller made convincing arguments. Only the fascists could deliver his vision of a re-armed Britain, so with military bluntness he proposed a whole new strategy for winning power. The BUF must change or die.

Chapter Twelve

Pat Hanrahan was amused by the selection of quiet cafes, ill-frequented bistros, and hotel bars Marcus Calhoun chose for their meetings. This week's choice was in Warren Street, run by a Greek Cypriot couple.

'Sir,' he laid his trilby down on the table. 'Where's M these days?' He found the reclusive Security Service officer who had recruited him more to his liking than this ex-Royal Navy commander who now appeared to be in charge.

'M's not very well,' Calhoun said. 'Pneumonia last I heard.'

'He probably caught it off his pet baboon, or one of his parrots or what have you. So do I work for you now?'

'For the time being.' Calhoun already had a pot of tea steaming in front of him and ordered the usual coffee for Hanrahan. It was a welcome treat that morning, as posing as a language teacher down on his luck meant that his cupboards must be stocked with only the cheapest of blends.

'You've been rumbled,' Calhoun said.

Immediately he tensed.

'Fortunately, by one of our own. You need to change that tie more often.'

Hanrahan touched the russet brown woolen tie. 'It's quite ordinary.'

'Buy a green one.'

'So I would look more Irish? Where was I rumbled, as you put it?'

'A riot outside the BUF meeting in Camden and at the affair in Kensington. You're known as Hook-nose.'

'Charming for sure. Is my admirer inside the Blackshirts?'

'You know I'm not going to confirm that.'

'So he is. Or she is—let's not forget the sisters.'

Calhoun muttered something about cricket whilst a couple tried to decide whether to take the next table, or the one by the window the woman worried would be too hot. Hanrahan had no interest in cricket. As soon as the couple plumped for the window, Calhoun leaned forward, speaking a little quieter than he had before. 'How is the shooting looking from your side of the fence? Why didn't we know this was coming?'

'There was no sign of it at all,' Hanrahan admitted. 'I've never heard even a whisper about rifles.'

'How about explosives?'

Hanrahan frowned. 'Explosives?'

'We kept it out of the newspapers during the King's Jubilee, but it will leak out soon enough. Half a ton stolen from a quarry in Cornwall back in May.'

'Jesus and Mary, you kept that quiet,' Hanrahan said. 'I've heard nothing about that either.'

'According to reports, there was none of the usual infiltration and stone-throwing before the shooting. You were just waiting.' Calhoun raised his eyebrows, demanding an explanation and Hanrahan searched for one.

'The word went out that it was not the day to cause a stir.'

'From?' Calhoun challenged.

'The Central Committee.'

'What was the excuse?'

'Our sisters were uncomfortable confronting a woman with violence. It would send the wrong message, as if we were against women having a voice in politics. Killing Mrs Symes would make bad headlines and cast the Blackshirts as being on the side of the angels. Which is precisely what has happened, helped by that fecking Nazi going all John Wayne with a six gun. Where did he come from?'

'Yorkshire, apparently. And with or without his intervention, the plan failed, indeed backfired. Mrs Symes is alive, and Mosley didn't even turn up. What I want to know is was he the intended target?'

'He'd be a bigger prize than Mrs Symes, for sure. But the Communist Party don't want to give Mosley legitimacy by fighting him openly, let alone shooting at him. It's the local organizations and the unions that galvanize the anti-fascist demonstrations, and they don't have trained killers on the books.'

'Moscow?'

'No – unless you're writing for Tory press.'

'But there's clearly a ring within the communists you're not aware of. Someone who has access to weapons, and now explosives. You need to start earning your salt.'

It was frustrating to have been reduced to a spectator at the shooting. Hanrahan hated surprises and was always wary of his back. If an armed group was operating beyond his knowledge, it added an unwelcome layer of danger that needed to be accounted for and planned for. He could not tell Georgie who he was meeting with, but he wished she was close by.

Calhoun stirred his tea. 'The explosives were not used to disrupt the Jubilee, but the terror ring may not have had the time to organize an attack. Bombs and guns are a change of tactics and change of tone for the left. If it wasn't the Jubilee, what's provoked them?'

'A Tory Prime Minister replacing a Labour Prime Minister without the courtesy of involving the electorate?' Hanrahan suggested. 'The National Government at last shown in its true colours.'

'But they shot at the Blackshirts.'

'Tories and fascists are one and the same so far as the left is concerned. Mosley just says things in public the Tories daren't.'

'Have you come across the BUF's Plan Blue?'

'Plan Blue! How the fascists love their plans and grand titles.'

'Well it exists, so it's worth keeping your ear to the ground. And if a copy happens to fall into the hands of your comrades, I'd very much like to read what it has to say. Meanwhile, find those guns and bombs please before there's a bloody massacre. Both ears to the ground. And get a new tie.'

Chapter Thirteen

Baroness Rockwell fell over herself to arrange the drinks reception, specifically at the request of the Leader. Sir Oswald Mosley was standing just two metres away from me, tall and imposing in his evening jacket. He carried off a dark moustache with far more panache than Herr Hitler. I noticed his limp as he came in, a relic of the Great War when he'd smashed his leg in an aeroplane crash. Since then, Mosley's career had featured more about-turns than the Trooping of the Colour; elected for the Tories as the youngest MP in Parliament, defected to Labour, split to form the New Party and failed utterly in the 1931 election before forming the BUF.

'Clifton, isn't it?' Sir Oswald offered his hand. 'Splendid courage you showed the other day, you're the kind of man this country needs. We're awarding you a stripe by way of recognition. I asked for you to be invited tonight, so more people could meet fascism's new hero. You're from the Midlands?'

'Yorkshire.'

'Yes, of course. Your father is in coal I believe.'

'He is.'

'The coal industry has been very hard hit by the slump. So many miners have been thrown out of work by the Old Gang, it's a scandal. But fascism will lead the way to recovery—led by young men like us.' He was just my side of 40, far younger than most politicians I'd bumped into. I was framing my next line when he turned to Howard Thring, who hovered close by his left shoulder like that angel in Islamic tradition that records evil deeds. 'Was

Clifton your find, Howard?'

'Indeed,' said Thring, offering the first threat of a smile I'd seen from him. 'Come and tell me about your trip. Oh, good evening Sissy.'

With a quick flash of her flawless teeth at the Leader, Sissy bobbed around Thring to take Mosley's place. 'Gosh Hugh, the Leader spoke to you! Isn't he just...well isn't this super? What did you say to him?'

'Just three words. It was hardly the dramatic speech I'd planned. But he knows roughly where Yorkshire is and how the coalfields are suffering, which is gratifying. And I'm getting a stripe too. Whether that makes me a lance corporal or what I don't know.'

Without being obvious I encouraged Sissy to drift towards Thring in the hope I could eavesdrop on the conversation he was having with the Leader.

'...collectively they achieve little, and individually even less...' Thring Senior grumbled. 'It's still a shambles top to bottom.' Mosley laid a hand on his shoulder and leaned close enough to say something inaudible to eavesdroppers. Thring nodded, a self-satisfied smile coming to his face. 'It is,' he said.

'But three words is a start,' Sissy put her hand on my arm, bringing spying to a halt. 'Handsome, isn't he?'

'Ah, hard to say being a chap myself.'

'Silly!'

'And he recognized you too—I hear he has an eye for attractive young women of quality.'

She glanced quickly away. 'I've just been speaking with Diana Guinness,' she said.

I let her words hang just for a moment, just to let her know I'd taken note of the evasion. 'The Leader's...ahem, special friend?'

'Yah. She's so beautiful, and younger than me too. Has the pick of the men, the lucky woman. She's married to Lord Moyne at the moment.' The Leader's latest mistress stood over by the windows; blonde and confident. 'Her sister's besotted with Hitler, and they visit his home regularly. Fancy that.'

'Are you besotted with Hitler too?'

'Of course not, silly! Unity is barely out of school, she's probably got that older man crush. Frankly…' She leaned in close. 'I don't know about you, but I find Hitler rather creepy. I've never met him, but he's not someone I'd want to chat to at a party. I've heard he can be terribly boring. Goodness knows how a funny little man like that became Chancellor of Germany.'

'He tells the people what they want to hear. Which is going to be our strategy too, I'll wager. And no one could call our Leader a funny little man. Give me Mosley over Hitler any day.'

'See,' she punched me lightly with her knuckle. 'He's charmed you too.'

The man did possess some kind of magnetism.

'Have you seen Julian this evening?' she asked.

'Over there, I think. Yes, talking to Diana Guinness now.'

'Men! Like wasps round a jam jar.'

'Are you and Julian old friends?'

'Of sorts. His father was my father's accountant before he died.'

'Was he killed in the War?'

'No, he just died, as people do. Daddy was always trying business schemes that didn't quite work and Howard Thring tidied up his mess. He's good at that. Julian and I are the same age, and I think he rather fancied his chances once. Then this flighty thing came in, Verity Laytham, all university and high ideas. Very much your type, Hugh. Books and big words. She swept Julian off his feet for a few weeks last summer. I sometimes wonder what happened to her. One week she was there, and the next she wasn't.'

She lowered her brow with mock severity. 'I should hire your Harry Bretton to find her.'

'His rates are reasonable. Five pounds a day, plus expenses.'

'I'll telephone his office in the morning.' She smiled. 'Julian still looks at me sometimes as if he made a mistake being distracted by Verity, then ending up with Melissa as consolation prize.' She now grimaced. She and Melissa were oil and water. 'They were engaged on Christmas Eve—it was quite a whirlwind romance. A total turn-around for him.'

'Your mother would never have let you marry an accountant.'

'Certainly not, darling. And as for Yorkshiremen who dig coal…'

'Now you're teasing. Where there's muck there's brass, as we say up north, and my father has plenty of both. And poor Julian will end up crushed between his father and his wife. Ah the wasp leaves the jam-pot. Julian!' I moved to meet our friend, with Sissy now on my arm. Julian wanted to know about Mosley too and received the same brief report.

'A stripe, jolly good.'

'Your father's been on a trip, I hear.'

'Yes, yes, you know; a lot of his clients are shipping people.'

After waiting for more exposition and receiving none, I tried to nudge more information out of him. 'That must be an interesting diversion from the office routine, steaming off to Europe on business.' Thring had not been away long enough to travel further than Europe.

'I like the South of France,' Sissy interrupted.

'Well he doesn't ship from the South of France,' Julian said.

'And I just love Paris, and Amsterdam.'

'I imagine the shipping business touches less artistic locations,' I said. 'Rotterdam, Hamburg...'

'Those sorts of places,' Julian said.

Playing guess-the-port was futile, but Calhoun must have contacts who could prove exactly where Thring had been.

'Now *that* man is from somewhere continental.' Sissy indicated a short, well-fed man standing by the curtains with only a half-empty glass for company.

'Oh yes, he's one of Father's German's.'

'Come on, let's say hello,' I said. 'He looks lonely in a big city.'

Sissy gripped my arm tighter. 'Oh Hugh, what about giving little me a little time? Or don't you like me?'

'Sorry, I'm still new to London, I'm trying to make friends. We can slip away in a while. Is there somewhere we can go dancing perhaps?'

'Indeed there is, and we can. So, the deal is that we meet a few more stuffy people until I am totally bored, then you can lead me astray.' She bobbed up to the short gentleman. 'Hello, I'm Sissy and this is my most heroic friend Hugh Clifton. You must have read about him in the newspapers.'

'I'm sorry,' said the man, 'I've not been in London for some months.' His accent was heavily continental, Germanic. 'Florian Kahn.'

Shaking his hand, I began a welcome in German, but quickly realized that my language skills extended little beyond asking directions to the railway station and ordering *brätwurst und bier* for two. Kahn's English was much better, although carefully phrased so that he spoke with a slow drawl. 'And Mr Clifton you are…hero?'

Sissy immediately recapped the story of Hugh Clifton-as-hero, which grew rather in the telling.

'It was a jolly good job the Leader wasn't up there with Mrs Symes,' Julian threw in. 'He was going to make a surprise appearance.'

But made a surprise non-appearance. Instead, the sniper shot the wall when he might have preferred Mosley. It still did not explain why he wasted a bullet at all.

'*Ja*, the shooting. Communists, we had one day the same problem in Germany, but *der Führer* brings order.'

'Do you work with *der Führer*?' It took little effort to make the question innocent and excitable, fitting with the tone Sissy used constantly.

'No, no, I'm *ein* merchant. I work with Julian's father, Hamburg.'

So guess-the-port had been answered.

'I ought to go to Hamburg one day,' I said. 'I'm writing a novel, there's a London detective, he's on the trail of something…I'm not sure what yet.'

'How about diamond smuggling,' Kahn suggested after Sissy and Julian had both tipped in a few ideas. 'The Dutch are good at that. Amsterdam.' He crooked a finger, grasping at the air. 'Your master villain is a Jewish diamond cutter who will stop at nothing. He values money above everything.' Kahn frowned to emphasize the evil this villain would embody. 'Human life means nothing to him.'

It was not a bad idea at all. Admittedly out in the non-fascist world, it was a *bad* idea, but it would serve the purpose. 'My hero is a Blackshirt, so the Jewish angle would be a really exciting twist.'

'The Jewish angle.' Kahn smiled. 'The Jewish angle troubles us at home. Many of the Jews that leave Germany come to England.'

'So your problem is becoming our problem,' Julian said.

'We have our German solutions.' Kahn shrugged. 'They are working. *Also* you need to find your English solutions.'

* * *

'Those poor Jews again,' Sissy said once they were in the back of a cab heading for that promised club. 'Harmless little men running junk shops and wearing little hats on Fridays, why do we have to attack them all the time?'

Perhaps she was testing me, but I would test her too. 'You're sympathetic towards the Jews then?'

'No!' she snapped. 'Don't say that, you'll get me shot! Not literally, but...' She snuggled up to me, which was welcome but unexpected. 'You won't report me to Department Z will you darling? I've heard they have a little black dungeon where they lock traitors in for days and days with nothing to eat, but that's probably made up.'

She should keep her illusions.

'Of course, I won't betray you. I don't understand the Jewish thing either; it's a miss-step for the Party if we go down that route. Antisemitism might excite the Germans, but it's lazy politics, masking real issues by blaming someone else.'

If Sissy's fascism was only skin-deep, she might even be trustworthy one day. A woman who did not have an irrational loathing for a persecuted minority was far more attractive than one who did. I squeezed her hand. 'You can be a secret liberal. I won't tell.'

She stage-giggled. 'Why is that naughty? Why is it even interesting? We could still go to the Party parties! And drink their champagne, and I could run their camps and you could be the famous hero, and it would all be a great joke and only we'd know.'

'Our secret.'

'But seriously, you'll still come to my camp, won't you? On Saturday? Our family home in Kent.'

'Of course. Will there be an invitation…to stay over.' I ran my fingers up the back of her hand, but she become tense. All the joking was over.

'You know I'm married,' she stated.

I pulled away from her hand as if it were a hot iron, but she grabbed mine back immediately. She gripped hard, her nails digging into my palm. 'My faithless husband is in Italy, with someone else. Lots of someone else's, probably.'

'Oh.'

'He bats for the other team, as Julian put it once. Everyone knew, apparently, except silly little me. His family wanted him married off to avoid scandal, they thought I'd put him back on the path God intended. I'd been a little wicked myself, and everyone said I should settle down, so I played their game. Vincent was positively the most beautiful man alive, a real Adonis. Cultured, thoughtful, the best dresser you'll ever meet.'

'Wicked?'

'I ran away to Paris,' she whispered. 'It was a little scandalous. After a few adventures, I found I was twenty-one, not exactly dusty on the shelf but they pushed me towards Vincent.' She paused, filtering bad memories. 'The honeymoon was horrific, as you can imagine, and that was just about it. One month and the dream was well and truly over.'

'I'm sorry.'

'Ah, don't!'

'And now I have to confess that I'm also married.'

'I know, I have spies, I've checked your pedigree.' Her tone was flat. 'Where is the honourable Leonora D'Auville now?'

'Oh, Home Counties somewhere.'

'Tell me about her.'

'I'd rather not.'

She leaned in and her perfume overwhelmed my senses. 'Just this once, then I won't ask anymore.'

'Leo wanted to marry a hero in uniform, but one with all his arms and legs and nerves intact. I was New Money, and very provincial, but once upon a time, I was a good catch. She was most disappointed when I didn't die out in India. We're not divorced, as that would add yet more stigma, plus my father's lawyer has told *her* father's lawyer quote, "the bitch is not getting a penny." He's more offended than I am.'

'Life can be so cruel,' she said. 'Do you still love her?'

'Report over,' I said. 'And I should get out of the taxi now. Married man, married woman...'

'But that's what makes this so perfect!' She gripped tightly again. 'A single woman can be positively ruined by having an affair, and a single man must be in need of a wife, but these days affairs are *de rigueur* for married people. Unhappily married people, of course.'

'Are we having an affair?'

'I jolly well hope so.'

* * *

Sissy purred at my touch. Pleasure ran both ways—I'd not made love for three years, and it may as well have been never. When she dug in her fingernails it was odd but not unpleasant. She urged me to *be careful.*

'But not gentle!' She chided, then bit my earlobe.

It was just after midnight, and we had been whisked by another cab from the 400 Club to Sissy's flat in Chelsea. The tunes we danced to had been forgotten, the label on the Champagne bottle that had fleetingly seemed important was now as significant as if it had been ginger beer. I could not escape her eyes, and her voice pushed the music into the background. Suddenly this was not an act, my body was not lying to Sissy. This was not part of the mission or any order from Calhoun. I nibbled her ear in turn, dislodging an earring and we laughed whilst we hunted it amongst the sheets. Play was delayed whilst she removed the other and placed it on the bedside table.

'Don't brag to Julian.' She settled back and I rolled to half-cover her, skin against skin.

'He'll work it out, he's not dumb.'

'Yes, but don't brag to him. Don't tell him I do this.' She slid a hand down to explore my buttocks, then ventured around under my hips. She grabbed hold, firmly.

I gave a little yelp for effect. 'Your reputation will remain intact.'

'And yours, cad. Seducer of married women. Invading London with your rough northern ways.'

'And you, the high-born lady, taming me.' I caressed her cheek.

She ruffled my hair. 'Not too tame, please.'

Chapter Fourteen

I judged the Dowager Baroness Rockwell's Kentish home to be modest compared to some I'd stayed at. If I correctly remembered what I'd once known about architecture, it was built in the same Palladian style as Moat Hall, with an entrance resembling a Greek temple. The Rockwell estate included rolling downland, small woods, and a stretch of a river which offered 'some fishing' in season.

Driving down from London that Saturday morning was pleasant, and as soon as my powder blue Alvis was parked alongside half a dozen other cars Julian Thring marched up resplendent in black.

'You're not in uniform,' was his first comment.

'I wasn't sure how clever it would be to drive around in it.'

'Ah, capital point. You might have taken a wrong turn and ended up down some side street you didn't want to be. Or be stopped by some officious bobby. They're not all on our side, you know. Not yet.'

Melissa had been part-concealed by Julian but now bobbed around him. Her blouse was also black and did not flatter her figure, and she wore a skirt of practical khaki. 'Hello again!' she thrust out her hand to shake mine with energy, but it was not a warm handshake. 'So the hero of the hour is come to teach us how to shoot the reds down like dogs.'

'Well, "hero" is pushing it a little.'

She nodded, her lips pursed.

'Sissy said we were to go and find her as soon as you arrived,' Julian said.

'We're down by the boathouse,' Melissa added and immediately started to walk away. She led down towards a hump-backed bridge where the little river emptied into the lake. Beside it ran a long wooden building of several phases of construction and a dozen or so young women dressed identically to Melissa were ranged on a mismatching set of chairs. A few were smoking and chatting and two read magazines. All came to the alert as we approached, and Melissa asked loudly whether Sissy was back. She was not, but I soon spotted her. An open-top green Bentley appeared, lurching towards us, clipping the grass kerb of the lakeside road as the driver oversteered in an attempt to keep to the track. Sissy rode in the passenger seat, gripping the door and windscreen grimly. 'Brake,' she called. 'Use the brake!'. The Bentley jerked to a halt with a loud creak and the engine stalled.

Sissy the socialite was transformed by that uniform into something so much more formidable. Shaking her head, she hurried from the car. 'You can take the next one Melissa. My nine lives are all used up. Ah Hugh, lovely to see you.' She held out a hand. It was trembling. 'Shake. We don't do hugs whilst we're in uniform, or those sweet little kisses the French do.' She glanced away as if embarrassed by how much we now knew of each other.

Melissa looked from one of us to the other, reading the signals.

'Melissa?'

Melissa let out a deep breath. 'Right-ho, I'll take the next one.' She yelled for someone called Eleanor.

'Death before dishonour,' Sissy said breezily, then set out with purpose along the road away from the bridge. I followed.

'Do you have a cigarette?' She asked.

'No, sorry.'

She screwed up her face. 'I so need one after that. Have you run out?'

'I don't smoke.'

'I did wonder. That's unusual in a man.'

'I think that's an illusion created by advertising men. Our regimental doctor was convinced fags cause all kinds of nasties and he had me stop after I had half a lung shot away.' I jabbed my right breast.

'Poor you. Just one moment in time and your whole life changed...forever.'

That was a little deep for a Saturday morning. 'So, tell me what you and the ladies are up to out here.'

'Well, for one thing, we're teaching them to drive. Women in the last war were ambulance drivers, and they drove staff cars and troop lorries.'

'You're not planning a war?'

'No, silly, but we need to be prepared. Next time we're not going to be the useless ones left at home, waving our hankies. My God, it's terrifying though. I was sure I was going to die just now, about ten times. Julia nearly tipped us into the lake at the end.'

'Are you teaching them to swim as well?'

'Yes, as it happens. And we're learning jujutsu.'

'My God, what's that?'

'Unarmed combat – an ancient Japanese martial art. It was developed to enable ordinary people to fight samurai warriors.'

'Well I hope you won't have to fight any samurai.'

'Me too—I've only had two lessons and I'm not very good. Did you bring your uniform? You look better in black than I do.' She planted her hands on her hips. 'Black isn't my colour, and khaki isn't anyone's colour.'

'You look fine.' To my man's eye, Sissy would have looked fine dressed in an old sheet and clogs, but unlike Melissa, she was blessed with that lithe body the tight blouse was designed for. A perfect vision of fascist womanhood. 'So I'm teaching the ladies to shoot?'

'Yes, but we'll take luncheon first on the terrace. Our wars are civilized.'

'Just promise me this is only for self-defence. You're training these women, these girls, simply to defend themselves.'

'Of course.'

Preparing the Women's Section to defend themselves occupied the afternoon. All were younger than 30; one worked in a London department store, another in a tax office and several were clearly Society girls. Two sisters from Bromley were middle-class stay-home wives who claimed they had 'nothing better to do'. Although some of the recruits were from the huntin' n' shootin' brigade, their experience was limited to bringing down defenceless birds with shotguns.

I was shown into the wooden shed whose doors were thrown wide to reveal two trestle tables laid with weaponry in the manner of a parish jumble sale. I checked each weapon; a couple of the familiar 0.455 Webley revolvers, an ugly nine-millimetre automatic pistol of foreign make, three Short Magazine Lee Enfield rifles that had probably seen military service, and a smaller calibre sporting rifle. It was hardly an armoury to bring down a government with.

'Is this all you have?'

Sissy was disappointed by my reaction. 'Do you know anyone who could supply better ones?'

'Safer ones, maybe. Don't touch the Luger. It's a museum piece more likely to kill you than a communist.'

'We can't afford more at the moment.'

'Surely with all this,' I swept a hand back across the estate, 'someone in the Party can find more funding.'

'Julian's father is working on it.'

Is he indeed?

'But for now, this is all we have. Sorry.'

Precisely 136 rounds of ammunition remained once the half-box of nine millimetre was set aside, enough to offer each woman five shots with one of the Webleys and a few with a rifle.

'All your women need to obtain Firearms Certificates if they don't already have them. And make this a formal shooting club too, keep it all above board. I joined the BUF North London club this week. Assemble your ladies, please.'

'Yes sir, lieutenant!'

I was by this time in Blackshirt guise. Before starting the demonstration, I unbuttoned my shirt front to gasps from the ladies. Two turned away.

An ugly spider's web of scars spread across my lower right chest. 'I have a matching one on my back where the bullet came out again. And I'm also short of a rib. This is what happens when the other man fires first. Or indeed, the other lady fires first.'

'I bet you were doing something heroic,' one of the shopgirls said. 'Saving the Colonel's daughter from a fate worse than death.'

'Ancient history.' I buttoned up my shirt and tucked it back in. The shop girl squeaked 'Aww.'

'I was given up for dead, and I'm only here through luck and through having a very brave Sikh corporal at my side. Never trust to luck when your life is at stake. And in battle, you watch out for the man next to you—or the woman next to you.'

'I'll watch out for you,' said the same shop girl. Sissy flashed her a glare.

Shooting lessons took place one-by-one with the others watching intently. Sissy and Melissa stood a row of champagne and wine bottles on a bench beside a wood-and-straw man-shaped target. 'Ten paces,' I said. 'Don't let them get closer or you're better off with a sword. Don't bother at longer ranges until you truly know your weapon. Don't try shooting when you are moving as you'll hit nothing you intend to.' I raised a Webley and fired two shots in quick succession, shattering two bottles to 'oohs' of appreciation. Turning attention to the straw target I hit it three times where the breastbone should be.

'Bottle shooting is a gimmick; shoot at the man. Aim for the centre of the chest because all you want to do is stop him. We don't care if he's dead, we just need him stopped. But if you do get a chance, shoot him a second time to make sure. In the head. Sissy?'

'Two shots,' she said uncertainly. 'One in the chest, one in the head.'

'Never risk anything clever like trying to just wound him with a shot in the arm; any shot is a shot to kill. Understand?'

Soberly, they nodded.

'Last weekend I shot to kill, as the whole world knows. I didn't enjoy it and I hope I never have to do it again. A pistol is for self-defence, ladies, that's all. Self-defence.' Training terrorists was not part of the mission. I handed the revolver butt-first to Sissy. 'You first, ma'am.'

With a half-shake of her head, perhaps to clear it, she stepped forward and accepted the revolver. She followed instruction to break it open, eject the spent shells and reload it with five rounds, but had clearly done it before. She clamped it closed, advanced to the firing line, and waited for my word to release the safety catch. 'Excuse me.' I touched her lightly, as if dancing, one hand on her back, one on her arm to encourage the correct stance. She gave a quick smile before closing one eye and concentrating on that target.

'Two hands, take your time, squeeze gently.'

She scored four hits – clipping one shoulder, hitting the other squarely as well as the target's neck and waist. 'I missed the heart,' she said.

'Don't worry. He wouldn't have got up again.'

* * *

I was pleased that Sissy proved to be a fair shot and as we walked across the estate late in the afternoon, I let her know.

'I wonder if I'll ever be as good as Verity, she was the tops. Said her father taught her using his service revolver. We came out one night after a bit of a party, it was pitch-dark apart from the moon, and we set empty bottles along the wall of the rose garden. She stuck the gun in her waistband and drew it like a cowboy and shot them out.'

'Gosh.'

'That's what I said. She did miss a couple, but we were rather squiffy.'

'It sounds positively hair-raising.'

'Oh, yes, I missed everything. Probably hit a squirrel up in the trees. V was lucky I didn't shoot her.'

It was a fine evening, and we looked down on a perfect model England rolling away from us. Water glittered as it escaped the lake and found its way through a little wood.

'I think that was the last time I saw her,' she said, with a hint of whimsy. 'That hideous man Parker was here, they had a bit of a tiff. That's before he got the scar to make him a bigger shit than he was before.'

'What was the tiff about?'

'Oh, he thinks the Women's Section is a joke. Women should just cook and stay at home and have babies and rot like that. Verity wanted to put a bottle on his head and shoot it off like William Tell, just to show him.'

I liked that image. 'Major Taylor's invited me to join Department Z.'

'Oh,' she said. 'That's…a bit of an honour. So long as you don't end up like Parker.'

'The scar wouldn't suit me.'

She tapped my chest lightly. 'You keep your scars hidden.'

Not to her.

'Being in Z would be handy,' she said brightly. 'You could investigate where Verity went to. Jules was terribly hurt when she just popped off without a word.'

'Did she send him one of those letters?' I asked. 'That sort of Dear Sweetheart my soldiers would sometimes receive from their girlfriends back home?'

'No, nothing. She just vanished.'

Chapter Fifteen

'Well I've met the top man, the Leader, the Prince of Darkness,' I reported as we strolled through Russell Square, chatting as old friends might. 'He shook my hand.'

'I hope you washed it afterwards,' said Calhoun.

'Like a true fascist I won't wash it for a week.'

'You're getting well and truly into the part. Careful with Mosley, he seduces men as well as he seduces women. Not in the same way, of course, but he's got more charisma than the whole Cabinet put together. That's what makes him dangerous; he's the kind of leader people are willing to follow without question. His truth becomes the only truth.'

It was not a large square, and ringed about by roads that carried cabs, busses, and private cars that circled like red Indians around a wagon train in that Gary Cooper movie. With constant movement came constant traffic noise. Reaching one of the cross-paths we turned and strolled back. Calhoun reviewed the inquest into the three deaths in Kensington. I'd given my evidence whilst proudly wearing Blackshirt uniform, much to the annoyance of the coroner and glee of the press. All we'd learned that day was the name of the man I shot was Richard Dennis, known as Dick, an unemployed dock worker.

'He had no criminal record beyond a bit of theft when he was a pup,' Calhoun concluded.

'I heard that Mosley was supposed to be at Kensington,' I said, 'but I never got chance to ask him about it—'

'No, no, be careful not to be too blatant.' Calhoun raised a hand in caution.

'Listen, but don't push questions too hard. The fascists are a suspicious lot, there are squads of them looking for spies simply to justify their own puffed-up titles. You'll be back in that black cellar before you know it.'

'Do they actually indulge in rough stuff down there?'

'Allegedly.'

'Torture?'

'Department Z would like to have that threat hanging over people. To create the idea that traitors will be punished. To whisper the idea that you might go down there and never be seen again. Fear is a powerful way to ensure loyalty.'

'Have they ever killed anyone?'

'If so, they've done a very good job of cleaning up the evidence.' Quickly Calhoun moved away from speculation. 'Tell me, are you getting anywhere on the question of funding?'

'That man Thring has links with Germany,' I stated.

'Shipping contacts?'

'There was one at the party, Florian Kahn.' I explained the gist of the conversation at the party. 'Someone called him Dr Kahn, but I don't know what kind of doctor.'

Calhoun nodded rhythmically, as if jotting notes at each fact shared. 'The Germans are fond of titles. Dr Kahn's a new name, so find out more about him if you can. Mosley's being very careful not to create visible links with Germany. It goes against his patriotic image, but he needs money. The Nazis could be the ones to give it to him.'

'Do you think that's why they're ramping up the anti-Jewish stance; to snuggle up to the Nazis?'

'A cynic would say yes, but there are some seriously unpleasant antisemites in the BUF. You've already had the pleasure of meeting William Joyce, their Director of Propaganda?'

'A strange character. I couldn't tell where the act ended.'

'He's an English teacher by day, but as an orator, he'd give Hitler a run for his money. Or Mosley.'

'Yes, I've heard him speak. I admire his delivery if not what he's saying.'

'Joyce and his cronies would have the Nazis running Britain tomorrow, but bluntly we have no proof of German support for the BUF; none at all. We were watching a businessman called Otto Bene, who we think was reporting back to a character named von Ribbentrop who runs this parallel Nazi Foreign Ministry, but I heard Bene was hit by a Berlin tram so we're back to square one.'

'Kahn could be a conduit for Nazi money.'

'That would be the easy guess, but we don't think the Nazis have that much money to throw around. Germany lacks gold and foreign currency reserves, which is one thing holding them back from causing mischief overseas.'

'So if you don't think Kahn came here with a suitcase full of fivers, tell me what to look for.'

'The BUF has official bank accounts as a legal political party, but we have a suspicion there's more, possibly a lot more. Perhaps they are using dummy accounts for companies that don't really exist, and trust funds that support supposed charitable causes, but it's almost impossible to follow the money once it's inside such structures.'

'Thring must have hundreds of companies on his books,' I said. 'Kahn could have the same at the German end. Can we raid Thring's accountancy practice and rifle his filing cabinets?'

'Not without legal cause.'

'So how about a little night-time intrusion?'

'Certainly not!'

'Why?'

'How extensive is your burglary experience? You haven't met K, Vernon Kell, head of the service. His watchword is that we don't protect the law of the land by breaking it. Half the spies he arrested in his early days were set free due to lack of admissible evidence. In some countries, they would have just been found in a ditch with a bullet in the head but this is Britain and we play with a straight bat. No burglary.'

Calhoun stopped and wagged a finger. 'I didn't order you to shoot that man last week and I hope you never have to do anything like that again. But, if you ever do anything underhand...and I say if...make damned certain you get away cleanly. And never tell me about it, not even a hint.'

That sounded suspiciously like a licence to misbehave, whatever the man called K might decree.

'Thring's son Julian might be the weak point,' I said. 'Shame he's engaged, as he's got a soft spot for a pretty face. I think he's marrying in haste after his previous amour threw him over. Verity Laytham – I wonder if she would be worth talking to?'

Calhoun started moving again, striding briskly now. 'Clifton, don't wander off the pitch.'

'But, with all that's going on and how important Howard Thring is, the fact that she mysteriously disappeared–'

'We know about Verity Laytham,' Calhoun stated abruptly. 'She's not important and she's off the scene now. You're inside the Blackshirts, they trust you. Just hold your end and bring me information, that's your job. Understood?'

'Understood.' I must have sounded surly as he gave me a hard stare, suppressing a further rebuke.

'If we're talking pretty faces. how are you getting along with Cecilia Poe-Maundy?'

Famously would be the honest answer. 'Oh, I'm helping Sissy out with her women's shooting club. She'd made this quip about machine guns...'

'Really? Mosley was blustering about stopping communist revolution with fascist machine guns.'

'Well, yes, it sounds like nothing more than bluster. For the moment it's just a dozen women with a few old small arms. But when I was trying hard not to be rude about their pitiful armoury, Julian let drop that his father is trying to raise money to buy more. Should I discourage him?'

'No, no, let's give them enough rope to hang themselves. Humour them as far as you can. A few gun-toting Debs are no threat to anyone, but don't let it get out of hand. Your Sissy is a useful contact. Work on her. She gets about and doesn't mind her husband finding out about it, typical of Mosley's circle. She should be an easy conquest.'

It would have hurt less if Calhoun had kicked me in the groin.

'There's no harm in having a little fun on our missions. For pity there's precious other reward.'

'So if I'm to...work on her...can I take her to Hamburg?'

'Monte Carlo would be more her scene.'

'I'm thinking to take her on a jaunt, invite Julian Thring, and see how many Nazis we accidentally bump into. Visit Dr Kahn on his home turf.'

Calhoun stopped walking and watched a bus pass by, as if interested in its advertising boards. 'I suppose it might be good to get you out of the country for a while and let the Blackshirt Hero fuss die down. Did you read about the Anglo-German Naval Treaty? And signed on Waterloo day too. It's nonsense to allow the Germans to break the Versailles Treaty in pursuit of a quiet life.

'I was in submarines, you know. And if I were the German naval minister, I'd build nothing else. You can get a dozen for the price of a battleship, and their U-boats nearly forced us out of the last War. So if you're going to be mixing with Nazis and shipping men, listen out for that word U-boat, won't you?'

'Does that mean I'm clear to go?'

'MI5 is not supposed to operate beyond our shoreline, and officially Britain doesn't run any spies abroad. However, you might occasionally hear rumours about our cousins in the Special Intelligence Service doing a little cloak and dagger stuff. Overseas is their playground.'

'Is that a rigid rule?'

'More of a gentleman's agreement.'

'I'm told I'm not a gentleman.'

'No. That's one reason we employ you.'

I felt a little more appreciated now, and it looked as if my adventure was approved.

'Take extra care over there. If you get into a pickle we can't help you. Be aware that the Germans take security seriously and don't penny pinch the budgets. Our equivalent is the SD, the *Sicherheitsdienst,* and there's a new outfit known as the Gestapo, the *Geheime Staatspolizei,* who sound rather like Special Branch but less loveable. And of course, there's the Nazis' private army the SS, plus several varieties of local police and political police, so plenty of reasons to look over your shoulder.'

'How do I tell which is which?'

'Once you're in a prison courtyard with a pistol against your head it will make no difference.'

Chapter Sixteen

Julian responded to the suggestion with one word. 'Germany?'

'Castles, Rhine maidens, pale beer in tiny glasses. Talking to that friend of your father's made me want to go back there.'

Out in the garden behind Black House we strolled along slowly, watching a squad of volunteers in shorts and vests performing press-ups under the command of an instructor.

'Melissa would love to come, she'll be in her element. Could we take Sissy and make it a foursome? We can have a boy's room and a girl's room so it would all be above board.' He winked. It would appear above board, at least.

'Good idea.' On so many counts. 'Do you know many people out there, who could show us the best restaurants, the places to be seen?'

'More friends of father's, I suppose. I hear there are some pretty racy clubs in Berlin, but I've never been.'

'Perhaps we should get as far as Hamburg and meet Dr Kahn again; he seemed an interesting chap.'

On command, the exercising squad stood to their feet, and in two ranks began stretching their arms skywards. Fine examples of British manhood plucked from the dole queues and dead-end streets were being drilled into a fighting machine.

'This can't be an official trip though; we can't be seen as representing the Party,' Julian said. 'The Leader has forbidden contact with Germany as it would damage our image to be compared to the Nazis.'

'I'm totally behind the Leader on that.' There was no need to lie this time.

'We need to build a uniquely British form of fascism, not a continental import.'

'Not that there's anything wrong with the Nazis,' Julian said, 'everyone who is anyone in Germany is joining them. Or anyone who wants to *be* anyone.'

Young men would be exercising like this in Germany right now. Newsreels showed German youth in their masses undergoing physical training, strengthening mind and body. Behind Black House, the recruits numbered just ten, but one day there could be hundreds being moulded into fascist fighting machines. Julian carried pride in his eyes, as if that was the vision he nursed.

Without any notice, Calhoun also arranged for a little training. I was collected by car and taken to a near-empty Territorial Army depot in west London. Two days in a row, a man and a woman, referred to as Mr Smith and Mrs Jones ran through some very basic concepts of how spies worked beyond the realm of paperback fiction. It was disappointing not to learn how to make invisible ink, poison darts or use a crystal radio set; instead, the concepts drilled into me were to watch, listen, report, and evade discovery. Other informers would have penetrated the BUF too, working for the communists, the unions, or the police and the fascists had their own agents, so constant vigilance was the key to succeeding. And the key to staying alive.

I made arrangements in just a couple of days, and we travelled to the continent via the boat train, with our first stop in Brussels. It was a long journey and Sissy became bored, or feigned bored, long before we arrived. I offered her a small selection of detective novels I'd brought along. She was quite smitten by Lord Peter Wimsey, thinking he needed a wife one day.

On the train, I read about a theft of explosives from a Cornish mine in *The Times*. Someone had clearly sat on the story for well over a month, probably the Home Secretary if not Prime Minister Baldwin himself. Waffle about Special Branch making checks served to excuse the delay, but the newspaper did not spare its criticism of those at the top. Baldwin was on the back foot even though not a single bomb had gone off. I recalled those men who appeared to be detectives searching doorways at the Kensington rally. Calhoun must have known—a warning would have been nice. I wondered what else he was keeping from me.

As a distraction I made copious notes for the Harry Bretton novel.

'What's your book about?' Julian asked.

'Diamond smuggling from Amsterdam.'

'We should be going to Amsterdam, then.'

'I bet Hamburg's like Amsterdam,' I said carelessly. 'Nobody will notice the difference.'

Make no notes was the order, but I could hold only so much in my head, so planned to bury clues in my scribbling hand as aide-memoires to faces and names. After Brussels we spent a night and a morning in Aachen, visiting the cathedral and the throne and tomb of Charlemagne. Over lunch, we enjoyed fresh and very sweet German white wines with labels unfamiliar in London. An afternoon train carried us to Cologne, perfect picture-book Germany with narrow streets of half-timbered houses and corner *gasthofs* serving beer in those tiny glasses or muscle-straining steins. I'd been before and delighted in showing my friends the cathedral and leading them up one of the famous double spires. If it had not been for that impulse to join the Army and see the world, I might easily have become a historian.

Everywhere we went the red, white, and black flag of the Nazi party was unavoidable. It flew from every flagpole and was draped down the walls of public buildings as so much dripping blood. The swastika motif was the same as the Hindu symbol for life, although I doubted that many of Herr Hitler's followers embraced eastern mysticism.

Julian indeed knew plenty of Nazis, and we dined with an expatriate English couple, of whom the wife was a music teacher and chairwoman of the local chapter of the BUF. Simple table talk over the next few days served to teach me much about the new Reich. Everyone admired Hitler, or at least said nothing against him. Every newspaper I glanced at was uncritical in its praise of *der Führer.* Bludgeoning the public with propaganda was the pathway to power that William Joyce and his associates wanted British fascists to follow.

The holiday continued with a cruise down the Rhine to Konigswinter and a jaunt up to the dramatic castle of Drachenfels. My new Rolleiflex camera came into play and I had my friends pose as a group, and singly. I'd treasure that picture of Sissy if it came out well. She insisted on photographing me too, then Julian posed us as a couple. That was another one to keep safe.

For all the Germans' martial reputation we had seen no troops of any description. The Rhineland had been demilitarized by the Treaty of Versailles, and the only uniforms in evidence were worn by police and border guards, so I did not expect to hear the tramp of marching feet. We were coming back down the steep slope from the castle, anticipating drinks before dinner, but stopped as the rhythmic crunch of boots on gravel came closer. A group of boys in tobacco brown shirts and black shorts marched around the corner, perfectly in step. Some were in their teens, some younger and at their head was a tall, blonde young man in similar garb. Proud faces radiated the joy of belonging. One or two were frowning, concentrating in keeping up with the bigger boys as they laboured uphill. A version of the Nazi flag was stitched to one swinging sleeve.

They were children, but they scared me. 'Boy scouts?'

'Hitler Youth,' corrected Melissa.

'They've disbanded the Boy Scouts,' Julian said. 'I suppose there's no point joining the Scouts now there's the Hitler Youth.'

Children were being trained to become Nazis. I knew that the BUF had a youth section, organized a few fascist playgroups, sports clubs, and boys' camps but the Germans had elevated youth indoctrination to a whole new level. Once those boys were old enough to vote there would only be one man they would vote for—or fight for. It was genius.

The youths provoked thoughts of my group of young women at the Kent camp. *My group of women*. Properly led they might be a useful force, and the men at the gun club I had joined were young and looking for leadership too. If I was to masquerade as a fascist, I may as well be an important fascist.

* * *

Back at the Dom Hotel in Cologne, all pretence of *Boys' Room/Girls' Room* was abandoned. Half sheepish, half cheerful, Julian confided that Melissa had said they 'should just get on with it.' Quite possibly 'it' was raising a brood of boys to feed the Mosley Youth.

The son of the couple who ran the Cologne BUF took us to a 'real' German *Lokal* the next evening. A few beers into the party, I noticed that a clean-shaven man of my generation had joined the edge of our group. Nobody seemed to know him particularly well. Eight or ten Germans attached themselves to us at some part of the evening, and by degree, the newcomer shifted stools to edge closer to us.

'Hugh,' I introduced myself forcefully, offering my hand. 'Sorry, my German is not very good.'

'Bruno.' He shook my hand. 'I like to practice my English.'

He also liked hearing about Mosley's progress towards power. Melissa became the self-appointed Director of Propaganda and talked at length, with Julian chipping in. Bruno listened politely, asking questions here and there, much as I might in his shoes.

It became clear we were wearing the same shoes. Bruno must work for one of those German agencies with exhausting names and perfunctory regard for the sanctity of life. In his company, listening would be a better strategy than talking.

Over beer and bratwursts, Julian raised the subject of the suppression of the Brownshirts in the 'Night of the Long Knives,' but Bruno shook his head. He was not a typical Aryan by a long chalk, slight of build with a sallow skin and half-closing his eyes as he talked. 'That's history now. The Brownshirts were criminals.'

I wondered what a future Mosley government would do with the Blackshirts once they had outlived their usefulness.

'The new Germany must have order on the streets. You need the same in England, you need to clear out the communists.'

'We're trying. Hugh shot one,' Sissy said.

Bruno's eyes opened now. 'Ach, are you the one? I read that story in the *Kölnische Zeitung*. You must tell me more.'

'No, I can't, I'm sorry.'

'Come, come! It sounds very heroic.'

'Yes, tell us!' said the young man called Hans who had a head start of a beer or two over everyone else.

'A friend who fought in the Great War refused to tell me anything about the trenches because he said I had to be there to understand.'

Bruno eased back. 'A good viewpoint. Men should talk about peace, not war.'

'Peace, hah!' chipped in Hans, already established as being a young army officer. 'Versailles robbed us of strength to defend the *Vaterland*. We must re-arm to face the Bolsheviks. England is re-arming, also?'

'Of course, we're not!' Julian said. 'Too many penny-pinchers and pacifists.'

'You should re-arm,' Hans urged. 'We need Britain's help against the Russians one day. They will come. When they see success of National Socialism in your country and ours, they are afraid and they come.'

'Well, I'm re-arming,' Sissy chipped in. 'I've formed a women's rifle club. Except we only have three measly rifles, and a set of pistols which darling Hugh tells me are too dangerous to shoot. Can you sell me some rifles, Hans? You must have a few to spare.'

'Hans!' Bruno tipped his head before the other had the chance to answer.

Hans switched to talking about how vulnerable Danzig was to attack by the Poles and Russians.

'I've never been to Danzig,' Melissa said. 'Or Hamburg. We're off there next. Do you know Hamburg Bruno?'

Of course, Bruno knew Hamburg. I could have kicked Melissa under the table, except that most evenings I was tempted to kick Melissa under the table at some point. How Julian put up with her for more than a minute I didn't know. She continued to say that as we had 'done' Cologne, we'd be moving on and Bruno offered to drive us all up there. He was so kind.

Somehow the holiday fell into Bruno's control. He would politely dictate where we went and who we saw, and his office would no doubt type up a report on me just as Mrs Ainsworth would type up a report on him. All this went unsaid. He smiled often and was always charming and obliging. I couldn't help liking the German, despite knowing that it might prove unwise.

The journey was a crush even in Bruno's huge black Mercedes car, with all the luggage in the back or on the roof, but it gave the opportunity to see the German countryside in full summer. It became flat and monotonous as we sped north. Hitler had an ambitious plan to criss-cross the Reich with new wide *autobahns* despite very few Germans owning cars, but Bruno explained how tens of thousands of workers had already found work on the scheme. That translated to tens of thousands more votes for the Nazis. It was the kind of project the Leader was always urging back home, and it had merits.

Bruno was so very helpful. Taking a turn in the front seat beside him, Sissy asked what he did for a living, and he laughed. 'I am in between jobs,' he said. 'Enjoying the summer.'

I translated this to mean that we were his job.

Hamburg had been the hub of the great Hanseatic trading network in the Middle Ages, Bruno said. I remember as a schoolboy being quite bored by that fact. It was Germany's second-largest city, and Bruno threw in the statistic that it was home to its greatest concentration of Jews. It triggered Melissa's usual pet theme, but curiously Bruno did not indulge her by sharing his own prejudices. He mainly listened and nodded, then moved the conversation on to the joys of yachting.

Sissy and I took a glorious room at the baroque Hotel Atlantic, looking west over the lake. I threw the windows wide open. 'If Mosley does it, I can do it,' I said, as we took in the late afternoon view, standing shoulder-to-shoulder.

'What can you do?' Asked Sissy.

'Swan off to the continent with a married woman.' I tapped her buttock lightly.

'Don't ask me if I was one of his women,' she said sharply.

'I wouldn't—'

She stepped away. 'Yes you would, it was on the tip of your tongue. It was what was coming next. You joke about being provincial, but sometimes you're clumsy. You don't take hints.'

'So?'

'So what?'

'Are you hinting I should ask you, or hinting I should shut up and mind my own business?' A further rebuke might come, or more likely a confession. I'd already guessed at the truth.

'One weekend, two years ago,' she said quickly. 'I was still getting over the wedding horrors, he was getting over losing Cimmie. Never ask again.'

Incompetent communist snipers might fail, but I should shoot the bastard the first chance I got. 'Right, we've got that straight,' I said, concealing any higher emotion. 'Do you fancy a stroll along the lake or champagne in the lounge?'

She did not move, so I shifted behind her and wrapped both arms around her waist.

'You don't care?' She asked.

'I may care but I don't condemn.'

'Why are you here?' She asked. 'Melissa, Julian, me—we're all here because of our families. What's your excuse?'

'I've read a lot, travelled a good deal and I want a better world.'

'But what are you doing about it?' She craned back her neck and our cheeks touched. 'You're smarter than most of the men I've met, but you're doing nothing with your life.'

'*Au contraire.* I'm with a beautiful, intelligent woman in Hamburg's finest hotel. I'm taking her to dine tonight at what I am reliably informed is the best restaurant in the city, with Dr Kahn and some of the most influential people in northern Germany. That can't count as nothing in anyone's book.'

She stroked the back of my hands. 'You're sweet.'

'And what are you doing about it? Why are you a fascist?'

'Fascism could see Britain rebuilt into the most fabulous civilization the world has yet seen,' she said. 'Modern, forward looking, but respecting the very best of our past.' Her voice almost choked with emotion. Perhaps she was quoting a line in a book, or perhaps this was her genuine vision.

'Imagine, if our friends end up ruling Britain, they'll have to find some job for you in the government. They could even find something for me to do.'

In the past few days, I'd come to realize I was backing more than one horse in this race. 'It could happen.' I hugged her a little tighter, almost tempted to forget Calhoun and make a bigger plan. Ambition and self-interest had surely led the Germans we'd met to throw in their lot with the Nazis. Men and women of influence all over Britain could soon be facing the same choice. 'And even if we fail, we can enjoy the ride.'

She slapped one hand against my hip. 'Ride! You're being crude again.' She inclined her head allowing me to kiss her neck from behind. 'Ride away.'

* * *

The *Altstadt* was a huddle of gambrel half-timbered buildings, ancient churches and spires. We filled two days enjoying its picturesque streets, cathedrals, riverside walks, and museums, and our new German friends engineered jolly evenings. Julian's fathers' contacts were limited in number, and I soon had them all memorized, supported by mnemonics scattered through my Harry Bretton notes; three shipping agents including Florian Kahn, and a couple of ship owners, one banker, some lower-tier Nazis and non-Nazi local officials, and even one Jewish financier hedging his bets. Nobody talked about U-boats.

Our guide-cum-Nazi agent told us his name was Bruno Vogel. He led our small sight-seeing party on a stroll through the streets of the *Altstadt* on the final afternoon, which was overcast and threatening rain. The German wore a calf-length black leather coat which Sissy had admired and asked where he had bought it. Not quite by accident, we passed Dr Kahn's office; Julian had to 'pop something in.' I took note of the address, the four floors and its position next to a very narrow alley in case Calhoun's cloak-and-dagger cousins ever felt inclined to make a nocturnal visit.

Bruno fell back until the two of us brought up the rear. 'I'm sorry about Kahn going on about the War last night.' Bruno said. Florian Kahn had been one of a few survivors pulled from the North Sea after his ship had struck a mine in 1917. According to the bitter anecdote his young brother had never been seen again. 'Do you know him well?'

'Not personally. Julian's father does business with him, I think.'

'*Ach, so*. Even after so many years, my English friends and I always end up talking about the War. It's strange to talk about what once divided us instead of what now unites us.'

'I was too young to fight.'

'And I just caught the very end, when it was too late for one sixteen-year-old to turn the tide of battle.' Bruno smiled.

'Everyone is certainly bitter about that Versailles treaty. Kahn must have mentioned it six times.'

'He was drunk, we were all drunk, but Versailles was unfair, foolish. The Allies wanted Germany to be the villains, as if we lost the war.'

'But, without wishing to sound insensitive, Germany did lose the war.'

'No, no.' Bruno wagged a finger. 'The *Wehrmacht*, the *Kriegsmarine* did not lose the war. The Fatherland was surrounded by enemies, and we fought to defend it. At the Armistice, not a single enemy soldier was on German soil. That is verified historical fact, not a piece of propaganda. The fighting men succeeded but were betrayed by the politicians and stabbed in the back by communists.'

Perhaps this carried some highly selective logic. When I was nine, I was knocked down by a bigger boy to the cheer of his gang. For what seemed an eternity I lay on the ground wishing for the will to spring up and the strength to hit back. Twenty years later I still remembered the humiliation. That was the Germany I saw.

Evening was approaching, heralded by the onset of a grey drizzle.

'You have the look of a bodyguard,' Bruno said.

'I do?'

'You watch your friends closely. You watch the room while we're dining or drinking, you watch the streets as we're walking.'

'Perhaps I do feel a little responsible for them all.'

Bruno gave a little laugh. 'You are a man to watch, Hugh. I mean that in the politest way, and with respect. Your heroism has already reached important ears even in Germany. You have a very good choice of friends. Julian's father, Sissy's mother are both very influential.' He paused to add gravity to his words. 'I would like you to think of me as a friend.'

'Of course.' Bruno was not someone I'd want as an enemy, not here in a narrow street far from home with night drawing near.

'We all need friends in dangerous times,' the German continued. 'And if your party succeeds in England as we have in Germany, the day will come when we will need to work together. The *Führer* has said that Britain is our friend. Our countries must never be at war again.'

'Agreed. Although I'm just an ordinary Blackshirt, with no rank or title.'

'Oh, dangerous times mean that men of talent rise swiftly.'

'Dangerous times eh?' I stopped walking, allowing the leading group to reach the canal well ahead of us. 'If I'm going to be any good at this bodyguard game, Bruno, I need to buy a gun. Something snug, not a hunking great Webley or Luger. Something I can hide in a rather smart coat like yours. I've noticed your police are armed – what are they using?'

'Walther, mostly. They call it the *Polizei Pistol*, the PP. It fires a small bullet,' he pinched his fingers to indicate how small, 'but it will get you out of trouble.'

I nodded. Calhoun would not approve, but that *Daily Mail* photograph could by now be pinned to the dartboard of every communist lair in Britain. Next time there wouldn't be a dead man's revolver to save me.

'Buy a Walther,' Bruno added. 'German craftsmanship.'

'Do you know where I could buy two?'

'One for you, one for your lady, yes?'

'I'm teaching Sissy to shoot, and I'd rather she fired something that wasn't going to blow her hand off. You heard her plea for more weapons.'

'The PPK is a good weapon for a woman. Not too heavy, not too much recoil and she could hide it in a purse. But how do you explain taking guns across the border?'

'Who would search Baroness Rockwell's daughter's baggage? And there's a curiously English understanding that a gentleman might need a gun when travelling abroad.'

Bruno rocked those leather-clad shoulders and allowed himself a little laugh. 'I'll take you to a man I know. Do you have enough Sterling? It would be more welcome than our Reichmarks, I'm sorry to say. You'll get a better price.'

'That will be no problem.'

I wondered if he was actually called Bruno Vogel. He said he would be coming to London at some point in the future, so we should meet for lunch and I agreed warmly. He did nothing to prevent our leaving Germany, but he'd seen through me, I was certain. My card was marked.

Chapter Seventeen

'Are you coming to Stratford?' Head on pillow, I was only just far enough away from Sissy to be able to focus on her brown eyes.

'No.' She rolled onto her back. 'I don't want to see any more fighting. Diana Guinness was telling me she never goes to rallies; she's not been once. Not in Britain anyway – I think she's been to some in Germany where things are under control. She's committed to the Party, but she doesn't like violence. I don't think the Leader does either, he knows it solves nothing.'

'He'd get more votes from the Middle Class without the brawling.'

'Well, I hope there's no brawling today.'

I reluctantly heaved myself into a half-sitting position. 'This is the start of the big push into the East End. Stratford's got a big concentration of Melissa's Jews, and the word is they're banding together with the communists to cause trouble.'

'So stay here, no one will miss you.'

'Oh, but they will—the Leader has asked for me by name. It's a great honour. God, it's past ten already.' I felt terribly rough.

'Are you going to join Department Z?'

'Yes, if they'll have me.' The logic had come to me in Germany, wondering how Bruno would categorize me in his report. By joining Z, I would at least have an alibi for being inquisitive, and something more edifying to do than act as a bouncer. 'Remember the chat we had about being important to the Party? I need a position where I can make a difference. Today I'm just a doorman.'

'Will you take your new gun?'

'Sadly not. For one thing that uniform is far too tight, I've nowhere to hide it. I need one of those natty black leather coats that Bruno has.'

'Mmm, that would suit you wonderfully, Mr Department Z agent. I think there's a place you might get one in Burlington Arcade.' She rolled over. 'It's your birthday soon, isn't it?'

'September the eleventh.'

'That's your present decided, then. We'll go into town next week and have you measured up.'

* * *

Delilah once discovered how to drain Samson of his strength and Sissy had performed the Delilah role admirably. Under the additional handicap of the after-effects of champagne, vodka martinis, and brandy, I reported for duty at Black House. Simply infantry for now, I dressed for action and joined two dozen more Defence Force Blackshirts in the back of that furniture lorry. Some managed to sit on empty crates down either side, but most remained standing, clinging to the frame of the vehicle or a few strops normally reserved for holding pianos or grandfather clocks in place.

Julian sat in a corner, saying little as his hangover was surely worse than mine; he could never keep up the pace Sissy set. The other Blackshirts stood slightly back from me, giving their hero space. I couldn't shake that badge, and it would do me no harm amongst these men. This was the core of Mosley's support, not the champagne-supping elite of Baroness Rockwell's parties. I discovered a few of their names and their stories. Some of the older ones had been in the army or navy, but most were young; paperhangers, bakery assistants, newsboys, and men who had not worked for a while. All their problems were the fault of the Tories, the unions, the bankers, or the Jews. It was a van full of discontent, bottled-up anger and resentment.

'But you're a toff, eh? Army officer,' one challenged.

'They threw me out,' I boasted with more Yorkshire than I would use at

Baroness Rockwell's. 'I didn't go to the right school. I wasn't one of *them*.'

Another delivered a slap on my shoulder. 'But you shot that fucking commie.'

'I did. Think there will be more today?'

'Plenty.' A cheer rumbled round the packed van as it lurched eastwards.

Yes, I was discontented too, and the Blackshirts accepted me as one of their own. The fates were trying to convince me that I was in the right place.

Stratford Town Hall in West Ham was our destination. We piled out of the van onto a street corner in the shadow of a tower that reared above us atop the grey stone building. Within this reminder of Britain's classical heritage and its follies, Mosley would speak about a new Britain. Perhaps two dozen policemen guarded the approach, and more were marching up to contain the growing crowd of protesters. Captain Parker saluted Julian and assigned his men to positions.

Together with one of the older Blackshirts I was given the *great honour* of checking tickets at the top of the staircase. Only ticket holders could have a seat, the rest must stand at the back. So much for front and centre; I was little more than a cinema usher. No doubt my next challenge would be selling ice creams during the intermission.

A tight knot of Blackshirts passed by, trotting down the stairs almost in step; the infamous I Squad, the stormtroopers of the movement. If there was no violence outside already, they would surely kick some off. At the foot of the stairs, Captain Parker issued their instructions. His idea of intelligence, no doubt, was to work out who was to be hurt and when and how. Sissy had been wise to stay away. For all her questionable morality, the lovely Diana Guinness had at least one good instinct.

Parker made his way up the stairs with a police constable in company. We made eye contact.

'Clifton,' he acknowledged me curtly.

'Captain Parker.'

Parker indicated a space beyond the second Blackshirt and the policeman took position, as if a third steward. It was far from clear who he had come to keep an eye on.

'Taylor says you want to join Z,' Parker said once he had come up to my eyeline.

'I do.'

'You'll need to prove yourself.'

'He already has,' the man next to me chipped in. 'Don't you know who he is?'

Parker took a step towards the man. 'You'd be surprised what we know, former sergeant Hills, so shut it.' He turned back to me. 'Monday, Black House, Taylor's office, eleven hundred.' After one more glare at the Blackshirt named Hills, he went into the hall to hear the speech.

My colleague raised his eyes. 'Watch your back if you're working with him,' he said. He offered his hand to shake. 'Danny Hills. I used to be a copper myself, made sergeant, so I know bad 'uns when I see 'em.' The police constable leaned in and asked which force Hills had been with, but he shrugged the question away. I guessed his career had not ended well.

Now a line of three, we filtered the entrants to the hall. As it was warm outside there was little excuse for heavy coats that might conceal a shotgun or rifle, but small pistols could be pushed into the backs of belts, into boots or jacket pockets and I had no brief to search people. Even then I could not in all decency search a woman, such as the one who smuggled in those cobbles at the Camden meeting. All that could be done was make eye contact and look ten feet tall at the top of those stairs. A man claiming to be a local MP had no ticket and made quite a fuss before I allowed him in on the proviso that he stood at the back of the hall.

'Disgraceful!' He wagged a finger at me. 'I'll be writing to *The Times* in the strongest terms.'

'I look forward to reading your letter, sir. Enjoy the speech.'

Out on the landing, only snatches of the speech escaped from the room.

Mosley attacked the Tories and their Jewish backers.

Mosley attacked Labour, the communists, and their Jewish backers.

Mosley's men attacked the communists and Jews outside.

Communists and Jews attacked Mosley's men and the hubbub grew.

Two Blackshirts dragged a man from the hall to the top of the stairs, letting him tumble to the floor. 'Throw him out,' one ordered.

The man's shirt was bloody and torn. 'I'm a St John's ambulanceman,' he protested, but was not in uniform to prove his words. Under the gaze of the police constable, I held out a helping hand, pulling the man to his feet firmly but not violently. 'Get up!' A little menace was feigned for the benefit of the so-called ambulanceman.

'I'd hurry on outside now, sir,' said the policeman to the victim.

'I'll take him. Come on, chum.' I escorted the injured man down the stairs and out of the building. Two more Blackshirts fidgeted by the main door, ready for action. Yells and police whistles echoed from outside.

'Off you go.'

The St John's man started to protest.

'You're lucky to be still in one piece. Now go find a real ambulance man to get that treated.'

Once he'd slunk away, I reinforced the pair on the door, watching the scuffles beyond the police line. A troop of mounted police trotted up to help contain the situation, then made it worse by charging the socialists and anyone else who got in the way, batons flying. Fighting spread and the commotion increased.

Blackshirts formed a rank within the police cordon, but now a half a dozen of them fell back and went into a huddle. One pointed in my direction and waved at me, calling me over by name.

'Lieutenant Clifton!'

I walked over to the huddle.

'This is right up your street, mate,' said the man who'd called me over. Two I Squad men were at the centre of the group, one holding a canvas satchel as a trophy, the other proudly twirling a pistol from his fingertip and laughing.

'We got another terrorist.'

I mustered all my officer-class authority. 'Where did you get that?'

'Out the bag,' said the man with the pistol. 'We laid into this couple of Yids, and one just ran and dropped this.'

It was an automatic pistol rather like an American Browning. A police constable pushed through behind me and saw the gun with horror. 'I'll take that.'

Reluctantly the I Squad man surrendered his prize. The constable took the dangling weapon and shouted to summon a sergeant.

'What else is in the bag?' I asked. Time was short.

'Looks like his sarnies.' The men were chuckling, nervous maybe that the muzzle could easily have been turned their way. The legend of the Kensington shooting had grown and grown.

'And I'll have that too, thank you!' The constable took the satchel

'What did the man look like?' I demanded.

'Well, he had to be a Yid. Short, and monkey-like,' the crop-haired man mimed scratching his armpits. 'Face all screwed up and ugly.'

'Yeah,' said the other. 'Just like a monkey. Wearing a scarf round his gob so we couldn't get a good look at 'im.'

An urge rose to smash both their heads together. I needed a sane description, not pat bigotry. Maybe the world would have been a better place if Monkey Man had shot the pair of them. That sergeant was coming across now, and only a moment remained to warn the squaddies. 'Get a sensible story together that doesn't start with you beating anyone up.'

The sergeant took the pistol from the constable and turned it over in his hand, clearly never giving a thought to fingerprints and allowing the muzzle to wander from one accidental target to the next. The pistol did not even appear to have a safety catch.

'You want to disarm that,' I suggested. 'Take the clip out.'

Coming very close, the sergeant growled into my face. 'When I want advice from a ponce who thinks he's Benito Mussolini, I'll ask for it. Did you find this, wop boy?'

'No, it was these chaps.' The I Squad duo had stopped guffawing and now looked apprehensive.

'Right lads, you're coming down the station, and no trouble.' The sergeant spared one last thought for me. 'And you, Benito, can fuck off back inside.'

Chapter Eighteen

Calhoun approached from the south end of Gordon Square as I walked towards him from the north. It was a quiet spot now the university term had ended. He indicated a bench and we sat at a polite interval from one another. Calhoun had called the meeting at short notice, as it was only a few days since we'd sat staring at the rain in some café while I related my German adventures.

'More fun and games yesterday,' he said.

'At least they didn't get a shot off this time. The pistol looked like a Browning to me.'

'It was a Tokarev TT33, seven-point-six-two millimetre,' said Calhoun, 'Russian. The same type as used to shoot those policemen in Kensington, you might wish to know. Likely the same weapon. Whatever his plan was, the assassin would have needed to get very close to use that against Mosley, protected as he was by your tin soldiers.'

'And a screen of very helpful policemen.'

'Yes, there are going to be questions in Parliament about exactly what they were up to. An MP was there. He didn't like the manners of the stewards.'

'Indeed?' I said, thankful he had not demanded to know my name. 'The I Squad men who found the gun described its owner in the least useful terms possible. They called him a monkey, which I thought was just ignorance and bigotry.'

'Ignorance and bigotry in the I Squad. Whatever next?'

'But the more I think about it, Monkey Man sounded familiar. Raincoat Man who shot at me in Kensington was, well...short, or he ran oddly and low to the ground.'

'Hmm, that's not a coincidence, is it? Did you check what was in the bag?'

'No, the squaddies said it was a packet of sandwiches.'

'Would it alarm you to learn that it was in fact a packet of three-inch nails wrapped around one and a half pounds of commercial explosive?' Calhoun waited for my jaw to drop, then recover, before continuing. 'It wasn't rigged with a detonator, so whatever he planned on using must still have been in your Monkey Man's pockets. Our friends in blue were so excited by the pistol they didn't investigate the dynamite sandwich until they were back at the station. It's a catalogue of incompetence all round.'

'So our security might be dumb and brutal, but it stopped another attack. I must say it was odd to see police actually coming into the building to join us, adding a second layer to our defences. Are the police colluding with Mosley, or did they know something was afoot? I had the same idea before the Kensington shooting. Can you check?'

'I may indeed already have checked; and if you need to know, I'll tell you.'

A man and a woman—clearly academics—sauntered closer at half walking pace, deep in conversation involving jerking hand movements.

'A fine day, again,' said Calhoun. 'Did you get to see the test at the Oval?'

'Sadly no.'

'The South Africans won by a hundred and fifty-odd runs. Still, I'm planning to see if we can pull the last one back at Lords.'

The academics faded from earshot, totally consumed in the world of ancient languages and taking no notice of the man who waited for them to leave before strolling towards us. Hook-nose wore a trilby today, but clearly his red tie was a favourite.

'That man—' I began.

Hook-nose sauntered closer.

'You're familiar with Hanrahan?' Calhoun asked.

'Yes, in a way.'

The hook-nosed man now had a name. 'Ah, so the fascist poster boy is one of ours,' he said. His Irish accent was obvious but subdued. 'Push up, but let's not make it look like a queer's convention.'

'We were just talking about ignorance and bigotry,' Calhoun said.

'Thank you, headmaster. But you can never be too careful. I saw two men get nicked just last week on this very bench. Just for being mates. That would take some explaining back in Charles Street.'

'Hugh Clifton, meet Pat Hanrahan. He's on the same mission as you, but on the other side of the fence. And he's been there a while longer. Quite gone native, haven't you comrade?'

'I have that too, sir.' Now his accent became much stronger, self-mocking. He was quite tall but not well-built and his little wispy blond moustache carried just a touch of red.

'As you surmised, Clifton is on the home team, nicely planted into the Blackshirts. He's been running through yesterday's incident at Stratford, and everything points to the same terrorist group being involved as in the Kensington shooting.' Calhoun reprised a few salient points for Hanrahan's benefit.

'You have a nose for trouble, Mr Clifton, I'll hand you that,' said Hanrahan.

'Special Branch have at last officially asked us to assist,' Calhoun continued. 'It looks like your exploding sandwiches were made from the explosives stolen from Cornwall in May. We're still checking, but it's a good assumption.'

'You never told me about the explosives robbery,' I objected. 'I had to read about it in the newspaper.'

'That's how being an informer works. You *inform*, I listen. And comrade Hanrahan has still not heard a peep about which left-wing lunatics now have the power to play Guy Fawkes.'

'Each faction suspects the others of being behind it,' Hanrahan said. 'Which is completely normal for the radical left.'

'Special Branch have been picking up rumours of an armed revolt being planned,' Calhoun said.

'That's nonsense. We're too scattered, too disorganized.'

'You say "we",' I challenged. 'Like you're on their side.'

'And you need to start saying "we" as well, fascist poster-boy,' Hanrahan snapped back. 'Live the part day and night, or someone will cut your throat.'

'Boys, I admire your pretended loyalty, but I need you to work together on this,' Calhoun said. 'We have a bungled shooting followed by a bombing so sophisticated it was defeated by a couple of dimwits who had no idea what they were doing. It looks like Mosley was the target twice, and we can't keep hoping they will cock up every attack. With this level of competence, they're as likely to kill a heap of innocent civilians as their intended victim, and we have a very nervous Home Secretary to humour. I need you two to work on this from either side of the fence. Make this a priority and collaborate when you need to.'

'If we're seen together, won't that risk exposing me?' I objected.

'Or me,' Hanrahan threw in. 'His face is all over the newspapers.'

'Last month's newspapers. And the people you'll be mixing with don't read the *Saturday Review*,' snapped Calhoun. 'Even then, how many would recognise that strutting buffoon in the photographs? I wouldn't usually bring two agents together, but we are critically short of men.' He inclined his head towards Hanrahan. 'Clifton here has already rumbled you, and I don't want him reporting you to their Department Z so they can have you worked over by the I Squad. Likewise, he needs to know if your comrades have plans to stick a knife in him.'

Hanrahan studied me. 'He's not popular.'

'I'll put together the intelligence we have, to give you a starting point.' Calhoun rose to go. 'Get to know each other. Hanrahan's an Oxford Man, but don't hold it against him. Buy him a cuppa, Clifton. You might learn something.'

Chapter Nineteen

The Metropolitan Line train clattered eastwards. I had popped into a couple of pawnshops, both amusingly run by Jews, and bought an old suit, knitted gilet, and a check shirt traded in by working men to pay the rent or buy beer. An 'honestly, hardly worn' trilby came from a market stall, and I became a northern engineer, down in London looking for work. I chose the name of one of my father's men and knew enough about his three children, his wife, his cousin who was gassed at Loos, and his fondness for pigeons to spin a tale. I also had a fair idea how pumps worked.

'If you don't mind me saying, it was a mistake to use your own name when you signed up as a Blackshirt,' Hanrahan said, quietly.

'Meaning Hanrahan isn't your name?'

'Call me Pat. And nothing I tell you about myself is true, beyond a few undeniable truths. But Hugh Clifton is just Hugh Clifton.'

'It's been easier to just be me. I haven't had to invent anything.'

'And what happens when this is all over? Pat Hanrahan will disappear as if he never existed. Pouf!' Hanrahan opened his hands as a magician might. 'But how do you remain Hugh Clifton? Out there for all to see and anyone to find.'

Having once been left for dead, the future had become an abstract concept not worth caring about. After a few months on this whirling roundabout, I wasn't sure I wanted it to be *over* let alone what I would do.

At Bank station we changed onto the Northern Line for London Bridge. Hanrahan resumed his safety advice. 'My other tip to keep you alive is not to tell anyone anything they don't need to know.'

'Including you?'

'Yes.'

'And Calhoun.'

'Especially Calhoun.'

'We have to trust the man we work for.'

'Who does? You trusted those arseholes who sent you to India and see where that got you.'

If it was good advice, it was unsettling. It was easy to still think in British Army terms – a strict chain of command with the tommies having blind faith in their sergeant, him in the lieutenant, then the captain, all the way up to the King. All empires were built on the assumption that the men at the bottom would obey orders without question.

'Who told you I was in India?'

'It was in the newspapers. You're famous—or infamous. Disgraced officer turned Blackshirt hero. I'd have stuck with disgraced officer.'

The train clattered onwards.

'Here's another thought to keep you awake at nights,' Hanrahan said. 'You know that we're working for an outfit known as M Section?'

'No.'

'Were you recruited by a man called Maxwell Knight? That's M.'

'No, I've only met Calhoun. He never mentioned M, but he talked about someone called K.'

'That's Colonel Vernon Kell. K is in charge of the whole service, Maxwell Knight runs M Section, but Calhoun's new, and I don't know whether he answers to M or directly to K. It could be that Kell has lost trust in Knight and he's letting Calhoun take over his agents one by one.'

'K, M... Calhoun's never even mentioned anyone called Knight.'

'M keeps himself to himself, doesn't even show up at the office, and runs everything from his flat. What nobody advertises is that he was in the British fascist movement in the twenties, before Mosley even thought of it. He joined some right-wing dirty tricks organization and William Joyce was his best friend.'

'*The* William Joyce, BUF Director of Propaganda?'

'The same. And M is also married to a leading fascist from the West Country. It makes me wonder sometimes who we're really working for.'

The old hand might have been trying to impress me, but if Hanrahan put much more doubt into my mind, I would soon know nothing at all.

* * *

Richard Dennis was known as Dick Dennis to his friends. He had lived in Southwark and was a sometime dock worker. Special Branch passed his address to K, who passed it to M Section, and Calhoun passed it to Hanrahan who now shared with me what he thought I needed to know. It was probably very irregular. Dennis was the man critically injured by the 0.38 bullet I fired from the sergeant's Smith & Wesson, but it was a pair of 7.62mm slugs that delivered the fatal shots, suggesting a Russian automatic.

Walking into East London opened my eyes. Back in West Yorkshire pit villages, miners' families lived in streets of two-storey terraced houses, each small, crowded, smelly, and very sooty from cheap coal. I never envied them, but occupants of London tenements just might, living stacked on top of each other in rooms that were smaller, more crowded, smellier. At least the Yorkshire air was fresh. Here, the proximity of the Thames, its docks, and marshes added damp to the misery and the onset of summer brought flies and extra stink. I was not political, I'd told Charles, but life was not being fair to these people.

Hanrahan bluffed his way into the second-floor rooms where Dick Dennis' widow survived in defiance of an uncaring world. A mean-cheeked woman, she stepped away from the door, small child in her arms, urging us to duck around the washing. One room served as kitchen, dining room, scullery, and living room, leaving just enough space for Mrs Dennis to talk to the two men 'from the union'.

A younger woman was called to take the baby. Still a teenager, her face was not yet scarred by this unforgiving life. 'What do they want?'

'Just take him.' Mrs Dennis sat in a chair in the corner, whilst Hanrahan took one by the little table. I merely lounged against the far wall, able to see Mrs Dennis around hanging sheets that hid Hanrahan.

The police had been, she said, and she hated the fucking police. Every cupboard and box had been opened and her things thrown around. It had taken the rest of the day to tidy it all up again.

This was tidy? No wonder revolution was only just over the horizon.

'The bastards shot him. The police shot Dick, the fuckers. They said it was that Blackshirt killed him, but I know it was the police.'

That Blackshirt simply nodded.

'You don't know who he was with that day?' Hanrahan sounded especially Irish this evening. 'You don't know who put him up to it?'

'You lot. Party people, filling his head with rubbish.'

'Do you know that as gospel truth? Because we're from the Party, and the Party knows nothing about it.'

'You'd say that, wouldn't you?' She twitched her suspicious eye from him to me, and back again.

'Could we see his cards?' Hanrahan asked.

'Police took 'em. His Union card and his Labour Party card.'

'Labour or Independent Labour?'

'Proper Labour - but that's you, in't it?'

Hanrahan nodded firmly. 'I thought just for a moment he might have been a communist.'

'He wern't no communist, just an honest working man.'

'He didn't have no work!' That young woman called back from deeper in the apartment.

'Shut up you!' Mrs Dennis shouted.

'Was 'e ever in t'army?' I asked, laying the coalfields accent on thick.

'He's Irish, you're from the north, what's this the bloody League of Nations?'

'The army, the War?'

'Yeah and wounded twice. And medals.'

'What regiment?'

She rose and after a little ferreting came back with a rusting tobacco tin, handing it over. 'Them's his medals.'

The lid creaked open to reveal a Great War Medal, once silver but now dirty grey, plus a brassy but tarnished Victory Medal with its rainbow ribbon. Both were handed out by the million at the end of the war and just about every man and woman in the Empire who served even for a few days was awarded these trinkets. Some veterans I knew also wore the Mons Star to complete the 'Pip, Squeak and Wilfred' trio, but the fact he didn't have one it meant Dennis had gone to the party late. He had waited until conscription gave him no choice but to serve.

His name, rank, and regiment were stamped around the rim of each medal. 'London Regiment.' I read aloud. It wasn't one of Britain's famous historical regiments, and I assumed it was one of those created by bulking up Territorial battalions during the Great War.

'I'll sell you them,' she said, spotting how my interest lingered. 'I thought about selling them to that Jew what buys things. Must be worth a lot of money, them medals.'

A few pints of beer at best; every household in the land must own a set. I knew men who had thrown theirs away, and widows who had burned the certificate of sorrow from the King and all. Who wanted to remember that war?

'Two pounds,' she said.

It was an outrageous price for bits of brass and silver. I ran my thumb across a tarnished silver oak leaf pinned to the blue, black, and gold War Medal ribbon. Not every soldier came home with one of those. An oak leaf meant 'mentioned in dispatches,' and the fact it was silver meant this had happened more than once. Dick Dennis must have fallen just short of a gallantry medal.

'What's t' story behind this?' I showed her the oak leaf.

'I dunno. He was in the war, weren't he?'

And like old soldiers the world over never talked about what he'd seen, I guessed. 'Did he meet up with any old army mates?'

'Them what's not dead you mean? Or gone mad? There's one called Robbie, he drinks with him down the Royal or the Lamb.'

'Robbie what?'

'Robbie Agnew—but don't tell him I told yer.'

I nodded and kept hold of the medals. 'Two pounds?'

'Each.'

Without a murmur of objection, I brought out a five-pound note from my wallet. The baby started crying in the side room and the young woman shouted at it to stop. Two children's faces appeared from the other doorway. Mrs Dennis took the five pounds eagerly.

'The Party is sorry for your loss.'

* * *

'Is that your own money you are spreading around, or His Majesty's Government's?' Hanrahan asked.

'There is little merit in being the heir to a mining fortune and not using the fact to best advantage.'

'Oh, sorry to have asked. Didn't have you down as aristocracy.'

'Far from it. New Money, very vulgar.'

'Exploiting the workers for the benefit of the elite? The beers will be on you tonight.'

'My pleasure.'

'You do know that when the revolution comes your family's mines will fall to the State? They will be operated by the workers, for the good of the workers. You'll have no fortune.'

'Then we need to stop the revolution, don't we?'

Robbie Agnew was not to be found in the Lamb and Flag, but he was an early customer at the Royal Oak, scratching his eye with the thumb of the same hand in which he held a burning cigarette. Leaning at the bar, he was gazing at the spirit lights. He was a shrunken man in shapeless working clothes and might have been aged forty but looked older through years of screwing up his eyes against bar-room smoke and staring into a beer glass as often as he could afford.

'Can we buy you a drink, comrade?' Irish-rich Hanrahan slid next to him.

I attracted the landlord's attention.

Agnew looked both of us up and down. 'And who are you then? And you, with your new hat?'

'We're here to talk about Dick Dennis,' Hanrahan said, keeping his tone low.

'You coppers? I've spoke to them already, I know nothing."

'I'm Irish; you want to know what I think of coppers? I fought against the Black and Tans.' From the little he'd told me about himself, there was a fair chance that Hanrahan was telling the truth.

'Whoever the fuck they are,' Agnew said.

'Do you think the coppers killed Dick?'

''course they did. Or they're letting Blackshirts carry guns and lying to us about it.'

'Dick did have a rifle when they shot him.'

'So they say.'

'Do you know where he got it?'

''course not. Where you going to get a rifle round here? Someone give it to him.' Agnew accepted a pint of beer. 'If he ever had a rifle in the first place.' He raised his glass to me in genuine thanks.

'You were in the London Regiment together,' I stated. 'Tell me about Dick.'

Agnew looked from one to the other of us, took a sip, then another. I dug change from my pocket and counted out four half-crowns before sliding them along the bar.

'Ten bob? What do you think you'll get out of me for that?'

'There's more. We're just filling in the last details, and you could help us.'

'But I don't know anything about no guns.'

'Just tell us about Dick.'

He scraped up the coins. 'If it's worth that much to you, Dick and me got roped in during sixteen, after Kitchener's army was wiped out and they'd run out of volunteers. Dick got gassed at Cambrai, but we was back in the line for the big scrap at Easter in eighteen and we both copped blighty wounds from shrapnel. War was over by time we came out.'

'He was mentioned in dispatches twice. What for?'

'Oh mention in bloody dispatches, that's just officer flannel trying to make us all into little heroes. Dick were a sniper, weren't he? A bloody good one. Said he killed seventeen Jerries, he scratched a tally on his rifle. They wouldn't let him keep it after the war, and he was bitter about that. He'd take his time and hit the Jerry in the head. One shot—whoof—goodbye Fritz.' Agnew took a swig of his beer. 'Clean way to go, if you have to go. I saw what their snipers did to our mates and Dick was just as good. He got this officer once, two hundred yards if it were ten. He waited for this whole bunch of Jerries to come out of this bunker then chose the officer. That took nerve, son. I bet you weren't there.'

'I was too young.'

'We were all too young,' he said.

'We want you to ask around, quietly,' said Hanrahan. 'Keep your ears open for anything about that rifle. Give him a pound mate.'

I took out a pound note and slipped it below the level of the bar, so as not to advertise. Agnew accepted it with the air of the guilty, glancing around.

'There's a fiver more if you hear anything.' Hanrahan pledged.

'A fiver?' Agnew's eyes widened. It was more than a week's wages. 'Cor you're serious about them guns.'

Hanrahan grimaced. 'Guns give the movement a bad name. Gives the coppers an excuse to crack down on honest working men.'

Agnew nodded.

'We'll drop by in a few days.'

Hanrahan checked each way as we came out of the pub. It was a sound practice worth adopting. This land was almost as alien as the Punjab.

'Dennis wasn't some lone lunatic,' I said as we walked back towards the station. 'The chap I call Raincoat Man would have acted as the spotter, allowing the sniper to concentrate on the shot without worrying what else was going on. Dick Dennis had all the time in the world. It wasn't like in the War; he wasn't tired and wet and nobody was shooting back at him. He probably rested his weapon on a table or chair-back deep inside the cover so nobody could see his face. The light was behind him, too. Mrs Symes was in the open, not moving about and she's hardly a small target. I reckon the range can't have been more than seventy-five yards. A raw recruit could have hit under those conditions.'

Hanrahan grunted.

'But they didn't use a raw recruit, they used a man who would hit exactly what he was aiming at. And that was not Mrs Symes, so much is clear. And he was a good enough shot to not accidentally kill a member of the crowd.'

'But they did kill two policemen.'

'Whilst getting away, because those two coppers were not supposed to get there so fast.'

'And it was your Raincoat Man who shot both the coppers,' Hanrahan said. 'The men in white coats dug out the same bullets as they did from Dennis, and more men in white coats say they were fired from the same gun you picked up in Stratford.'

That was neat; almost too neat to be true. 'So Raincoat Man is also well trained. Unless something messed up their plan, Mrs Symes would have been dead if they had wanted her dead.'

'And you'd be dead if Raincoat Man had wanted you dead.'

It was sobering but true. 'Silencing Dennis was more important than adding a Blackshirt to his bag.' I offered the best excuse I could think of to explain why I was still alive.

Hanrahan glanced behind him.

'What?'

'Just checking we're not being followed.'

Now he mentioned it, I also had that odd sense we were watched and had to check to make sure I was wrong. We were not alone on the street, but the East Enders were minding their own business.

Hanrahan dug his hands deep into his pockets, his shoulders relaxing as if now feeling safe. 'The police have been edgy ever since that explosives robbery. It's not lone lunatics as you call them, there are similar stories coming in from across the country, so it's not just London. Someone is organizing.'

'Your communists, presumably.'

The streets were better lit as we approached London Bridge station.

'Everyone says so, but I heard nothing about gun attacks being planned and nothing about that explosive. The CP Central Committee is being careful in how it confronts your fascists. It was officially against confronting Mosley in Stratford, so not to give him publicity.'

'His widow said Dennis was a Labour Party member. If he's not one of your communists, that explains why you didn't hear a peep. Are we inside the wrong parties?'

'The Security Service and Special Branch together don't have enough people to penetrate the Labour movement effectively. It's embedded in communities with loyalties going back generations. It takes months, years, to get deep enough inside a party to learn its secrets.'

'How long have you been *inside*?'

'That question would require an honest answer, and I'm not giving any honest answers. You tell the truth, I'll keep my secrets close, and we'll see which strategy works best.'

The tube station was now in sight. 'You can't be a total fake,' I said. 'What's your cover story? How do you explain the money in your pocket to your comrades?'

Hanrahan dropped any hint of an Irish accent. 'I tutor ladies and gentlemen of quality in German, Russian or French in the comfort of their own homes. Or…' He added back the accent. 'I give lessons to the idle rich, the monied middle class, and capitalist businessmen. I can be here and there, so nobody knows where I should be at any given hour. And nobody knows how much a language tutor earns cash-in-hand.'

'Impressive. I think William Joyce does something similar.'

'Joyce, by Jesus, I'm in quality company there.'

'So, you're a teacher, that's one fact. Fact two is that Calhoun said you went to Oxford.'

'And he told me you were at Cambridge, like him, as if that will matter after the revolution.'

'You like to joke about this revolution, like it's all a bit of a jape and it's never going to happen here. But with what we're hearing, isn't the chance of a revolution increasing?'

'Since Labour did so badly in the '31 elections, activists have been saying that it's impossible to achieve socialism democratically. Our system is slanted against it; the Police, the Courts, the Church, the House of Lords, the King. Revolution will come if the government doesn't help the working people – and the people who should be working. And the honest truth is that the real fascists are the Tories, not your mates the Blackshirts.'

'They're not my mates.'

'Stay in your role, always. Think fascist…and sleep fascist.'

It wasn't an offhand remark, which meant that someone had told Hanrahan about Sissy. Calhoun surely wouldn't be so careless, even if my private life was being intimately documented in a manilla file. 'Still, Russian pistol, Labour party shooter, fascist target; this has the hallmark of a left-wing plot. You're going to have to chase that Labour Party lead, I won't get close.'

'Typical aristo, getting the workers to get their hands dirty while you go back to chasing titled ladies.'

'I'm actually going to chase Scotland Yard and see whether I won any friends by stopping that police killer. And I'd like to get into that building the shots were fired from. Do you think Calhoun could pull strings?'

'No, he wouldn't, and there's no reason your new mates at Scotland Yard would allow you to conduct your own private investigation.'

'Yah, I suppose.'

'It doesn't stop us getting inside that flat though. I've strolled by and the place is empty by the look of it. Shall we say Sunday morning? The shops will be closed, and the God-fearing people of Kensington will be at church.'

'I was instructed specifically not to break the law.'

'That's K and Calhoun talking. M taught me there's only one law; don't get caught.'

Chapter Twenty

Journalists finally caught wind of the Stratford bomb story and splashed it across the newspapers that Saturday, throwing in excitable links to the Cornwall explosives theft and the Kensington shooting. Mosley was even quoted in newspapers that normally shunned him. It was a communist conspiracy inspired by Moscow, and William Joyce's propaganda section made great play of it in the *Blackshirt*. I made sure the names of the men who found the pistol and satchel were mentioned to the Defence Force commanders, and of course to my new masters in Department Z. Credit was given where credit was due. One day, I might need friends in I Squad.

Inspector Renton agreed to meet in one of the better public houses at the edge of Mayfair, as 'none of his usual clients' would be found there. I no longer had a club to invite the Inspector to, as my name had been crossed out when rumour came that I was dead, then I'd been blackballed when attempting to rejoin. I vowed I'd make no more attempts to break into those bastions of snobbery.

'Let me get this right, Mr Clifton.' Renton spoke slowly and deliberately over his bitter-and-mild. 'You're asking these questions as an ordinary citizen.'

'That's right.'

'Not as a Blackshirt agent. What's your security section called? Section Z?'

'Department Z.' Surely Renton knew that and was only testing. 'And no, I'm just out to protect myself. The whole country knows it was Hugh

Clifton who shot that assassin.'

'It made you a bit of a star.'

'Well, that's not welcome because it also makes me a target. A juicy target for someone's revenge, someone who wants to score a political point. This communist conspiracy is real, you know.' A little verisimilitude never hurt. True Blackshirts should believe their own propaganda.

'You could leave London and go back north.' Renton raised one of the fingers that was gripping his pint. 'I would.'

'Communists can catch trains too, and there's even more of them in the north than down here. So I'm staying and it would be really helpful to know what you know about the killers. Where they got the rifle and pistol, and who the second man was.'

'And third man, because there was a car waiting,' the inspector added.

Yes, of course, there would have been. I'd heard that car. 'You had detectives sniffing around beforehand and your men on the scene were armed, ready for trouble.'

'We armed one or two. You might have read about that explosives robbery? And we had heard someone was looking to buy rifles. Our usual London gangs prefer shotguns to Lee Enfields, so it smelt political. And it turns out the man you shot was an ex-soldier.'

'Dick Dennis, yes, I've worked that one out. What about his accomplice? He was a good shot, so ex-army too?'

Renfield took another sip. 'There was a group of men from the same division as the shooter, which I can't name, thrown into military jail in early '18. Different battalions, territorials and conscripts, and the scrapings of the London streets who would have been in jail if the army hadn't got them first.'

'Scum of the earth, what?' I referenced the Duke of Wellington with maximum irony.

'This mob were. Passing Karl Marx around and spreading Bolshevik ideas.'

'Including Dennis?'

'No, the military police must have missed him. There must have been more missed, and the army only made examples of the ringleaders.'

'I never read about this incident.'

'You'd be surprised what never makes it into the official histories. The whole gang was discharged at the end of the war, cases dropped. It looked bad, would spoil the parades. Everyone just wanted to go home and forget. I know I did.'

'Have you got their names?'

'Sorry, Mr Clifton, you're already close to costing me my rank. I agreed to meet because it's useful for you to know the kind of men you might be up against. It might just keep you alive and save me another corpse to scrape up.'

Viscount Wickersley would be the man to discover those names, as he must have the connections. 'We could exchange information.'

'No, we couldn't. You're not one of my regular snitches, and I have no intention of becoming one of yours.'

I toyed with my pint, wishing I had information to share.

'Unless you have anything of value to tell me.'

'Not yet.'

'You're wasting my time.' Renton finished his own pint in a couple of long gulps. 'It's a good pint here, but I don't recommend you become a regular. For the good of your health, quit the Blackshirts and get yourself back north.'

* * *

I awoke in Sissy's Chelsea apartment. A wave of nausea swept through me to think that the woman slumbering by my side was part of a mission; luring a woman to bed using a portfolio of lies verged on the criminal. My excuse was that seduction and sex was for King and country, and the King better be grateful, as my head was thick from the drinking, the late-night dancing and more drinking. Reaching the apartment at what, four o'clock, we had barely had the energy to kiss goodnight, and she began snoring in a most unladylike manner within minutes of her head meeting that pillow.

She opened her eyes one at a time.

'Good morning Sissy.'

'Is it? Oh, I must look hideous.' She shut her eyes again.

'No, you look delightful.'

'Liar.' Now she sat half upright and pushed aside unruly strands of hair. 'And I feel hideous. You are so beastly, you won't let me smoke even if I feel like death.'

'It's not a question of me *not letting you*. Your choice. Melissa doesn't smoke.'

She let out a groan. 'You'd never have got along with Verity, she smoked all the time – much worse than me. One after another. She'd drink you under the table too, V would be a complete mess this morning. I miss her you know – she was chummy, witty, funny…' She was lost momentarily in some thought or memory. 'Have you been able to find out much more about her, now you're in Department Z?'

'I'm not precisely *in* yet; that's the joy for tomorrow morning. Have you got anything I could use as a starting point, such as Verity's address?'

'She lived in Kensington, near the museums, I never went to her flat. But I do have a picture somewhere.' She swung out of bed, adjusted her nightgown then ferreted around in a drawer. Taking out a box decorated with a collage of old greetings cards she sat on the end of the bed, sorting through a dozen photographs of different sizes. With one in hand, she scrambled back to a sit back against the headboard.

'This is us last June, or July. We went boating on the Serpentine.'

Sissy was to the right of the picture in a light-coloured cloche hat with ribbon, and beside her was a slightly shorter woman wearing what looked like a straw boater pushed well back so that her face was not shaded by the brim. She was wider of face than Sissy, with high cheekbones giving her an almost Nordic beauty. Full, dark hair fell to her collar. While Sissy held that ear-to-ear smile with eyes that loved the camera, Verity kept a more serious expression, staring straight out of the picture, her gaze burning into the beholder.

'Stunning, isn't she?'

'What colour are her eyes?'

'Blue—so very striking with that raven hair.'

'Raven hair? You should be the novelist. Who took the photo?'

'Julian.'

'Poor chap—and he carried a torch for both of you?'

'Oh, not by then. I've known him for years, but we were always friends and never more, whatever he might have wanted before I got married. He's lovely but he can be quite wet- goodness knows how he manages as a Blackshirt when things get rough. Verity would have eaten him alive.'

'So she was a man-eater?'

'Well, she had a wonderful way with men. She had this little lever she could pull that made them just come to her, as if she was about to lead them straight up to her bedroom. I bet she'd be fireworks in the sack.'

'Lucky old Julian.'

'Maybe not so lucky Julian. I'm not sure he was ever invited home—things he said, hints he dropped…'

'Poor chap.' Much about this blue-eyed raven-haired dream woman did not ring true. 'Were you two friends before she met Julian?'

'No, I didn't know her before and I'm not sure if you'd call us friends even after she popped up. We rubbed along but we only had half a dozen girls-only outings. I'd tease her a bit about Julian and she'd tease back about… well, whoever I was seeing at the time.'

'But she didn't open up with tales about her family, her school, her parents?'

'Gosh, I was usually squiffy and we just talked fluff. And politics.'

'Did she have a job?'

'Job, no, well she ended up working as a typist at Black House, but they don't pay very much, if anything.'

'Family money? Where did she come from?'

'I can't say. She didn't have an accent I could pin down to one of the regions, so I'd guess Home Counties. She wasn't as plummy as me, *dahling*, apart from when she put it on for a show. I think her family were boaty; she met Julian at some regatta. He introduced us – what—in the autumn of '33.'

'You said you talked politics, so what brought her into the Party?'

'Well, like me she was a mad keen anti-communist. She was up for forming a women's militia and shooting them down in the streets. That's how my little group started.'

'So what happened to end her friendship with Julian?'

Sissy screwed up her delicate chin. 'She just upped sticks and went. Never heard of her again. Jules was most cut up about it, poor thing.'

'She never turned up to another Party event after she'd tipped Julian over?'

'I never saw her at one.'

'Despite being, as you say, mad keen? And working at Black House.'

'No, she just dropped out of circulation all together. So you see why I'm worried? It looks odder each time I think about it. It's like…' she paused. 'It's like you started making up a character for your book but then never got round to finishing the story.'

I ran a fingertip gently across her shoulder towards the nape of her neck. 'Verity wasn't just a penniless good-time girl who smelt Julian's money, and only pretended to like fascism to make him happy?'

'No, silly. Who'd fall for that?'

One day Sissy would find out what I was, or I'd have to tell her. 'I'll see what more I can find out,' I said. 'Could you get her address from Julian?'

'Jules doesn't even want to hear her name.'

'Could you find a reason for him to hear it? Be subtle though—don't share your worries with him or anyone else. For whatever reason, she may not want to be found, so this could be tricky.'

'I'll make up some story,' she said. 'Ooh, this is like being one of your detectives.' She rolled towards me and snuggled up. 'I'm awake now,' she purred into my ear.

I tensed at her touch, glanced at the clock, and groaned. 'Sorry but I have to go.'

'Go?' She pulled back, playing hurt.

'I arranged to meet a friend.'

'On a Sunday?' What friend?'

I had lied to her enough. 'Pat.' Sharing a made-up name shouldn't hurt.

'Male Pat or Female Pat.'

'Male, he's Irish. He's helping me with…with research for my book.'

Chapter Twenty-One

Hanrahan and I paced into the dead-end street with purpose. At its darkest end reared the back wall of some shop that fronted the High Street beyond. On the left was the closed cobblers' shop and beside that, by the very corner, a black door. In the opposite corner gaped the getaway alley. For Hanrahan's benefit, I described where the Wolseley had been abandoned and where the policemen fell.

'They came from this door. Raincoat Man must have stopped to fire at the policemen first, which gave us time to run in from that end. Then he ran this way…' I re-enacted the flight of Raincoat Man for a couple of paces. 'Dennis came out second and I shot him here.' I dug a finger into the chipped brickwork where my bullet had passed straight through Dick Dennis' body and left its mark four feet above the ground. 'By this time Raincoat Man is in the alley. He turns, then he fires twice. It's what ten yards, he couldn't miss.'

Hanrahan looked up at the building. 'Shoot, miss, run downstairs, two shots at the cops… How long did they have between the first shot and you getting here?'

'Two minutes? Less maybe, time does funny things when all hell breaks loose. We could run it and time it on my watch.' As I said this, my body was in no mood for running.

'No, we'd look too suspicious out there. We need to get inside.' Hanrahan took a canvas pouch from his jacket pocket. 'Stand close.' He gave me a swift lesson on how to pick a lock, and the black door opened to a firm push. 'Did you follow that? You should buy your own set – I'll tell you where to go. One day you'll need it.'

Immediately inside the door was a bare wooden staircase, narrow and steep. Musty air sank down to greet us. I pushed the door closed after me, which left a window at the half-turn as the only source of light. Hanrahan led upwards, each step creaking. His toe brushed an empty beer bottle that lay on the first-floor landing. What looked like a door was long since sealed up and painted over, so we continued to the end of the landing and another staircase. After climbing past another half-turn we came to the top, where a cobweb-draped window offered a view down on the scene of the police killings. A single door hung partly open with its handle hanging off.

'The police have no class,' Hanrahan muttered, running a finger down the fractured door jamb and broken lock. He pushed the door fully open, and we took a few cautious steps into what looked like a living room of a flat. It stood empty and unloved. Another beer bottle took pride of place on its mantlepiece, and the cold grate hosted screwed-up newspaper and cigarette packets. The only furniture was a single chair with a broken seat. To one side we found a bedroom, with an abandoned bed stripped of its mattress, to the other a tiny kitchen and a bathroom. The lounge window looked straight down the market street.

I pointed to where Mrs Symes had stood. The sniper's position was so perfect that he must have known where the target would stand, which meant he must also have known in good time that the council would ban the BUF from the hall.

'This took some planning.' Hanrahan was clearly thinking on the same lines. He fiddled with the sash window and the lower pane slid up easily. To make sure, he worked it up and down twice. 'It's been oiled.'

I pulled the chair over and rested my arm on it, as if it were a rifle. 'Bang! Close the window.'

He slid it down. 'Pick up the cartridge so there's no evidence.'

'No, he didn't reload, so there would be no cartridge case ejected,' I said. 'That's what gave me the chance to shoot first, Dennis was pulling his bolt back as I fired. If Dennis' sights were off, he'd have needed to correct with a second shot. Perhaps they debated firing again, losing seconds. The second round could have jammed, and they gave it up as a bad job.'

'If...perhaps...you're guessing.'

'Yes, and Raincoat Man could have stood where you are right now calling Dennis an incompetent bastard for missing, wasting time they didn't have.'

He smiled. 'Even the best plans go wrong.' Hanrahan nodded his head as if counting. 'Bang, realize they missed, shut window, run for it, out the door, down and around those stairs, tuck the guns in their coats before they go out, check who is outside.' He put up his hands in horror. 'Holy Mother Mary there's two coppers with guns waiting!'

I could picture myself covering the ground to the scene of the murders in that time.

'If that police driver hadn't been on the mark, the shooters would have been out that alley before any of you arrived. The plan didn't account for that police car. Or a Blackshirt fanatic with no fear of death...'

He was having another dig at me. 'Are we done?'

'Yes.' Hanrahan made for the door but stopped as he reached it, frowning. He tried to ease it closed. When it squeaked, he stepped away and held up a finger to his lips. Someone was ascending the stairs steadily but slowly. For a moment I contemplated climbing out of that window, then opted to retreat to the bedroom. Hanrahan followed and pushed its door to. Some draught prompted the flat door to bang closed.

Simultaneously we drew our weapons with perfect Buzby Berkeley choreography. Hanrahan glanced at the Walther, taking in its make. He was armed with a larger style of automatic, perhaps even another Tokarev.

'Hello?' Came a woman's voice. She had stepped into the living room. Nobody answered her. Harahan slid his weapon away and I copied the move with less confidence that we were under no threat.

'Hello?' She was close to the bedroom door now. We stepped back and allowed her to open it.

'Good morning,' I said, with all the innocence I could muster.

Startled, holding her hands to her mouth to suppress a gasp, the woman shrunk back into the living room, allowing us to follow. She was old enough to be my aunt, overdressed for the season and with grey hair pulled back into a bun. 'What are you doing?'

'For sure this is up for rent?' Hanrahan said.

'Yes, but you need to see me first, not just barge in. Who gave you the key?'

Hanrahan shifted to block any escape from the flat.

'We want to ask about the shooting, back in June,' I said. 'In the week before the shooting, how many people did you show around this flat?'

'None, I told the police. I told the police everything. Who are you?'

'There's police, and there's police,' said Hanrahan.

'Do you have a badge?'

'I have this.' I withdrew a pound note.

'I don't want any trouble.'

I rustled the note.

'I don't need your money.'

'Put it on the church plate, then. How much did he offer you to say nothing?'

She pressed her lips tightly together.

'We won't hurt you,' Hanrahan said, in a manner which suggested he just might.

'I never saw him before. He had a foreign name, Shattensomething. He was American.'

'What did he look like?' I asked. 'Short?'

'Not so tall as you, but yes, and dressed a bit like you are.'

'Foreign-looking?'

'A bit. He looked Spanish.'

'Why didn't you tell the police about him?'

'I never gave him a key, like I never gave you keys. And he scared me, like you're scaring me. I could scream you know, there's lots of people will hear me.'

'That would be...unnecessary,' said Hanrahan.

Her eyes were wet, pleading. 'Just go, and I won't tell anyone about you.'

'How many days before the shooting was this American here?'

She looked at the mantlepiece for inspiration. 'The day before, two days before.'

'How much did he give you?'

'That's my business. Now will you leave?'

'To be sure, we will.' Hanrahan inclined his head to summon me.

I tipped my trilby to the nameless woman. 'Thank you for your help ma'am.'

For all her protestation, she accepted my pound note and stood rigid until the door was closed. Hanrahan clattered down the stairs with urgency. 'Well, I'm so glad I'm partnered with a rich boy.'

'If your revolution comes, I won't be a rich boy, as you've pointed out.'

'Do you believe the American with the made-up name she's forgotten already, or is he a Spaniard?'

'There's lots of Jews in America.'

Hanrahan stopped mid-stair and turned. 'What? Have you been indoctrinated already?'

'Looks Spanish, sounds American, has German-sounding name. There are lots of Jews in America, and lots of money behind them.'

'Oh please! Don't start believing that worldwide Jewish conspiracy crap. I know nobody likes the Jews, but don't swallow the fascist line that they're behind everything.'

'It was just an idea.'

Hanrahan rounded the corner leading to the ground floor. 'It's an idea that stinks.'

Chapter Twenty-Two

My meeting with Major Taylor proved to be painless. His office was on the second floor of Black House, the Z on the door probably dating back to the teacher training college days and innocently granting a name to a far-from-innocent department.

'Sorry about that affair the other day,' Taylor said. 'It had to be done, you know.'

'That's perfectly fine, sir. I'd have done the same in your shoes.'

He introduced me to Lucy Parmentier. Young and severely blonde in that Unity Mitford way she served as his secretary and sat in the front left of his little office acting as gatekeeper. 'I'm so excited you're joining us,' she said as I shook her hand. 'Now we'll see some action!'

As Taylor ran through who was who and how often they showed up to work, it was clear that Department Z had a title and ambition greater than its resource, so was pretty typical for the BUF as far as I'd seen. Taylor explained that I would not be paid. 'We're ah, a little short on the old...,' he rubbed two fingers and a thumb together. 'But then, I understand...' He was embarrassed to say it out loud.

'I'm not short of a bob or two,' I said with a smile that probably came across as cocky.

'Quite, quite. You'll be a useful member of the Department. Whatever time you can give to the Party, spend it here. My men don't waste their time selling newspapers and sticking up posters.'

'What exactly do we do?'

'Well...you've seen yourself.' He gave a self-satisfied laugh. 'Let's write that afternoon in the cellar down as a training exercise, ha hah?'

* * *

Mrs Ainsworth was far less bubbly than Miss Parmentier and never expressed an opinion of her own, or indeed said anything about herself. She came around to Havelock Mansions that Monday afternoon as usual. I had not yet been invited to Calhoun's office over in Charles Street and remained an outsider, just one notch up from the snitch Robbie Agnew. I dictated a formal account of the interview with Agnew and embroidered the story of how information about 'the American' came to light via a script Hanrahan had agreed precisely. The minor offence of housebreaking was omitted from the narrative.

The secretary, if secretary she was, paused and sipped her tea. Sitting in the armchair, she accepted my apology for the lack of biscuits. Lounging on the sofa, I finished off the debriefing by adding titbits of information picked up in the yard at Black House, in coffee-rooms or jazz clubs and even things learned in bed. The Security Service files on Julian and Sissy grew thicker. I was handing these people power over my friends—or the closest I had to friends.

'Did you ever open a file on Verity Laytham?' I tried to sound nonchalant.

'I couldn't possibly tell you.' She answered without a flicker of emotion to give away what she really knew.

'It would be useful to see it, that's all. She was close to Julian Thring last year. They might have gone places too, met people...'

Mrs Ainsworth gave a broad, almost patronizing smile. 'I type, I file, then in the evening, I go home. I don't ask questions about any of this.' She indicated the shorthand notes in her little notebook. She closed it, then slipped it into the bottom of a wicker shopping basket beneath a bundle of knitting. 'They might pick my pockets, but even these days, no one will try to steal half-finished knitting.' She offered a steel-hard look suggesting that anyone who dared might rue their decision.

* * *

Calhoun telephoned within two hours, instructing me to go to the ticket hall of Kings Cross station. Untypically, the spymaster was fifteen minutes late, wasting my time purely for theatrical effect. He said nothing by way of greeting and simply stood with his hands in his pockets, watching the to-and-fro of passengers and porters.

I broke the silence between us. 'You wanted to see me urgently.'

'Hmm. I'm wondering if we made a mistake with you.'

'Pardon?'

'You don't interrogate my staff; clear? You're to obtain information that we need, full stop. You don't see our files, you don't stray from the fairly straightforward mission you have been given, is that clear?'

'No, not in the slightest. I think Verity Laytham would be worth contacting.'

'She's not important, she's left London. Young Thring is marrying someone else, so file closed. From now on, just follow orders, Clifton.'

'I'm not in the Army anymore.'

'If you can't follow orders, you're no use to us. This isn't a hobby you've taken up, it's not another front like your writing. You've taken the King's shilling and you'll follow orders.'

'I don't need that shilling.'

'You may not, but don't think you can just walk away from this any time you please. You're a leading Blackshirt now, people know your name. When this all falls out, you'll need us to protect you.'

'Who from?'

Calhoun's smile was not pleasant. 'In our game, there are no gentlemen, only players. No umpire, no boundary and it's all long grass. The most interesting part of your report on your jolly to Germany was when you met that character Bruno Vogel. What did he say? We live in dangerous times.' He said nothing more and simply walked away.

Chapter Twenty-Three

Being a secret servant left a bad taste in my mouth that day. Almost as bad as on Sunday morning after visiting three clubs or had on Saturday morning for that matter. Right then, London felt a nasty, unwelcoming place but Kings Cross Station offered an escape. Renton had hinted heavily that I should go back north. I held not one shred of nostalgia for the bleak hills, the coalfields, and the soot-black villages but for once felt a desire to go home. Hanrahan could be left to grub around for leads amongst his socialists, whilst Viscount Wickersley was busy hunting out a list of names of the would-be Bolsheviks of 1918. All that would take time.

The Director of Propaganda had more than once suggested I make a speaking tour of the northern branches, so on my next day at Black House, I called in to see William Joyce. The demagogue accepted without grace that I had finally come into line with his idea. He spent at least half an hour delivering a lecture on how to speak to an audience, and how I must stick closely to the script on how the communist plot was stopped. I should really attend one of the BUF's speakers' courses, he said. Joyce was frighteningly young, and his arguments left little room for discussion. I'd heard that hooked scar that carried his smile almost to his right ear had been inflicted by a 'Jewish communist' with a razor a decade before, adding extra cause for his invective.

It was time Sissy saw how the other half lived, and she happily agreed to get away from the sticky London summer. I preferred to take the Alvis rather than the train as it offered flexibility. It was a pleasure to drive, and the top could be opened in the heat of the day. Communists could indeed catch trains north and Hanrahan was right in that I should never have used my real name, so I put both Walthers in the glove box.

Progress was slowed when we stopped to pick up a couple whose Austin Chubby had broken down and then ran them to a garage in Stamford. Sissy expressed a wish to share the driving, enjoying the freedom. Clearly, she had been sheltered for much of her life, bracketed by limits on what women of her class were supposed to do with their time. One of those limits was not to pretend to be 'Mrs Clifton' as we booked into an old coaching inn in Grantham. She produced a wedding ring from her purse, which proved a handy prop.

The bed was small and creaked with every movement, which provoked laughter amid the lovemaking. Half the pub must have heard.

After a full English breakfast, Sissy commented how flat the landscape was and I promised she'd see the Pennines once we left the A1 and turned west. The roof stayed up that second day as wind noise had grown tiresome at speed and Sissy lost control of her hair more than once.

* * *

'Welcome to Rotherham.' A meeting of twenty-four members brought together hurriedly in rooms above a shop greeted Hugh Clifton, hero of the Party. I spoke for no more than fifteen minutes on the shooting incident, keeping away from any areas of doctrine as instructed, and was enthusiastically applauded.

We stayed in a country hotel near Wentworth Park as a respite from the industrial towns, then I made a repeat performance the next evening at a hall in Sheffield. My audience this time numbered well over a hundred, and another fifty men gathered outside to make sure that I knew that fascists were not welcome in that city. I used the chanting and shouting as cues for my story, which added humour to the grim tale. Sissy sat at the front, beaming all the time, and was the first to applaud. I'd never be a Mosley or Joyce but these first attempts at public speaking passed off well.

The sun was setting over the Pennines as I drove the last hour or so through the coalfields that stretched north of Wakefield, and we reached Moat Hall in the dusk. I'd given my father little notice, as otherwise he'd pull out all the stops to invite a gaggle of influential friends which could only embarrass Sissy by putting her on show. However badly we might behave in private, she was still a married woman with a position in society.

Moat Hall did not have extensive grounds, but the next morning we walked around such land as my father owned. In a quiet spot behind the little wood that masked the ancient moat, we fired off a few dozen rounds from our new Walthers at an old sign warning off trespassers, getting used to the feel of the unfamiliar weapons. It was a pleasant day, with the sun playing hide-and-seek behind bobbles of cloud, so we took lunch in the orangery and drinks on the terrace afterwards.

'I say, she's prettier than the last one,' Father observed when Sissy excused herself, leaving us seated outside. 'A little skinny for my tastes but that's the fashion these days eh? Where do you find them? And if she's this what, Baroness's daughter, and you married her, what would that make you?'

'A bigamist.'

'Oh, very funny lad. If you divorce the other one and marry this one, you don't become a Baron or anything?'

'No, it doesn't work like that.'

'Well, she looks like a good catch, so it's time to ditch the other one legally; she's bound to have disgraced herself by now. You'd have grounds for divorce.'

'And she'd have grounds too, which means Sissy's name would be in the newspapers, and that would embarrass her mortally. And I'm far from popping the question. Sissy and I have only been friends for a few weeks.'

'Come on, son. Do something with your life.'

'I am doing. London is treating me very well, as you can see.'

'My money is treating you very well.'

'And I'm grateful. Sorry if I've been the prodigal son of late, but I'm back on my feet now, keeping busy.'

'With the...old soldiers' hospital,' father waved his glass in a little circle, as if mixing a cocktail. 'And Wickersley tells me you're writing a book too?

All is forgiven, lad. You're welcome any time. Especially if you bring that pretty one with you.' He frowned, hiding his thoughts before spilling them out. 'I hear you nearly got yourself shot again. Was all that guff in the *Mail* true? You, in with the Blackshirt crowd and having this shooting match with communists.'

'Yes, in a way. I was in the wrong place at the wrong time.'

'But you shot a feller dead?'

'Wounded him. I picked up a copper's gun and brought him down. It was all over in a moment—it wasn't like some of the stories out there. The newspapers make things up to please their readers' tastes.'

'Made up eh? I don't always believe the *Mail*. Say I do fancy a cigar. You?' He rose to his feet.

'No, sorry.'

'Of course, of course, I thought you might have changed.'

But I had changed. When Sissy returned, I'd take her for a walk beyond the moat to a bridleway that led up to hilltop outlook. There was beauty up here and I was tempted to stay, leaving the city and the hate behind me.

My father emerged from the orangery holding not a cigar but an envelope. 'I had this rubbish through the post.' He passed over a cheap manilla envelope with the address of Moat Hall written in block capitals for the attention simply of MR CLIFTON. 'They didn't say if it were for you or me.'

I withdrew the contents, a folded sheet of newsprint. It was a torn-out extract of the front page of the *Daily Mail*, with a familiar Blackshirt posturing in the photograph. Across the picture someone had scrawled DIE FASIST BASTARD in red crayon.

'A dire indictment of state education,' I pronounced. 'We need to teach those people to spell.' I glanced instinctively out to the hydrangeas, then over to the long hedge. Any idea I could leave my brief spell as a spy behind me was an illusion. Nowhere was safe. I tried to pass the offending newspaper clipping back but it was refused.

'If you think that London business is over, it isn't,' my father said. 'The buggers know where you live. Everyone up here knows it was you that shot that man, whether or not you killed him. Bit of a hero, they say to my face, standing up to them Russian terrorists. But I know what they're really thinking, they can't fool me. The pit villages are full of union men, socialists, layabouts and troublemakers. Your Mosley's not liked round here.'

'The British Union of Fascists stands up for the working man,' I stated. 'Our message is very popular in the old mill towns. We've branches in Huddersfield, Wakefield, Leeds.' Gosh it was hard peddling this rot, but not even my father could be told how insincere my commitment was. I continued in this vein until Sissy returned, by which time I'd torn up the offending newspaper clipping. My father went to find his cigar and we left to find that path to the hills.

* * *

Over dinner, Sissy asked about the coal mines and my father was only too happy to talk about mining at length. His expression lifted and fell as he talked of the War, the depression, the false dawns, and the new slumps. The dining room overlooked the garden and could accommodate twelve at a sitting but only we three ate that evening, with Sissy sitting opposite me. My father sat at the end with his back to the life-size painting of my mother commissioned from a photograph after her death.

'Are we working full-time again now?' I asked. My fortune was also imperiled by the struggling economy.

'No, now it's summer we're back to part-work most weeks. This bloody government is killing business.'

'Do you make sure the miners have three down days in a row, so they count as unemployed?'

'Can't do that, mucks up the shift pattern.'

'You need to. Lay them off in a pattern that allows them to claim dole for those three days. It keeps them from drifting off.'

'Where are they going to drift to? There's men walking from Huddersfield to Halifax looking for work, passing men going t'other way from Halifax to Huddersfield.'

'When the recovery comes, you'll need those men,' Sissy said.

'There's always plenty of men,' he growled.

'But if you're loyal to them, they'll be loyal to you.'

'Loyal to the publicans and bookies more like. They're turning into thieves the lot of them. Do you know that curve beyond the pit, where it starts going uphill? The buggers climb on the coal trucks when they're going slow and chuck coal down to their mates, then jump off before the train picks up again.'

'Working men are struggling to feed their families, Dad, all over the country. That's why I joined the BUF.'

Father threw down his napkin. 'B-U-F, I ask you. Are you in this party too, my dear?'

'Oh yes,' Sissy said.

Her bright response deflated the attack that was being pumped up. 'BUF—I don't understand why we've suddenly got to have new parties springing up everywhere. It's the same villains in different hats. Why on earth have you two joined Mosley?'

'Economic policy. Imagine if Britain re-arms; aeroplanes, tanks, lorries, battleships all need steel and steel needs our coal. Re-armament means our mines will be working every day, every shift.'

His father looked off to the distant hills, now gathering dusk. 'More coal, eh?' This was the acid test of how deep his conservatism ran.

'We restore the pride of the working man,' Sissy added. 'And the working woman. No more hunger marches.'

'You sound more like you've turned into a socialist, my dear, for all your good family.'

'It's National Socialism,' Sissy explained. 'It's a bit like socialism in that we don't want families starving, but we want Britain to be strong again and not just follow orders from Russia.'

'A committee of experts will run each sector of the economy,' I said. 'Scientists and businessmen, not just clueless politicians.' The pitch sounded as if I was rehearsing for my next public meeting.

'So, a Coal Committee would be run by mine owners?'

'Something like that. And we control imports, so we develop our domestic market and home industries.'

'And we keep the communists out,' Sissy added. 'If everyone is in work, what do they have to rebel about?'

'Where do I sign?' Father chuckled.

Sissy made her move. 'It would be wonderful if you could make a donation. I'm organizing a women's action group...we're terribly short of funds.'

'A thousand quid Dad, you wouldn't miss it.'

'A thousand... you must be joking.'

'Five hundred?'

'It would be very sweet of you,' Sissy purred.

'What are you going to spend five hundred of my pounds on?' he asked cautiously.

'Training and organizing.' It was not politic to say *pistols and rifles.*

* * *

A second night at Moat Hall was enough to thoroughly exhaust the common ground between my father and myself and given that it would take ten or twelve hours' driving to return to London we set off east in good time after breakfast. Summer had peaked and afternoons saw thunderstorms gathering over the Pennines. We planned to stay in that same Grantham inn to break the journey south. A lie repeated comes easier than a new one dreamed up afresh.

As I eased the car from the gates and into the lane, I caught sight of a distant flock of sheep on a hill slope and a black shape darting around that must be a dog. As a boy I'd been taken to sheepdog trials where clever collies had rounded up sheep on command, even splitting off part of the herd or one specific sheep. It might not be necessary to destroy the BUF at all if the darker elements could be removed sheepdog-like from the well-meaning flock. Not everything in Mosley's manifesto smacked of evil. Quite possibly Sissy, Julian, and the more decent members I'd come across could be herded down a more constructive path.

After a few twists, the lane went through one of the half-a-dozen villages that fed miners into the Clifton family's enterprises. The older buildings were of local sandstone whilst the colliery terraces were of brick, but all were sooted almost black. A group of four men loitered beside the road, then I spotted five on the other side. It was busy for a Sunday.

'Is it church this early?' Sissy asked.

'No.' I slowed the Alvis as a battered open-backed truck with green cab reversed into the road from behind the little grocer's store. I stomped the brake with only a last-moment warning and the car shuddered to a stop. Sissy gripped the dashboard to save hitting her nose on the windscreen.

'Christ Hugh!'

The truck blocked any forward progress. While Sissy was still rebuking me, men who had been waiting for us came around the truck. In the wing mirror, I could see more moving into the road behind, perhaps ten of them. By reversing I would surely hit several and escape would not be guaranteed even then. I pulled on the handbrake but allowed the motor to keep ticking over.

'Hugh?'

'Let's see what they want.' I stepped out and confronted the nearest man. 'What's this?'

'We don't want your sort up here.' The speaker wore a collarless shirt of a dusty hue, sleeves rolled up, with braces keeping his black trousers in place. A ubiquitous flat cap covered his head.

He looked familiar. 'We've met before; you work for my father's company.'

'When there's work.'

'I've just been to see him about that.'

Men closed around the Alvis, peering in at Sissy. Her head vanished as she ducked down.

'We're going to end the evils of short working,' I announced, nowhere near as convinced of my words as when on that platform in Sheffield. 'My father will re-organize the shifts so you men can claim the dole if laid off.'

'That's bloody good of him, but we want work. Proper, full-time work.'

'Nice motor,' one of the other men said. Sharply he took two steps back and his comrades shrank away with him. Sissy had been ferreting in the glove box and it was clear why. The words 'She's got a bloody gun!' rippled through the group.

Silence fell as the engine of the Alvis chose that moment to stall. I needed a plan instantly. There were far too many to fight off, but if I laid out the ringleader with a sharp cut to the jaw the rest might be cowed. With luck, Sissy wouldn't kill anyone, but she could take my training advice seriously and pop six of them in a panic amid some fascist fantasy that the revolution had started. She'd put fifty rounds into targets the day before and hardly missed one.

Only a fool would ignore the glint of the Walther held close to Sissy's breast. It waited to punish anyone unwise enough to touch her door. The ringleader looked sharply at Sissy, then back at me. 'We don't want you no harm, sir.' At least he now remembered some respect for rank, or perhaps he respected a firearm. 'But we don't want your sort up here. Mosley and that.'

At last, I remembered the man's name. 'A man's politics is his own Mr Horley. You're all Labour, right?'

'A man's politics is his own.' Horley turned up one corner of his mouth in a smile.

'Fair enough. You vote your way, I'll vote mine. That's democracy.'

'Democracy? Yer make me laugh, bloody fascists. Get out the north and stay out if you know what's good for yer.'

Threats grumbled around the mob. Checking one face, then the next, I edged back to the car and laid my left hand on top of the open door. Nobody tried to stop this retreat, so issuing a warning was hopefully the limit of the gang's commitment, or the limit of their orders.

'My business up here is concluded. As I said, we'll have you all back working soon.'

One then another jeered in response. I edged to put the open door between me and the ringleader. 'Now, Mr Horley, if you could kindly remove that vehicle, we'll be on our way.' I promptly sat inside and closed the door.

Sissy's face betrayed her fear. I gave her a quick grimace.

'Keep calm.'

'Jolly fine for you to say—you've done this before.'

'It doesn't make it any easier.' I turned the key and the engine started the first time. 'Here we go, cross fingers.'

The green truck visibly shook as its engine came to life, then it was driven just far enough aside to allow me to drive the Alvis past if I climbed the kerb. I eased the car forward, not wishing any final drama, but the men parted, sullenly watching the rich people go. At a loud thump on the coachwork, I pushed down hard on the accelerator and shifted the gear. Jolting as it hit the kerb, the Alvis swerved around the truck. Rushing through the gears I jerkily achieved a speed of fifty miles an hour down the empty main street. A little dog nipped from a gate and unwisely risked its life yapping at the speeding wheels until left far behind.

'Thank God we're out of there,' Sissy said. 'I thought they were going to lynch us!'

'And I thought you were going to start shooting them.'

'Only if they'd touched me...or you.'

Two children without shoes waved from the side of the road. Sissy waved back with the hand that still held the gun. Realizing what she was doing, she pushed the weapon back into the glove box hurriedly.

'Safety?'

'Grief.' She took the Walther back out again and put the safety catch back on, double- checked she'd actually done it, then slid it away once more.

A lower speed was in order now. 'Someone put them up to that. One of the Hall staff with a loose tongue must have told them I was coming up.'

Another child at the side of the road waved, and a more relaxed Sissy waved back. 'These are the people we have to save,' she said. 'They are what it's all about, even if they don't know that's what we're doing yet.' Sissy still held that naïve belief of the Upper Class that they had a divine mission to save the ordinary people.

'Well I tried, but it wasn't the time or place to start debating economic policy.'

'You knew those men, didn't you?'

'I used to play with Horley as a child, out in the fields and the woods before we knew any better. Before we were divided into *us* and *them*.'

'Will you write to your father, and tell him what happened?'

'No, he'll start sacking people. Then he'll talk to his friends high up in the police and have men arrested as an example. It's not what we want. So, no I won't tell him.'

'That's probably for the best. We need to win their hearts.'

Chapter Twenty-Four

Summer rain lashed the windows of the Lyon's Corner House. BUF men normally boycotted the whole chain, which I suspected its prominent Jewish owners did not mind one bit.

'I wondered whether you would come back,' Calhoun said.

'In for a penny, in for a pound.' I did not have a great deal of choice.

'Your seed cake, sir,' said the Nippy, sliding the cake towards me. 'You won't have one sir?' Calhoun patted his waistcoat to indicate that it was fuller than he'd like it to be. The Nippy smiled, then she was gone with the speed for which the Nippies were famed.

'Department Z, P G Taylor and his crop-haired crew? That's a clever move.'

'I thought huddle close to the enemy and all that.' I bit into the cake.

'Take care though, Z is the least secure security organization I've ever come across. It leaks more than a ten-bob dinghy, as my old captain used to say. What have you got for me?'

It is difficult to deliver meaningful intelligence whilst biting into seed cake and Calhoun fidgeted as I took time to clear my mouth and speak politely. 'The Word at Black House is…' I finished swallowing. I told how Mosley was away on one of his long Continental vacations with his friend's wife, Baba Metcalf, and that Diana Guinness had been injured in a road accident whilst rushing to join him and break up the tryst. 'It's all tittle tattle, I'm afraid.'

'What's he up to?'

'Champagne, caviar, and extra-marital slap and tickle. Nothing more sinister as far as I've heard.'

'They're not in Italy? You know we're worried about Italy, and their designs on Abyssinia.'

'I don't understand why you're worried; most people don't even know where Abyssinia is. And I think Mosley's gone to France, whatever is happening anywhere else in the world. His party is in a mess, they're nearly bankrupt but somehow he finds the time and money for holidays with titled ladies.'

'As do my agents.' He was teasing rather than rebuking me.

'It's useful to find out what's happening in the regions.' I defended my little holiday and took a very small nibble of cake so to allow conversation to continue. 'The BUF is very active in the small towns and the shires. We need ears and eyes beyond London.'

'You're it, I'm afraid,' Calhoun said. 'And for the moment, it has to be London. Wickersley has been doing his homework whilst you've been up north. Four men of the London Regiment were arrested for sedition late in '18. One died of the Spanish flu and the rest cooled their heels for a while before charges were dropped and they were simply discharged.'

'Dick Dennis wasn't one?' Renton had already confirmed this, but I avoided telling Calhoun I'd met with him.

'No, but plenty were missed,' Calhoun said. 'Nobody wanted an enquiry that would undoubtably uncover more communists amongst the conscripts. Tens, hundreds, thousands...a witch-hunt would spread the idea that revolution was in the offing. It was best to let each little nest of reds think they were on their own.'

'Do you have the names of the three that survived, at least?'

'I do.'

* * *

Hanrahan said that every name on the list was new to him. None were known agitators anymore, even if they once had been. It was time to go east again, back to that other world. For comfort, I now had a snug little holster to conceal a new Walther PPK beneath my jacket. Quite how I would explain this to an over-inquisitive policeman was another matter.

Robbie Agnew occupied almost exactly the same spot of the bar as he had on the previous occasion. He recognized us at once, but only warily acknowledged our arrival, saying nothing even when a beer was slid his way.

'I've got three names for you,' Hanrahan said. One by one, deliberately slowly, he listed them. Agnew shook his head at each one, but his pupils widened on the second name, falling back on the third.

'So, tell us more about Ewan Williams.'

'Never heard of him.'

'Come on.'

Agnew shook his head.

'There's more money,' I said. 'A fiver.'

'It's not much use if I'm dead,' Agnew turned away and took a long gulp of beer.

'We're wasting our time,' Hanrahan said.

A cough came unbidden as we emerged into the night, a reaction to the smoke in the bar followed by the dank London murk outside. A sultry August evening pressed the polluted air of the city down to suffocate the streets without offering a cleansing breeze.

Hanrahan waited for my spasm to pass. 'We can hardly keep quiet with you around can we cough drop?' He pointed to an alleyway across the road. 'You're fine with the rough stuff, Mr Clifton?'

'When needed.'

'Agnew's not some socialist girl you know; I saw you that day in Camden too. It was a clever move to pick on a little one. Robbie might not come so quietly.'

'He'll be six beers down by closing time.'

'So ready for a fight. Never misjudge a drunk man, they don't know when they're beat.'

'I think the fight was knocked out of him a long time ago.'

It was a fair wait until 'throwing out time' and we said little to the other.

At last, it was 'time gentlemen, please', although there were no gentlemen among those who stumbled out into the night. Agnew came our way, head down, sauntering if not swaying. I stepped in front of him.

'Oh fuck, what do you want?'

Hanrahan slipped behind Agnew and in the same movement grabbed his arm and locked it high behind his back, then dragged him into the alley as a spider pulls a fly into a crack. The ex-soldier cursed and protested. 'Some fucking union men you are. Fucking coppers that's what you are.'

'Shut up,' I said. A strong northern accent carries menace well. I was a good six inches taller than Agnew and squared up as if ready to punch the daylights out of him. Just possibly I might have to. 'Those names. One of them shot your mate.'

'How do you know?'

'Which one? Ewan Williams?'

'Dick knew him. Let go that arm, yeah?'

Hanrahan tightened his lock and Agnew cursed again. 'Leggo, I'm helping yer! Williams he'd been made a lieutenant for a few weeks, but they put him back into the ranks. Not posh enough.'

'Was he a communist?'

'Fuck knows.'

'We'll ask Fuck next time we see him. In the meantime, where can we find Williams?'

'I don't know.'

'Hit him,' said Hanrahan.

'Oh come on mate, don't hit me, I don't know! He's a cabbie.'

'Cabbie?' I asked. It would be a good job for an agitator; moving around with few questions asked about where he would be at any time of night or day and impossible to keep under surveillance.

Agnew gave a grunt of pain as Hanrahan again jerked his arm higher. 'You'd not be lying…mate? My northern friend takes real offence to being lied to. I've seen him in a fight. He don't take no nonsense.'

'He's a cabbie, honest as the day is long. But he calls himself Jones now.' Hanrahan loosened his grip. 'Can't hide the Welsh, can he?'

Hanrahan bundled Agnew to the end of the alley and allowed him to pull away from the grip. 'We'll be back to say hello again, Robbie, and we expect a little more respect next time.'

Agnew cringed as if about to be punched, but Hanrahan straightened up and unclenched his fists. I offered the man a five-pound note.

'I'm not a police snitch.'

'No, you're our snitch.'

Hanrahan passed a slim piece of card over. 'We're your friends Robbie. If you hear anything, telephone that number. A woman will answer; just tell her you want to meet the Irishman.'

No more license was needed for Agnew to turn and bolt.

'There's an Englishman, and Irishman and a Welshman,' I said. 'Sounds like a music hall joke. Are you sure you don't know this Williams? Or Jones? Not that there's a shortage of Welsh men called Williams or Jones.'

'I don't know the cabbie, but if there's a cell of militants planning armed action they will keep their heads down. You don't parade those ideas around. The left's not as united as it pretends to be and I'm not the only man the government has on the inside.'

'Cabbies are licensed so should be easy to track down. Do we report to Calhoun first, or find our man first?'

Hanrahan started to walk back towards the tube station. 'Let's find him.'

Chapter Twenty-Five

Taking a cuppa at one of the green cabman's shelters was part of Ewan Jones' daily life.

'We've got some Rich Teas too,' said Doris as she handed the cup of tea over the counter.

'Oh, ta Doris.'

She offered a biscuit straight from the packet. 'There was a copper asking after you.'

'Copper?'

'You could tell 'e was a copper. No uniform though. He must be one of them *detectives*. What have you been up to then? Robbing diamonds?'

Ewan glanced anxiously back at his taxi.

'You workin' late tonight?' She continued, as if detectives quizzed her so often it was of no account.

'What did you tell the copper?'

'Just that you came by from time to time. Nothing more. I didn't tell him that I'd seen you this morning, I wasn't going to drop you in it. He asked if you used to be called Williams, but I said you'd been a Jones so long as I knew you.'

He sat inside the shelter to think, to drink his tea, and take his biscuit. A man popped his head around the door, a snap-brimmed trilby on his head. 'Could you take me down to Limehouse?'

'I'm on my break.'

'I'll wait.'

Limehouse was a decent fare and the man looked well enough dressed to be good for a tip. Ewan finished his tea hurriedly and munched the last third of his Rich Tea as he walked to the cab and opened the rear door. The man and a colleague got into the back, and he followed their directions east, then south towards the river. It was growing dark, so he turned on his lights. The men were quiet, and he guessed they were in business as Limehouse was mostly warehouses and offices where it wasn't slum housing. It was gangland too, but the London gangsters respected cabbies and were good tippers – see nothing, say nothing. Yes, the men had that look about them.

'Do you know the Old Swan?' The first passenger asked.

'Yes,' he replied. The pub was a little rough, but these men must know what they wanted. Gangsters without a doubt.

When the pub came in sight, the passenger modified the directions. 'Carry on past...now left.'

For the first time Ewan held a doubt. This was a place he had never had cause to come. It was a narrow street between high warehouses, with no name as far as he knew it and no exit at the far end. He slowed to little more than walking speed, awaiting the next instruction.

'And stop.'

As he pulled on the handbrake, cold sharp metal pressed against his neck.

'Switch off.'

He switched off the ignition.

'Now get out, Ewan. We're going to have a little talk.'

Chapter Twenty-Six

The Muse had completely deserted Vincent Hammer. A sub-plot involving a missing woman, blonde, Dutch, amounted to just half a page, and I knew I wasn't making up half of what I typed. It was little more than inaccurate reportage. Now was the moment I needed that absinthe, but instead, I took a little splash of ten-year-old single malt that would have counted as a double or a triple pub measure. The phone jangled for attention.

It was Bass, the night porter. 'There's a gentleman to see you, sir.'

'Does he have a name?'

'He's a police officer and he'd like you to come down at your earliest convenience, sir.'

A muffled voice in the background said, 'Right now.'

From the window, I could see a black car stopped directly in front of the porch, and by the sound, its motor was still running. A uniformed officer sat behind the wheel, waiting. A quick glance around the room checked for anything remotely incriminating, then I pulled on a jacket. Thank goodness I did not live on the sixth floor. A brass-grilled lift served the building, but it creaked and was achingly slow. I trotted down one floor into the hallway where Bass stood almost to attention. He was ex-Royal Artillery and 'very sound' according to Calhoun.

Inspector Renton paced across the mosaic, clearly impatient.

'Good evening inspector,' I said with as much cheer as felt appropriate.

'Mr Clifton, would you come with me.' It was not a request.

'I'll just...'

'Now would suit me dandy.' Renton touched my jacket sleeve, suggesting he would lock his grip if there was the least resistance.

Bass was watching closely. Both he and Lilley, formerly of the Coldstream Guards, knew what number to telephone if the tenant of flat 64 ever got into difficulties. Renton continued that discomforting light pressure, encouraging me out of the building. A black Wolseley stood at the kerb and its police driver stepped out, allowing the engine to keep running. I was urged into the back seat and the officer closed the door as Renton went around the other side.

'We're just going to drive.' Renton said. The Wolseley pulled away from the kerb and headed towards Holborn. 'Have you met a man called Ewan Williams?'

'No, I don't think I have.'

'Ewan Jones, then. Cab driver, union man.'

'Ringing no bells.'

'Have you any plans to speak to a cab driver named Ewan Williams or Ewan Jones? 'Cause you'll need to cancel them, 'cause he's dead. They pulled his body out of the Thames at Greenwich this morning. I'm talking to you because if we'd ever met in a pub last week we might have talked about him. Except I gave you no names, but if we had met we might have talked about the Mutineers.'

'London Regiment, 1918.'

'So you do know. You and the rest of the chocolate detectives of Department Z. I was right guessing you were one of them.'

Joining Z had made a handy screen for my real role.

'And now you're going to tell me you've no idea who killed him? Aye, he didn't drown, he was smacked around first, and then they sawed his arms off.'

'What?'

'Ah, you're shocked. Good, it'll teach you what nasty people you're messing with.'

'Any idea who it was?'

'I hoped you could tell me.'

I fell silent, as no doubt Mr Newburn would advise me to do. I didn't have the telephone number of that hard-nosed solicitor who had fenced against Renton last time, but he should be reachable through Black House. Someone manned their telephone until late into the night in case the biff boys were needed to save a speaker's hide at some rally.

'It looks like this cabbie, whose name you do know else I'm a Dutchman, fell foul of the wrong people. They wanted to make him talk or shut him up, or one followed by the other. They sawed both his arms off at the elbow and let him bleed to death. We haven't found the arms, but we did find his taxi. No clues, of course.'

'Shutting him up,' I said.

'Mmm? Go on.'

'Like they executed the man I shot.'

'Do you know that for a fact, or is it a guess?'

'Hunch.'

'Hunches don't convince judges,' Renton said. 'We're going down the station, and you're going to make a statement about where you've been for the last three days. Every hour.'

'I'm a writer, I work on my own.'

'That's so very convenient.'

'And I have been socializing with a married lady, who I wouldn't want to compromise.'

'Also convenient. We'll pull her in too unless you co-operate. And her husband.'

'He's in Italy.'

'You're a bloody clever arse, Clifton. Or you think you are, but you're out of your depth whatever game you're playing. Three days, a complete life story. A writer should be able to manage that.'

* * *

'So who killed Williams?' I asked. 'Or Jones, or whatever name St Peter has written in his book?'

Hanrahan shook a puzzled face, then masked it with the lip of his beer glass.

'I've just completed my finest piece of fiction to date for the benefit of Inspector Renton. The fact he pulled me in shows the police were working on the same lines as us, and Jones-Williams was the third man in the Kensington shooting.'

'They're cleaning up,' Hanrahan said at length. 'In the same way that Dennis was shot.'

'I thought that too, but sawing his arms off? That's rather extreme. A bullet in the head I can understand if they just want to shut his mouth. If they wanted information, then yes I'd expect him to suffer a good beating, but sawing his arms off is simply medieval.'

'Spreads fear though, doesn't it? It sends a signal to the others to stay in line, not get careless. Stalinists can be dramatic.'

'So this is a trademark of Stalinists? Forgive me, I don't know many.'

'Or some of your mob learning from Hitler's henchmen.'

For all the sinister threat of the black room, my experience down there had proved to be entirely theatre; faux-evil. 'Department Z play at it, but they wouldn't torture and mutilate someone.'

'You don't think? There's some nasty pieces of work in your movement. Just because you haven't met them doesn't mean they're not there.'

The glint in the eye of the Director of Propaganda and Parker's unforgiving stare came to mind.

'I mean that.' He leaned forward. 'If you put a foot wrong, someone will be sawing your arms off. Or worse.'

'Worse?'

'Have a drink and think about what you would do in their position, if you had to make someone talk or shut them up. If you wasn't an officer and a gentleman, and if the person in front of you was expendable, like this Ewan.'

'I thought that he'd turn out to be the one who shot at me. That he'd turn out to be the ringleader, as he'd once been an officer, albeit briefly.'

'No, taxi man. He drove the car, that's all. Your ringleader is still active and making sure nobody gets to the truth.'

'I had to give Inspector Renton the rest of those names that came from my source. I'm making out this is a Department Z investigation so that he doesn't guess my real game. He might already know the names, but it gives him the idea I might be valuable.'

Hanrahan agreed. 'You know, I wonder if we honestly want to stop someone shooting Oswald Mosley, or blowing him up? They'd be doing us all a favour. Your mission is to disrupt the fascists, so if someone else is doing your job for you what's the worry?'

'Oh, come on, you're winding me up now. We don't want war on the streets. And when you assassinate a leader, you often get someone even worse in his place. And a martyr to the cause to celebrate, more use dead than he was alive.'

'Makes you wonder if there is someone worse, who would want a vacancy in that top seat,' Hanrahan mused. 'Francis-Hawkins, Joyce, Box, Fuller?'

'Nobody needs to kill Mosley, or Mrs Symes for that matter,' I said. 'They're struggling for money and membership has fallen from fifty thousand last year to ten now.'

'So what are those forty thousand people doing?' Hanrahan said, a sparkle in his eye. 'Have they really fallen out of love with Mosley? Did you see all those fascist salutes for the King on the Jubilee parade? I did. Some days I think it's not the men strutting around in black uniforms that we need to worry about. Do you remember the Titanic, when we were still lads? That unsinkable ship steaming at full speed for an iceberg that's nine tenths under the water. In the dark, waiting. Is there a party within your party, one you haven't found?'

'Or one within yours,' I challenged. 'One you haven't found.'

Hanrahan gave a slow and deliberate laugh. 'Aw, we're just guessing.' He drained his pint and wiped froth from his little 'tache. 'Don't you have a high-born lady to go to? I have places to be.'

Chapter Twenty-Seven

Darkness fell, then midnight passed. Police officers drew arms and received their orders. Black-painted vans and cars moved into position without the drama of clanging bells.

'Did you tell Clifton this was going down?' Hanrahan asked.

'It's not his place,' Calhoun replied. He was behind the wheel of the discreetly black Humber half a street away from the target address.

'No. He'll be with his *fascista* by now, on his second bottle of champagne in some swanky club.'

'If he is, it's what we've asked him to do. I regret that your mission is restricted to dockland barmaids and corned beef sandwiches. Our list of names has proved interesting, and the police didn't have them. Special Branch are hitting all Ewan Williams' and Dick Dennis' known associates.'

'But not Robbie Agnew?'

'No, we're leaving Robbie for you, swimming free.' Calhoun checked his watch. 'Clear decks for action.'

A police van shot past, and the headlights of one of their Wolseley's grew from the opposite direction. Doors banged and dark figures swarmed towards the tenement where an ex-soldier called Moulton should live.

'Wait here, I don't want Inspector Renton seeing your face. He's already too familiar with Clifton.'

'Half the country is familiar with Clifton,' said Hanrahan. 'He's a liability.'

Calhoun closed the door quietly and walked steadily towards the scene of the commotion. Policemen were pouring into the building now. Others should be covering the back to prevent escapes. Shouts came from within.

A second police van drew up with less urgency, a Black Maria awaiting its charges.

The Security Service man held back. Some of the police would be armed, and so might the men inside, and accidents would happen. No shots came. A police sergeant stood by the parked Wolseley, a plain clothes officer by his side. It was Renton.

'Ah, Calhoun. Thanks for the names, they're all on the shopping list for tonight. The score is four-two so far. We've had two empty nests; the birds had flown already.'

'Tipped off?'

'Or scared of getting their arms sawn off. We've got four, but they don't feel like the men we're after.'

'No Americans?'

'Of course not. Where's your source for that one?'

'Oh, you know,' Calhoun shrugged.

'I know, I know, you protect your grubby sources.'

Hands in pockets, they stood and watched as silhouettes passed briefly across lighted windows. More doors banged, men shouted, a woman shrieked. Glass shattered, then more glass. An officer in plain clothes hurried down the front steps and made across to report. 'Moulton's gone, sir.'

'So what's the roughhouse for?'

'Got to make sure. Some smart-alecs in there were giving us a bit of gob, and the local boys have found a pickpocket they've been after for months.'

'We didn't do all this to nab a pickpocket.'

'No sir.'

'The cupboard is bare,' Renton shared his news with Calhoun. 'Someone's told them to scatter, so I don't hold much hope for the last two tonight. Have you any idea who we are dealing with?'

'Amateur terrorists with a grudge against the Blackshirts.'

'And the Conservatives,' added Renton. 'There was another bomb today, under the car of the MP for Harrow. He was opening some fete. It was just slipped under the car with a crude contact detonator which would have gone off if his chauffer had driven over it. The chauffer was a proud military man and was inspecting the shine on his wheel hubs when he spotted it.'

'Luck saves us again.'

'We can't hope these amateurs won't learn from their mistakes. The men who pay our wages are becoming nervous and we can't keep the Harrow bomb out of the papers; a hundred people saw the sappers turn up to defuse the thing. I'll dress tonight's raids up as being connected to the bombings, so at least it looks like we're taking action.'

Calhoun returned to his car slowly. He shared the news of the failure and of the latest bomb with Hanrahan. 'It's not your Irish cousins back to haunt us, is it?'

'No.'

'You sound certain. Shooting policemen, bombing politicians, it sounds right up their street. Do you have any evidence that this is *not* a new move by the IRA? We know they're active again on their home turf.'

'If it had been the IRA sir, the bombs would have gone off.'

Chapter Twenty-Eight

I only learned about the raids by reading an account in the *Evening Standard*. Calhoun would not even have mentioned them if I had not queried the story, and he made clear I had no role in such an operation. So much for the line I'd typed in Chapter 3:

...everything now relied on one man, one Blackshirt Detective.

When Sissy asked to see Vincent Hammer's output, I showed off the first three chapters with a suitable level of author's pride. She sat in the armchair, quickly reading page after page, trying to smile at my little jokes, but mostly with an increasing level of pain on her face.

'Well?' I asked as she laid it aside.

'It's a start,' she said, summoning a little brightness.

I mimed crestfallen. 'It's not very good, is it?' Indeed, I'd thought I was making a decent fist of it, but clearly not.

'I don't like the girlfriend, she's silly. All she does is ask questions and get in the way.'

'It's a way of explaining to the reader what's going on.'

'Show the reader what's going on! You don't need a pretty blonde fluffy thing acting dumb.'

The girlfriend on the page bore more than a passing resemblance to Lucy in the office.

'Give her some life, give her a gun, give her some character and some spirit!'

'I could base her on you.'

'Don't you dare! Do that and I'll sue.'

CHAPTER TWENTY-EIGHT

Taking the papers back was demoralizing. Cruel as she may have been, Sissy was not half as critical as a London publisher might be. Life as a novelist might be just a cover, but it was cover that may have to be maintained for months, if not years. I needed to improve my game.

'Just write *must try harder* at the bottom,' I muttered. 'In red ink.'

'Sorry,' she said. 'I thought you'd have written more.'

The telephone rang. It was Captain Parker. 'Be on the Mile End Road, nine sharp tonight. No uniform, working man's dress. We're using the bread van, you'll see it.'

'How long will we be?'

'Not long.' Parker hung up.

This was the test, surely. 'I have to go,' I apologized.

'Not your friend Pat again!'

'No, that man Parker. Something is going down in the East End.'

'Oh God, what have you got into now?'

'I'll drive over, I can drop you at Russell Square tube station.'

'Forget that. I'm coming too!'

I took my Walther from its drawer. 'Are you sure?'

'Is mine in there too?'

* * *

I did not want to see Sissy in danger, but perhaps it would not be such a bad idea for her to see what the Party was up to after dark. It might dent some of her enthusiasm. There was no time to get hold of Hanrahan, and the last thing I was going to do was head off into the night with Parker and his gang with nobody knowing my whereabouts. A BUF meeting was held somewhere in the capital most days of the week, many being no more than a street-corner gathering, and more often than not, a meeting met resistance. Violence would abruptly terminate legitimate political debate, then the vans would roll from Black House and the biff boys would ride to the rescue. It's what I expected from the evening's entertainment.

Sissy joined me in the Alvis, and I put the second Walther into the glove box. It could be the ace I would need to get away without my arms being sawn off, if somehow Parker was onto my game and this rendezvous was some form of trap.

'Please don't touch it unless you're in dire danger. I'm so glad you didn't start popping shots at those miners.'

'I'm not sure I would have if it had come to it.'

'Then it was dangerous to even take it out. Never pull a gun if you're not ready to use it. You're raising the stakes to no purpose.'

'Oh, you're right, you're right. The man is always right.'

'You don't believe that for a second.'

'No, I don't.'

I parked the Alvis behind the bread van which I found halfway down the Mile End Road, silent with no lights showing. Parker came from the dark. I closed the door and moved to join him on the pavement.

'Who's that with you?'

Sissy wound her window open. 'It's me, Captain Parker!'

'Christ Clifton, this is no place for a woman.'

'Sissy can look after herself. Department Z should recruit more women.'

'She stays here.'

'Oh, you boys run along and play!' Sissy settled back into her seat and started to wind up the window.

'Driver's seat,' I suggested quietly.

'Yes sir.' She began the inelegant task of shuffling across.

'Whatever you hear, you heard nothing,' Parker warned her with a jabbing finger, then led me away. 'Why did you bring her?'

'We were already out, and Sissy is not someone it's easy to say no to.'

'Pah!' Parker swaggered down the pavement. Shadows moved in doorways and four men joined us, wearing an assortment of caps and jackets. 'Meet the Action Squad.' From a distance, we could be any old group of East End bruisers off for an evening of malice and mayhem.

'Round the next turn is a kosher grocer,' he said. 'Simple plan. Two men smash the plate windows, and I do the door with this.' He took out a hammer. 'I empty the till to help the funds, then you finish the job. Give it to him, Reece.'

The man called Reece handed me a bottle heavy with the smell of petrol.

'You've got a lighter with you?'

'No.'

'What kind of man are you?' He fished in his pocket. 'Here, I want it back.'

I was about to commit burglary and arson, with little option to refuse. My loaded pistol would surely add years to the sentence if we were caught.

'This is your rite of passage Clifton. This is how we're going to win the East End.'

We rounded the corner. Clubs appeared from beneath jackets, and one man wanted to smash the first window he came to.

'Next shop, fool!'

I took a deep breath, then glass cracked under the impact of two men bashing at the display window. It was tougher than I'd have guessed, and it took several blows to bring it crashing to the pavement. A horn sounded, then again, closer. Parker moved to the door with his hammer. A pair of lights swept around the corner and the Alvis jerked to a halt beside us. The engine stalled.

'What the bloody hell?' Parker declared.

'Police,' Sissy snapped, leaning across to speak through the part-open window. 'Two officers are coming this way.'

Parker held up a hand to restrain my enthusiasm to burn the place down. 'Another time, Clifton. You lot, that way! Get to the pub. I'll circle back round for the van.'

Sissy tried to start the engine as I pulled open the passenger door. She turned over the engine again and it refused to start.

'What have you done to it?'

'Nothing, I just...'

Two constables came around the corner, breaking into a sprint when they saw the glitter of broken glass on the pavement. One leaned to speak through my window. 'Sir? Did you see what happened?'

'Yes we saw some ruffians,' Sissy piped up in her poshest of posh voices. 'They skedaddled when I hooted. They ran that way.'

'Sir?' The policeman clearly was not going to take the word of a female driver.

'My ah, wife is correct constable,' I said in my best officer-speak. 'Three or four men were breaking into this shop. Naturally, I asked my wife to stop and I challenged them. They ran off.'

'That was brave sir, but…'

Sissy succeeded in starting the car at the third attempt.

'We'll motor that way and see if we can still see them.'

'Sir…'

Taking my cue, Sissy crunched the gears and drove away as fast as she could before the constable could veto my suggestion, ask my name or even take the registration number.

'Wife?' asked Sissy.

'It was a quick and easy fib. Well done back there, it saved my bacon.'

'You can't do this Hugh. You're not a thug.'

'Parker was just testing me.'

'He'll see you in jail more likely.'

Chapter Twenty-Nine

Pat Hanrahan rarely said anything openly at political meetings. He saved his thoughts for the quiet of a walk in the park or when covered by the hubbub of a pub. For King and Country or whatever, he sat through another fractious, volatile meeting of the East London branch of the Communist Party of Great Britain. Thirty-three people only filled half the seats set out over the Hackney pub, but they managed to fill the room with noise.

'The Police are cracking down!' insisted the Chair, in response to a pair of Jews demanding more action. 'Don't give them the excuse.'

'You're a sell-out!'

'Guns and bombs is not the answer.'

'It's the only answer,' a bearded student asserted. 'If we'd killed that reactionary woman when we had the chance it would give us one less fascist to hang when the day comes.'

'She's a traitor to women everywhere,' added one of the women.

Others cheered.

'No, no!' A union man butted in. 'That's the Trotskyite view! We don't need anarchy we need to organize centrally…'

Hanrahan looked out of the window and let it all flow past him. As soon as the meeting was over, he offered to buy the bearded Trotskyite a drink. Then another, then a third. Unlike Clifton, he was not spending his own money, but the pub was a cheap one with no pretensions of luxury.

'You're ready for the fight, then?' Hanrahan asked.

'I'm ready.'

'These bombs, these guns. You don't think it's a put-up job by the establishment?'

'No, it's real.'

The Trotskyite could easily be in the pay of Special Branch, the Trades Union Congress, or the Labour Party. Hanrahan had attended one splinter group meeting where he was convinced every person present was on the payroll of another organization. Some days it felt like the Communist Party of Great Britain was a fiction sustained entirely by its opponents' agents.

'But if I wanted to…y'know…join the revolution? Where do I sign?' Hanrahan asked in his lowest conspiratorial whisper.

'Sorry comrade, I can't help you.' Perhaps the student doubted his commitment, perhaps he was also paranoid about spies and informers.

'So you don't know who's behind it?' He would tease the student, hoping for bravado to overcome his caution. 'Who's organizing?'

'Nobody,' the student declared, with a gleam in his eye. 'These are spontaneous acts of frustration by the jobless and the hungry.'

This sounded like wish-fulfilment, the sort of thing the CPGB wanted everyone to believe. 'Which college are you at?'

'University College.'

'I'm an Oxford man myself.' It was hard not to feel loyalty to a university he'd never attended, and it was a lie he could be proud of. 'Have you been to Oxford?'

'Yeah, I went to a few rallies in the summer term.'

Oxford was the centre of Marxist Britain, according to the Tory press.

'So you'll know the student body is ready for revolution?' Hanrahan spun out a line more worthy of *The Daily Telegraph*.

'Yes, yes, it's so exciting. Revolution in the air! The comrades were talking about this American adventurer you know?' The student hushed his words. 'Recruiting.'

At last, there he was—the American. 'For revolution?'

The student nodded.

'Did you meet him?'

'No. In fact the guy I was talking to he hadn't met him either, but his girlfriend had.' He paused. 'Or her room-mate.'

Oh, one of those, Hanrahan thought.

* * *

Georgie was waiting for him outside and took his arm. 'Whoa, Pat, you've had a few! I turned down two good offers standing out here in the rain, waiting. I could have made a quid.'

'You, what are you?'

She laughed, and they walked slowly back to the underground station in the light drizzle. He matched her pace as she had a heavy limp and would be limping for the rest of her life. She would be an outcast forever and was perhaps the only person he could trust. And then, only perhaps. Her blonde hair drooped from under her favourite beret, and she listened intently as he shared what little he'd learned.

'There are American leftists around,' she said. 'But I've heard men from South Africa or Australia referred to as "Americans" by people who don't travel. All they know of the world is the movies, and most are American.'

'If this American is recruiting, organizing, he'll be spending money and Moscow are very tight with theirs. Clifton thinks he's a Jew.'

'No, really? Is he that deep into the fascist mentality? I don't trust your friend Hugh Clifton. He sounds too confident to be just another informer – you must be careful.'

'Hugh's very green, he's blundering his way through, a model British Empire Boy's Own hero. A pair of fists and pistol.'

'But he's got money, a shiny car, and there's that lord that gets his information – you know the class the Security Services recruit from. He's got establishment printed all over him. He wasted no time falling into bed with that Sissy, and she'll be winding him round her fascist fingers. Have you met her?'

'No.'

'Watch her if you do. She's clever but she hides it and given half a chance she'd take Diana Guinness' place at Mosley's side. She'll charm your pants off, so don't underestimate her.'

As they continued to walk, he could tell by the pause she was preparing to skewer him. 'You knew about this American before, didn't you? If Clifton thinks he's a Jew, he must know about him as well.'

That was a stupid slip, Hanrahan was getting careless. 'Yes, we did pick something up.'

'Where did that come from?'

'Oh around, chatter.' He wouldn't give her the exact sources of his information. Some days he could trust Georgie with his life, but there were things she'd be better off not knowing. Or he'd be better off if she didn't know.

Chapter Thirty

Using those grubby mining profits, I ordered a dozen Westley Richards 'Take Down' rifles; refined, almost beautiful weapons designed for hunting so making the purchase appear less military. I also knew that the BUF would struggle to stockpile enough of the required 0.318 ammunition to become a nuisance. Twelve rifles would allow *my women* to drill as a little platoon and I rose a notch in their estimation.

Four rifles had arrived by the next weekend I spent at Baroness Rockwell's country seat. Each woman was allowed ten shots. I ran through some dry loading/unloading exercises, cleaning, dismantling, and basic stripping and enjoyed the experience more than I should. I'd also purchased six new civilian-pattern 0.38 Webleys. It was a heavy pistol for a woman, but I told them it was best to train for self-defence on weapons they were most likely to come across. I wasn't training terrorists, and it was a big gun to conceal in a handbag or a woman's coat pocket. Five hundred rounds of ammunition allowed twenty-five rounds each of pistol practice that weekend, the trainees reloading five times and always leaving an empty chamber.

'Just so you don't shoot your foot off.'

It was crucial that Sissy became competent with a firearm. Dangerous waters swirled around us, and she could be pulled down with me. She shot only with her new Walther. Quizzed by the other women she simply replied, 'Buy your own gun.'

Sissy copied my instruction closely. Almost casually she fired a whole clip at the target, two-handed, and hit with each one. Over the whole morning, only three of her rounds missed the 'human' target entirely. A little learning might be a dangerous thing, but her instinct to pull the pistol in Yorkshire had showed that a lot of learning might make *her* a dangerous thing. Those miners would have been dead men.

'Excellent,' I accepted the Walther and checked it was fully unloaded. It was not too large to be concealed in a handbag or a woman's coat pocket.

She was simply beaming as she removed cotton wool from her ears. 'Oh, I forgot to tell you, I got V's address out of Julian over lunch yesterday. I had to lie rather a lot and spin some story about her borrowing my hat and never giving it back. He said she'd probably moved, and I would be wasting my time for a silly little hat, but I did love that hat I never lost and gave a good account of why I needed it back.'

'That sounds like a good piece of subterfuge. You still want me to hunt her down?'

'Five pounds a day, plus expenses, as agreed.' She smiled. 'None of the girls have seen her, nor Mother; she was quite drawn to her.'

'What did she do, in the Party? I know she was behind your women's militia, but did she have any official role when she was working at Black House?'

'No, she did a bit of typing or filing, the sort of thing women are allowed to do down there. Boring things to be honest.'

* * *

Yes, Black House could be boring, but it was always a busy place, with its printing presses churning, men and women coming to-and-fro for meetings, and 'FH' and his administration team working all hours to bash the organization into order. Unemployed lads slept in the barrack rooms, emerging for the seven-thirty reveille, physical jerks in the garden, drill, and inspections. Almost everyone was a volunteer and I tried to appear occupied whilst avoiding as much real work as possible. My first job at Department Z was amending files on who now held which overblown job title. There was a good deal of turnover in the movement's topsoil as regional officers were sacked for incompetence, fiddling the books, or running Blackshirt branches more like cosy tea parties. It was all no doubt of interest to Calhoun, but it took me no closer to discovering anything about the BUF's money.

Casual conversations indicated that this officer or that found need to travel to Italy, drawn ostensibly by the ruins, the art galleries, and the fine weather. I passed their names to Mrs Ainsworth, accompanied by little more than speculation; men named Dundas and Tabor who I'd never met but seen from a distance were the ones I most suspected. What I needed was a date and a time when one of them would step off the boat train and could be arrested with a suitcase stuffed with Mussolini's money.

Lucy Parmentier had a strong Essex accent and was quick to display her crooked selection of teeth in a smile. In her smart black silk blouse, she was quite the most cheerful fascist I had ever met. When my first reports were ready, I presented them to her.

'I'll show you how to file.'

As an initiate to the dark art of office work, I needed to be inducted into its mysteries. Lucy went over to a row of wooden filing cabinets five drawers high, running her fingers along it. 'It's all alphabetic by subject.'

'So if I wanted to read my own file that would be under C?'

'You mustn't read your own file, it's naughty.' Lucy showed her teeth – not a perfect smile but a winning one. 'And the keys are behind the door. Numbered per cabinet. We have to keep things neat for Major Taylor.'

A ten-bob dinghy indeed.

'I'm going to pop down for a cuppa, you comin'?'

'No, I'll just file these. Get the hang of the system.'

With another cheeky smile, as if plotting the overthrow of democracy was all great fun, Lucy left for her tea, closing the frosted glass door as she went. I was alone in the little office. A quick inspection showed the drawers were indeed usefully lettered. After only a moment's thought, I took the third key and unlocked 'K-N'. Everyone referred to it as the 'Kensington Shooting' so logic dictated the file should be under K, and in the top drawer. As it was. With one eye out for movement beyond the glass door, I hurriedly flicked through the file. It was padded by a dozen newspaper cuttings, several featuring a familiar handsome chap's photograph. Time, place, and basic facts in the written notes all seemed to tally. Someone had drawn a little diagram which was out of scale. The typed-up report of my interrogation was extensive and too painful to more than skim through and notes of interviews with other Blackshirts added little to my own recollection. A communist 'Red Front' was blamed. As investigations went it was worthy more of a cub reporter than a Blackshirt Detective of the Harry Bretton calibre.

I slipped the file back and pulled open the drawer marked L. Someone moved in the anteroom. I shut the drawer quickly and flicked through my slim pile of notes for one I could legitimately be filing under K to N.

Parker came in. 'No Taylor?'

'Not seen him, sorry.'

'I see Miss Parmentier's got you at work.' Was that twitch of his cheek an attempt to smile? 'Taylor likes his paperwork, but I've no time for it, I'm not an office boy.' Parker flicked a finger towards the window that looked down on the central quadrangle. 'The battle is going to be won out there, on the streets. Shame about the other night—you'll get another chance though. Things are going to heat up if there's an election before Christmas.'

Parker left, having unwittingly shown me the weak spot in his armour. I was still grinning when Lucy returned. 'I've finished filing—I hope I got it right. Sorry but I have to go out for the rest of the day now.' Unpaid staff came and went as we chose.

'Back to your novel writing? That must be more fun than typing this old stuff.'

'Indeed it is.'

'Inventing crimes and murders and things. You have an exciting afternoon Mr Clifton.'

'I will.'

Chapter Thirty-One

It was easy to find 16C Brompton Villas, placed on a genteel square between the Brompton Road and the Natural History Museum. Six flats were accessed through its front door, and the brass plate for 16C was marked 'Harrison'. Around five o'clock would be a good time to gain entry, I judged, assuming someone in the building worked office hours. This area of London was provided with little gardens for the use of residents of each square, so offered a pleasant place to loiter. A gardener looked my way, but I merely tipped my fedora, quite fitting the setting in a broad-shouldered, tan plaid summer suit with handkerchief projecting in a neat triangle from the breast pocket. Stylish but not flashy had become my personal dress code, and Sissy made sure I wore nothing that was out of fashion. Anything she disapproved of was never worn again.

A photographer in Holborn had made copies of that photograph of Sissy and Verity by the Serpentine, including isolated images of Verity herself. The original would soon wear out after being pushed into a wallet then passed from one hand to another, and the search for her could last some time.

At almost half-past five a man of about my age wearing a pinstripe suit and carrying an overcoat slung over his arm hurried towards the building. Matching his pace, I engineered to reach the door just behind the resident. He politely held the door open for me to follow him, much as one sheep after another enters a pen.

'Thanks awfully, old chap.'

Everything about him shouted *office worker*. 'Do you live here?' asked the office worker, narrowing his eyes.

'I've come to see Verity.'

'Verity?'

'16C?' I pulled out a photograph immediately, with the kind of excitement a suitor might show.

'Ah, third floor,' said the other with just a hint of wistfulness. 'But she's long gone. Mr Harrison is up there now; I travel into the City in company with him some mornings.'

'Oh, that's a pity. Have you any idea when she went?'

'Sorry. I haven't seen her since last autumn.'

Sissy had said much the same, allowing Julian just a couple of months to wallow in the throes of rejection before he was drawn in by Melissa.

'Who's the landlord?' I took out a pencil and a notepad.

'The Estate,' the man said with some reluctance and growing suspicion. He nodded down the hallway. 'Mr Levin's their man here. He lives in the basement, but he uses the outside steps.'

'Thank you so much.'

I wrote a note for Mr Harrison and left it on the sideboard in the hall where a few other letters awaited the residents. Returning to the pavement, I opened the gate in the iron railings and took the dozen steps down to the basement. Levin was in later middle age and walked with a stoop that emphasized the low basement ceiling. He was far from a caricature Jew, but all the racialist pamphlets I'd pained myself to read over the past few months had made me sensitive to clues such as his accent. Yet another false name served as an introduction. Mr Horley came fresh to mind.

'And what can I do for you Mr Horley?'

'Ah, I'm looking for a friend of mine. Verity Laytham.' Levin was shown the photograph. 'I understood she lived at 16C. She said if I was ever in London I should call.'

'You're from the north, yes? And it's a long time since you've seen the young lady?'

'So has she moved out?'

'The second week of October 1934.'

'Did she leave a forwarding address?'

'No, and she didn't leave the six weeks' rent that was owing. I kept her deposit, and I pawned her things for the rest.'

'She left her things, what things?'

Levin offered a shrug. 'Everything she owned, for all I know. The shop owner is a friend of mine, she can buy them back if she comes back.'

'Could I have the ticket?'

The man raised one eyebrow.

'I'm in touch with her sister. She's worried about her too. I rather think Verity would rather her sister looked after her things until she returns. She never mentioned where she was going?'

'No, we never talked. She was quiet.'

So far from fireworks, then. Not the hard-drinking party girl Sissy made her out to be. 'I know she wanted to travel; France, Italy, you know...'

'I don't know. Send this sister and she can have the ticket. I'm sorry not to be trusting, but Miss Laytham didn't talk about any sister to me.'

'She had plenty of friends though?'

'No callers at all, no men running in and out like with some girls. She was very quiet. She was a very good tenant, I never thought she'd be one to run off without paying the rent. But it's the quiet ones you need to watch, they say.'

* * *

Sissy was amused to play the sister, and sufficiently resembled the image of Verity in black-and-white for the ruse to work on Mr Levin, whose attitude was at best indifferent once shown the photograph of the two of them together. He said that his wife had cleared the room and thrown out a small pile of things 'not worth pawning'. She'd taken two books back to Kensington library, adding the cost of the fines to Verity's debt.

We drove to Earl's Court where it was only ten minutes' work to find the pawnshop which held Verity's things, stored in a valise and a small trunk. I redeemed them for thirteen pounds and seven shillings. Returning to

Chelsea, we parked in the street below Sissy's apartment and unpacked the cases in her sitting room. Both were locked, but with a little force and a selection of implements bought on Hanrahan's advice, both came open.

'Where did you get those?' Sissy asked.

I put the lock-picking kit away. 'A disreputable friend.'

She shook her head in amazement. 'What's your disreputable friend called? It's not this Pat, is it?'

'As it happens,' I replied. A little truth served to dilute the lies I had to tell Sissy. 'He's a useful man to know.'

'An underworld contact?' She flashed her eyelids. Fictional crime was so more glamourous than the real thing.

'He's been around, and if you happen to bump into him by accident, let me know. He's an inch or two shorter than me, sort of hooky nose like the Duke of Wellington, can sound Irish when he wants to. Touch of red in his hair and a little moustache. He's a good friend, but he's also a bit of a socialist.'

'A red-haired red?'

'So, if you ever meet, just be careful what you say.'

'You're very mysterious, it's no wonder Department Z wanted you.' Kneeling, she turned her attention to Verity's belongings which had not been folded with any great care and some simply had been shoved into the corners of the case. Mrs Levin had presumably packed everything she could find as quickly as she could when she cleared the room. Perhaps she was the one who locked the valise and may have retained the key as the pawnbroker did not have it. The first item Sissy took out was a practical summer dress in light blue. 'I remember her wearing this.' Indeed, Verity was wearing that same dress with white openwork buttons in the form of flowers and little turned-out collar in the Serpentine photograph.

'And this.' It was a pink-and-white striped short-sleeved jersey. 'And this,' she added pulling out a deep blue skirt. 'I never realized she had so little to choose from. She never seemed to be poor.'

Each item was checked, then re-folded in a pile. However limited Verity's wardrobe might have been, the underwear and nightwear were of quality silk, and the few skirts, dresses, blouses, and one coat Sissy laid out all came from London's better stores. Two perfumes carried Parisian labels.

'These are fine stockings,' Sissy said, counting out three pairs. 'No ladders.'

I shrugged.

'I suppose that to you, ladders are something that firemen use?'

A black sequined grip was empty other than for a small compact. One book of poetry, a small amount of writing apparatus, and a single photograph in a tarnished silver-plated frame completed the paltry inventory.

'You notice that there's nothing at all with her name on it,' I said. 'Not even on the luggage label, or inside that poetry book.'

'Yah but who cares about a little poetry book?' Sissy swung around to sit with hands around her knees. 'She just left these old things when she scarpered. It wasn't worth lugging it all.'

'But these things are far from old, and even pawned worth what, two or three months' wages to a working woman? A year's savings? Not many people would leave so much behind unless they had money to burn.'

'Or were in a tearing hurry,' she added. Sissy picked up the photograph. It featured a man in naval officer's uniform. 'He has to be family, it's such a boring picture. Could it be her father?'

'It's someone's father. From the cut of that uniform, it's from the Great War, so he'd be fifty or sixty now.'

She gazed at the old sailor thoughtfully. 'Well, even if you don't care about a few old dresses, you don't leave a photograph of your father, because it's probably the only one you have. It's like she went out one day meaning to come back but didn't.'

I moved from the floor to sit on the sofa and survey the evidence. 'Can you remember her wearing anything that isn't here?'

'Hats. And she had a summer coat, quite light, with a big belt. And there's no town shoes.'

'Or money, or passport...could she drive?'

'Oh yes, we took a tourer out once round Oxfordshire.' Sissy swung her legs around and stood up, looking down on the collection with hands on hips.

'There's no driving licence either.'

'None of this makes sense,' she said.

'Did you know her at all before she met Julian?'

'No, she just appeared. An instant chum, as if I'd ordered her from a catalogue.'

It was a good analogy. 'So, a beautiful woman appears from nowhere and takes an interest in our friend Julian, who for all his charms is not Clark Gable. A sudden interest, I'll bet. Then she vanishes just as completely. Nothing about your catalogue order friend rings true.'

'She was a gold-digger, as I said.'

I did not challenge her conclusion. The less Sissy's thoughts strayed down the path of spies and conspiracies the better.

Sissy paced slowly towards the window, counting off facts with chops of her hands. 'Verity comes to London with just enough to survive on whilst she snags Julian. Last September she went out...in her summer coat and a hat. She took her handbag with her purse and all the clutter that goes with it. She left a photograph of her father and clothes that an ordinary shop girl would die for, so she meant to come back.' Sissy stopped pacing and stopped tallying the evidence. 'She's dead, isn't she?'

'There's no evidence that she isn't.'

'Oh God! But someone would have found her body. The Police or...'

'Who knows?'

The one who surely did know was Calhoun, and he'd been quick to brush off my inquisitiveness. Verity Laytham could have taken several leaves out of the same book as Hanrahan and masked her real self. If true, this implied she was not christened Verity Laytham and she'd bought, borrowed or stolen that photograph of the old sailor to add a little depth to her story. No wonder Julian had never made it so far as her flat, as he'd have found it half-empty, a barely lived-in shell, and exploded the charade. No wonder he didn't want to talk about her, if he had any inkling of what she really was. Or indeed, what became of her.

Chapter Thirty-Two

If my days at Black House were dull, the late summer nights were filled with theatre, the cinema, restaurants, dancing clubs, and jazz clubs. Off duty at last, Julian and I leaned against the bar of the High Ace Roadhouse, just clear of the space where several dozen young people made stabs at the latest dances. Melissa hated jazz. 'She calls it Nigger Music,' Julian said, barely audible over the sound of the Jamaican band.

An American journalist once explained to me what a poisonous word that was. One day Melissa was going to spout her views in the wrong company and receive a hefty slap. Verity must have been so much more appealing, whoever she really was.

'In the canteen, Parker told me that jazz was decadent Jew music,' I said, 'which doesn't really tally with its roots in Africa or wherever. People who just don't like it have to frame political excuses. I hope that doesn't mean we're going to ban jazz when we come to power.'

'Certainly not.' Julian took a large swig of his martini. 'We're not puritans.'

'A love of jazz is not incompatible with being a good fascist,' I stated. 'We should write that into the constitution. We rule the Empire, and those chaps are from the Empire, which makes them British. So jazz is British!'

Julian frowned.

Perhaps I had already enjoyed one more vodka martini than a secret agent should consume on duty. 'Imperialism is a sword that cuts both ways. We'd never rule India without the help of the Indians. I had one white sergeant in my platoon, the rest were Sikhs. The Romans ran their Empire exactly the same way.'

So not in exactly the same way, but Julian wasn't the one to be pedantic. Saturday night logic dictated that we both needed another drink. It must be a legitimate tactic for an agent to get his source drunker than he is, especially when Julian did not know he was a source.

'Hire the Empire to run the Empire.'

'We won't have an Empire now the India Bill has gone through.'

The barman took my money and in return I received a martini in each hand.

'Mmm, thanks.' Julian accepted his new drink and took a large swig. 'Bet Mussolini wouldn't just let go of India, he's got it right. Sticking it to those slave-owning savages in Abyssinia and putting two fingers up to the League of Nations. Bet Italy didn't have a *Peace Ballot*. We should just let them have Abyssinia and forget all this sanctions nonsense and war talk.'

'What about the Abyssinians? Don't they get a say?'

'What about the Indians—hah, touché!' Julian clinked glasses again.

Sissy should be here, but a second night on the trot had been forsaken for some family crisis involving an aunt. 'Shame Melissa wouldn't come along, jazz aside. Bit of a whirlwind romance, you two, by all accounts.

'Why, why yes,' Julian said, blinking as if he hardly believed it himself.

'You won't have met your intended in a jazz club.'

'Father, you know...families.'

'So marrying Melissa was his idea? I can't imagine your father as a matchmaker.'

'No, no, mother did the Jane Austen thing. She's been trying to marry me off since I was about twelve.'

'I saw that photo of Sissy with that Verity girl. She's very stunning you lucky dog. I'm surprised your family didn't hurry you both off to the altar before Melissa got a look-in.'

'I say, are you serious with Sissy, old man?' Julian said, looking away. 'I've known her for years and wouldn't want her to get hurt again. Her husband treated her shockingly. He's a pederast, you know. Like half of Headquarters before Father cleaned it out. Before *Plan Blue*.' He uttered the name as if it was a great secret that he'd only let loose to a close friend in the confidence of drink.

'Plan Blue?'

'You missed it all, you joined after all that. Black House was ruled by FH's pretty boys... it's being cleaned out, top to bottom, Cornwall to Glasgow, root, and branch. Father's organising us, getting us ready for the election.'

Plan Blue could not be the most tightly guarded secret, limited to a few men in the know, if both Julian and Mrs Symes were familiar with it. A copy would be filed somewhere in Black House if I only had the excuse to go hunting for it. For some reason, Julian had decided to blurt out its name now, mixed in with that homophobe rant about Francis-Hawkins' cabal. Even part-sozzled, Julian had steered sharply away from the subject of Verity, masking one secret with another.

'Wait...we were side-tracked. You were telling me why you didn't marry Verity.'

No, he wasn't.

'No, well she didn't...'

'Didn't?'

'Didn't.' Julian waved his drink.

'Didn't have what? Family, money, breeding, a full set of teeth?'

'No, no, she just didn't stay around.'

'How very mysterious. Whatever happened to her?'

'I say, I don't want to talk about it.'

'Oh, go on. I might bump into her, tonight even, and fall for those blue eyes and raven hair.'

'The what?'

'Raven hair.' I mimed tumbling locks. 'Sissy's romantic description. She sounded quite jealous, as if I'd fall for her too.'

'You need to drop it, Hugh.' Julian delivered this as the opening shot of one of those arguments that spiralled into broken glass, broken friendships, flying fists, and being ejected into the street.

'Sorry, sorry.' Gosh, that nerve was raw. It was time to divert my friend, whilst Julian was still what passed for a friend in my new world. 'So with Melissa not here and you still technically being single, are you allowed to dance?'

'Um, yes.' Julian looked moodily at his empty glass.

'Two along, behind you. Tall blonde, plus petite redhead, very pretty. I'll dive in with the tall one and you back me up with her friend. We'll dance our cares away.'

Julian twisted around to survey the targets. 'Now you're talking, old man.'

It was a chance to play sheepdog and prize Julian away from Melissa.

* * *

I'd never made it into the office in Curzon Street where the top ranks of the Party plotted and conspired, but that Tuesday Thring Senior came over to attend a meeting of the Research Directory at Black House. In a party overflowing with ego and machismo, this grey man in an accountant's suit slipped into the building almost unnoticed. He nodded as he recognized me in the hallway, then made straight for the large meeting room, left hand gripping a tan briefcase. Perhaps it contained the secret of *Plan Blue*. I dearly wanted to rifle its contents. A street thief might be persuaded to grab the bag, but then Thring would know his secrets were out—if indeed the bag contained more than a notebook, pencils, and an apple.

I bought myself a briefcase in tan leather, much like the one Thring used. Up in Department Z, I casually set it down resting against the filing cabinets as I chatted to Lucy. 'I've had some ideas on the future of the Department and I'm going to make a formal report of it.'

'Do you want to dictate them to me, so I can type it up?'

'I can type, I just need a machine.'

'You can use the spare.' She nodded towards a typewriter that sat unloved on top of the filing cabinets. 'The ribbon's a bit tired though. The carbon paper is in my middle drawer, but we're down to about six sheets.'

'What shall I do with the report when I'm finished?'

'Leave it in Major Taylor's tray.' She indicated the wire basket on the heavy desk by the window. 'He's lunching now so we won't see him before two. There's so much going on I bet we won't see him back at all today.

I'm going to get myself some tea and have a sandwich. How about you, Mr Clifton?' Her smile hung there.

'I'll pop out later,' I said.

'Make sure your spelling is good because he gets particular, Major Taylor.'

Lucy was a creature of habit and left her desk for lunch as close to the stroke of noon as she could contrive, which made eleven fifty a perfect time to call on her. She was allowed forty-five minutes and usually took no less than forty-four. Her last job had been working for a school. FH hated what he called 'clock watching' and I'd heard Taylor spring to her defence more than once.

As soon as I was alone, I went for the third key and unlocked 'K-M'. Swiftly I pulled open that bottom drawer where L lurked. Even drunk, Julian had remained coy about Verity, implying he suspected not all was well in the way she had disappeared. If Department Z had any credibility as an internal security unit, they should at least have opened a file on her. Thring Senior must have been in on the act, judging by how swiftly he wheeled the politically appropriate Melissa onto the scene once Verity was consigned to history.

Laytham, Verity Dorothea, came to hand swiftly. I closed the drawer, locked the cabinet, dropped the manilla file into the briefcase, and walked along the corridor to the toilet. There was one marked for ladies on the ground floor, but all the others were for the gents.

Verity's file was marked with a black gummed sticker. I'd spotted red and green stickers on other files, and the Kensington one was marked in red. The black blob might mean Spy, as that is what the file called her, much in the way pirates gave traitors the Black Spot. Inside was a familiar photograph, selectively snipped so that only the woman in the boater was still shown. Julian had taken that photograph so must have supplied a copy to Z – Possibly his only copy. The file contained her correct address in Brompton Villas and a guess at her age as '25 to 30, claims to be 26'. Hair was 'black' not 'raven', eyes blue, height five feet five. Odds-on Julian had also provided this information. Quite possibly one day last autumn he'd found himself down in the black room with its single lightbulb facing icy questions.

Her nationality was given as British, with a question mark. In a separate hand, someone had written 'Russian?'. Sissy had said her accent had not been distinctive, as might happen if English was not her first language. Verity did have those high cheekbones I'd thought of as Nordic, but was that a Russian characteristic too? Department Z suspected her origins were fabricated but had no idea of who she really was or whose agent she had truly been. Whoever had compiled the record had written 'Special Branch', then another hand had crossed it out.

The two pages of sketchy facts and guesswork were possibly the product of paranoia rather than justified suspicion. A charge of spying was based on slight evidence; unauthorized access to a file referred to as 'UJ' and asking questions about 'Blue,' which must be Plan Blue. A further note in that second hand read 'refer to JEB'. At the foot of the last page and without a question mark was written 'Deceased'. Her date of death was given as September 1934.

Something grabbed at my heart, just for a moment.

Clipped to the back page was a cutting from a newspaper with 'Herald 4 Oct 34' written in the margin in pencil. The short, single-column story told of 'a woman's badly decomposed body' being found near Hammersmith Bridge. A cold sensation ran through my soul. If 'Verity' was dead, it gave a lie to the assertion that this was not a suicide mission.

Chapter Thirty-Three

Sissy bought me a coat for my birthday, calf-length in black leather, double-breasted and belted. 'It Emphasizes your broad shoulders,' she said, stroking her hand across it. As promised, it was roomy enough to accommodate the shoulder holster under my left armpit without a tell-tale bulge. She treated me to an early supper, then we went to see the new Fred Astaire/Ginger Rodgers musical comedy *Top Hat* at a cinema.

I wore the coat, but not the holster, when I walked to the British Library the following afternoon. I'd become a familiar face when I began my research into fascist literature, and staff briskly assisted my search of newspapers from September 1934. *The Daily Herald* was the obvious one to start with, keen on a good scandal to excite its working-class audience, then I'd check its counterpoint the *London Evening Standard* with its conservative tone. Despite that 4 Oct date pencilled in the file, I began with September in case the lazy researchers of Z had missed something. Moving on to October, the first article I found in the *Herald* was indeed that dated Thursday the fourth. I read impassively of that woman's 'badly decomposed' body. What had I asked Sissy to do?

Follow-up stories over the next few days speculated that the woman had jumped from the bridge, had been drowned by a lover, or stabbed to death by a lunatic, but such stories faded without resolution. Some ferreting was required in later editions to find the tiny report of the inquest, where the coroner returned an open verdict on the unidentified woman.

Of course, she remained unidentified. The body of the woman who was not Verity Laytham would carry nothing to betray who she really was. I telephoned the Metropolitan Police headquarters and after several attempts and a couple of coins was able to speak to Inspector Renton and arranged to meet him on the Embankment in the late afternoon.

September was moving on and the summer heat had been replaced by scudding, threatening skies over the futuristic Shell Mex Building. On its tower, the huge clock dubbed 'Big Benzine' read ten minutes past four. Inspector Renton was there before me.

'Mr Clifton, I'm surprised to see you still in London.'

'It's pleasant at this time of year.'

Renton scowled at the clouds that would unload rain before the evening was out. 'Don't mess about, son. What's your game now?'

'Can we work together? As I've offered before.'

'Work how? If you see me as one of Mosley's bought men, I'm telling you I can't be bought. If you want information to share with those biff-boys so they can saw more men's arms off, forget it.'

'I want to share information.'

'What information? Is there anything in Department Z's files I'm likely not to know? If you want a deal, Mr Clifton you need to start offering *me* something. Not your detective story mysteries, but real information. What do you have?'

I breathed in before launching my pitch. 'You can't share this with anyone in the BUF, especially not Department Z if you've got friends there.'

'I'm picky with my friends. What's your highly secret real mystery?'

'Did you find a woman's body last October? She'd be unidentified, late twenties, dark hair?'

'Sorry, is this you giving me information, or me giving it to you?'

'Bit of both. Here, look at this.' I passed over one of the copy photographs. 'She's called Verity Laytham and she'd not been seen since last autumn.'

'Verity Laytham,' Renton repeated the name. I saw no flicker of recognition, but he would have honed a card player's skill to keep a straight face over many years' experience of the interrogation room.

'She was close to Julian Thring.'

'Thring? Not the Blackshirt accountant?'

'His son. I've checked suspicious death stories in the papers from late last year, and this one fits too well.'

I passed over a brief note in pencil with her last known address, all the newspaper references, and the date of the inquest. Renton glanced at it. 'I'll look into it.'

'And you'll let me know what you find?'

He pocketed the note. 'I'll look into it.'

Chapter Thirty-Four

'Britain needs a strong ally in fascist Italy,' Julian expounded. We were taking lunch on the King's Road once out of uniform. 'And that's what the BUF needs.'

It was a small table, so we were seated almost knee-to-knee. The Foreign Secretary had been speaking out against Italian ambitions in Abyssinia, and amid all the excitement this caused at Black House I hoped that someone would be careless and I'd at last pick up a lead on Mussolini's money. Any hope that Julian could be lured into being indiscreet about his father's links to Italy was dashed when he shifted topic. 'I say, did you hear about Sir Malcolm Campbell?' Julian asked. 'Three hundred and one miles an hour!'

'I couldn't do that in the Alvis, that's for sure.'

'And,' Julian held up a finger, 'he was carrying the BUF pennant on his car, *Bluebird*. In America. Spreading the message.'

Mr Symes had wittered on about *Bluebird* over dinner earlier in the summer. Perhaps there was truth in the coming together of racing aces and airmen to build the fascist future.

'Oh, and Florian Kahn is coming over from Germany again. Father is putting together a dinner; would you like to come?'

That was more like it. 'Certainly. Sissy too?'

'Of course. It's Tuesday, next week.'

Just possibly my focus on Italy had been wrong. Even in his most unguarded moments, Julian had made no comments about his father going there or having any Italian business associates. Beyond his reluctance to talk about whatever happened to Verity, he was trusting and often careless.

He was also proud of his father, his company, and his influence, which Melissa would echo and amplify. Perhaps the key was Germany, after all. Perhaps it was Florian Kahn that should be arrested as he stepped off the boat train.

* * *

It was time to act. Sooner rather than later Parker would drag me down into his world of Jew-baiting and red-bashing. I'd already joined Julian's Squad on a couple of occasions, riding to rescue street-corner rabble-rousers from the hate they had sown. At some point, I'd either be arrested or end up with one of those livid scars or eye patches too many Blackshirts wore as badges of pride. Any risk in my next move was counterbalanced by the chance it would buy my exit from the spiral of street violence and save me from dying of boredom waiting for a loose fact to float into my ears at Black House.

I'd stayed at the Grosvenor Hotel by Victoria Station on a couple of occasions and was familiar with the grand Baroque vestibule and the smart cut of the porters and concierge. Julian had dropped the name of the hotel lightly into conversation as he discussed the date of Kahn's arrival. Common sense, and enquiry about times of the boat train suggested the German would arrive in the afternoon. Calhoun had no grounds to arrest him and had dismissed my suggestion.

'Puerile.' Had been his comment.

'I'm sorry?'

'It's an idea fit for that novel you're supposed to be writing, no more.'

'We have to act.'

'No, we have to *observe*. We'll get one chance to break up this funding chain, one. If we show our hand too soon, the best that happens is they know we're onto them and they completely change the plan. At worst, I lose my job and Lord Rothermere splashes our incompetence all over the front page.'

'So there's nothing else we can do?'

'Just tell me what you find.'

Even if it was puerile, and fit only for a cheap novel, I used that day's edition of *The Times* to provide cover for me to sit in the lobby of the Grosvenor and observe the comings and goings. A copy of Agatha Christie's *Lord Edgware Dies* was on hand too, given that nobody would legitimately read a newspaper for three hours. In two years of disgrace and convalescence reading had been a lifesaver, or at least a brain-saver.

Calhoun's rebuke stung. Hanrahan was always putting me in my place too, taking any opportunity to say I was an amateur if not always in so many words. It was time for *Action.*

If I was seen by plenty of hotel staff, they might remember my face later and assume I was also a resident or at least had legitimate business there. Each new arrival merited a glance, then sure enough the rounded figure of Kahn arrived. I swapped book back for newspaper, glancing furtively around it as Harry Bretton would surely do at this point.

Kahn did not have a great deal of luggage. A bell boy took his single leather suitcase and led the way to the elevators, but the German kept a firm grip on a pigskin valise a little larger than one a doctor might carry. As soon as the polished wooden doors closed, I was on my feet sharply. The brass hand of the indicator betrayed that Kahn was staying on the second floor. When the elevator returned it was without the bell-boy.

'Second floor,' I requested.

Just after leaving the elevator, I paused mid-corridor as if lost. After a few moments that bell boy came from the right, silently whistling and checking a coin in his hand.

'Ah, I'm meeting Mr Kahn. Two oh six isn't it?'

'Two hundred and fourteen, squire.'

'Of course, thanks.' The boy received a sixpence for his unwitting part in the subterfuge and I took the stairs back to the lobby before leaving the hotel.

Dinner would be at eight at Simpsons in the Strand, but the customary drink beforehand offered latitude to arrive late. Returning to the hotel before seven, I again prowled the lobby, dressed for dinner, as smart as any other guest. Kahn came from the elevator at seven-thirty sharp. He left the key for 214 at the desk, then one of the staff immediately hung it on a hook. More guests departed for dinner, or for a show, and I went out into the street and allowed time to pass. A few new guests arrived. I was wearing my homburg and grey coat with fur collar which gave me the most European look I could manage. As if in a hurry I dashed into the lobby, slightly out of breath. Two men manned the desk, and I chose the one who had not taken Kahn's key a short while ago, feigning a German accent. 'Kahn…*Ach*, I'm going to miss the show…Ah, two fourteen, please. *Schnell*, quick.'

The key was handed over with a minimum of ceremony, as I was clearly a continental gentleman in a hurry. So many people had seen my face now, I must ensure no trace was left of what happened next. Quite probably I would be breaking the law, but three men had been shot dead and another had his arms sawn off and someone was liberally scattering bombs that only by the grace of God had not killed anyone yet. The other side had scant regard for the law, whoever they were. I took the stairs up to the second floor to avoid being seen by the elevator boy and moved smartly to unlock room 214 as if it were my own, snapped on the light, and locked the door from the inside. Goodness knows what I would do if Kahn returned; almost anyone else might swallow a lie, take a bribe, or be subdued by a firm sock on the jaw.

Yes, I'd punch Kahn too, if it came to it. He was a Nazi, I'd tell the judge. And then I'd be the hero on the front of left-wing newspapers for a change.

Kahn had unpacked his suitcase into the wardrobe and drawer. He was clearly only here for two nights. Very cautious exploration of the clothes and drawer revealed nothing. The suitcase was on top of the wardrobe and felt almost empty; it was certainly not stuffed with Nazi money. Kahn's pigskin valise sat on the floor by the dressing table. It was of course locked, but after trial and error with Verity's luggage, picking the lock with the toolkit took less than two minutes. Any faith I'd put in locks over the years vanished. They were not worth the brass they were made of.

Ten minutes was all I could risk in that room. The valise carried documents in English, German, and what, Russian? There were too many to read and stealing any would alert Kahn and kick over the not-very-sophisticated train of subterfuge used to gain entry.

Instead of money, I found what appeared to be shipping contracts. After all, what else would a German shipping merchant be expected to carry in a document case? Momentarily I felt stupid, then jotted down names of companies, ships, dates in case any of it was relevant. A note in German was from a Hamburg bank—a man named Engelmann was writing to a London banker named Abrahams at Muller and Abrahams of Lombard Street. Engelmann was the Jewish banker who had stood out from the other Germans I'd been introduced to in Hamburg, and he seemed to be providing some kind of assurance or *bona fides* for Kahn. Abrahams also sounded Jewish, as did a typed list of twenty-three names clipped to the letter. The names were in twelve groups, with a German town listed beside them. Each group had the same family name as if husband, wife, and children.

Russians, Jews, Nazis, and British fascists made strange bedfellows; Kahn truly was playing all sides. Invoices detailed goods travelling from Hamburg to London, to Rotterdam, Bilbao, or returning the other way. The Russian document had an address, what looked like names, a date, plus lists of things and quantities. At least the Russians used Arabic numbers. I slavishly copied the Cyrillic lettering of the 'things' in the list and what looked like origins and destinations. Hanrahan should be able to read basic Russian if he had been at all truthful about being a language tutor.

From outside the room came a clatter, then footsteps and voices. Kahn? He should be on his second cocktail by now. A maid? If I was caught breaking the law Calhoun would disown me and Renton would use that flimsy statement distancing me from the Williams murder to build a bigger case. Plenty of hotel staff had seen my face and could describe me loitering with intent. If someone arrived with a key, the only other way out was a suicidal route via the window. Playing the innocent might work, but as a final resort, I'd shoulder-barge my way out of the hotel and hope none of the staff were foolish enough to try to stop me.

The voices faded. That cough which came on when I became excited had to be suppressed. Excited, yes. The riot, the shooting, the chase, Sissy…it was a long time since I'd felt this alive.

I checked through the valise again, willing it to contain more. Kahn was no money courier, or at least not on this trip. After snapping the lock shut again and placing the valise exactly where I found it, time was come to leave. I locked the door, took the stair again and slapped the key on the counter with only a gruff grunt as a foreign gentleman in a hurry would do.

Chapter Thirty-Five

A taxi whizzed me to the Strand, but I only just made dinner in time for the soup, taking my place hurriedly across from Sissy whose punishing frown did not bode well.

'Apologies. I was in full flow, typing a gripping scene. I just had to finish it.'

'Is it getting any better?' She delivered this more as a rebuke than interest.

'Yes, I hope so.'

Sissy sat between Julian and his father. Kahn was opposite Thring whilst Melissa completed the party on my left. The empty chair between Melissa and Kahn must have screamed my absence. Soup had just been served and a waiter promised to bring another bowl, with only a hint of condescension for the latecomer.

'I was telling Dr Kahn how well our membership is thriving,' Julian filled in the gaps.

'Your escapade in Kensington did us no harm at all,' added his father. 'The next challenge is to get the wretches in the regions to pay their subscriptions.'

'Is that a problem?'

'Constantly.'

My soup arrived, appearing to be tomato with something green floating in it, perhaps basil. I made to catch up for lost time whilst Thring carried on talking. '...now Lord Rothermere is back on our side and has closed his ears to those Jewish advertisers of his, we are picking up new force.' Thring turned back to Kahn. 'I'm lunching with Lady Huston this week, after she's met with the Leader.'

'Is it true she's building a bomber?' Kahn asked.

'A bomber?' Julian echoed.

Kahn mimed an aircraft swooping over his soup. 'RAF bomber, all paid for by Lady Huston and her friends.'

'I didn't know that,' Thring admitted, or pretended to admit. 'It's a very interesting development. A supporter who can fund a *bomber* is a very good one indeed. Hugh, your father is in mining?'

'Yes.'

'Do you think he'd join us? Is he good for a contribution?'

Indeed, he had already made one. 'He is a staunch Conservative unfortunately, and a Freemason.'

'A lot of our supporters are Conservatives or pretend to be Conservatives because we're…ha ha.'

'Not respectable?' I suggested, hurrying to take another spoonful of soup before I was quizzed again.

Thring frowned. 'Too novel. Our ideas unsettle the conventional mind that has lost hope of a better future.'

'My father is conventional, I'm afraid. And I must say that he'd probably shed blood before money, but I could arrange a meeting the next time he's in London. I'll warn you he can be very…ah, direct.'

'I like direct. He sounds like a man who can't suffer fools.'

'And sadly, some people who are not fools either.'

'You don't strike me as inheriting his directness, Hugh. I imagine you didn't fit into the Army very well—they don't encourage young men to think. Hugh is a thinker,' he explained to Kahn. 'A writer. An intellectual.'

'I wouldn't go that far.'

'Oh for God's sake, you read more books in a week than most people do in a year!' Sissy objected. 'If you're not an intellectual, who is?'

'You're very kind.'

She kicked my shin under the table. The momentary pain was ignored.

'Myself notwithstanding, Sissy is right in that the movement needs more of…what you might call intellectuals,' I advanced. 'The left's got them ten a penny, a socialist poet on every corner, but we haven't. A revolution needs money, but it also needs damn good songs; the Red Flag, La Marseillaise.'

Thring senior gave a forced laugh.

'Have you heard the *Horst-Wessel-Lied*?' asked Kahn. '*Die Fahne Hoch*... that's an inspiring song for you. And for the *Red Flag*, the *Kozis* steal the music of *O Tannenbaum*.'

'There you go Hugh, write us a song.' Sissy waved her spoon a little, conductor style. 'Blackshirts tra la laah.' This suggestion was another punishment.

'What a capital idea!' Julian said.

'That should keep you busy,' added Melissa.

Every expression at the table pinned me as if a prize butterfly. There would be no escape. 'I'll listen to your Horst...your song, for inspiration.'

'You can buy it on gramophone record,' said Kahn.

This conversation must be steered somewhere else. 'You're here on business again, Dr Kahn?'

'Meetings, yes, with Howard, and my contacts, and my banks, you know.'

Banks, interesting. It had been a guess that Kahn would be bringing money to aid Thring's fund-raising drive, but perhaps the money was already in London. How international banking worked was a mystery.

'Tell me about the Nuremberg rally,' Melissa interrupted. 'I heard Diana Guinness and Unity were there.'

'I was not there, I have business,' Kahn said. 'I have not too much time for politics.'

'But the New Nuremberg Laws sound fascinating.'

'*Ach*, yes, yes, necessary steps.'

'To contain your Jewish problem?' Melissa's enthusiasm for systematic repression lacked all shred of decency but at least my clumsy attempts at intelligence-gathering would now pass unnoticed.

'You're making being Jewish illegal, or something?' Sissy said, with an edginess that was short of polite.

'No, no,' Kahn said. 'It's only a step to protect German blood. No mixing of the races by marriages.'

'That sounds like a brilliant idea,' said Melissa. 'We need laws like that in Britain.'

I cleared the last of my soup, wishing I'd brought my Walther to silence the lot of them. Conversations such as this could be taking place at restaurants and chic bars right across the capital at that moment. Antisemitism was a kind of disease, toxic and spread by mouth. Defeat the communists, certainly, but it was anyone's guess which impure or nonconformist group would be added to the hate-list next. These people needed to be stopped.

* * *

'Well, that didn't go too badly,' I lied as we stood on the pavement outside Simpsons.

'Where are all the cabs?' she snapped. 'You missed that one.'

'Sorry about being late.'

'You were horribly late, and I was so embarrassed and so was Julian. I don't want you to come back with me tonight, I have a headache coming on.'

'Sorry again.'

'You did yourself no good with Julian's father.'

'He liked the song idea.'

'Don't be naive, he was humouring you. He trusts nobody and writes people in his bad book for any old reason. He's *important*, Hugh!'

'I know that.'

'If you want to get on in the Party, you don't start by offending Howard Thring. *Not respectable*, what were you thinking? I don't want to be back on the outside, the Party means something to me.'

'And me too, I'm sorry.'

'Stop saying sorry, you're wearing it out. I thought we were getting somewhere, you know, in Germany. You're just too damn flippant to be taken seriously. If it wasn't for Melissa starting to prattle about the Jews again you could have dug yourself a proper hole.'

'So, shall I forget about that song?'

'Oh, no, no you're writing a bloody song now. Just make sure it's a good one. Something with marching and flags and stamping feet.'

'I'll get on with it tomorrow, then.'

'You can do what you want tomorrow, I don't want to see you tomorrow.'

My coup at the Grosvenor had come at a price. 'As you wish.'

Chapter Thirty-Six

Hanrahan was the man to help decipher the Russian, so we agreed a meeting via the Mayfair office which was our usual route. I had no idea where he lived, and I'd told nobody my own address other than Sissy.

It was a fair guess that Kahn would be visiting that private bank whose name was on the letter of introduction. I telephoned Muller and Abrahams the next morning, aping Kahn's German accent and throwing in some decorative *ja*, and an *ach so*. 'Kahn' received confirmation that his appointment was for five o'clock. That seemed late for a bank; everyone surely would be ready to go home, which might suit both Kahn and his contact.

Time was tight, but action was possible.

It was shortly before noon by the time I met Hanrahan in the arcade above South Kensington tube station. An impromptu brass band had set up at one end; three unemployed men desperate for pennies or the offer of a job. We dived into the nearest pub and found a corner to talk.

Hanrahan looked at the Russian words. 'I need the whole document.'

'This is the essence. I copied it letter for letter, the best I could.'

After an intake of breath, as if his Russian were rusty, Hanrahan rattled off the shipping list. 'Agricultural tools of some sort, 600. Tractors, no it must be spare parts, also 600. More parts… 48 boxes in total. Leningrad is what was St Petersburg, and this word is Bilbao.'

'Destination, then. Other shipments were heading for Bilbao.'

'*Pavel Denisovich* looks like a ship name, so it's odds-on it's taking cargo all the way from Leningrad to Bilbao rather than the other way around. The Russians make fine tractors. Sorry it's not what you're looking for.'

'Wait, wait that ship was on one of the other contracts.'

'Which you didn't copy?'

'I only had ten minutes.'

'Amateur.'

'Come on, I could have gone to jail if they'd caught me in that hotel room, and I'd have got five years if I'd had to fight my way out. I need to look into the case again after Kahn has visited that bank. I suspect the owners are Jewish, which is very strange.'

'It makes me wonder which side your Dr Kahn is on.'

'Both sides, is my guess. He could be withdrawing money from some secret account, but even if he isn't it would be useful to know which of the papers he's going to hand over to the bank, and what he takes away with him.'

Hanrahan looked at my note carefully, weighing it almost. 'You really need that case again. You need the full details about those ships and those names so you can spot anything hidden in there that isn't obvious in a quick glance. You should repeat your trick at the hotel tonight.'

'That would be pushing my luck, and Kahn might be doing the rounds of all his associates today and bring nothing back to the hotel at all.'

He smiled. 'So, how about we recruit a couple of eejits to knock Kahn down as he comes out of the bank and grab his bag.'

I'd already entertained this idea. 'Action,' I said distantly, forming a small fascist fist.

'Unless you're too worried about going to jail.'

'Oh, we're well past that now. Dennis, Williams...there's going to be more bodies before this lark is over, I just know it.'

'For sure, but let's make certain they're not our bodies.'

I sat back, quelling the surge of excitement and resisting the urge to cough. 'Well, there's three men over the road, playing trumpets to ward off starving. How about we recruit them? I'll give them a tenner each. They're your constituency, so you'd be the best person to sell a little street revolution.

Kahn's a businessman and a Nazi, so a perfect target. If they get caught, they have sound political motives.'

'I can't get some poor jobless men thrown in prison for a few pounds, no matter how desperate they might be. This is more a job for some of your Blackshirt biff boys. Tell them Kahn's Jewish. Give them a chance to beat up a Jewish banker and you won't even have to pay them.'

It made sense, and a well-dressed foreigner coming out of a Jewish bank was easily damned by association. 'We'll still pay them to make sure they keep their mouths shut.'

'*You* will pay them to keep their mouths shut,' Hanrahan corrected. 'All that dirty family money put to a deserving end.'

'If I show you where to go, you'll need to do the recruiting, I'm too well known.'

'But they don't know me from Adam, why should they trust me?'

'The biff-boys are not the sharpest tools in the shed, and you could talk a snail out of its shell. Mention Tommy Moran, he's one of the hard men out East. Hint that this is one of his ideas, totally secret, and it will make them too afraid to brag about the job afterwards. Ask if you saw them at the Camden bust-up, and even if they weren't there it shows that you were. Try Kensington Library. Lads without jobs spend time there when not needed at Black House.'

'Not reading Shakespeare I'll wager?'

'Keeping dry, it's raining.' I checked my wristwatch. 'We don't have much time. You recruit the men, take them out to the City and find the bank.'

'Me? Now you want to get me arrested?'

'I need you—I can't do this on my own.'

'I'm not supposed to be fighting the fascists.'

'In the end, it's all the same, two sides of a coin as Calhoun once said. We need to defeat them all. Don't you want to know what Thring and Kahn are up to?'

'I surely do.'

* * *

Larger banks joined the ancient tradition of hanging signs over the narrow, canyon-like Lombard Street but Muller and Abrahams advertised its presence by little more than a modest brass plate beside a black door. Kahn would probably arrive by cab, then after his meeting hail another from the kerb.

Hanrahan recruited a broad-shouldered bruiser and a wiry young man still in his teens and gave them five pounds each, which I'd learned was the weekly wage of senior BUF officers such as Joyce. For an unemployed man, it was more than a month's dole. The bank door was some seventy-five yards down from the junction with Gracechurch Street, at a point where four-and five-storey office buildings threw everything into shadow. It was no longer raining. I stood with Hanrahan at the corner, backs to the traffic, alternately keeping eyes on that front door and checking that we were not in turn under observation.

'There's a lot of standing around in this game,' I commented.

'It's ninety-nine parts boredom and one-part sheer fecking terror,' Hanrahan said.

Kahn duly stepped out of a cab at seven minutes to five.

'Time for that terror.'

Hanrahan touched the peak of his cap. 'I'll go and get your men.'

I returned to the Alvis, which I'd parked in a small side street pointing towards Cornhill and away from trouble. I sat with one hand sweating on the wheel, hoping the engine would start the first time when the need came. Owning a car of quality and dressing as if I belonged in the City allowed me to blend with the surroundings. When a policeman strolled past, he gave car and occupant no more than a glance. If I'd been a bank robber, he'd never have guessed.

Chapter Thirty-Seven

Pat Hanrahan brought the two hired men from a café to the corner. Each had already pushed five white one-pound notes into their pockets and was tense for action. Each pulled his hat low over his brow and kept his face turned away from the thoroughfare. Idle working-class men on street corners were commonplace and the trio were deliberately ignored by the office workers who began to fill the pavements on their way home.

'Where is he?' Asked the wiry one.

'Where's that fucking Yid?' The bruiser was keen for action.

'Just wait,' Hanrahan said, suppressing his usual Irish accent to a point it was barely perceptible. If anyone were caught, he would put as much distance between himself and this caper as possible.

Kahn came out of the bank, glancing to right and left as if looking for danger. He failed completely to spot it.

'That's him, go.' Hanrahan touched the burlier man on the shoulder.

At the kerb, Kahn halted and started to seek a cab. The big man walked briskly towards him, head down, weaving between the bank staff making for their bus or train.

'Go.' Hanrahan gave the youth a little push, setting him ten paces behind his comrade.

A cab appeared at the far end of Lombard Street and rumbled its leisurely way towards Kahn. He raised one arm to hail it as the big man picked up pace with a few yards to go. The bruiser struck Kahn at a run, his shoulder striking the middle of the German's back, sending him sprawling and rolling onto the pavement with the bag skitting away from him. Kahn let out a shout, then the wiry one was on him, grabbing the pigskin valise. He was fast that boy, sprinting for all his life in the wake of his comrade. Bankers stepped aside in surprise as the thief hurtled past. Hanrahan turned and walked away.

* * *

My watch hand moved to twenty-seven minutes past five. I had by now pulled the soft top of the Alvis fully open to make the powder-blue car an unmissable target for even the dimmest thief in a hurry. Thank goodness the rain had not resumed.

When the big man appeared around the corner, I turned the ignition key and kept looking straight ahead, not wishing to catch the running man's eye. Sweetly, the engine burst into life. The bruiser ran past and ran onwards, not even glancing my way. Only a few steps behind, the little chap followed, that bag hugged to his chest, panting loudly as he ran. Someone was shouting. He barely paused to swing the bag into the back seat of the car then rushed on to his rendezvous with Hanrahan where another five pounds would be waiting for him. The bag landed with a thump just as a police whistle blew back in Lombard Street. Without screeching the tyres or clashing the gearbox I gently steered the Alvis out from the kerb, slipped behind a Model A, and eased off down the street.

Havelock Mansions should have been only ten minutes away, but traffic was building up. Threading westward behind busses, taxis and private cars was not the swift getaway I imagined. More police whistles joined the first and the jangling bells of a police car approached from the opposite direction. Other vehicles veered aside to make room as the black car jinked between them. With luck, nobody would connect the powder-blue Alvis with a common street robbery. With luck. My hands sweated inside my gloves that gripped the wheel. Beyond a doubt, I was now a criminal and could go to prison for ten years. Oh, for the thrill of it all!

I parked directly in front of Havelock Mansions.

'Good afternoon, sir,' said Lilley.

Now something of an underworld mastermind, I simply nodded in acknowledgement before making for the stair. Stranger things might have happened in this building. Kahn's pigskin case was heavy and much fuller than it had been at the hotel. Hefting it onto the table beside my largely decorative typewriter, I was about to retrieve my lock-picking tools but paused. Picking the lock should be child's play now, but no such subtlety would be needed, and indeed would be counterproductive. A street thief would surely just cut through the leather strap and dispose of the bag as soon as it had been emptied. Sawing through the strap with my breadknife took less than a minute.

I had never seen so much money. Even rich people rarely handled five-pound notes in wads; I was in the preserve of bank robbers now and counting the loot into stacks was satisfying beyond expectation. My swag came to eight thousand two hundred pounds, mostly in five-pound notes. It was enough to buy a dozen houses in a smart new suburb or fund the whole BUF operation for a month or two. This was it. This was mission accomplished.

But wait. A Jewish banker in England hands over money to a German who worked with the Nazis, with a nod of approval from a German Jewish banker. I was looking for funds coming *into* the country to fund the BUF, not out to benefit the Nazis. I fidgeted bundles of notes from hand to hand trying to work out what I was seeing. Who did this money even belong to: Kahn, the BUF, the Nazis, or the banks themselves?

Several documents remained in the case. All the shipping notes were still there, as far as I recalled, but not the list of names nor the letter of introduction. That Rolleiflex camera proved to be a good investment and I set it up to take photographs of each of the letters. My table lamp and standard lamp were brought into play to offer the best light. Perhaps the technique would work. Once photographed, I then transcribed each document in detail, which took all evening. I did this longhand which was faster and more accurate than my typing and left no tell-tale evidence on my typewriter ribbon or carbons.

Calhoun wouldn't want to know anything about the string of petty offences leading to this point. Once the facts were together, the names and dates tied up, and a plausible methodology to explain the findings had been concocted, only then it would be time to present another report. My final report, presumably. Hanrahan had agreed to say nothing. It was not his mission.

A blow had been struck against the fascists—Kahn's plans would be in tatters, and there would be panic over the money being taken. Accusations, recriminations, and traitor-hunts might follow and heads would roll. Howard Thring would be incandescent, which was no bad thing. His was the kind of organized mind the BUF needed, and therefore precisely what democratic Britain did not need. I felt pretty chuffed at my day's work.

All the documents went back into the case, together with a few loose fivers shoved into the corner as if the bag had been hurriedly emptied. Long after dark, I drove close to the scene of the crime, finding a leafy square near Moorgate where a constable was strolling sedately on his beat. Parking out of his sight at the far side of the square, I walked back to intercept the policeman with the pigskin bag tucked under my arm. It had been cleaned of any incriminating marks such as sticky fingerprints, and by wearing the finest pair of gentleman's driving gloves I ensured it stayed clean.

'Constable, I just bumped into two ladies on their way home, who say they found this bag over by the park. They asked me if I'd kindly take it to a police station.'

The constable accepted the bag, then looked off into the darkness where any pair of ladies would be masked by the trees of the square.

'It looks as though there's some money in there and some papers. It was hanging open, but I didn't want to pry.'

We moved under a streetlamp. 'It looks stolen, sir; see how the thief has cut through the strap? Lord yes, a fair amount of money. The villain must have dropped this in a hurry and scarpered. Could I take your name?'

'I'd rather not be involved constable, I'm only in town for tonight.'

'There could be a reward.'

'No, no, I didn't even find it.' At least that much was true. 'And I'm sure those ladies wouldn't want to be involved.' Also true. 'So, I'd be obliged if you just make sure it gets back to whoever lost it. Goodnight.'

No policeman would expect a thief to hand over a stolen bag with twenty-odd pounds drifting around in the bottom. Few would doubt the reluctance of ladies of quality to come to the station at this time of night, nor for a gentleman in a fine homburg to hanker after a few pounds' reward. Snobbery was such a useful weapon and reinforced an excellent piece of improvised theatre. Kahn would think he'd been robbed for his money by opportunist thieves. He'd try to restore whatever plan the money formed part of, but now I would be watching.

The exploit had reaped another benefit. No longer need the Security Service be subsidized by Yorkshire mining profits. I had a fighting fund.

Chapter Thirty-Eight

Black House buzzed with even more intrigue and discontent than usual. I went directly after visiting my bank, who had happily accepted both the story of a good week in Monte Carlo and a briefcase full of my winnings.

Julian Thring was already uniformed in black from head to toe when I came into the locker room to change. 'God, the fox is in the henhouse,' Julian said. Under his breath, he whispered. 'Dr Kahn was attacked and robbed last night.'

'No! At his hotel?' I stripped off my civilian shirt.

'Just walking the streets, taking the air. There's a hell of a stink though, it could be the reds. Kahn said they looked like reds. Two of them, big brutes by the sound of it.'

As though this was news, I pondered the development whilst slipping on my all-black disguise. 'I'd better skip upstairs and see if Major Taylor's there. Department Z needs to launch an investigation.' This was already a half-formed plan. 'You should help us. You know Kahn, he's a friend of your father's and, if I can be candid, they could use an accountant's brain up there.' The last thing I needed was being paired with someone like Parker.

Major Taylor stated he would flog then hang the criminals who had insulted Dr Kahn, and afterwards set their heads on pikes for good measure. 'What this country lacks is order on the streets!' With real power at his disposal, he might be frightening. He'd started investigating the case, he said. Lucy had opened a file already.

Julian and I sat before him, much as excited schoolboys desperate to be picked for the first eleven. 'Did you read my paper sir, about how the Department operates?'

'Yes, yes, I'm thinking about it.'

'From what I've seen Z doesn't do much actual investigation. The files mainly contain cuttings from newspapers and trade directories.'

'Yes, but we're very short of men.'

'Not anymore sir!' Julian said, sitting upright and pushing back his shoulders.

'Julian's skills would be a positive boon in a complex investigation. As I said in my paper, we should grow Z beyond...whatever it is Captain Parker does.' *And in the process spare me from being dragged into any more of his escapades.* 'Julian and I make a good team.'

Taylor nodded, weighing us up. 'We're telling people that Dr Kahn was simply taking the air, but in fact, he was robbed leaving a bank. That's highly confidential information.'

'Oh,' I said with as much surprise as I could feign. 'So having an accountant on the investigation of a bank robbery would be useful.'

'Indeed, indeed.'

'Which bank was it?'

After only a few more minutes' discussion, Taylor sent his new investigative duo on the trail of Dr Kahn's stolen money. I said I had a hunch which police station might know more about the robbery and, as luck would have it, Dr Kahn's case had been handed in by a public-spirited civilian the night before. I signed for the case using my real name, fortunately not encountering the constable who I'd met walking the beat.

Kahn added an extra day to his sojourn in London to complete his business and agreed to come to Black House for a half-hour interview in the small meeting room that afternoon. He was grateful to receive his case and checked its contents as we watched him. He passed four five-pound notes from one hand to the other as if counting them. Then he admitted that he had been robbed. 'This is secret, *ja*? Do not tell everyone. This is secret, commerce, business.'

Julian took written notes as his hand was so much neater than mine and it gave him an immediate purpose. Kahn put his bag aside and said that the thieves had taken 'a few things and a little money,' but that was all. *No wads of banknotes, then.* He'd seen nothing unusual when he'd come out of the bank, except perhaps three men on the street corner. He was bashed to the ground by a 'big rough man' then robbed by another. His suit had been torn and his left hand was still red raw where it had arrested his tumble onto the pavement.

'Someone knew,' he stated. 'They waited for me, those three men.'

'Three men?'

'I think three of them. One was in charge, *vielleicht*? They were waiting for me. *Ich.*'

'Reds?'

'Ja, *Kozi*, Who else?'

'Perhaps you were just unlucky?' I suggested. 'Lombard Street is lined by banks, so they waited for someone to come out at the end of the day when the streets are busy with people going home. You dress well and desperate men are everywhere. For all they knew your bag could have been stuffed with money.'

'It was they that was unlucky,' Kahn said. 'They left twenty pounds and all my papers. It is an inconvenience, nothing more.'

'I must apologise that your visit to London ended this way,' Julian said.

'*Ach*!'

'But if I might add…' Julian hesitated. 'That bank is Jewish. We're curious…'

'Many banks are Jewish.' Kahn made a familiar grasping motion with one hand. 'They have us in their grip—for now.'

'But they're happy to do business with a member of the Nazi party?' Julian asked. His innocence was a positive boon.

'I am in London as a businessman, nothing more. Sometimes it is convenient to be a Nazi, sometimes not.' He flashed gold-capped teeth. 'You don't walk into your bank wearing that uniform?'

'No.'

'I didn't wear my Nazi pin. It was business.'

Julian was happy to set off on a wild goose chase to Kahn's hotel to discover if he had been followed or unusual visitors had been seen. I did not want to show my face again at the Grosvenor, but it would be useful to hear if my subterfuge had been spotted. The Thring name might raise warning flags if Julian went to Muller & Abrahams, so I made an easy case for that to be my task alone. No appointment was possible before the early closing on Friday.

Whilst I'd been going through the charade of initiating a Department Z investigation, a photographer in Holborn had been busy blowing up the photographed documents to life-size. My excuse was that the original documents would be lodged with my bank, but I wanted a record of my own. Two prints of each to be secure. The well-paid photographer was asked politely not to read them, and it was in his interest not to demur.

I would indeed lodge a copy at the bank on Monday, but for the meantime finding a home for the photographic prints in the small apartment where Mrs Lilley or her daughter would not find them whilst cleaning was a challenge. The furniture was austere, but after removing the bottom drawer of the tallboy, a foolscap envelope containing one set of photographs and my original notes could be slipped onto the base of the unit before re-inserting the drawer. An envelope containing the second set went into the bottom of a suitcase. That's the copy I'd deliver to the bank. After a moment's thought the negatives were dropped into a tea caddy that I had not got around to filling with tea.

* * *

The hubbub of a London pub on a Friday night served to hide my meeting with Hanrahan. He preferred crowded places to lonely parks with nowhere to run and no witnesses if an encounter went sour. And what could be less suspicious than two men enjoying a pint together?

'So, comrade what was in the bag?' he asked.

'What you'd expect,' I replied.

He smiled. 'Well done, you're learning. Don't share anything you don't need to share. It's your case, and I was happy to help push a stick into the fascist's wheel.' He eased back into his chair and sipped his pint. 'Now with you being cosy inside Department Z, can you share what they've already found out about the shooting and bomb plot?'

'I would if they'd found anything we didn't already know. They just snip pieces out of newspapers, and everything is blamed on the Red Front. Have you discovered anything new?'

'All I've learned is that Ewan Williams-Jones was a local Labour Party organizer, low level. Dennis was Labour Party too. One of the men who got away from the police raids was a union man, one was a former CP member, the others were unknowns.'

'So we're back to your side having a party-within-a party. Is the Red Front real?'

'People like to think there's a united socialist front, but there isn't. They're even less organized than your fascists.'

'But does the CP have cells sleeping inside the Labour Party? Or Moscow even?'

'That's my mission you're trespassing on now.' Hanrahan formed his hands as a wall across the round, beer-stained table. 'That's your side, this is my side.'

'Fine.'

'One comrade—just the one—said there was someone he called the Adventurer picking and choosing the comrades for anti-fascist activities. He hadn't actually met him, because nobody meets him. You know, like that tipster your friend's cousin knows who always picks the winners in the Derby. A Bogeyman.'

'My Raincoat Man, I Squad's Monkey Man, the American who looked Spanish, now this Adventurer of yours could be the same man.'

'Or that's what they want us to believe. It's easier to imagine one villain causing mayhem all over the country than a whole underground movement. Look.'

Hanrahan collected up several beermats and shuffled them into a deck. 'They're operating just like a Bolshevik cell network.' He set one beermat down. 'Command cell.' One by one he laid out a row of mats underneath the first. 'Propaganda cell, fund-raising, recruiting, quartermaster.' Then he laid a third, widely scattered row. 'Positive Action.'

'Shooting people?'

'Strikes, protests, bombs. Each cell has a few men or women who know and trust each other, but only the cell leader is the link to the next level. Few activists outside the cell would be known to its members, and even other cells would not know of its existence or purpose. The Kensington shooting cell has been broken up.' He snatched away one of the mats. 'Ewan Williams and Dick Dennis are dead, and the rest are in hiding.'

'Didn't Special Branch arrest some?'

'All released without charge. The men in the know got away. Special Branch have just cut off one tentacle of an octopus.'

'And octopus tentacles regrow,' I threw in.

'Do they now?'

'Apparently. I did a lot of reading when I was in hospital.' I ran my hands over the remaining beermats. 'How do we find the other cells?'

Hanrahan sat back and blew smoke out heavily. 'With difficulty. If there is a network where's its support base? The police are pulling in leftists all over the country and what are they finding? Nothing, or it would be all over the Tory press.'

A mirror etched with a scotch whisky advert hung on the wall directly behind Harahan's head. Just for a moment, a blonde-haired woman in a beret was reflected in the mirror. She was looking our way, then she moved and was lost in the smoke and masked by shoulders.

'I'm not going to turn round, but is there a woman watching us?'

'Where?' Hanrahan moved his eyes but not his head.

'Near the door, to the right of the bar from your seat. Blonde, plum-coloured beret.'

'Sorry, I can't see any women at all.'

I checked the mirror again and there was indeed no woman to be seen.

'Being on your guard never hurts,' Hanrahan said by way of excusing me.

'I see why you like to sit facing the door.'

'I don't want some bastard stabbing me in the back. Literally, as well as professionally.'

Now I cautiously turned around and confirmed that there were no women anywhere near the door. 'I was sure she was watching us.'

'Don't be surprised if there's someone keeping an eye on you from time to time. Special Branch have you in their black book and your Department Z is probably being watched by Department X.'

'There isn't a Department X.'

'How do you know?' He smiled to emphasize that he was teasing, or perhaps to underline that I had to take care. 'We might have one new lead.' Hanrahan brought my attention back from seeking ghostly women. 'Our friend Robbie Agnew has asked to meet us again.'

'How did he contact you?'

'I gave him a contact number, remember? Royal Oak, no time agreed yet. Which means that tonight, we are off duty. Another Drink?'

Being rather full of beer, I decided against going out for supper somewhere. Dining alone can be miserable. Sissy had said she 'had plans' for that Friday but had agreed to come out the next night after a little resistance. She was still acting sore over that one late arrival for dinner so goodness knew how she would react if she knew just half the truth. Training her to use that Walther might prove to be a bad idea.

A little bread and cheese I kept for light lunches whilst struggling over the typewriter should still be edible, so that would make do for supper. With perhaps a little port. Hailing a cab, I took the seat on the pavement side and watched London slip by. It was past ten when I climbed out at Havelock Mansions, so the porter would be in his flat with a mug of Ovaltine by now.

Not being a smoker had its advantages in not ruining my sense of smell, and months in hospital wards made me sensitive to odours of any kind. The thick fug of the pub radiated from my coat when I hung it on a peg in the little hallway. Entering the sitting room, I switched on the light then paused. Normally the room smelled vaguely of furniture polish, or hot dust if the heating pipes were just warming up, or coffee if I'd abandoned a cup half-drunk. Tonight the air held an alien twang, as if perhaps Sissy had somehow sneaked in having just disposed of one of her cigarettes and helped herself to whisky or dabbed on some scent. More likely, someone else had dashed around the room wearing a pub-heavy coat.

I drew the Walther from its shoulder holster and took gentle steps forward. The script of the Harry Bretton novel still poked from the typewriter and the fibbing balls of paper remained in the basket that Mrs Lilley and her daughter had been instructed never to empty. Everything looked perfectly undisturbed. Nobody lurked in the kitchen, nobody waited for me behind the bedroom door and the bathroom was almost too small for anyone to hide in, but I nudged the door open with my toe anyway. That smell lingered in every room, but the person who brought it here was gone.

Immediately I went to the tallboy, removed the bottom drawer and saw the envelope of documents resting untouched. Relaxed now, feeling annoyed for the misplaced anxiety, I went to the bedroom and took down my suitcase to confirm that the second envelope of prints was still there.

Of course, it was gone.

Chapter Thirty-Nine

Harry Bretton would not have been such an idiot. He would not have been played for a fool.

Or maybe he might. That would be a good twist.

Either the phantom woman in the pub was real, or someone had been watching Havelock Mansions waiting for me to go out. Or indeed, both. They had known exactly where my flat was and had either bluffed their way in or picked through several locks to enter it. Bass the Night Porter had seen nothing when I asked him about anyone loitering outside or trying to gain entry.

It was likely that the intrusion had been set up over several days, first discovering where I lived, then establishing the time Bass came off duty, and finally pouncing when there was something worth pouncing on.

Hanrahan had warned me, cryptically, but my trust in him faded. Calhoun did not know about our escapade in Lombard Street, surely, and I couldn't see him burgling his own agent's flat. Unless he had no trust in me and was taking what he could at a time that suited him. Renton might be more interested in me than he pretended. Worse, Department Z could be more efficient than I imagined, or indeed there could be a Department X watching my every move.

Then there was the mysterious M who I had never met, supposedly off sick, but who played by his own rules.

Edgy, self-critical, continually re-playing the events of the past days, I must have been no fun before the theatre or at dinner afterwards. Sissy and I made little conversation of consequence, and she offered no more than a polite good-night kiss before she got into her cab. Flowers and Belgian chocolates had made minimum impact and that breach of etiquette had still not been forgiven. As she was driven away, I watched the taxi become lost amid its brothers.

Sissy knew where I lived. I'd given her a slight excuse for my being out on Friday evening, so she knew I'd not be at the flat. She resented being shoved into a box, categorized as a fluffy society girl and nothing more; she chafed for a role and was smart enough to have found one. If I was acting, she could also be acting. Trust nobody, I'd been told. I would need to be on my guard all the time.

* * *

I did not wear my uniform when visiting Muller & Abrahams private bank on Monday morning, nor state my BUF affiliation when asking to see Mr Abrahams. I was simply investigating the theft on behalf of Dr Kahn and no more. Abrahams the banker inspected the note of authority Kahn had signed permitting him to speak to me.

'Everything is completely confidential, Mr Abrahams.'

The impeccably dressed banker nodded quite slowly. Without knowing his family name, no one at first meeting would challenge his pedigree as an affluent member of the English middle class.

His collar studs and cufflinks were in gold, as fashion dictated, and although fashionable men often affected regimental-style ties, Abrahams' appeared to be genuine, and a Guards regiment at that.

'I'm going to step back a little, as if taking a photograph of the scene,' I said. 'So step back with me, so we can take the right picture. This wasn't Dr Kahn's first visit to your bank.'

'No, you know that.'

'Indeed, your relationship goes back many years.'

He screwed up his mouth to disagree. 'Not that many years, no. Surely you know that too?'

Feigning a little surprise helped the act. 'Dr Kahn gave me the impression you were firm friends, so I assumed it went back some years, I'm sorry.'

'We've only done business this last year. Perhaps Dr Kahn makes friends quickly.'

'Indeed he does. Now, if I may say this is very, very confidential. Dr Kahn has not told the police about the missing money. We have not told anyone.'

Abraham did not react.

'And I trust you have not told anyone either?'

'I made a very short statement to a police constable,' said Abrahams. 'I made no mention of the money, as that is entirely Dr Kahn's affair. We pride ourselves on discretion.'

It would be a mistake to betray that I knew the exact sum that had been in the bag, as it was a fact Kahn had not shared. 'The thieves dropped Dr Kahn's bag, but there was only twenty pounds in it. They left his papers, which would have been very inconvenient to lose but had no value that a thief would see.'

Abrahams still did not twitch.

'I'm wondering where we stand legally on the loss of the rest of the money. Would you regard it as the bank's–'

'No. Once money leaves that door, it is a client's responsibility to do with his funds what he will.'

I asked more formulaic questions on who knew Kahn was visiting, whether there had been any indication he had been followed or that the bank was being watched. Of course, there was no such indication, and of course, all the bank staff could be trusted.

'I'm going to say something that Dr Kahn might not approve of, and please don't repeat it to him although it's in his interests that I ask it. You know of his political views, in Germany?'

'You mean do I know he is a member of the Nazi party?'

'Indeed. And that doesn't cause you any difficulty?'

Abraham's look suggested he could have my tongue cut out and fried. 'I have a client whose factory turns diseased horses into dog food, but I don't intend to start eating dog food. Forgive me but I don't have to like my clients' politics.

'So the Nazis don't worry you?'

'Now they have power, it might civilize them. Being in government concentrates your thoughts once you have real decisions to take and you're not just chanting slogans on the streets or writing bad books in prison.'

'So where does this unfortunate incident leave those people?' I would not be more explicit about the list of names, leaving Abrahams to fill the blanks.

'The money is paid, so I expect the arrangement to stand. Even the Nazis hold to agreements, and I was dealing with Dr Kahn directly, not the Nazis. He has a business reputation to maintain.'

'And your people?'

He was a hard businessman and could read faces well. 'You know the Jews are used to persecution. Three thousand years of being blamed for everything; it's happening here in London sadly, with Mosley's Blackshirts on the streets. It comes, it goes, we ride out the storm and it passes. If I can help families in Germany, I'll do what I can.'

'If someone wanted to disrupt your plans–'

'No, no these are not my plans.' He blinked. 'I am a banker, pure and simple.'

'Dr Kahn's plans, then. Let us say there's someone who doesn't like Dr Kahn, or the Germans, or the Nazis indeed. Communists, say, who wanted to put paid to his work here, disrupt his schemes. After stealing his money, what would they do next?'

'I don't know. I'm not a revolutionary.'

'You were Army?'

'Grenadier Guards. I stopped a bullet in the summer offensive of '18, but it didn't make me hate the Germans. The War was a long time ago.'

'I wasn't suggesting that you would disrupt the plans personally.'

'That's very good of you, young man. Now, I need to bring this meeting to a close, if you have heard everything you need to hear.'

I rose from the chair. 'As a former military man, offer me a battle plan. Could someone attack Kahn's ships?'

'Warehouses.' Abrahams smiled and joined the game. 'Ships move, but warehouses sit inviting attack. If I was Dr Kahn's enemy, I'd attack his warehouses. There's something for you to investigate next Mr Clifton. Good afternoon.'

* * *

The latest rendezvous was a tourist café overlooking the Serpentine, offering a view of Horse Guards in the distance. I approached warily, and Calhoun was already seated at the last table on the terrace. He folded his paper and invited me to sit with a wave of his hand.

I expected a reprimand, or some revelation that he knew what I'd been up to.

'Busy week?'

'The usual.'

'Are you feeling unwell Clifton?'

'Oh, a little hungover. A touch of a cold, perhaps.'

'Where are you on Plan Blue?' he asked bluntly.

'I've still not seen a copy, but I think I understand what it is. Thring is in every Research Department meeting I've seen at Black House. He's re-organizing the BUF in the regions, and still trying to raise money as he mentioned struggling to get members to pay subscriptions.'

'And there's just Plan Blue. No more colours?'

'Should there be?'

'It's worth keeping an ear out.'

'Plan Blue might also extend to what Thring is up to with Dr Kahn.' Some careful manipulation of the truth was required to summarize what had been learned about Kahn meeting Thring, and his links to Muller and Abrahams.

Calhoun did not betray whether he already knew it all, but he also did not ask how the information had been obtained. 'So Kahn smuggles money into the country, and deposits it with Muller and Abrahams for the BUF to draw on?'

'No, I don't think that's what's happening. Germany still has poor foreign currency reserves, isn't that right? Kahn and Thring were talking about it over dinner, while the rest of us were–'

'Having a good time?'

'Trying to look as if we were having a good time without actually eavesdropping.'

'So what is he doing?'

'Do you have a coin on you?'

Calhoun was puzzled, then pulled out a half crown from his trouser pocket.

I tapped the saucer of his teacup. 'I am Germany, and your saucer is the BUF. I want to give the BUF half a crown, but I don't have any English money.' I took out a pencil. 'But I have plenty of pencils, so I'm selling you this pencil for half a crown. Here it comes on my ship across the North Sea.'

I slid my pencil point-first across the table. Calhoun cocked his head, poised to pass the half-crown in return.

'But you give your half-crown to the BUF. Into the saucer, please.'

The half-crown chinked into the saucer. 'Very clever.'

'No money has to come into the country at all. I can write you a receipt saying you've paid for that pencil, but in the end, it's just paper. Even if the police raid the bank's records there is no transaction linking them to the BUF.'

'I imagine Kahn isn't selling pencils to Muller and Abrahams.'

'No, I think he's selling Jews. I'm guessing they are families who want to get out of Hitler's Germany and for whatever reason can't just leave.'

Calhoun's eyes flicked away. This was a new idea to him, and he was thinking it over. 'The Nazis have rounded up communists, trade unionists, and others they class as politically undesirable. Some must be Jews. A lot have been shunted to a place called Dachau near Munich. They've built a large concentration camp down there and I can't imagine it's pleasant.'

'These families could have accounts here in London, or friends with money here, who could wangle it for Muller and Abrahams to pay off the Nazis.'

'But you're guessing though; have you any proof?'

He was testing me now. Either I admitted to street robbery or I lied to the boss, and he might know I was lying. I chose to lie. 'With my Department Z hat on, I've seen a list, briefly; two or three dozen names. There's no other reason for Kahn to carry it around, and no better reason for a Jewish-owned bank to deal with the Nazis.'

'You don't have this list?'

It sounded as if he was asking for it, condoning the actions. I'd made a hand-written report and started to draw it from an inside pocket.

'Lord don't carry that around town. Put it away, I don't want to see it or know how you got it. Be careful what you touch and how you touch it. We'll only get proof when these Jews of yours step off the boat. Do you know when they're due?'

'I have a list of ships, and some dates. Can you discover when they are next due in England?'

After a moment's hesitation, Calhoun said, 'Give me the ship names. Just the ship names. Whatever else you've got, knock it into some sort of shape so that Mrs Ainsworth can type up a report. And for God's sake keep it safe in the meantime.'

Chapter Forty

The idea that Robbie Agnew had asked for a meeting was unsettling. When last seen he had been ready to run a mile and Robbie owed Hanrahan and I no favours. Just possibly he had found some information he judged would be worth more than a few pounds. Just possibly it was worth the risk to find out, but from now on I was going to take every precaution I could. I was not going to trust to a concealed Walther being my only friend that night.

Darkness fell. Brick tenement blocks closed in on both sides of the narrow streets and a stench of sewage cut the air. Hanrahan and I fell subconsciously into step as we strode side-by-side. It was an area hostile to Blackshirts, and that old soldiers' art of being alert to threats came to the fore.

'Man in the entrance,' I said, 'over the far side.' The figure was barely distinct, mostly in shadow and in sight for only a moment. Even then, his hat brim was pulled down to conceal his face.

For all his nonchalance, Hanrahan glanced off to the left. 'Not your beret woman?'

'Hat. Gone now.'

As we turned a corner, the Royal Oak lay ahead. The traditional working-man's pub was on a more human scale than the warren of tenements. Yellow lights glowed from the windows promising warmth, comfort, and conviviality. 'This has the makings of a trap,' I said.

Hanrahan made a growling sound. 'Do you have a plan if it is?'

'After a fashion. Do you?'

'I always have a plan.'

Agnew was not in the Royal Oak. 'He could have meant the Lamb and Flag, like last time.'

'He was clear, Royal Oak.' Hanrahan said. It was a little before ten, so we waited, taking a scotch each but lingering over the drink. The bar was unsettlingly quiet, with only three other customers.

'Are you armed?' Hanrahan asked.

'Indeed. You?'

Hanrahan nodded. 'Let's hope we don't have to shoot our way out of here. Calhoun won't support us. He'll make up some story that fits the politics of the day.'

Robbie Agnew opened the taproom door cautiously but came no closer.

'Robbie, come join us,' said Hanrahan.

'You need to come outside,' he said uncertainly.

Yes, it was a trap. The landlord froze in his action of wiping out a glass.

'I'll go,' I said. From the window, I could make out a group of men gathering out in the street. The odds would be two against twenty. Hanrahan barely budged from the bar. He was the one who had taken the call, and he was the one keen to come along at Robbie Agnew's bidding. He was the one who shrugged off that watching man in the doorway and he was the one who knew I had taken Kahn's briefcase. Hanrahan moved his right hand to find the inner pocket of his coat. In this new world of spies and traitors, it might be one man against twenty-one.

Stepping through the taproom door would put me out of Hanrahan's sight and safe from a dirty shot in the back. I nipped after Agnew into the little vestibule in front of the outer door, and the snitch retreated into the street. The waiting gang were ranged in a half-moon, allowing enough space for me to venture outside but not to escape. Barely visible in a doorway some houses back towards the tube station lurked that figure again, then in the opposite direction, another was watching and waiting from the shadows. One at least was the Ringmaster come to control the show.

'So what's this, Robbie?'

'We don't like police spies.' Another man spoke in reply, stepping forward. In his hand, he carried something small, a cosh perhaps. Using a knife would show intent to kill and few men would risk hanging. I might have to risk that rope. Shooting four of the gang in as many heartbeats would create a big enough gap and sufficient confusion to allow a sudden bolt for freedom. It could work, but it would be murder.

'My friend and I should perhaps just go.'

'No, you don't. You fuckers are getting a lesson first. You won't come round 'ere again.'

Fuckers plural. That put Hanrahan on my side.

'Ready for yer lesson, spies?' One had a hammer, another a bottle, the next a length of two by two. It would be a painful lesson.

I closed the outer door sharply and pulled the bolt across. In an instant I drew the Walther and rushed back into the taproom, levelling the gun at my colleague, or the man who purported to be my colleague.

'Hey, isn't there enough people out there wanting to kill us already?' Hanrahan did not take his hand out of his inner pocket.

The landlord started to move, but I twitched the gun barrel his way. 'You stay there!' The bid to escape halted. 'So Pat, did you know this was planned?'

'I'd be stupid to still be here if I did. Coming tonight was always going to be a punt. Robbie's talked to someone with links to the top who has the power to set this up. This is bigger than just one rogue gang, it was worth the risk just to find that out. Now point the Nazi gun at the bad boys, there's a pal.'

'Cover the door.' I lowered the Walther so I could still take out a knee if Hanrahan made a wrong move.

Hanrahan moved to take up a position close to the door, still not producing a gun.

'Do you have a telephone?' I demanded of the landlord.

'No.'

In a moment the Walther was pointing directly at the landlord's head. 'I repeat, do you have a telephone?'

The landlord rolled his eyes towards Hanrahan for help.

'If he doesn't shoot you, for sure I will,' said my ally.

'At the back.' A slight twitch of the head indicated a passageway linking through to a back room. A phone hung on its wall and I took the receiver in hand in moments. I asked the operator to connect to the number and prayed she'd be speedy. A woman answered, and I could hear the sound of another East End pub in the background.

'Julian Thring. And hurry please.'

'Oh yes,' she said, as if crisis was a nightly event. 'Mr Thring! Here you go.'

'Hello?' Julian said hastily.

'Royal Oak as described. Come now, immediately. Twenty of them, armed.'

As soon as I was done, the landlord slipped past into that back room, watching the Walther all the way. Both remaining customers scuttled after the landlord to safety. The door slapped closed behind them and the bar fell silent.

No attempt was being made to storm the pub. None of the men outside had seen my gun and Hanrahan's remained in his pocket, if indeed that hand inside his coat was not all bluff. Hope remained that the men did not want to wreck their local.

'Come out you bastards!' The muffled threat was shouted from close to the window. 'Come out like men and take what's coming!'

At some point, their resolve would stiffen. If the landlord intended to escape from the back, attackers could also come in that way. Perhaps a warning shot would serve if they came so far.

'Didn't you have a plan?'

'Mmm.' Hanrahan said, without his usual swagger. 'We could try the back. It will be covered, but not by so many.'

'So we'll rely on mine.'

A distant motor vehicle engine grew closer, then another. Doors slammed and shouts arose.

Hanrahan lifted his eyebrows. 'You called the police?'

'Better.'

A window shattered as a half-brick came straight through it. The outer door thudded with the impact of a thrown body and more pressed against the glass. Julian's men surged down the street yelling death to Jews and communists. Whether or not the gang were Jews or communists made no difference to the punishment meted out with wooden clubs, lead-filled rubber coshes, and hobnailed boots. This is what Blackshirts did best.

'Time to go?' Hanrahan tipped his head towards the door

It was the work of a moment to leave the taproom and unbolt the outer door. All was uproar in the dark, with men jostling and fighting. I put my pistol away lest someone try to grab it, or I was tempted to use it.

'Julian!'

He ran up with a trio of Blackshirts. One had a bloodied nose, another made to set about Hanrahan with a cosh.

'No, he's on our side!'

Hanrahan clapped me on the shoulder. 'And aren't I fecking glad.'

'Let's get away from here. Don't leave any wounded!'

'We never would,' one man growled.

Hanrahan slipped behind me as the Blackshirts pulled back, their enemy shrinking away in a surly mob, with some lying bleeding. The shadowy Ringmaster beyond them was gone. One of our injured was helped to his feet and back to the vans. All my allies were on board by the time distant police bells began to clang. Everyone except Hanrahan; after all, he had his own plan.

Chapter Forty-One

The call from Inspector Renton came as a surprise, considering the policeman claimed not to want a relationship. 'This missing woman of yours,' he said, 'Verity Laytham. Why did you start chasing the idea that she was dead?'

'That's confidential, I'm afraid.'

'Listen, laddie, once you're down my nick it won't be confidential.' Renton gave time for this to sink in.

'Sir, I'm in Department Z and if they discover I'm talking to you they'll throw me out.'

'At the very least.'

Yes, he had me rattled. 'Either way, I'd be in no position to discover anything else.'

'Aye, you're more use with both your arms attached to your body,' Renton agreed. 'And you might be interested to learn that Department Z are not the only detectives in London. We've done a little investigation of our own, you know, as the police do from time to time. Do you know Sir Bernard Spillsbury?'

'The pathologist?'

I'd read his name in connection with major murder investigations. Sir Bernard was a growing legend in the new field of forensic science, as Renton went on to spell out for the benefit of my education. 'Get yourself to University College and ask for Dr Pascoe, one of Spillsbury's disciples. Mention my name and say you're a cousin of this Verity. And Clifton, anything you learn comes straight to me first. Understood?'

Serving many masters was becoming routine, so it was easy to agree. Calhoun couldn't be told what I was learning from Special Branch, and I certainly would not share every detail with Department Z. As Special Branch might already have ears within Black House it would be a challenge to keep the story straight for all the files I fed. By offering this chance to meet the pathologist Renton was clearly letting out some line, but I had no doubt that at some date he would reel me in.

University College was only a short walk from Havelock Mansions, but Dr Pascoe came as a surprise. Women struggled to be accepted into the medical profession and the idea that a female would make a career of cutting up dead people would be a mystery to most of conventional outlook.

Dr Pascoe might be no more than my age. The white coat drowned her frame and she kept her hair well above her collar, perhaps to stop it trailing in anything unpleasant. In an office shared mostly with cupboards and shelves of medical journals she put on a pair of spectacles and studied the photograph of Verity, unconvinced. 'Her hair was coming out. Sorry, I don't mean to be insensitive about your cousin, but if you want answers to your questions, you're going to need to hear unpleasant details. And they are all unpleasant.'

'Oh, I'm ex-army. I've seen a few things.'

Perhaps this was too much bravado, as she raised an eyebrow. 'The body was cremated so there is no chance of a second opinion. Sir Bernard allowed me to lead the post-mortem, and he simply read the file afterwards.' She shared a few pages of notes across the desk. 'The height and age and general build seem to be correct. Did she have any distinguishing marks such as moles, birth-marks, or scars?'

'I didn't know her that well.'

'Was she married?'

'No.'

Dr Pascoe took an intake of breath. 'Are you ready for this? My conclusion was that she died during or soon after an illegal abortion.'

I was completely wrong-footed by the off- spin.

'And she had scars suggesting it may not have been her first.'

I really was the amateur in the room. 'This isn't my area… if she was pregnant… would it have shown?'

'Probably not. Most women forced into this deal with the Devil do so before it shows. We had her down as a back-street abortion gone wrong and thrown into the river in panic. It's no wonder nobody claimed the poor woman.'

A pregnant young woman came full square to the centre of my suspicions. 'And was she a *poor* woman?'

'I'm not sure, to be honest. She was wearing what looked like a quality skirt and silk underwear. They were in a better state than she was, if you pardon me.'

'Fully dressed? So not taken straight from an operating table?'

'Operating table?' She dismissed the idea with a raspberry. 'You've clearly no idea what happens in a back-street abortionist's house. But you're right in that they must have dressed her again, after whatever went wrong. Her underwear was not bloodstained. She certainly didn't drown so suicide or an accident is ruled out.'

'Perhaps they dressed her to disguise how she got into the river? To make the police think it was a suicide or an accident.'

'Overlooking the fact that Sir Bernard and myself devote our lives to deducing the cause of death beyond a policeman's hunch?'

'I doubt it crosses most people's minds. Not people in a panic.'

The overlooked professional nodded. 'That's true. But if they wanted to dress her like a suicide, she wasn't wearing a coat.'

'In late summer she might not have worn one.'

'Clearly, you don't observe women's fashion very closely. I'd expect her to have been wearing a coat, buttoned or belted, unless it was good enough to steal.'

Verity's summer coat had been missing from that valise. 'Fair enough, so the lack of a coat is inconsistent with a suicide.'

'And the fact that she did not drown, as already explained.' For someone who dealt chiefly with the dead Pascoe had a jolly smile. 'Was your cousin adventurous?'

'Oh gosh yes, a real tomboy.' So this was made up, but it was easy to imagine the sort of woman who might become a spy.

'You see I wondered about the silk underwear, because yes that would be expensive, but it didn't fit with everything else. She'd had a hard life, lost a couple of teeth, had a couple of ribs broken then healed. It all only made sense to me if she was...you know... a lady of the night.'

These facts and suppositions were all very inconvenient. 'Did she have both her arms?'

'Why ever wouldn't she?'

'No saw marks, no marks from tools or weapons? You didn't find any evidence of foul play, no stabbing or strangling or poisoning?'

Pascoe frowned. 'You know more about this case than was made public, don't you?'

'I expected you to tell me she'd been murdered.'

'The police thought that at first. If you must know, I didn't understand the puncture in her right leg or the one on the back of her left shoulder. Possibly there was also a gash across her lower abdomen, around the kidneys although her stomach had burst.' Dr Pascoe grimaced, and I tasted my breakfast.

'Gash,' I tried to visualise the mutilated corpse. 'And by puncture you mean stabs?'

'The untrained eye would say she was stabbed in the leg and in the shoulder and had her side ripped open by a blade. But she didn't have any cuts on her arms which I'd have expected if she had tried to defend herself. She wouldn't have died straight away from wounds like this, she would have struggled and fought back and there was no sign of that.

'But the evidence for the abortion was so clear. That's what killed her, either by blood loss or shock. Those other injuries occurred sometime after death, days possibly. My surmise is that she was bashed and scraped and impaled on objects in the river. Her blouse was so torn I'm surprised it stayed with the body.'

'So not a murder?'

'No, I'm certain she was killed by the abortion.' Colour rose in Pascoe's cheeks. 'I'm also certain you're not her cousin. Let me guess; reporter?'

'Writer. But I do know the family, or her fiancée at least. Or he would have been her fiancée if she'd lived. Did Sir Bernard read the file?'

'He did,' she looked defiant. 'And the Coroner returned an open verdict as there were too many questions and not enough answers. The police lost interest as soon as it was clear we didn't have Jack the Ripper back on the streets and the deceased was, in their words, just a knocked-up tart.'

She removed her glasses and blinked at me. 'You're not going to claim I've missed a murder, are you? A year after all this was done and dusted, your Inspector Renton calls. I don't know him, but Sir Bernard does and I'm told he's Special Branch. I'm no expert on the fine question of who does what in the police force, but don't they concentrate on Irish terrorists?'

'At times.'

'And now you turn up, armed with lots of new information you're not sharing with me. Don't deny it, because otherwise, you wouldn't be here.'

'I won't deny it. You have a body without a name, and I have a name without a body.'

'So you're telling me this has become a murder investigation?'

'It should be.'

She put back her glasses and gave some attention to a pile of papers on her table, then sifted another, as if she had better things to do. 'It's been fascinating meeting you Mr Clifton, but I can't tell you anything more.' Now she looked straight at me. This young professional's career was suddenly in danger of collapsing. 'I'm going to have to be terribly careful if this will all end up back in court. The Coroner was happy, the file was closed.'

'Fair enough. I'm grateful for what you've shared with me.'

'I do hope you're not going to upset the apple cart.'

'I can't promise that I won't.'

Chapter Forty-Two

The state of the Empire, or at least the state of the Italian Empire, was a topic of conversation everywhere, and provoked the idea to invite Sissy to Veeraswarmy restaurant in Regent Street. Its Indian cuisine, its décor, and traditionally dressed staff brought back memories both good and bad.

Sissy was resplendent in a red halter neck dress. She blinked at the spiciness of the curry but took it as a challenge. 'Did you use to eat this all the time in India?' she gasped, reaching for the water.

'Occasionally. Most of the time we ate in the mess.' I mocked an upper-class officer accent. 'Honest old-fashioned English cooking, and none of your foreign muck.' Then tucked in.

She smiled. Perhaps I had been forgiven at last.

'Mess food was often awful. This is better.' I tapped my plate. 'Indeed, it's better than the Indian food I had in India.'

'I feel I'm there, right now. Oh, I do love coming out with you. You talk about such interesting things.'

Yes, I'd been forgiven but did wonder how much of this new Hugh Clifton was made up. Perhaps Sissy was actually having dinner with Vincent Hammer, and it was Hammer's ego she was flattering.

'How's your song coming along?'

I was hoping she'd forgotten that.

'It's coming along,' I fibbed. 'I'm calling it *The Fascist Marching Song.*'

'And Verity?' She asked. 'Have you found out anything in Department Z?'

'Let's leave Z out of it.' She would be safer if I did not share what I had discovered, or how. I would be safer too.

'But it's what Z does, investigate...'

'No they compile information on people they want to hurt. Officers that need to be sacked, Jewish shops they want Parker and his friends to smash up.'

She shrugged her bare shoulders. 'Silly me.'

I reached across and touched her arm. 'Sorry, but for the time being we must keep this as our own little project.'

'Of course. What would your Harry Bretton and his stupid girlfriend do next?'

'Connect the facts.' I took another deliciously spicy mouthful and considered where this investigation was leading. 'Think back to last autumn. When did you find out she was gone?'

'She just didn't turn up for dinner one night, and that was that. It was just me, and Julian and...well another chap. No one serious. Don't worry about him.'

'Verity is the one who worries me. How did Julian react when she didn't show up?'

'Cross, embarrassed—it was his treat. Then, pretty sad. I think he mooned around outside her flat for a few days, but when I asked how he was feeling he was so miz about it I never raised the subject again...no, no, I did once, at a party at his parents'. I asked if he'd heard from her, but Melissa was there and took his arm and said "now, now, forget her" or something soothing like that.'

Just as if Melissa had been well briefed on how to handle the subject of Verity. I drew the attention of the waitress in a sari, and she poured more wine. 'When men are out together, we talk about politics, or cricket or horses, but I think you girls talk about deeper things.'

'Men, a lot of the time. And what beasts they are.'

'Present company excepted?'

She gave a snort.

'So, say when you were with Verity, she'd talk about Men?'

'Ah,' she pondered. 'No, actually.'

'Did you go out partying? The sort of two am cab home, totally squiffy party?'

'Is there any other kind?' She gave one of her sweet laughs.

'Back in my university days, my friends would open up after a pub crawl or late night's revels in someone's digs. They were all stiff upper lip in the daytime, chaps don't blub, but in the small hours, you'd meet the real man. They lost their father in the War, or their mother hated them. One even lost his virginity to his nanny.' I paused. 'Honesty in their cups.'

'You're asking what Verity was like in her cups?' Sissy stared into the distance. 'She stayed Verity.'

'Did she ever mention another man, someone other than Julian?'

'No, she was all about the moment, the future. She never talked about the past.'

'I don't mean the past, I mean right then, last summer. Was she seeing another man? Someone important perhaps.'

'No.' Then her eyes widened. 'You don't mean...'

Up to this moment I'd had Verity down as a spy, a female version of myself making one fatal slip and coming to an untimely end. 'I don't know who I mean. Everyone is at it in your circles.'

'Our circles,' she corrected. 'You're *at it* too.'

'Have you come across anyone called Jeb? Or perhaps initials J.E.B.? Or UJ? Could be someone in the Party?'

'No. Have you heard something juicy?'

I paused, made sure no staff were in eavesdropping range, leaned across the table and whispered the question. 'Could Verity have been pregnant?'

'Gosh, you have heard something juicy!' She sat straight upright, eyes popping.

'Truly, Sissy. Think.' I touched her hand. 'Was there any hint she could be...you know... last September? The act would be I don't know, May, June. Could it have been Julian? Was that why he's so wounded and why he so hurriedly moved on to Melissa?'

She looked away. 'I need another drink. And I need a cigarette.'

'Sissy?'

Her expression hardened. 'Melissa thought she was a fraud, a gold-digger as the Americans call them. Where did you find your latest piece of scandal?'

'Amateur detective work. I pulled a few strings, people who know people. I found newspaper articles about a woman's body being found in the Thames last October. It sounded like Verity.'

Sissy almost threw down her fork. She covered her mouth to stifle a cry.

'It gets worse. The dead woman had been pregnant.'

'Oh no. Jesus Hugh, are you serious? This is horrible. She grabbed at her wineglass and stared across the room for perhaps a whole minute. After another large gulp she gave her sober assessment. 'I suppose if she was preggers and Julian wouldn't do the decent thing, she might have been so horrified she threw herself off a bridge in a total funk.'

'Would she do that? The Verity you knew.'

'No, she was fearless,' Sissy admitted. 'She was brave. She'd go it alone or find a way to do away with the problem.'

'If she did try to do away with it and died when something went wrong, she didn't get to the river on her own. Somebody carried her body and dumped it. An abortion might have solved one problem but making her death look like a bodged abortion would solve all of them. After a couple of weeks in the river, even the experts would be fooled.'

A silence fell as she digested the implications.

'Verity was just too perfect all round, appeared abruptly, then disappeared abruptly. I wonder who she upset.'

'I'm going to have to ask Julian.'

'Do you think he'll tell you? I've tried myself and he clams right up.'

'As you said, I'll get him into his cups. We'll have dinner and I'll get him very drunk. Two drinks for him, one for me. He'll remember how much he used to fancy me and might one day wake up to what an ugly mind Melissa has.'

'Be careful what you tell him.'

'Do you honestly think Verity was murdered?'

'I think it's pretty likely. She upset the wrong person, or she slept with the wrong man, or both. There are people who are certain she's dead, as if they knew it as a fact. As if they ordered it.'

***

Nobody at Black House questioned the purpose of my visit to the Royal Oak, nor why the Defence Squad had been called out. Street fights in the East End were commonplace. A victory for his squad did Julian's reputation no harm at all and I'd won friends by buying drinks all round afterwards.

Lucy had been typing industriously but stopped the moment I went into the office. News of the Italian invasion of Abyssinia gripped Black House. People were talking of little else, which offered hope that their attention was elsewhere. 'Do you think it will come to war, Mr Clifton?' she asked.

'Oh, I doubt it.'

'But they're saying we need to stop the Italians from taking over Africa, and that's a problem innit, 'cause they're Blackshirts and we're Blackshirts.'

'Indeed that puts us in a bit of a fix.'

'Cos if the Party supports the Italians, we're like traitors. But Mussolini is our friend.'

'Well I tell you what, I'm glad I'm not on the Political Committee and have to sort that one out. Let's stick to good old investigation.'

'I'm glad there's someone here interested in that. There's them like Captain Parker that just wants fights.'

'Whereas people like us...'

'Proper investigators,' she said with a smile. Yes, I had another ally on my side of the fence.

The ever-helpful Lucy went out for her short lunch at 12 noon and Major Taylor routinely enjoyed a longer one. Few people at Black House were paid anything approaching a proper salary, so Z was always thinly staffed. At least it had one diligent member who made sure he was there when others were not.

Today I opened drawer 'T'. Julian's file read pretty much as a school report, but a single line referred the reader to 'see Laytham, V'. In front of it was a file marked with a green gummed sticker and named for Thring, H L. The green sticker presumably meant 'Good Egg' as the file contained nothing but his photograph, address, and office address. Thring & Winter had its own file, curiously, containing just an introductory sheet with a couple of press cuttings from August 1934 relating to a break-in at the firm. Calhoun had specifically warned me off trying to burgle the offices, but now I gained a strong conviction that M Section had already tried.

I went back to the stairwell to check I was still alone, then took out the Verity file again and looked at those cryptic notes, UJ and JEB.

No file existed for 'UJ'.

JEB proved less of a problem. He was not under J, but there was a Baxter, JE. I took the file to the gent's cubicle and settled down to read. Born in 1888, Jeremiah Erskine Baxter had been a party member briefly in 1933. 'Known as Jeb' said the note, a *nom de guerre* based on his initials. The file's main content was an article clipped from the *Illustrated London News* plus a number of shorter cuttings from newspapers of his appearances at the Royal Geographical Society and other meetings. He'd apparently cavorted with Lawrence of Arabia, adventured in Russia with the Whites, 'served in Ireland' and once vanished up the Amazon for sixteen months. His life had been a highly irregular Cook's Tour of the world's most dangerous places, and newspapers had reported his death on two occasions.

The photographs were small and grainy and showed him in a variety of garb and headgear suited for the jungle, mountain, or desert backdrop. He owned 'more scars than he could count,' a true son of the Empire. If not a sheer fantasist, JEB would be a dangerous man. He was not shy of publicity, so should be an easy person to find.

Chapter Forty-Three

Life had changed for the Hon. Cecilia Poe-Maundy. For the past two years, she had discovered a purpose in fascism, with its athletic young men and women, chic parties, and adventure camps. That uniform gave her a sense of belonging so much more than being part of a nebulous Society set that drifted from one social occasion to the next. Life was now so much more than belonging to a worthless, faithless husband and playing up to norms on how a woman of her class should behave. She could pick and choose the England she wanted to see—vibrant and forward-looking, not harking back to the good old Edwardian days of class and privilege and everyone knowing their place. The future was for everyone and buzzing with cars, aeroplanes, radio, and perhaps even televisions one day. Under fascism, everyone would be happy.

But she was troubled. Hugh Clifton had upset the equilibrium she had restored after the disaster of her marriage. She'd fallen in love with this rogue, this kind-hearted intruder from the north, this hero/coward who embodied everything fascism was meant to be. Yet he wore his politics as lightly as a silk shirt that he could shrug off at any moment. Just talking to him had cleared her mind, as if all the windows in her stifling princess' tower had been opened. She was still an enthusiastic fascist, but she was no longer an unquestioning fascist.

Hugh kept his cards close to his chest. He wasn't telling her everything that was going on, and she was determined to find out. Verity had played her for the fool too, whilst trying to steal Julian's heart. And surely, a true gold-digger would aim higher than an accountant's son.

Bert Ambrose's dance band had paused, and Julian was talking, but Sissy was only half-listening, thinking of Hugh and his amateur detective work. He'd taken on too much of the persona of that sleuth of his; Harry Bretton blundering his way across Europe. It was a slim hope that publishers would show mercy on that book as the chapters she'd seen were awful drivel. Detective work was thirsty work, and she called a waiter across and ordered two more gin martinis.

'Say, steady on girl!' Julian said.

'We don't often get the chance to talk.'

'Because you're always glued to Hugh, the lucky dog.'

'And you to Melissa. Are you really going to marry her?'

'A chap should get married.'

'That wasn't what I said. I never liked the way she just latched onto you the moment Verity was gone, it was too soon. I can't imagine you forgot her that quickly?'

'Of course, I didn't.'

'Then why?'

'Aw.'

'Just hurt, lonely?' Adopting her playful puppy-face might stop him taking offence. 'Missing her?'

'She was too good for me.'

'In what way?'

'Oh, so beautiful and clever and...you know what she was like. It was if you had a big sister, livelier, cleverer.'

'Cleverer? Oh, thank you.'

'Sorry, that came out wrong, I didn't mean you aren't bright but she was terribly well read. A bit like Hugh, you know? Classics and things. Those heavy political books like Marx we all pretend we've read but haven't.'

The band struck up another tune. It came from a recent Hollywood movie, but neither the film nor the name of the tune came to mind. Sissy accepted her cocktail and made the count four. In drinking terms, Julian boxed at lightweight whilst she could go ten rounds with the heavyweights.

'Was she sexier than me?'

'I can't answer that,' he said. 'There's no answer that will get me off the hook on that one.'

'I think...' Sissy feigned squiffy now. 'I think she could wind you around her finger every time she wanted.'

'Oh, I'd have let her, willingly.'

Bingo! Sissy was inside the confession box. She moved her lips close to Julian's ear, as the band was trumping its trombones and thumping its snare drums. 'Do you think you'd have married her if she'd stayed around? Would your family have let you?'

'Father loved her, they hit it off wonderfully.'

So she had even fooled Thring Senior with her raven-haired wild-girl classic scholar ways. Verity was too damned perfect for Sissy's liking; no wonder Hugh had latched onto her suspicions.

'And she was already in the Party.'

As she leaned over, it was so in character for Julian to glance down at what cleavage her halter neck displayed. 'How was she in bed?' She purred.

'What?'

'Go on, you can tell me. She was so good at everything else, I always thought she'd be, I don't know, a real tiger in the sack.'

'Tiger.' He stared at his drink.

'Oh,' she said. 'You never...' She sat back, acting prim.

He shook his head sadly. 'Just strung me along.'

'Poor Jules.' She patted his hand.

He took a drink to drown the memory, extracted the olive, and ate it in two chews.

'Was there someone else? Did she have another lover?'

'Of course not.' He took a drink. 'I don't know.'

Now she was pushing the limits. 'She wasn't one of those girls who fell for the Leader?'

'Mosley? No, no, why would she? I don't believe all that rot about him bedding this woman and that anyway. Verity wasn't a slut, she was... principled.'

A great whoosh of alcohol hit her brain. All this must be remembered in the morning. 'You don't know anyone called Jeb?'

'No.'

'Some sort of adventurer, explorer.'

'Oh wait, yes, Jeb Baxter, father knows him. He's speaking at something soon...'

'Did Verity know him?'

'I don't know. She was quite cagey about her private life. And I think we've talked enough about Verity.'

The licence to pry was running out. It was time to play the ace. 'I heard she was pregnant.'

'No.' Julian was pale at the best of times but lost what remained of his colour.

She gave a very quiet affirmative nod.

'Where on Earth did you hear that?'

'Oh, some club,' she lied. 'Someone I hardly knew.'

'She can't have been.' A tear seemed to be forming in Julian's right eye.

'It does happen.' She took both his hands in hers. 'Poor darling Jules. Have you any idea where she's bolted to, any at all?'

'You sound like Hugh now, he's got all interested in Verity too. Why is that?'

'He writes detective stories and he picks up clues.' Now for that other ace. 'He thinks she's dead.'

Julian's face turned blank.

'You mustn't tell anyone this, or we'll all get into hot water, seriously. Understand?'

'Yes.' He hardly seemed to care.

'Hugh found a newspaper article from last October about a woman that sounds like Verity being found dead in the river.'

The tear was released and coursed down his cheek.

She gripped his hands harder. 'I'm sorry Jules.'

'No, no, it's what I dreaded. Going so suddenly like that, without a word, without even a miserable postcard from wherever she'd run to. To be honest, that's why Melissa appealed. She's honest, she's lively, I know her family and where she's from…'

'Do you think your father knew Verity had died?'

Another tear followed the first.

'Do you think that's why he introduced you to Melissa?'

Julian bit his lip. If he was frightened, he was not the only one.

Chapter Forty-Four

Hold high the Fascist flag, my friends,

Hold the standard high!

We'll march to victory today,

The Blackshirts marching by

For sake of Britain, God and King

Our Leader's aim is true

So hold the standard high my friends

The old red white and blue.

Sung to the tune of *Auld Lang Syne*, this draft of *The Fascist Marching Song* was my best effort yet. Except I'd used both 'march' and 'marching' and the fascist flag wasn't red, white, and blue. Drat. Writing with my pad resting on the restaurant table, I crossed out the draft and vowed to get a crowd of drunken Blackshirts singing the final version before I dared show Sissy, Thring or anyone else. Calhoun was late, which was out of character. It was also out of character for him to call a meeting in the evening, and even more unusual for it to involve dinner in a half-empty French restaurant at His Majesty's Government's expense.

The MI5 man came striding through the doors, carrying an envelope under his arm and slapping a newspaper against his thighs as an irritated banker might when his stocks are falling. A waiter indicated that his guest had already arrived. The reserved table was particularly narrow and set in a small booth with special appeal to lovers or spies.

'Bad news?' I asked as my handler sat on the bench-seat opposite.

'That's the only kind these days. Things are moving fast, faster than we'd like. Your chum Mussolini is bombing Abyssinian civilians with mustard gas and all decency says we should stop him. What do your Blackshirts think about him now?'

'They still admire him, perhaps less now than they did. Mosley's in Italy right now.'

'Is he, by Jove?'

'Begging money from Mussolini is my guess, and Mussolini will give it because if Mosley is opposed to sanctions or military intervention it puts him halfway on the Italian side. But that in turn puts the BUF in a fix. How far do we appease our Italian paymasters whilst simultaneously being loyal subjects of the King?'

'So if we go to war with Italy, whose side are they on?'

'Britain's, to a man. We're patriots.' Saying *we* had become a habit. 'But Mosley is anti-war through and through. He wrote a piece about the outbreak of the Great War, saying that when the crowds cheered the announcement the men were celebrating their own funeral. Even if he wasn't in Mussolini's pocket he'd campaign for peace and for negotiations because he doesn't want to see thousands of our young men killed.'

Calhoun ordered veal and I followed my host's lead. He selected a suitable wine from what he claimed was a good vineyard, which suited me fine. I had never made a study of wines, vintages, and all that. Once the waiter had retreated, Calhoun leaned forward over the table. 'I'm going to give *you* information for a change. Things are getting very sticky, politically. Baldwin doesn't want a confrontation with Italy, so he's ordered the Mediterranean Fleet into harbour. The First Sea Lord agrees with him because he's worried about what the Japanese might get up to in the Far East if our fleet gets tied up in a scrap with Mussolini. Between them, they've handed the whole pond over to the Italians.'

'The Romans did call it *mare nostrum*—our sea.'

'It gets worse, much worse. Junior officers and ratings mutinied on three Royal Navy ships in Alexandria this morning.'

'Grief! Is it in the paper?' What looked like a *Times* sat well-folded on the end of the table.

'Not yet, but it will be by the morning editions.' Calhoun sat back to make space when the waiter proffered the bottle. 'Just pour,' he said.

'Is this why we're…' I raised my glass.

'To bloody war or sickly season,' Calhoun toasted. 'If the Sea Lords don't want to fight the Italians, the petty officers and fresh-faced young lieutenants are saying that Nelson would have put to sea and damn the Sea Lords. And Winston Churchill is sharpening his cutlass ready to stick it in Baldwin's back. We played down the Invergordon Mutiny in '31, but it was much more serious than we allowed the newspapers to think. A mutiny in the Royal Navy…' For the first time, I saw Calhoun display genuine emotion. 'It's a national humiliation. Cutting sailor's wages, cutting back the fleet, agreeing to that treaty with Germany and now hiding in port whilst the Italians run riot. The government could fall.'

'And will it?' I took another sip of wine, not quite keeping up with the boss, who was most of the way down that first glass.

'Baldwin's not a man of action. He's not the man to start a war and not a man to stop one.'

'But honestly, without being brutal, how many people in Britain care about Abyssinia?'

'It's more the threat to the Suez Canal and the flaunting of the international order. Britain is expected to be the world's policeman and we're standing by watching daylight robbery, rape, and murder. Stalin and Hitler are watching too, to see what they can get away with.'

'You're saying the mutineers are right and we should go to war with Italy?'

'No, no ...we need the Italians' goodwill to keep the Germans in check.' Calhoun puffed and looked away. 'I know that sounds ridiculous, but that's international diplomacy for you. Hanrahan's communists are mobilizing for peace marches; what are your shower up to?'

'The same, ironically. I can't imagine I'll be marching side by side with Hanrahan though.'

'Peace is the only option,' Calhoun muttered, more to his wine than to me. 'Britain isn't ready for war and frankly, Five isn't ready for war. Do you know how many officers we have?'

'About two dozen, plus the typists and the clerical ladies.'

'Not far off. To think we had seven or eight hundred in the Great War. And now we have to watch the Blackshirts, the Communists, the IRA, Russian agents, Italian agents, and German agents with one man and his dog.'

'Sounds like I'm the dog.'

He smiled. 'So nose to the ground, or no biscuits. I need to know how Mosley is playing this crisis, day by day if you can.'

I nodded, imagining a world collapsing in flames.

'Oh, and you'll need this.'

The large envelope contained documents making me an official of the Board of Trade.

'Those four ships of Kahn's are due to dock between tomorrow and November the first. Get yourself down to the docks, keep an eye on who's coming ashore and what's coming ashore. If there was ever a time for the Germans to stir up trouble, it's now. Ah, here comes our veal.'

Chapter Forty-Five

National Government Betrays Britain!

Blackshirt trumpeted indignation at Britain's humiliation in the Mediterranean, forgetting how it had lauded Mussolini's victories a few weeks before. Britain must 'Mind Britain's Business' and stay out of the conflict. The Leader summoned every BUF supporter who could afford the train fare or who could be squeezed onto hired motor coaches to join a Peace Parade.

Forming up four abreast, we were to march from Black House towards the West End of London. Julian's Squad was placed two dozen ranks back from the front, with him taking the right-hand file and me immediately to his left. For a week the BUF had mounted a strident campaign against the sanctions imposed on Italy by the League of Nations, but today the word went around that it had been quietly dropped. Sanctions were preferred to war. It was not 'peace at any price' but there would be a price.

'Baldwin's calling an election,' Julian said through his teeth. 'It should be four weeks from now, mid-November.'

'Are we ready?'

'Wish we were. Father says we need another six months, and no bloody Abyssinia.'

'The mutiny might help.'

'But help who? If the Tories look like arses, the winners will be Labour.'

'Ay up, we're off.'

Orders were barked and the band struck up a tune. Standard bearers led the parade, followed by the marching band and then the BUF leaders with forty I Squad bodyguards in close attendance. Next came Blackshirts in our hundreds, marching in clean military style. Sissy was further back with the uniformed Women's Section and Melissa was carrying their standard. The youth section in grey shirts followed, then party members in civilian clothes, marching untidily and waving placards. Other organizations tagged on at the back, including a few churches and women's groups.

Brash militarist peace-campaigners crunched their hob-nailed boots through Chelsea with the band playing Souza's 'Stars and Stripes'. A woman yelled abuse from the pavement. I glanced her way. Who could be against peace? The order came to halt. Word came back that the Leader was negotiating with some high-ranking police officer who wanted to steer us away from the trade unions' march.

'Our peace will be more peaceful than their peace,' I said under my breath, and Julian grinned. Over to one side, a figure in the thin crowd was watching our halted parade, keeping low, moving from behind one spectator to the other. He stopped and raised his head so that the peak of his cap no longer concealed his eyes, but the rest of his face was masked with a scarf. For just an instant, our eyes met.

'It's him. Monkey Man.'

Julian looked anxiously towards the crowd, where no Monkey Man was now visible. 'Who?'

The Leader was already some distance ahead, and out of immediate danger. 'Can I have the squad?'

'It's my squad, old man.'

'So tell them to follow me.' I broke ranks with purpose, heading for that place in the crowd where Monkey Man no longer stood. I sensed a rush of black shirts behind me, and the civilians parted. Left or right? A gap between two shops was filled by plain wooden hoarding, and in its centre was a re-used house door that hung open.

'This way men!' It was all eerily familiar.

Behind me streamed Julian and eight more of his squad. I spotted Parker near the head of the parade, glaring at me.

'Parker!' I shouted. 'Time to prove yourself.'

To his credit, Parker called to the I Squad without a moment's delay and they peeled off in my direction. They had a nose for trouble. I was the first to barge through that door into a patch of waste ground where some building project had been abandoned to weeds. My quarry nipped around the back of one of the standing buildings and into a back-alley. I was after him like a greyhound chasing a hare, but a racetrack hare was never meant to be caught.

Men streamed into the building site from both sides. It was an ambush—devised for one specific victim. A man in a flat cap and scarf-wreathed face pointed at me directly. 'Get that tall one!' he shouted, remaining stationary as the flat-capped mob broke into a charge. Bottles and cudgels sprang from inside coats while bricks and broken timber strewn on the ground offered more weaponry.

Julian took a hit immediately from a bottle aimed at me. It shattered as he batted it aside with his arm. I pulled my friend over to a gable wall to protect our backs, but our squad was overwhelmed in moments; knocked over, pushed back, or running for safety. A man swung a hunk of wood and I blocked it with my left arm, recoiled with the pain, then socked my assailant on the jaw with such force that he was hurled back onto the ground. Another attacker immediately stumbled over the man on the ground, and Julian kicked him in the head.

My left arm had gone numb and wouldn't block the next attack fast enough. A man punched me just where there was no rib to take the impact and it was my turn to stagger back coughing—into the brickwork and into Julian. No black shirts could be seen; it was all greys and browns and chants against the fascists on every side. The mob burst out into the main street, arrowing into the Peace Parade in a wedge of pure hate. I kicked my attacker on the shin, then punched him untidily on the top of his head; once, twice, three times. The man lurched forward, grabbing my waist and locking us together against the wall. I pummelled that head with the back of my fist, again, again and again. Sweaty and tobacco-pungent, the man clung on.

Julian grabbed my attacker, yanking him back by the collar. The man broke contact, shaking his head, giving me a split second to make a clean punch and break his nose. Black uniforms now pinched off the attack, the I Squad surging forward in full cry through that little door and knocking it off its hinges, driving the attackers back before them. If there were once fifty socialists, they were suddenly outnumbered as the hoarding collapsed before a great surge of black army-ants. The men in flat caps began to run. One of the I Squad delivered a rugby tackle that would not shame a Halifax man at the Thrum Hall ground. Another laid into the prone man with his boots, which was much less sporting.

Dizzy, my right fist hurting from my own punches, and my left arm useless, I doubled up in a bout of coughing. I was out of the battle.

Flat caps lay on the ground as their owners left them behind. Trapped men were punched, and those on the ground kicked repeatedly. The fight had turned the way of the fascists and the violence turned excessive.

The crack of a pistol silenced the shouting. All fights froze. All eyes sought the new danger. Monkey Man had fired that shot, without doubt. He'd ducked back out of sight immediately, but his shot checked the Blackshirts for the seconds needed for the leftists to break contact and stream away.

'Fucking shit, fucking shit!' A Blackshirt fell to his knees, then pitched forward into the weeds.

No second shot came, and all possible shooters had fled. If I'd brought my pistol, I could have found the energy to chase Monkey Man and bring this duel to an end. Perhaps that's what my nemesis wanted and was even now waiting in a place of his own choosing. For some reason, the villain had not contrived to shoot me during the melee, and for all the wisdom about any shot being a shot to kill, that I Squad man had been hit in the leg.

Only fascists were still on their feet, so men moved freely to aid the casualty. He had by now rolled onto his back, clutching a bullet wound in his thigh. Plenty around him had been serving soldiers or had attended one of the BUF training camps so knew how to treat bullet wounds.

'Julian?'

My ally was shaking away pain in his right hand, had a nasty weal on his left cheek and green glass fragments were embedded in the seams of his shirt. Julian was panting and shaking. Half his Squad were down, and one was clearly unconscious. Two of the attackers remained inert on the ground. If nobody had died today, it was only down to chance.

'That's a fearful cough, old man.'

'Yes, when I get excited.'

'By Jove, I thought we were done for there.'

'Peace is worth fighting for,' I panted. A quick check confirmed that my left arm was not broken. Several more coughs came before I could control them, then I tested that sore patch under my ribs. My knuckles were raw, my trousers were torn and I could feel blood drying on my cheek.

The two enemy casualties left behind were at last stirring, and a Blackshirt was poised to resume kicking one into oblivion. 'Oi, leave him!' An idea formed. 'Julian, keep the coppers away. And make sure the Leader is well clear of this as well.' On impulse, I summoned a clutch of Blackshirts towards the injured leftists. 'Come on, you, you! We need prisoners. Grab those two.' They quickly got the idea and seized both men, jerking them still half-conscious to their feet.

Only now did policemen arrive at the scene, shouting at random, but arresting nobody. Ambulancemen were called. Pulling the captives behind a mound of abandoned bricks amid a huddle of Blackshirts I demanded rope, scarves, anything to bind and gag them with.

Julian came back, red-faced, his eyes wide with exhilaration. 'What the hell are you going to do with these two?'

'Take then back to Black House. Find us a van can you?'

* * *

Crop-haired men in black bundled the captives out of the baker's van and down into the cellars of Black House. Sacks engulfed their heads, and they would be entitled to think they were about to die. All the big names had remained with the parade, pressing on, so Julian pulled what rank he had. The least injured man was dragged into the black-walled cell, and the other was given some rudimentary treatment for his injuries by a former soldier.

Our prisoner was in his thirties, dressed now only in soiled blue-green collarless shirt and trousers of mucky brown. His boots and belt had been confiscated and his jacket and coat were being searched. His hands were tightly bound.

It was hard to deny the thrill as I removed the sack from the captive's head. I was tempted to slap him, just to show him who was the boss, just to show him how hopeless his position was. This was power, true power. The man before me had no idea where he was and no idea if he would ever see the sun again. I tasted bile; how easily I could become the evil I was supposed to be fighting. Down in the black room, I was the master, the terrible inquisitor and anything I did would be for the greater good. A dangerous slope led down into darkness and the Devil beckoned me.

Julian offered a tin cup half-full of water to eager lips. Hastily we had agreed to play a form of doubles tennis. I would deliver the forehand smashes from close to the net, whilst Julian would hang back, an unknown quantity in waiting.

Blood had stopped running from the wound across the man's brow and now congealed in a mess around his eye socket. He looked with some expectation towards Julian, the kind one who had offered the water.

I imagined I was Parker, nasty and brutal. Channelling that pain in my arm to enhance my menace I leaned in close. 'Tell us who organized the attack. We want the names of everyone involved.'

No response came. So, the next move was to do what; strike him? I wanted to so dearly; my arm bloody hurt. 'You need to tell me.'

'I know who you are,' said the man. 'You was in the paper. You shot that comrade.'

'Then you know where this is heading.' I stepped back.

The man glanced at Julian again, as if the boyish face offered him hope. The two stone-faced Blackshirts by the door certainly didn't. 'You can't do this.'

'But I am doing this.' I took the tin cup from Julian, paused as if to offer the man a drink then splashed the remaining water onto his face. I hurled the cup so it bounced off the wall and rattled across the floor and he flinched, expecting a blow.

'I've done nothin'.'

'Attacking my men with bricks and bottles? Then shooting at us? Who is to know you didn't die on that miserable patch of land? Head crushed in by a brick. Who is going to tell the police that they were causing a riot and they left you behind?'

If I was Parker I'd be reaching for the rubber hose and the pliers, or a saw…this could have been the place Ewan Williams spent his last hours. Even as I ran through ever more extreme tortures in my head my captive remained insolently silent.

'Come on.' I made for the door, taking Julian and the guards outside. I locked the door, then flicked off the light switch. It was as if the builders had placed it on the outside for that specific reason. 'Cup of tea anyone?' I asked cheerfully.

'What?' asked Julian.

'It's that or beat him to a pulp. Let's give him some time to repent, and meantime see how the other one is faring.'

At that moment Sissy hurried down the stairs, with Melissa and Lucy straight behind her.

'Hugh! Are you hurt?'

'Bumps and scrapes that's all. What are you all doing here?'

'We saw the fight and heard you'd come back. Everyone else just formed up again and carried on as if nothing had happened.'

Melissa checked Julian's grazed cheek, and even admired it. He told her it was nothing. Who says accountants are soft?

Sissy spotted the injured man lying on a bench under guard. 'What the hell are you up to?'

'Shhh.' I put a finger to my lips.

'Yes shhh,' said Julian. 'We could really get into hot water for this.'

'Is what we're doing right, sir?' the oldest of the men asked. The half dozen Blackshirts were excited but apprehensive.

'Are we going to give him another kicking?' asked another.

'No, we'll try something else.' I raised my voice above the hubbub. 'Ladies, chaps. We keep this to ourselves for today, agreed? I'll sort it out with the brass. Lucy, could you arrange some tea?'

'Yeah,' she said. 'But you need to look at 'im down 'ere else you'll have a dead 'un on your hands.'

The second man was the more badly injured. He had lost three teeth and had suffered what the older Blackshirt suggested was a concussion. 'I've seen this, before,' he explained.

Melissa knelt by the casualty and felt his brow. 'Commie or not, he should go to a hospital.'

'Julian,' I said quietly. 'Can you make sure that van's still handy?' I clapped my hands to gain attention. 'Ladies, could you give us some room? Everyone else step back. If I get carpeted over this the fewer of you are involved the better. All of you, go and get a cup of tea.'

'Tea? With all this going on?' asked Sissy.

'Please,' I came close to her. 'There are things you are better off not knowing.'

She glanced towards where Julian was now trotting up the stairs. 'Like what happened to Verity?'

'*This* might be what happened to Verity. Down here, in that room. So be a darling and have a cup of tea.'

She gave a mockery of a salute. 'I obey, oh great leader.'

Once alone, I knelt by the bench serving as makeshift stretcher and spoke softly to the casualty. 'Now, here is the deal. You tell me what I need to know and in five minutes you'll be on the way to hospital. You have my word as an officer and a gentleman. Understand?'

'My head...'

'Who was the man with a scarf across his face? The one who organized the attack. The one who shot at us.'

'I never saw him before,' the man murmured. 'He was with Dingle.'

'And who is Dingle?'

'Union.'

'Give me the names of your other friends there.'

'I just, I just…'

Both the clammy skin and the paleness of the invalid's face were worrying. 'Just tell me your own name then,' he said gently. 'So we can tell the doctors.'

'Travis, Gordon Travis.'

'That was easy.'

Only a couple of minutes' gentle questioning were needed, which were as many as could be risked. Julian returned with four men and confirmed that the van was ready.. Travis had served his purpose.

Six Blackshirts and three women sat in the canteen waiting for me. Lucy brought out a plate of my favourite squashed fly biscuits to share around, and we sipped tea and made awkward, halting conversation. Wounds were compared, dabbed clean and Band-Aids applied. Melissa told everyone how she was a trained first aider, issuing instructions on how to conduct this most basic of first aid and the men were too drained to do anything but comply. Only the women's uniforms were clear of blood or rips.

Exactly one hour was allowed to pass, then I stood up abruptly. 'Ladies, time to leave. Julian, time to resume play.'

'And what are you going to do now?' Sissy asked. 'Uh-oh, don't tell me, it's better if I don't know.'

'You've got it.'

One hour spent in total darkness with no idea of what the future held would warp any man's mind. I staged a magician's return to the room, snapping on the light and allowing the prisoner no time to spring any kind of plan he might have hatched. He was lying in a corner, obviously not planning anything, so two of my Blackshirts dragged him back to sit facing the inquisitors once more. *My Blackshirts.*

I dived straight into it. 'Your friend is being more talkative than you are. We have Dingle, and we have Travis but we need more names. Four more will do, then you can go. My promise.'

'And mine,' echoed Julian using a tone that was far from reassuring.

We let silence fall. It was all he had to look forward to if he said nothing.

'Names. Let's start with yours.'

Chapter Forty-Six

'Been in the wars?' Hanrahan pointed to the scabbed knuckles on display as I laid my coins on the bar.

'Stopping the communist revolution in its tracks. The usual?' It was also usual for me to pay. Hanrahan used words like 'redistribution' to justify it.

With a pint of painkiller in my fully functioning right hand, I passed another to Hanrahan and followed the Irishman to a quieter corner. Over a few minutes, I offered an edited-down story of the ambush, excluding the part where two men were illegally imprisoned and threatened with torture. Grief, my left arm ached. I'd been carrying it in a sling around Black House to enhance my status.

Hanrahan leaned forward in the cheap pub chair. 'You're sure it was your Monkey Man who sprung the ambush?'

'Yes, he looked me in the eye and dared me to chase him to where his comrades were waiting. He knew I'd follow him.'

'How close was Mosley?'

'He'd passed within twenty yards of that door a minute or two earlier.'

'So he didn't shoot Mosley, and didn't launch his attack until he was well past.' Hanrahan was clearly puzzled.

'He was after *me*. And I'm not being egotistical.'

'Monkey Man wants to cause mayhem... but not hurt Mosley.' Hanrahan was trying to understand what I was trying to understand. 'Make him look weak but not a martyr? And he chose you because he knows you're getting close to him.'

'That's more or less what I've concluded. And it makes sense if it was he who set us up at the Royal Oak too. I saw someone far off when the balloon went up; I bet that was him. Saturday was another attempt to see me in hospital rather than on his trail.'

'But not kill you.'

'No, I don't understand that.'

'He might come round to it, you know. Take care pal, you won't always have fifty Blackshirts on hand to pull you out of the shit.'

'You didn't hear about an attack being planned?'

'No. I was at the TUC parade, which passed off quietly. A peace march is supposed to be peaceful, for sure.'

'Well, the upshot is that I've got a little further. Monkey Man takes a different name, a different guise each time he pulls a stunt, and the little men he's recruiting don't know who he is. He organized that little riot claiming he was from the TUC. He's going for cheesed off old soldiers and men on the edge of the unions.'

'That sounds about right,' Hanrahan agreed.

I made a barrier of my hands then slid them apart. 'Remember that wall of yours? I'm putting a gate in it. I've got six names from that riot yesterday.'

'Can I ask how you got them? I did hear two comrades went missing.'

'Fascists don't play by the rules, and scared men find those black uniforms pretty intimidating.'

'You're becoming a scary man, for sure. Stormtroopers at your command and...well...you're a paid-up Department Z petty tyrant now.'

'As long as everyone believes that, it helps us. Now I'm checking this list for ex-soldiers. I'm using the British Legion to find them.' I slid a list of names across the table.

Hanrahan glanced at the names. 'I don't know any of these.'

'Check the unions and the party lists. If Monkey Man can find them, we can find them. Once we've got some addresses, we'll split the list. If there are any old soldiers, I'll play the ex-officer, welfare and all that as I couldn't talk about unions for longer than a minute.'

'You've not given this list to Calhoun?'

'Like last time when it ended so well? Do you think these men will still be there when Special Branch come knocking? The fewer people who know, the better.'

'And I suppose you don't want awkward questions about how you got the names.' He indicated my scabbed knuckles.

'No.'

'I have my orders.' Hanrahan said, pocketing the list and standing up. He drained his pint. 'Don't get carried away with the fascist thing. They'll hang you out to dry.'

* * *

With the help of the British Legion, I had three addresses to check, using my role at the hospital as a legitimate reason to seek men out. Arnold Dingle could not be found. His neighbours said he hadn't been around for a few days and his landlord had already let his room. His *Jewish* landlord, they emphasized with a spit. Mind, Dingle was trouble—he'd been a shop steward in the General Strike.

Charlie Watkins said he was far too young to be interested in the hospital. 'I've worked at the docks, an' no need of your charity.' He stood in the door of the two-up two-down terraced house, unmoved.

'As an old soldier, you'll always be welcome at the Hospital.'

'Old soldier? I never cared for soldiering. When they sent me medals I threw them in the river, and my brother's. We got a letter from King George saying how sorry he was my brother died. I took it to out the privy and wiped my arse with it. I shat on King George.'

'I see.'

'And what kind of captain are you? You can't have been in the War.' Watkins challenged my alias as Captain Smythe.

'Not the Great War, no. I served in India.'

'Cushy posting then. Oppressing the poor bloody blacks.'

'Maintaining the order of the Empire.'

'As I said, oppressing the blacks. I've no use for your kind of charity, captain.' Watkins closed the door.

It was growing late, but next on the list was Billy Rich and he lived only two streets away in a near-identical terraced house of sooted brick. His old mother said he was not home. 'Gone to that club,' she said.

'Which club?'

'Oh that club, you know, for the old soldiers. Did he call it the Wipers Club?'

'I've never heard of it.'

'Or he's at the Marquis of Granby. He'll be there, I'll bet a crown on it. He don't like officers, though, but you don't sound like no officer.'

'We're not all toffs who went to Eton. I worked my way up from the ranks.' It might be an idea to keep control of these lies so they didn't catch me out one day.

'Well, good for you sonny. Marquis of Granby, down there, left then left again.'

The Marquis of Granby stood on a major road, taking a prime corner position, and was fairly packed for so early on a Friday evening. My damaged lung would be challenged again. As a Great War veteran, Billy Rich should be at least in his forties. Several men fitted my imagination of what he should look like, so I enquired at the bar and he was pointed out.

At first impression, Billy Rich did not look like an honest working man who had hit hard times. His shirt appeared to be new, if not fresh. His jacket was not frayed, darned, or patched like several I'd pushed past in the bar. Thinking back, Watkins had also worn a decent shirt and his wife had answered the door in a dress that was far from the washed-out look so common in these streets. Someone had been spreading money around. I bought half a pint of Ind Coope beer and took my time. Rich stood drinks for two of his mates, who raised glasses to his health.

As Captain Smythe I weaved my way through the men by the bar; the few women in the room sat by the walls. 'Billy Rich?' I asked.

'I didn't do it and I wasn't there!' His friends burst out laughing. 'Who are you, then?'

I went through my Captain Smythe routine.

'Do I look like I need charity?' Rich stroked the back of his hand down his jacket.

'Flushest bloke on the road,' his friend said.

'To what do you owe your fortune?'

'This and that.'

'Well, excellent, but I'm keen to meet other men who might need assistance. Do you know Arnold Dingle?

The jolly drinking face fell away. 'No, I don't.'

'Might he be down the Wipers Club?'

'No such place.'

I started to ask the other men the same question, but Rich took hold of my lapel. 'Look mate, mister Captain Smythe. This is an honest pub for honest working men and you can just bugger off.'

Rich released my lapel as I stepped back. It would have been a good idea to bring Hanrahan along; I was in need of one of his plans. Rich and his friends might be advancing in years, but there were three of them plus goodness knows how many more confederates in that pub. My left arm was not up to punching my way out of the bar and that Walther suddenly became a liability. If I didn't draw it, they would find it in a fight. If I did, there were simply too many witnesses to whatever happened next. I backed away a little more, glancing in that big mirror behind the bar to make sure no more East Enders were sneaking up from behind. All were engrossed in their Friday night.

...Except for one woman. I'd seen her before, in another mirror in another bar. Blonde, possibly Nordic, with high cheekbones. Today she wore that same plum coloured beret but a different coat, of wrap-around style. Immediately following eye contact she left the pub, closing the door in a swirl of smoke.

'I'll say goodnight,' I said, touching my hat brim, making more space between Rich and myself. The old soldier eased himself away from the bar, taking a step closer. I put bodies between me and any attack, then a vacant stool, then a whole group of drinkers. Rich and his friends advanced another pace or two, before allowing me to leave. I heard a cheer of derisive laughter.

A cough came the moment I reached the street, but I suppressed the next. The woman had turned left and was already some distance away. She walked with an uneven gait as if she had a lame right leg, so I should be able to catch her with ease. I made to follow at a quick pace, soon closing the distance. She crossed the road, looking right and left and possibly behind her. My pace increased. Death by taxi was coming my way and I dodged back. A bus hid her momentarily behind a blur of red and once it was gone, so was she.

The evening sky ahead was still bright, and I could not see her further along the road. She could not have skipped onto that moving bus and no cars had stopped to pick her up. Beyond a set of closed shops was an arch-roofed alley, possibly an escape route she had planned beforehand. I broke into a jog to reach its end, then edged perhaps ten yards inside. The alley smelt of urine, and fresh cigarette smoke hung in the air. A torn poster advertised a circus. Another promoted a BUF rally and glancing at it almost proved my undoing.

In a rush, she came from an alcove, and pushed a blade against my neck. 'Don't follow me!' She had a soft, almost whispering voice. Harsh tobacco on her breath overwhelmed her perfume. 'You're careless Hugh Clifton.'

'Verity Laytham,' I managed to say, my Adam's apple grating against the blade. 'Just, just move that would you.'

'How's this?'

Her other hand pushed something metallic into my gut and she slowly withdrew the blade. Upright, back against the brickwork, I was transfixed by the pistol she gripped in her left hand.

'You're supposed to be dead.'

'Good. Let's keep it that way—or you're the one who'll be dead, on your own, out here. Find the wrong men and they'll kill you, like they think they killed me.'

'Who are you, really? Did you used to have my job?'

'Well done, detective,' she said. 'Your Commander Calhoun recruited me. Save the country from fascism he said. Get friendly with the Thrings, he said.'

'I guessed as much.'

'So tell me what Union Jack is.'

'A flag.'

'Don't be stupid.' She pressed the gun muzzle harder into my gut, just where the bruise from the riot was still tender.

'Can you take that gun away? I won't hurt you.'

'No, you won't hurt me.' She stepped back two yards deeper into the alley, knife still free in her right hand, gun still threatening in her left. Lunge for the pistol and the knife would be in my ribcage, go for the knife and I'd be shot at a range where it was impossible to miss, even if Verity wasn't the top-notch shot Sissy claimed she was. Relaxing was not an option.

'Last summer I came across a document called Union Jack,' she said. 'Three sections; Red, White and Blue. Endorsement by Mosley, preamble by General Fuller, but that's as far as I read in the moments I had. I developed a contact who could get me a copy, but all he did was set me up for the Blackshirts to kill me, or MI5 or Special Branch or whoever up there in the establishment is in league with the fascists. Calhoun will get you killed too.'

'Why would MI5 want to kill you?'

'You think there are just two sides here, good and evil? Maxwell Knight is a neighbour of your Major Taylor—they were in the British Fascists together. Knight runs M Section, your handler Calhoun works for Knight, and the best dupe they can find to infiltrate the fascists is you.'

The shadowy woman took another step back. 'You think you're the hero, but maybe you're just what American gangsters in the movies call a patsy. So tell me, Hugh Clifton, master spy, what's Union Jack?'

That file note 'UJ' came to mind; it must refer to Union Jack, which meant that Department Z had known that Verity knew about it.

'What's Red, White and Blue?' She asked.

If she was going to shoot, she would have pulled the trigger by now, even if the knife had not already done its work first. By sharing a little, I might survive and even learn something to boot.

'Plan Blue is some kind of economic project; boring things, raising money, making people pay their subscriptions, sorting out the paperwork. It suits Thring, the accountant.'

'So Thring is running Blue, that makes sense. What are White and Red?'

'Are you still working for Calhoun?' *Calhoun did ask if there were any more colours, so he knew about Union Jack too.*

'The woman with the gun and the knife asks the questions. What are White and Red?'

'No idea, I never heard about them until just now, but we could work together–.'

'No we couldn't.' She stepped back another yard, step-step, awkwardly on that injured right leg. 'But I might call on you again and see what you've found out.'

'Like you raided my apartment?'

'You're careless Hugh Clifton, and careless people get killed.'

'Is that a knife wound in your right leg by any chance?'

'Carry on guessing.'

'Last September you were stabbed three times; in your back, in your gut and in your leg. Were you left for dead or rescued at the last minute?'

'You write novels, don't you? Put that in the next one.'

'Somehow you got some poor woman's body from an abortionist, dressed her in your clothes, stabbed her in all the right places, and threw her just far enough into the Thames that she was bound to be found and reported in the newspapers. You included sufficient clues to make whoever ordered you killed think that you were dead, but not enough to encourage the police to investigate more.'

'Or men at the top ordered the police not to investigate more. If you're going to write a thriller, don't forget the twists.'

'What's the Wipers Club?'

'Never heard of it.' She took two steps further down the passageway. 'And for the sake of your health, don't tell anyone you've seen me. I won't play nice next time and you won't even see me coming.' She turned to limp away. 'Good night, Hugh Clifton.'

Chapter Forty-Seven

If Calhoun knew about Union Jack, it was likely that Verity was the one who had told him. No wonder Plan Blue came as no surprise, but how much he knew about Plan Red and Plan White could only be guessed. Julian clearly thought that Verity was dead, as did Department Z and Calhoun wanted everyone to believe it too.

I noticed she talked about 'MI5' like the old hands did, but I had no idea if she'd been one of their trained officers or just an informer as I was supposed to be. Perhaps she had taken that one chance to betray the Blackshirts for money or under some illusion she was helping save the country. Her alleged skill with a pistol and eagerness to use a knife showed Verity was no amateur. If she truly believed MI5 were the ones who ordered her killed, she could be just waiting for her moment to creep up on Calhoun with her blade when he chose a favourite restaurant once too often.

...Or follow his latest agent home. If she knew Calhoun's habits, she could have tailed me from one of our little lunches or walks in the park right back to Havelock Mansions. She wouldn't always advertise herself with that beret.

On my way to meet Hanrahan, I took care there was no woman lurking in the shadows by Havelock Mansions and changed the rendezvous away from the first Victoria pub he proposed to another in South Kensington. I wouldn't mention Verity to the Irishman, and indeed her name might mean nothing to him, but it felt wise to keep secret anything that did not need to be shared. Within this caveat, some facts needed to be aired.

'My contact in the army knows nothing about this Wipers Club,' I said.

'It might be the place we need to find, or the group we need to find. Or it might just be a worthless bit of tittle-tattle.'

Hanrahan nodded slowly at the name. 'It's not worthless, I've heard it too,' he said.

'Where? You never told me.'

He inclined his head. 'It came up once before...one of those late-night conversations in someplace like this, you know, when I was asking here and there. I didn't think it had any relevance.'

Certainly, Hanrahan had caveats too.

'So is it a place or a group? My contact is checking old soldiers' clubs.'

Hanrahan fiddled with his cigarette packet, turning it one end on the other on the table. 'How about both a place and a group. A place old soldiers can go, but where they are screened and selected. Or a place the cell can meet openly without it looking suspicious.'

'But only one cell? Even if we find this club, we can't crack the whole organization.'

'Let's find it, then we'll see.'

'I'm meeting a top man in the British Legion on Thursday. If we get a lead by the weekend–'

'–that's when we go and have a look. If it's a real club, it should be busy.'

'Are you seeing Calhoun before then?'

'No, let's find your club before we get him excited. And if there's trouble, you can call your Blackshirt pals to smash the place up. That will make their weekend.'

* * *

In the back seat of a black Wolseley, two men sat in conversation whilst the police driver took a cup of tea in the café close by. Rain drummed on the roof and the windows quickly misted.

'So how is trade at Charles Street?' Inspector Renton asked.

'Brisk,' said Calhoun. 'Now Baldwin's called the election we're going to have a busy three weeks.'

'Are any more mutinies planned by your naval comrades?'

'I hope not. It's fitting they chose Trafalgar Day to call it off.'

'That's Mr Churchill, isn't it? Flying down there and making his appeal to patriotism.'

'Making his appeal for votes more like. Naval scuttlebutt runs that the mutineers had this date in mind all along; have the mutiny last exactly one week, ending on Trafalgar Day to make their point. Baldwin wouldn't have gone for the election with a mutiny hanging over his head. There will be some kind of deal to save face all round, but Baldwin has been torpedoed.'

'But there have to be court martials? They can't get away with it.'

'Mutiny is mutiny, but like all mutinies the sailors have a point.'

Renton huffed as if he'd have the whole lot hanged. 'But can I take it there will be no more trouble in naval bases for the time being? I can cross that worry off my growing list?'

'Yes, cross it off.'

'How about the communists, what are they planning for the next three weeks – more bombs and shootings?'

'We've had no hint of what they're planning or who is behind it, beyond a sort of Moriarty figure who pops up here and there whenever there's trouble. His last game was disrupting the Blackshirts' Peace Parade.'

Renton was unimpressed. 'I don't like the idea of a single criminal mastermind behind it all. And if there is, he's not going to come out into the daylight. We wouldn't see him once, let alone popping up here and there.'

'Perhaps not.' Calhoun tipped his head. 'But you've had a good run of success in the north, I hear.'

'We've got about a quarter of the Cornish explosives back and a few firearms. Every result was through a tip-off though, not one was due to local police work. We've made no significant arrests and had nothing more from you boys to guide us.'

'Yet,' said Calhoun.

'Bide your time, do. And if you've nothing to offer me on the left, do we need to worry about the right?'

'No, they're the usual shambles. In-fighting, chest-thumping...'

'Shambles? Have you heard of Plan White?' Renton asked.

After a moment Calhoun admitted that he had but could hardly admit to being ignorant of its contents. 'How does Plan White fit into the picture?'

'I'll tell if you tell.' Renton saw straight through the bluff. 'If you know of it, you must have a man inside the fascists.'

'By the same argument, if you know about Plan White, that means you have also someone on the inside. So what is it?'

'You first.'

Squeakily, Calhoun cleared a circular patch on the misted window beside him with a fingertip. 'It's not just White. An accountant called Howard Thring has written a thing called Plan Blue which sorts out the financial and organizational mess the BUF have got themselves into.'

'So no longer the usual shambles?'

'Perhaps not. Your turn.'

'As it happens, I read Plan White at the weekend. It's going to change the rules of the game.'

* * *

Major Taylor called Department Z together, and the dozen or so attendees just about filled the small meeting room. 'As of oh seven hundred this morning, Plan White is in operation,' he announced.

My heart raced and my mind along with it. Plan White was no longer secret; surely that meant that the BUF was going into action. I'd need to inform Calhoun as soon as possible and work out how to disrupt the plan.

Taylor opened a foolscap envelope with a flourish, taking out a sheet of paper, and started reading aloud. 'The Leader has decided, in consultation with the Research Committee, that the Party is identified too closely with Italy and as a party of British patriots this cannot continue.'

Julian shot a glance my way. Everyone fidgeted, and the murmuring continued as Taylor read out order after order. 'Quiet!' he growled.

Plan White unfurled in less than a page of notes. The party would be re-named The British Union of Fascists and National Socialists, British Union for short, ending once and for all the idea it was a puppet of Mussolini.

'What?' Parker had been sitting stone-faced and cross-armed until this point.

'Listen carefully, Captain Parker. This is for the good of the Party.'

'But *socialists?*'

'Hitler's a National Socialist,' Lucy added helpfully.

'Quiet, please. We have a lot to consider here.'

The Party would be patriotic (National) and for all the people (Socialist, without actually being socialists). The British Union would drop the Roman *fasces* symbol immediately, and in its place would be a standard of red, white and blue. Taylor passed around an image of the new flag drawn hastily in crayon. A white lightning strike within a blue disc stood for action, and the white circle around it represented industry. With its red ground, the flag did not look so different from the swastika flag used by the Nazis, which might be the point.

At least it meant that the 'red, white and blue' line in my *Fascist Marching Song* now worked, although I'd need to change the title. As Taylor continued to drone the dull facts of the re-organization, I knew that dropping the word 'fascist' might prove to be the sharpest move Mosley had made since adopting it. It made sense if the British Union were ever to win power. Plan White had Thring's dry, practical fingerprints all over it, and General Fuller's military eye for victory as its foundation.

Candidates in the upcoming election would campaign in suits, but black shirts with collar and tie may be worn underneath. We would not be parading in uniform.

'No uniforms?' It was my turn to make a token protest. I'd just bought a new shirt to replace the one ripped in the ambush and paid to re-equip three men who had helped me that day.

'If there's war with Italy, we can't be the Blackshirts. That's the order from the very top. If people think we're on Mussolini's side nobody will vote for us.'

The British Union needed support from women and needed to regain the trust of the Middle Class, so public brawling must be curbed, 'unless the Reds start it.'

'They always do,' snarled Parker.

'The Defence Squad is confined to barracks when not stewarding meetings. I Squad will cease active operations. And sorry, Parker, that means the Action Squad too.'

'What shit!'

'That's the order, Parker; like it or get out.'

Parker folded his arms over his black shirt, which also looked newly purchased.

Taylor's words fell like lead filling the souls of the other men and the lone woman in the room. 'It doesn't change what we think, or what we believe, just what we look like. And the Jewish Problem will not be a campaign issue, except in the East End of London. The time's not right. Any more questions?'

Nobody had the heart to ask any, so the meeting was closed. 'My office, Clifton,' Taylor said.

I followed Taylor upstairs then stood at ease in the Major's office whilst he sat down and read through a note. 'I heard about your unauthorized interrogations.'

'Yes sir. Sorry but there was nobody here to authorize it. I had to use my initiative.'

'It was a good move, wish I'd been here myself. What did you find out?'

'A few names, but not much more than that. I'm trying to find out more about them.'

'Excellent, make up a file won't you?'

'Certainly.'

'But, ah. Don't write anything about the business downstairs.'

'Certainly not.'

'Things like that are not for the file. Have you got anywhere with the investigation on the Kahn robbery?'

'I've been keeping an eye on his ships as they come in, as we discussed. Two have come and gone without mishap and the third is due.'

'Good man. Once this election's out of the way, we're going to expand

Department Z. I'm thinking of making your investigation team into a section of its own. Could you handle that?'

'I can sir.' Indeed, it had formed a specific recommendation in the paper I'd written. Taylor had adopted my idea as one of his own and I was not going to argue over the credit. I left Black House pleased with my morning. Plan White had been revealed and Plan Blue as I understood it had pretty much run its course. Neither were worth anyone killing Verity to protect, which just left Plan Red. Nobody was talking about Plan Red.

Chapter Forty-Eight

Stephen Wain was a retired Lieutenant-Colonel heavily involved in British Legion activities for London. Back in the early summer I had attended my first trustees meeting of the Woolwich hospital and voted to have one of its wings redecorated, adding the suggestion that the existing mint green was rather septic. My role at the hospital helped secure the introduction to Wain.

Both Wain and Viscount Wickersley were members of the Army and Navy Club in Pall Mall, and a hurried change out of my black uniform and into smart attire allowed me to join them for luncheon. The viscount soon excused himself, citing pressing matters, leaving Wain clearly wrong-footed. I'd only met him on a couple of occasions when seeking the address of this man or that, so we'd established no particular bond before now.

Wain chatted about the recent visit to Germany by Legion representatives, and the return trip by old soldiers of the *Frontkampferbund.* 'United by our common experience,' he said. The British delegation had reputedly met Hitler.

'I'm looking for a place called the Wipers Club,' I said. 'Do you know where it is?'

'Wipers Club? I've never heard of it,' he said. 'Is it new?'

'It could be.'

'Well, most of the clubs were set up straight after the War, or in the early twenties once all the men were back. The War didn't just end on eleventh day of the eleventh month like every schoolboy is taught. It dragged on for us—we were in Iraq until twenty-one and there were chaps stuck in Russia beyond that.'

'I've come across a number of sporting clubs and social clubs; does the Legion support them?'

'We have our own clubs, but members might of course join whatever other outfit they like. Every now and again we get asked for money to support one which has fallen on hard times. Old soldiers are quickly forgotten and there are so many without work some local clubs can't keep going.'

'But no Wipers Club?'

'Who would want to remember Wipers? I wasn't there but Ypres was a shocking show. Not many men walked away from that one.'

'So the name could be ironic, mocking the misery and futility of war.'

'I say, what?'

'Formed by people who hated the war and everything it stood for.'

'Like who? Pacifists? Defeatists? Communists?'

'Or all three. Have you had any requests to support any new London-based old soldiers' club or association in, say, the last year?'

'One comes to mind, but it wasn't called the Wipers Club.'

'Can you remember its name?'

'Ah, the East London Sporting...no, Sportsmen's Club. Not sure we could help in their case. Why the interest, may I ask? More spare beds going at your hospital?'

'Indeed, old soldiers die as well as fade away. I need to reach out into corners of the capital that might not know that we're there for the old boys. Could you find me the address of this club?'

'Yes, I suppose I could ask one of the office ladies to search the correspondence when I go in next week.'

I glanced at my watch. 'Could we go this afternoon?'

'You're in a dashed hurry, young man.'

'I do have some rather urgent business with that particular club.'

'You have...' Wain paused, sensing perhaps that he was being asked to play a small part in a wider game. '...an urgent need to fill a bed?'

I smiled.

He looked first puzzled, then amused. 'Wickersley does mix with some interesting fellows these days. Then with elections and mutinies and God knows what else happening on our streets...'

Saying nothing at the right time can have the impact of a speech.

'I say, come down after lunch tomorrow. I'll have the ladies hunt through the letters first thing, and we should have something for you by the afternoon.'

Friday evening would be an ideal time to pay the Wipers Club a call.

Chapter Forty-Nine

The East London Sportsman's Club appeared to be nothing more than a basement and ground floor of an end-of terrace house where old soldiers could meet up. Across the road, we sat watching and waiting in the Alvis.

'It doesn't have a licence,' Hanrahan said. 'And it isn't called the Wipers Club.'

'I think it's an ironic nickname.'

Night had fallen and only two men had entered the club so far. The second looked like Billy Rich.

'You need to replace this motor with something in black,' Hanrahan said. 'Something modest that stands out less.'

'I'm mixing with the aristocracy. Even my Alvis looks plebeian compared to the Rolls Royces.'

I had asked Hanrahan not to smoke in the car for the same reason I'd once fretted about carrying my aunt's wet dog. The smell would penetrate the upholstery and hang there. And as for powder blue, one can be too inconspicuous.

'That cough of yours is fecking annoying.'

'Sorry, did I cough?'

'All the time.'

'Nerves, sorry. Is fecking a real word?'

'I make it a real word. Look at him, wouldn't you?'

A man was walking down the pavement on the opposite side. Caught in a streetlight he seemed to be rather short, stooping or holding his head down deliberately. He wore a wide, flapping raincoat of American cut and his hat also had that smart States-side look. He crossed the side street beside the club and came to a door in the gable end. He paused as a lone woman walked slowly past, then rapped once, twice, three times. It opened sharply.

'Recognize him?' Hanrahan clearly did not.

'Raincoat Man. I'd need to see his face to be sure, but everything fits if he turns up here. I think he let me see him deliberately during the Peace Parade. He knew I'd chase him into that building site, and he was waiting.'

'He could easily have killed you.'

'Maim me must have been the plan – scare me off without all the fuss of a murder investigation.'

'And without putting your pretty face all over the newspapers again, a fascist martyr to those nasty communists.'

'We're not fascists anymore. We're national socialists.'

'For sure that makes all the difference.'

After only two or three minutes the man came back out, then walked briskly back the way he had come.

'We should follow him,' I said, putting a hand on the door handle.

'He's gone already. Where the Jesus did he go?'

Raincoat Man was indeed gone.

'Damn, he's got a habit of vanishing like that. With luck, he'll be back.'

For a club, it was not proving popular. Hanrahan offered me a flask, but I produced my own and we clinked them together and took a drink against the night.

A sharp rap on the window made me jolt my flask mid-sip.

'You two bastards hold as still as still can be.' His voice carried through the glass, as would the bullet from that muzzle he pressed against it. Nothing is more terrifying than having a gun pointed at you at close range. Hanrahan would die first, then I would have only a heartbeat to live. The man may have been short, but he was broad. His face remained invisible in the shadow of his hat and was half-covered by a scarf pulled over his nose and mouth. He held his gun as if it came naturally and he would shoot without hesitation. One side-step took him beside the front wheel, allowing himself more space in case Harahan suddenly opened the door.

'Out, this side, both of you.'

Hanrahan complied slowly. 'Just do as he says, pal.'

It was up to me to make a move. At best my chance was one in two, which were terribly long odds with my life at stake. Raincoat Man would fire before I even had the Walther out of its holster. Reaching for my whistle would be even more suicidal. Even though Julian and his squad were sitting in a furniture van two streets away they may as well be on the moon. I had to comply. Raincoat Man wouldn't want to fire—not out in the street at least. He too would be gambling with his life. Automatics have a habit of jamming and even dying men can shoot back.

Hanrahan eased slowly out onto the pavement with his hands half-raised. I crawled across and copied him, hoping the wily Irishman had an idea better than this. Was there nobody watching who could reach a telephone and call the police? So much for always having a plan.

'Hands down, don't make a pantomime of it,' Raincoat Man growled. There was a tint of the colonial in his accent. 'Over there, now, as you're so interested in our club.' The barrel twitched to indicate the side door. It opened just as we reached it.

Urged down a half-flight of stairs we came to another open door, where a man stood ready with a rifle. It was Charlie Watkins. A rifle was not the best weapon for fighting in an enclosed space, but it would be a terrible risk to assume it would miss. He stepped aside so we could enter the room beyond. The floor was of bare boards, the walls undecorated and the only furnishing was a trio of benches, a couple of chairs, and a table. A window screened by thick curtains must open onto a light well. I'd been to better clubs.

Billy Rich was waiting for us with another rifle at the ready. 'You again,' he said. 'Captain fucking Smythe.'

Raincoat Man glanced at me and gave a laugh. 'Promoted are we?'

Watkins patted our pockets and removed first Hanrahan's pistol, then my Walther.

'Sit over there,' said Raincoat Man, still holding his own pistol with intent.

The two riflemen edged back and kept their fingers on the triggers of their weapons, held at the hip but ready to shoot. Both Watkins and Rich were veterans of the Great War and would know how to use a Lee Enfield. Raincoat Man did not recruit novices.

I sat on the bench in front of the window and Hanrahan joined me on my right.

'I've stalked lion, tiger, jaguar. You two were easy meat.' His hair was blonde, his blue eyes deeply sunken and lined by creases, but his accent was hard to pin down and muffled by that scarf.

I was tempted to blurt out the name I'd guessed, but that could be enough to see us both killed. Let him think he was nothing more to us than a bogeyman with a set of nicknames.

'Tie their hands.'

'Wiv what?' Watkins asked in his strong cockney accent.

'Your ties. Tie them with your ties.'

'I've just bought this,' Rich grumbled.

For a moment I hoped the squabble would be resolved by them coming over to take our ties to use. It would bring them nice and close and their bodies could be used as shields, but Raincoat Man knew that too. Watkins bound Hanrahan's wrists with his own plain brown woollen tie whilst Rich remained ready, then Rich bound mine with a military-looking tie in red and blue stripes. 'I want that back,' he said. 'Don't bleed on it or snot on it.'

Once satisfied, Raincoat Man nodded his pistol barrel in my direction. 'This, gentlemen, is former Lieutenant Hugh Clifton.'

'He told me he was called Captain Smythe,' Rich said. 'I never believed him even then.'

'No, he's a front-page Blackshirt hero. And armed with a Walther PP straight from Nazi Germany. How appropriate.' His own pistol barrel drifted to point at Hanrahan in turn. 'But who are you, with your Tokarev TT-thirty?'

'Thirty-three,' corrected Hanrahan.

'Oh, sorry, Professor. Or is it comrade? You can't buy the latest Russian automatic on any street corner.' He took it from the table and slid it into the pocket of his raincoat, making it a partner for the similar weapon he was already holding. 'Who are you two clowns working for—the communists or the Blackshirts?'

'There was a village bus, in Ireland, County Armagh,' Hanrahan began. 'Gunmen stopped it one evening and ordered everyone off. Protestants to one side of the road, Catholics to the other. If you were on that bus, and you never went to church, which side of the road would you choose?'

'If you believe that giving the right answer means I'll give you a big hug, and if you're wrong I'll shoot you, you're mistaken. I may just shoot you anyway. Rip out your toenails first and cut your bollocks off for good measure. I could keep you alive for days.' He paused and looked from me to the Irishman, weighing our souls.

Raincoat Man had not removed his scarf; if he intended to kill us he wouldn't worry about exposing his face. This was a terrace of thin-walled houses and those Lee-Enfields would make one hell of a noise in that cellar. So much gave me comfort. His mention in the files back at Black House suggested where his allegiance lay.

'Department Z,' I blurted. 'British Union of Fascists and National Socialists.'

'Oh, well, in that case, there won't be any balls to cut off. You're useless wankers, P.G. Taylor and the whole lot of you. Is he a Blackshirt wanker too?'

'He's a friend of mine, sort of my bodyguard.'

'You're a bloody useless bodyguard, mate.' He spoke directly to Hanrahan. 'Is he telling the truth?'

'He pays me two pounds a day.'

'You can get a whore for less than that, Mr Department Z Clifton.' Raincoat Man stepped back.

'He'll pay you a lot more just to let us go,' Hanrahan said. 'He's loaded.'

'I don't need his money.'

'There are forty Blackshirts sealing off the streets,' I said. 'As soon as they miss us, they'll be here.' I stretched the truth a little, but if Raincoat Man had been the ringmaster watching the battle of the Royal Oak he might believe this. 'You need to let us go.'

'Watch them; shoot them if they move,' he said suddenly. 'Don't wake the neighbours unless you have to and don't listen to any rubbish they come out with, like offering you money for their sad little lives. I'll fetch the van and see if he's lying about those Blackshirts.'

Raincoat Man clattered up the side stairs. Watkins sat down with a grunt on one of the chairs, perhaps ten feet away, his rifle pointing loosely at me. Rich stood further back, with his barrel relaxed and aiming at the floor. A chance might come, and I tensed ready to act in case Hanrahan suddenly took the lead.

'Why do you call this the Wipers Club?' I asked.

Billy Rich took a moment before deciding to reply. 'It's a joke,' he said. 'Because there's not many of us left. Ordered over the top by you lot. Toffs, officers, Tories. I lost every single mate that joined up with me. Every one of 'em.'

'And tossed on the scrap heap when we got back,' said Charlie Watkins, the man who had shat on the King.

A knock echoed down from the side door, a sharp rap one-two-three. It was a simple signal, but effective. Surely it was too soon for the gloating Raincoat Man to be back with his van, unless he had a further monologue of vitriol to deliver. Rich left the room and his footsteps sounded on the stairs. There was a muffled grunt, more footsteps on the stairs, then another Tokorov pistol came into view, jammed hard into the neck of Billy Rich. His rifle dangled uselessly from his left hand. As Watkins twitched in his chair, a woman's voice commanded, 'Sit!'

Nobody moved, but that rifle barrel was still dangerously close to aiming at me.

'Be calm, gentlemen,' she said. I recognized her clear, accent-free voice, but only risked a blink in her direction. Verity spoke straight into the ear of Billy Rich. 'You, comrade are going to drop that rifle. Don't jump at the noise, boys.'

Billy Rich let his rifle thump onto the old carpet.

'I'll shoot him,' said Watkins, his eyes not leaving mine.

'I'll blow your friend's head off and yours before you've even pulled that trigger.'

Rich was unarmed now – she'd choose to shoot Watkins first. I was closest to Rich and made ready to dive for him with a shoulder if he tried to pull away from Verity.

'Play things properly and nobody is going to get shot,' Verity said. 'We're coming into the room. Nobody else move.'

Rich came first, making small shuffling steps, a gun to his head. Verity followed, keeping the gun touching his neck but allowing herself a little more space and a free hand to go for her knife if she needed it. Rich now formed a shield between her and Watkins' rifle.

'Now, Clifton. You first. Slip behind me and get out of here—the door's open.'

I gingerly rose, wary of that rifle barrel still pointed my way. Maybe it would only take off one of my knees. I coughed and everyone flinched.

'Steady!' Verity cautioned. 'Once both my comrades are out, I'm leaving you both here, unharmed. Don't follow us, there's no need for anyone to die.'

'My pistol,' I hissed.

'Just get out.' She snatched the Walther from the table, arming herself twice over. I barely made the stairs before Hanrahan bumped into my back. 'Out!' he urged.

Verity soon followed us into the side street. She kept the door partly open, the Tokarev pointed down the stair. 'Back inside, idiot!' she shouted into the darkness.

'Georgie!' Hanrahan held out his bound hands. 'Great job, perfect timing.'

'You would both have been dead men without me.' She pocketed the Walther and with her left hand took out a familiar flick knife. Awkwardly she sawed at Hanrahan's bonds, then he, in turn, freed me.

'Get to your car and start the engine,' she ordered.

I ran to the Alvis as the man-and-woman team held the doorway. They were a team, clearly. I no longer had to wonder who had saved her from death and concealed her resurrection. Once the motor was running, I pulled around in a half-circle and pushed open the passenger door. Verity passed my Walther to Harahan and darted for the car in an awkward half-run, diving into the front seat and scrambling over into the back. Hanrahan followed a moment later and no rifle shot chased him. I accelerated the Alvis into the night.

'Always have a guardian angel,' Hanrahan said.

'You're working together?'

'We're all working together,' said the voice from the back. 'Where are your Blackshirts?'

'Two streets the other way. I never got a chance to blow my whistle, and I can't send them in against rifles. We need to reach a phone and contact Calhoun. Get MI5 to raid that place before they clear out.'

'We *are* MI5,' Hanrahan said wearily. 'Calhoun doesn't have any stormtroopers. Special Branch kick in the doors.'

'Well, Calhoun will have to ring them, then.'

'Don't mention me, I'm dead,' said Verity. 'You two men can invent some heroic way you got out of that jam.'

'Best not even mention the jam,' Hanrahan added. 'Just that we've found the terrorist cell.'

I spotted a phone box, pulled up beside it, and spoke briefly to the Security Service switchboard operator. After a long two minutes' wait, Calhoun came on the phone. I was ordered to return to my flat and stand by. Verity must have walked away whilst I was in the phone box.

'Well, she's a box of surprises,' I said.

'A wonderful woman, all round,' Hanrahan said. 'You might want this back.' He handed over my Walther.

'So, you…and Verity?'

'She's not called Verity, she's called Georgina at the moment, and no, we're not dot-dot-dot.'

'Are you the one who saved her? When they tried to have her killed?'

'Oh, I'm a regular knight errant. There's a story, but I'm not going to tell you.'

'One day?'

'Not even one day.'

'Tell me at least who attacked her.'

'The man she was going to meet was a Blackshirt, nobody important, some clerk who's not been seen again. The other two…well. I'm not sure any of them are still alive to tell the tale.'

Chapter Fifty

Calhoun insisted on seeing me the next morning in Hyde Park. I made sure I took my pistol, concealed by the new swish black leather coat. After what I'd learned from so-called Verity, I was trusting nobody, although sowing discord may have been her intent. Hanrahan was certainly playing a deeper game, but he was the veteran and I still had much to learn. Failing to learn could see the lessons ending abruptly.

Some left-wing rally was being held at Hyde Park Corner, and men were lugging red banners towards it.

'Not your usual quiet spot,' I observed.

'Not your usual fashion.' Calhoun frowned critically at the leather coat. 'We're here because in ten minutes or so I want to hear what Mr Attlee has to say. He's only led Labour for a fortnight, and it will be interesting to see how he plays the Mutiny. Let's walk that way, and you can explain what happened last night.'

I re-told the story rehearsed with Hanrahan. 'They call it the Wipers Club, so far as we can tell. Ex-soldiers with leftist sympathies. Hanrahan claims not to know who's controlling them.'

'Claims? You mean you don't believe every word that comrade Hanrahan says?'

No answer was needed.

'About this Wipers Club?' He asked.

'Well the person I've called Raincoat Man and I Squad called Monkey Man is one and the same, and that club is where he recruits. We saw him arrive, we saw him leave. There was a side way in, so we went to have a look, got into a scuffle with two chaps; Billy Rich and Charlie Watkins, I'd seen them before. They were careless, long in the tooth. I laid one out with a good old sock to the jaw, Hanrahan wrestled the other to the ground and then we legged it.'

'That's was Hanrahan's story too, word perfect. Did he mention he'd dropped his gun?'

'Yes, I ribbed him about it.'

'This isn't a public-school jape. And you missed out on the point-blank executions.'

'The what?'

'Special Branch went straight to the address you gave. They found four rifles, Lee Enfield, some ammunition, money...it looks like you're right about finding our assassins' ring. But dead assassins. There were two of them, shot in the head, then through the heart. Or the other way around as if it makes a difference. Your Watkins and Rich, it appears.'

My warm satisfaction that I had escaped both the cellar and exposure of my ineptitude evaporated. I was stumped for words.

'I was hoping you could revise your story to explain what happened.'

'We heard no shots.'

'The police also found a Tokarev automatic pistol that was still warm, with four rounds missing from its clip. Hanrahan was issued with a Tokarev, so if he was ever caught we had the option to blame the Russians for whatever he'd been up to. Do I have to blame this on the Russians?'

'Does that mean you're going to issue me with a Luger, so if I cock up you can blame it on the Germans?'

'Don't try to be witty.' Calhoun rapped a knuckle against the spot on my leather coat that should have concealed the Walther. 'What's that, if not a Luger?'

'Walther.'

'Be careful Clifton. You got away with shooting one man in hot blood but it's not open season. We're keeping last night between Special Branch and ourselves until we have a straight narrative. The last thing we want is the press blaming the deaths of two ex-servicemen on foreign agents or over-zealous police officers. Or a bloody Department Z death squad. The last thing you and Hanrahan want is to be arrested for murder.'

Facts needed to be knitted into hypothesis, and quickly. 'Suppose Raincoat Man came back, found we'd got the jump on his squaddies and didn't see the funny side. We know he's happy to murder his comrades when he thinks he's been compromised, and he did use a Tokarev to shoot Dick Dennis.'

'That's plausible. And you'd have a good defence in court if you could identify this man and give him a name. Could you?'

The truth had to be strained a little more, but who these lies protected was open to question. 'He was short, wore an American style raincoat and hat and a scarf across his face. We've picked up a few other clues here and there. He's some sort of adventurer, a mercenary, or a big game hunter. A South African, Australian, or an American. He's got a vicious streak if he can so easily shoot men who thought he was on their side.'

Raincoat Man had not been the only person with a vicious streak that night, but Verity could not be mentioned. She had walked away carrying her own Tokarev pistol when I'd been in that phone box. Goodness knows what she had done next.

'You're certain this is the same man who shot at you in Kensington all those weeks ago?'

'It's a fair bet. And he's the one who lured me into not one but two ambushes and dropped that dynamite at I Squad's feet.' I had an idea of who the man might be, but not what was driving his campaign of mayhem. 'He's not one of yours, is he? If Mosley is a problem, paying a bunch of disgruntled ex-soldiers to shoot him would clear your desk a little.'

'For goodness sake, Clifton! Who do you think we are? This isn't Germany – we're not allowed to go around shooting people no matter how much they might deserve it.'

By now we had reached the edge of the throng. Clement Attlee had already started speaking, his every pause greeted with a cheer. He was no Mosley, but he had no need of a phalanx of black-clad troops to guard him either. Union banners and the flags of affiliated groups waved, and the working people of London cheered for Labour.

Calhoun stood well back, perhaps looking for men he had placed in the crowd, infiltrating the Labour movement as Hanrahan had the communists. Indeed, Hanrahan was there, in familiar flat cap and rust-red tie. He ignored us and we ignored him. Fascists in civilian clothes should be here too, mingling with the masses, watching and learning.

'We need to split up now. Usual report to Mrs Ainsworth tomorrow. The fourth of Kahn's ships, the *Pavel Denisovich* is due at Southall Docks on Friday the first, so you need to meet it. You know the form by now,' Calhoun said. 'I say what's happening over there?'

A group on the edge of the rally were no supporters of Attlee. He'd said something about building peace instead of re-arming, and persuading Herr Hitler to do the same. 'Heil Hitler!' a woman shouted, then another. A handful of people wearing quality coats made the fascist salute towards the podium. Foolish did not even begin to describe it. A ripple of anger flashed around the audience, then socialists surged towards their enemy.

'Good lord, that's Diana Guinness!' Calhoun said. 'They'll kill her.'

I was away in an instant, running around the edge of the crowd as they swarmed close to Diana and her companions. The socialists stopped short, barely a punch away from the Leader's mistress and began to hurl abuse. I pushed through to her. 'I'm a friend, Lady Diana.'

Spinning around to block the way, I stretched out my hands as Canute attempting to stop the tide. 'Hold, hold!' That flapping black coat must have lent me a veneer of authority as no one came any closer. 'Ma'am you need to leave here now.'

More allies were concealed in the crowd than I dared wish for, and yet more lurked close by Marble Arch hoping to cause trouble as the socialists dispersed, so I was quickly backed up by a dozen men. Slowly we gave ground, facing insults but no physical violence. The men and women screaming at me were unarmed ordinary Labour voters or we would have been overwhelmed. Militants had not yet had time to concentrate and to flood in to attack. Diana and her friends hurried away, and the undercover fascists formed a screen beside me until she had escaped in a taxi. The rear guard fought a few scuffles before our opponents returned to the park, cheering a victory.

Diana did send a very nice note of thanks.

Chapter Fifty-One

Britain's left-leaning newspapers saw straight through Plan White, but the conservative press welcomed this sudden lurch towards respectability. Mosley would stand as the British Union candidate for Evesham, south of Birmingham, and by some back-room chicanery, a strong Conservative candidate was nudged into choosing an adjacent constituency and replaced by a sacrificial goat to be devoured by the Leader.

Black uniforms may have been discretely hidden away, the name, the flag, and the creed changed, but across the country violence between left and right intensified as the election approached. I made sure I did not volunteer for any more rescue missions for the British Union, or to steward any campaign meetings. I was not risking being crippled for the benefit of Mosley's election chances, let alone have my new coat ripped. Based on the form in the 1931 election, the Party was in for a drubbing, no matter how it was wrapped up. Defeat could see it simply fall apart and that would be the end of British fascism and the end of my mission.

With all that was happening, I barely needed the distraction of an invitation to a reception at the German Embassy, but then again, I needed the distraction. I had enlisted in this spy rigmarole almost as a lark, for something to do. Claptrap about king and empire and patriotism only provided the excuse, but visions of embassy parties and beautiful women on my arm had drawn me out of lethargy and self-pity. The invitation came as a surprise, but now I was at an embassy party with a beautiful woman on my arm. Sissy was wearing the same deep blue crepe evening gown with the Chinese style buckle as on the night we had first met.

A slight man in an excellently tailored evening suit greeted us.

'Bruno!' Sissy exclaimed. 'I never knew you were in London.'

'Sissy, so glad you could make it.' Our invitation was perhaps explained. Bruno kissed Sissy's hand. 'Hugh.' He gave a polite continental bow of the head and we shook hands.

'Welcome to London, Bruno. What brings you here?'

'I've been attached to the embassy staff.' He beamed with what must be pride. 'Remember, when we met, I was waiting for a new post?'

So he is a spy was my immediate thought. 'In what capacity?' I asked innocently.

'Cultural liaison. And the Anglo-German Fellowship is just the start, Von Ribbentrop is going to establish a sister organization in Germany. We'll have cultural exchanges, meetings between your industrialists and ours... And plenty of dinners.'

'How marvellous,' Sissy said.

The Germans were out to impress, and the embassy ballroom was fairly packed with people. Over on one wall was a head-and-shoulders painting of Adolf Hitler, given the prominence a British embassy would only afford to a king or queen. I had contrived to arrive late to be less conspicuous and forced to make small talk with little idea why we were there. British Union officials were still under a directive not to fraternise openly with Nazis. It created the wrong impression.

'Oh God,' I exclaimed.

Bruno followed my gaze. A short, wide-shouldered man appeared to have been squeezed into someone else's evening jacket and his blond hair was barely tamed by brush or Brylcreem. He was almost overtopped by the blonde woman in the soft pink dress who stood with her back to us.

'Who's he?'

'Let me introduce you,' Bruno said and ushered us towards the short man and his companion.

'Double God.'

The companion turned and was revealed to be Leonora. 'Hugh, my, I didn't expect to see you here.' She flicked her eyes towards Sissy. 'And with a charming young friend.'

'Sissy, may I introduce Leonora.'

'His wife,' she said, tilting her head to one side.

'Charmed,' said Sissy, both hands now gripping her wineglass in the manner I'd taught her to grip a pistol.

'Ach, this is awkward,' Bruno said. 'I didn't realise. Hugh, do you know Sir Jeremiah Baxter? One of your great explorers.'

Thickset, with wild sun-bleached hair, Baxter hesitated then held out a hand to shake. His bright blue eyes were deeply sunken, and his weather-beaten and creased skin made his true age hard to judge. For some reason, perhaps an old back injury, he did not stand perfectly upright. Unmasked, he looked little like a monkey at all.

Baxter smiled. 'No, we haven't met. Everyone knows me as Jeb—they'll only get away with calling me Jeremiah at my funeral.'

So that was the game. 'Hugh Clifton.'

'You may have read about Hugh's exploits in the newspaper,' Bruno said. 'He's a leading Blackshirt, fighting communist fire with fire.'

'Yeah, Blackshirts. Men of action.' His drawl was slow and not quite British. 'I think I recall reading something about you in the papers, Mr Clifton.' One could easily imagine he was American. A lifetime travelling the world and surviving in dozens of languages, had obliterated his original accent allowing Baxter to adopt any he chose.

'You don't share our politics?' Dry mouthed, I joined the game.

'No, no, I'm not political. Barely in England most of the time. Don't care which set of rascals ruins the country.'

Leonora intervened, 'Jeb is a famous explorer, he's been all over the world. Quite a career.'

'Yes, I also recall reading a thing or two about you in the papers, Mr Baxter,' I said.

'Nothing true I hope.' Baxter looked unsettled, as if this meeting was not part of his plan either.

'So are you in London long?' I asked, far too bluntly for polite society.

'Only so long as I need to be.'

With the skill of the diplomat, or the instincts of a spy, Bruno sensed the tension. 'Jeb, you wanted to meet…' he began.

'Oh yes, yes,' said Baxter. 'Good to meet you…Clifton. I'll keep an eye on your career from now on. You're clearly a man to watch.'

As Sissy had contrived to slip away from any embarrassment, only Leonora remained. 'She's young,' was her first comment.

'I'm fine, thanks for asking,' I said. 'Recovering nicely.' I brushed my right chest.

'Ah, the wound,' she said, tilting her head to one side.

'Sorry I didn't die, dashed ungallant of me.'

'Oh stop it! You're clearly better, and you're finally…finally moving up. She's an heiress, isn't she?'

'I've never asked.'

'Oh rot, she's Baroness Rockwell's only child, everyone knows that. You know how to pick them, you're just like bloody Mosley.'

'From that barb, I gather you're not a supporter of our party.'

She screwed up her face in disgust. 'Certainly not! Is your pretty little thing a *party girl*?'

'Indeed she is.'

'Jeb's got nothing on you. You're quite the social mountain-climber.'

'Pit village boy made good. How is the impoverished landed gentry?'

Her face twitched in the way it did when she became angry. 'I'm at the same reception as you are. With your Nazi friends.'

'And Jeb Baxter.'

'Ah, a man amongst men. Our conversation was just getting started when you turned up.'

'You didn't come at his invitation?'

'No, would that make you jealous?'

'I just wondered why you're here if you're looking down your nose at Mosley and the Nazis? Who invited you?'

She gave a little laugh. 'Aha, that's a little mystery. When I saw you, I thought this was some practical joke of yours, rubbing my nose in it with *her*.'

My blood ran cold. Some puppet-master had brought together a most unlikely group of people in a way that defied coincidence. It was a warning—a demonstration of how powerless little people are when the fate of nations is at stake.

'I know hardly anybody here,' she said. 'Anglo German Fellowship, indeed. My brother would turn in his grave.'

'I think the whole point is to keep people's brothers out of graves. This is about peace.' As I spoke the words, I began to doubt them.

Leonora looked about herself, lost. 'I had a chaperone and he's vanished. He's something in the Foreign Office.' Anxious as ever, she now had good reason and she searched for the nameless man.

'Is it time for a divorce Leo?'

'You want to talk about that here, honestly?'

'We can both move forward.'

'And then you can marry your titled lady and enjoy her estate in Kent? I suppose I'd have grounds enough by now—if I wanted to see my name spattered across the gutter press.' She gave a tiger's smile, deploying the last power she had. 'No, I think perhaps not. You might become a big man in this party of yours, or a coal baron in your own name.' The man she sought appeared and she waved him over. 'You might grow up.' Her escort drew close, and she turned away from her husband after her Parthian shot. I simply let her go.

Sissy nipped back by my side the moment I was alone. 'You never told me how good looking she was.'

'I'm not brave enough to discuss one woman in front of another.'

She hooked her left arm through my right, knowing that my other was still a mass of yellowing bruises. 'What was all that with the old explorer? I thought you were going to punch him, or he was going to pull out a big jungle knife.'

'Something dangerous is going on. I can't explain it, not here. Sorry, but we have to leave.'

I went to recover our coats. Even asking the question of who Baxter was working for could be perilous. An explorer could set off at a moment's notice for some far-flung corner of the world, but surely everywhere worthwhile had been explored by now. There might be other reasons he would suddenly need to be in Venezuela or Iraq. He'd walked smiling into the German embassy, at an event that was a thinly veiled propaganda exercise by the Nazi party. He associated with militant former soldiers and led them against the BUF. He appeared to be a communist agitator, but Hanrahan claimed to know nothing about him. If he knew Bruno, there was a fair chance that Baxter knew Dr Kahn too and probably Howard Thring. Verity had stormed his headquarters without compunction and Leo had been in the company of a man who was 'something in the Foreign Office'.

The complexity was baffling. I needed to write it all down on a big chalkboard and keep rubbing out the links until it made sense.

We walked away from the embassy as quickly as Sissy's heels could carry her. 'Apart from being terribly embarrassed by meeting your wife, we hardly met anyone,' She complained. 'So tell me why we're leaving and what the dangerous thing is.'

'That man, Jeb, Jeremiah Baxter, I've seen him before wherever there is trouble. He disguises himself but he's the one who shot at me in Kensington, he dropped the gun in Shoreditch that I Squad found and he shot that Blackshirt on the Peace March. And I bet he's behind lots of other things as well.' I wouldn't mention the Wipers Club cellar.

'You're sure? So he's what, a communist?'

'I don't know what he is. Goodness knows why the Germans invited him to their soirée and I can only guess why they invited Leonora.'

'Surely not to embarrass you? But why would Bruno want that?'

'Not to embarrass me—or Leonora—or you—or Jeb Baxter. The message is—'

Sissy completed the thought. 'It was a threat.'

'Exactly. But was the message for me or Baxter? Or for that matter, both of us. And who from? Baxter has had three, even four chances to kill me now and he hasn't. I'm useful to him somehow, or to his masters. I may have to ask Bruno straight out.'

'In that blunt northern way, you can't help.'

'If I must. We need to invite him to dinner as soon as we can.'

She gripped my arm tightly. 'This is why you bought the guns, isn't it? We're in danger. Is this all because of Department Z?'

'It's complicated.'

'Humour me. Don't treat me like some stupid floozie you've picked up at a dance hall. You bought me a gun, you taught me to shoot, and it wasn't just 'cos you wanted to show off—although I thought it was at first. You did it because whatever is going on, I'm in danger too. Tell me I'm right. I need to know now Hugh, tell me what you are up to.'

'You're safer if you don't know.'

'Oh rot. If they dragged up your ex-wife they must know all about me and where I live and it sounds to me as if they are saying "you behave Hugh Clifton or we'll do something nasty to your wife and your lover and you." Like they did to Verity. You have to be honest with me. Don't just string me along as you play your detective games like bloody Harry Bretton's brainless girlfriend.'

'Sissy...'

'We just need to run away, run away now.'

It was tempting, but the warning could have been far more subtle than it seemed. 'I thought you wanted to fight the communists?'

'I want to stop them, but I don't want to fight them with knives and bricks like you've been fighting them. And that man Jeb is dangerous. If you'd met him anywhere else you'd have been shooting or stabbing each other, and it will happen for certain if you keep chasing whatever you are chasing, and he keeps doing whatever he's doing. I mean, why was he at that party? You think he's working for the Russians but to me, it looks like he's working for the Germans.'

'Or the British,' I added.

Chapter Fifty-Two

The fourth and last of Kahn's ships was due on the Friday. I had now welcomed three to London using the spurious Board of Trade papers, and each had berthed at a different quay within the sprawling docklands that spread east from the city. My reception in Harbourmasters' offices varied from suspicious to accepting, but I proceeded to check the manifest of each ship and review the passenger lists.

Pavel Denisovich steamed up the Thames on the first of November. Its final destination might be Bilbao but it had stopped off at Hamburg, and was now working its way through the labyrinth of dock basins on a rising tide. It was an unremarkable vessel other than for its prominent red star and the Cyrillic name painted on the bow. Although a cargo ship, it carried twenty-three passengers and their extensive luggage. After witnessing the arrival of three vessels to no profit, this was the one that most exercised my imagination.

Using the usual papers, I gained entry to the wharf, forsaking my black coat for a less conspicuous grey overcoat. A rusting crane leg offered enough discreet cover for me to stand part-concealed and watch officials go aboard. One seemed familiar, perhaps because of his stylish black leather coat; Bruno. After close to half an hour, twenty-three adults and children of various ages, came down the gangplank, glancing anxiously about themselves. They were Europeans and appeared well-dressed, neither workmen nor impoverished refugees. Immediately after them came Bruno. Despite the cover of the crane, he caught my eye and tipped his hat.

I strode out from the shadows. '*Guten Morgen*.'

'Good morning Hugh.'

'You've been on board the ship?'

'Yes.'

'I'd be interested to hear why.'

'Would you? I am interested to hear why you are interested.'

For a moment it was as if we were the only two men on the dockside, two yards apart, eyes locked in challenge.

'Do you have a café near here?' Bruno broke the silence. At least he remained polite, and it would not be a question of who could draw his Walther first. Not that morning.

'There's one outside that the dockers use. It's rough and ready.'

'We will go there.'

A pervasive fug of tobacco smoke and the smell of fried eggs and bacon filled the café. Fresh coffee added to the overwhelming assault on my senses. Bruno scowled at the first taste of what the English considered to be coffee. '*Scheisse!*'

'How the common man lives, I'm afraid.'

Bruno added a full spoon of sugar to the coffee, pausing when he noticed how brown-stained the sugar in the bowl already was. 'I like meeting you, Hugh but I don't understand why you are here.'

'I'm a member of the Party's Department Z and they want me to keep an eye on Dr Kahn's ships. He was robbed, you know. He's a valuable friend of the Party.'

Bruno did not act convinced. 'Department Z is for intelligence, no? So what intelligence have you learned about Dr Kahn's ships?'

'That Germany has a new export commodity. The Nazi party is charging Jews to leave Germany.'

He shrugged. 'It's a convenient arrangement. The fewer Jews in positions of power, the fewer need to be watched.'

'Or arrested, beaten up, or shipped off to camps.'

Bruno grimaced at the coffee again. He did not rise to the bait.

'What are you? Gestapo, SS, SD, Abwehr, –'

'I'm a cultural attaché to the German Embassy.'

'And your cultural role at the docks is?'

'To see your new guests pass immigration procedures, customs for luggage. That all is in order.'

'And then what happens to them?'

'They have friends in England, you know. People with money. Jews will survive, they always have.'

'Just not in Germany?'

'We are unimportant men, Hugh, we can't hold back the tide of history. We follow orders, but we don't have to enjoy what we do.' Perhaps he was being honest.

'You're certainly not enjoying that coffee.'

Bruno set down his cup.

'As a friend, I have to warn you that we hang spies in England.'

Now Bruno gave a little smile. 'England is our friend. The *Führer* has given specific orders there must be no spying in Britain. So, I cannot be a spy.'

'And I just take that at face value?'

'The *Führer's* orders must be obeyed,' he recited. 'And something tells me you are more than you claim to be. As a friend, you can tell me. What are you, British Secret Service?'

'Department Z, British Union of Fascists. Sorry, British Union of Fascists and National Socialists.'

Bruno nodded. 'Very good…as you say spies can be hanged, or worse. Very much worse. But even though neither of us is a spy we can still be useful to one another.'

If it was a game, it was a lethal game that Bruno was playing.

'So tell me something useful. I need to know who is pulling the strings. You invited me to your embassy party, which was very kind. Someone also invited my ex-wife and made sure that I met a certain explorer face to face. It can't be coincidence.'

Bruno held up his teaspoon and wagged it in emphasis. 'As I said, we're unimportant men. Even that explorer. There should be peace between you.

You both have Britain's best interests at heart.'

'Not Germany's best interests?'

'Britain and Germany are friends, so our interests are the same.'

'Well as friends we must have dinner tonight,' I said.

'Oh, I couldn't.'

'We can talk about being useful to one another. There's an excellent Parisian restaurant that has relocated to London. I've never been but I hear their fish is excellent.'

The German weighed up his options. 'Will you bring that lovely lady of yours?'

'Certainly. Shall we say eight o'clock? Pruniers, St James.'

Once Bruno had walked off into the drizzle of a gloomy November afternoon, I strolled into the goods handling area. Working men tend to simply ignore men in clean coats and sharp hats waving official documents, but supervisors on the other hand proved eager to please. That word luggage was troubling me.

I kept watch from the cover of a harbour office where the dirt-smeared glass and fading light might serve as a mask. Those twenty-three people appeared to have shipped half their houses with them, as two canvas-backed lorries arrived to collect the luggage. Both drivers and their mates stood by as stevedores loaded the crates, but the official who should have been in this office taking an interest in all this was absent. Afterwards, he could honestly claim to have no knowledge of whatever was being done.

One man did take an interest, coming from the shadows and walking around the lorries once they were fully loaded. He was a stooping fellow who checked that no one was watching him from the cover of a crane. Despite the shabby greatcoat and grey homburg it was clearly Jeb Baxter in a new guise. That must be very important luggage, and Bruno must be fully aware of what Baxter was up to. Once the last crate was loaded and the lorry backs roped down, Baxter left and only one stevedore remained, chatting with the drivers and offering a light of their cigarettes. In a few minutes, the lorries moved off, through the gates and away. My Alvis was parked nowhere near enough to offer hope of giving chase.

The subterfuge had been subtle. *Pavel Denisovich* had not been unloaded at night at a provincial dock by an irregular workforce. The lorries proudly carried the owner's names and they had been loaded by unionized labour. Customs men and officials within those harbour offices must have stamped all the right forms for that luggage to be unloaded, even if money had bought blindness on the part of some. Only an investigator in possession of the trail of evidence would be suspicious and, even then, paper could tell lies.

I returned to my apartment to take a bath then dress for dinner. Pausing with bow untied I leafed again through my copy of the shipping manifests. Nothing more to arouse my interest was bound for London on the *Pavel Denisovich*. Or was it? I'd only shown a quickly copied summary to Hanrahan, and perhaps lost the subtlety of what the note actually said in Russian. It needed to be translated in full.

Chapter Fifty-Three

Dinner at Pruniers of St James was the plan. Madame Prunier's restaurant had only opened the year before and had an excellent reputation for fish dishes. Even the Prince of Wales sometimes ate there. Howard Thring had recommended it, but he'd warned that almost all the staff were foreign; quite what else he would expect from an establishment set up by a leading French restauranteur was unclear. Amongst those undesirable foreigners, it was just possible that one spoke Russian.

I collected Sissy deliberately early and travelled back to central London by cab. The Maître d' observed that we were early in that polite way the serving class have of expressing disapproval to people considered to be their betters. He seated us at one of the less fashionable tables.

As the waiter took an order for drinks, I suggested that we wait until the others arrived. I excused myself and went to find that Maître d'.

'Monsieur?'

'This is rather unusual, but I happen to have a cable here in Russian, and I can't speak a word of Russian. I don't suppose any of your waiters...'

The Maître d' accepted a florin and glanced around. 'If you'd like to follow me, monsieur.' He led the way to the kitchens.

I was partly expecting to find an Ashkenazi Jew, of which there were many in London, but the man who appeared was a Ukrainian who told me he once served with the White Russian army.

'I go to Paris when the reds won.' He concluded, his weather-beaten face hiding a lifetime of struggle. 'Not so many rich people live to Paris now, they worry war with Germans, so Madame come to London.'

'You can read Russian?'

'Yes, I speak to Russian guests if they make trouble with waiters.'

I unfolded the copy of the manifest from my pocket. The print had creased badly. 'Read this to me, please. I'm just the shipping company accountant. I wondered what's on this ship.'

'Ah, yes, see this ship name.'

'*Pavel Denisovich,* sailing from St Petersburg?'

'Yes. To Bilbao…I don't know that place.'

'It's in Spain.'

'Ah yes, things to go for the Spanish police, *carbinari.*'

'Tractor parts?'

'No, no, *vintovka,*' he mimed shooting a rifle.

Deep in my heart, I had expected an answer of that nature. It did not stop me feeling a bloody fool.

'And you say pistol. And bullets, lots of bullets for those police to shoot, hah? I hope they shoot communists.'

'Oh, not tractor parts at all then? Silly me.' Pulse now racing I strained to keep my tone light. 'Well thank you for your time.' A shilling seemed a good tip for such a tiny, unimportant piece of information and the man was pleased.

'Next time, come to me, I read all your Russian.'

'Next time I have something, I'll be straight here.'

Bruno, Julian, and Melissa were by now seated at the table. Sissy glared as I reappeared, and my false grin did nothing to break her expression.

'Sorry, Sissy something important has come up. Julian, I need to speak to your father, urgently.'

'He's probably dining at his club.'

And Calhoun might be dining at his. Unless an operation was afoot, the Secret Service worked office hours. At best I could ring the all-night number and have a message passed on. The waiter was waved away with an apology.

'I'm sorry, I have to go. Sissy could you look after Bruno.'

'Hugh this is so rude, what's happening?'

'I'll explain tomorrow. Now, honestly, I have to go. Julian, we need to find your father.'

'I say this is very mysterious, old man.'

'Julian!' I made a Z-sign in the air, in the style of Douglas Fairbanks in *The Mark of Zorro*.

'Jules, this is outrageous,' Sissy protested. 'Tell him to behave.'

'We live in outrageous times, love.'

'What in the world is going on?' Melissa exclaimed.

'I'm sorry Melissa, you'll have to excuse us. Bruno could you order, please. I hear the fish is excellent.'

'No, I'll go too.' Bruno said.

'No, no, it's not necessary. I only need Julian.'

'Oh, the whole evening is ruined!' Sissy threw down her napkin. 'I don't want to sit here while you and Julian go off on some boy's night out.'

'Nor me,' Melissa added. 'Where are your manners tonight, Hugh?'

I'd never truly cared for manners. 'I'm sorry Melissa. Party over, with apologies.' Yes, it was Party Over if my conclusions were correct. 'The doorman will summon cabs for you ladies.'

'He jolly well will not!' Sissy retorted.

I crumpled a pound note into the hand of the Maître d' and we collected our coats, leaving the restaurant in a huddle, squabbling one with the other. Bruno hung back, and I turned and seized his arm. 'Where did the luggage go? The crates from that ship.'

Bruno jerked his arm back, glaring.

'It's not luggage at all, is it?'

'It has been nice meeting you again, Sissy, Melissa.' Bruno gave a little bow to each of the women. 'I am going to return to the table and have a drink.' He drew back towards the security of the restaurant, his glare daring me to make a scene.

'The reds know what the cargo is, and where it's going.'

Bruno gave a shrug. 'It is a pity about dinner.'

Julian insisted on putting Melissa in the first cab, which arrived after two or three minutes we could ill afford to lose. He gave her a little wave, but she did not wave back.

'So where's your Father's Club?' I asked.

'It's the Gresham, in the City.'

Miles away—too far for a wild goose chase. 'Be a chum, go back inside, and call ahead to make sure he's actually there so we don't waste more time.'

'I'll do no such thing until you tell me what's happening.'

I took Julian's arm and led him a few yards clear of Sissy's earshot. 'Your father is mixed up in something. He thinks he's being clever, but someone else is being more clever. I came across a document when we were investigating the Kahn robbery, and now I understand it. I was stupid and didn't spot the obvious, and I was lied to by someone I trusted.'

'But what's so crucial?'

'If this goes wrong, your father will be up for treason and they will hang him. And it will sink the Party.'

Julian's mouth made an O.

'Union Jack; Red, White and Blue. You've heard of Plan Blue and Plan White? There's another one, Plan Red. Heard of it?'

'No.'

'And you never did, understand? Never ever tell anyone you heard of it, or your head is in the noose too. Now phone him, please. And don't say anything to Bruno, he's mixed up in this somehow.'

Sissy fidgeted as Julian went back inside. 'Treason? Honestly?' She had not been quite out of earshot.

'Department Z stuff, you don't want to be involved.'

'Like hell I do. What was all that training for? This is what you've been chasing for months, isn't it? If this is it, if this is the night—'

'Sissy, it's not a game anymore.'

'It never was. You've been up to something from day one, from the day I met you. Shooting a terrorist, making enemies of famous explorers, locking people in a dungeon...then all that time when you were supposed to be writing but could only turn out a few chapters of drivel in six months. You were never just an ordinary Blackshirt, were you? And I don't want to be ordinary either.'

I reached for her hand and held it until Julian burst back from the restaurant.

'He's at the Travellers Club, just around the corner in Pall Mall.'

A touch of mist was in the air. We strode the short distance from St James' to Pall Mall as quickly as Sissy's heels would allow. 'Sissy, have the doorman hail a cab. Tell the driver to wait, we'll only be a minute.'

'Aye, aye sir.'

Julian led the way inside but made it no further than the lobby, where he asked for his father. As precious minutes ticked away, we distracted ourselves by admiring the baroque opulence of the place, its statues and columns.

Thring emerged fully dressed for dinner, radiating disapproval. 'What's the meaning of this Julian?'

'Sorry, sir,' I said. 'Department Z business.'

'Department Z, you make me laugh. Does Major Taylor know you're chasing around London tonight?'

I stepped away from the porter's desk and drew Thring after me. 'On behalf of Department Z, I've been watching Dr Kahn's ships as they come in. Forty-eight crates were unloaded from a Russian ship called the *Pavel Denisovich* today. Where are they now?'

'Don't interfere Clifton.' Thring was clearly in no mood to use my Christian name.

'Six hundred rifles, six hundred pistols, and enough ammunition to start a civil war. Bought from the Russians by the Germans using Jewish money. Strange bedfellows. I can see the need to supply weapons in penny lots to our rifle clubs out in the shires—God knows we need decent weapons—but enough to equip a battalion? That's revolution, that's treason. Forget losing the election, you'll get the whole leadership hanged.'

'That's not the plan, Clifton.'

Of course, it wasn't and it never had been. The truth hit me like a train.

'In a few days, it won't be a problem.'

'So, this is Plan Red? Yes, I know about Union Jack too.' All those pieces finally fell together. 'Let me guess; you're going to somehow get the weapons into the hands of known communists, then the police will receive a timely tip-off? Communist revolution thwarted a week before the election, and a lovely paper trail leading back to Moscow and Jewish bankers.'

Thring smiled. 'If that happened, it would do no harm to our vote at all.'

'Except in a few days, the guns won't be there. The reds know your plan already, the real reds, the ones who actually work for Moscow, not ones you've duped into joining your plan. How many dockers saw those crates loaded? Which communist agent talked to the drivers, asked them who they worked for or where they were going?'

Thring frowned.

'It's a paper-thin plan once you see through it. The communists will be down there tonight, tomorrow at the latest, dispersing the guns amongst people they trust. Your tip-off will mean nothing, and you will have created a genuine communist revolution. Not this week or next, but when they are ready.'

Now he looked flustered, and I had never seen Thring flustered. 'How do you come to this conclusion?'

'When Kahn was robbed, it can't have been an accident that he was picked by the thieves. He was carrying some papers pertinent to this labyrinthine plot. Papers which communist agents read, then put back in the case to make it look like they were only after money. When I interviewed the banker Abrahams, he gave away the fact that Kahn was also carrying cash even though Kahn denied it on record.'

'And what makes you think guns are involved?'

'I glanced through those papers, as any agent on his toes would do,' I admitted. 'My Russian is pretty rusty, but *vintovka* means rifle. It didn't make sense at the time, but it does now.'

'You're very clever Clifton, I admire your tenacity. You'll go far in the Party.'

'You need to tell me where the guns are.'

'I don't know, and frankly, I don't want to know. By the way, I'm here as a guest. You might want to speak with my host. We're still dining but I'll bring him out.'

The man who emerged was as out of place as an ape in the dinner jacket. It hung from his shoulders and his shirt looked the wrong size. We locked eyes but Thring stepped in close, as if to part us. 'I understand you've met, so there's no need for introductions.'

'Baxter,' I said.

'Jeb Baxter, the explorer?' Julian asked.

Thring simply turned to walk away, 'Jeb tell him, but don't tell me and Julian mustn't be involved. Julian, come away.'

Reluctantly, Julian followed his father partway across the lobby, then stopped to protest. 'Father!'

'Julian, if you know what's good for you…'

Baxter walked a few paces towards the main door. 'So,' he growled, 'You were telling the truth and it was Department Z on my tail all that time. I never knew you wankers had it in you. And there's me thinking you and your Irish friend were Special Branch stooges.'

'Where are the so-called personal effects of those Jews stored?'

'In a Jewish-owned warehouse in the East End. Shipped there by a heavily unionized transport firm, with a top communist shop steward.'

'Well, the communists know about your store and what's there. Remember when Kahn was robbed? They can read Russian shipping invoices and they've been onto your plan ever since.'

'Is that so? You'd better get down there, then.' He started to speak quickly, snapping out the address of Levi & Company in Wapping and some basic directions. There was a large sign over the gate. 'You can't miss it.'

'Is it guarded?'

'Just an old Jew with a club. Even you can handle him.'

'There could be a lot more than just one Jew down there by midnight. The reds are bound to move fast. You need to come too.'

'Your Department Z must have some muscle you can send down there? Someone got all my men killed or nicked.'

'You killed them yourself. Dick Dennis, Billy Rich, Charlie Watkins, Ewan Williams–'

'Not Williams.' He blinked slowly. 'I don't saw men's arms off, even if they deserve it. I'm not a bloody savage.'

So much for Hanrahan's confidential sources—and no wonder he had heard about the Wipers Club before. He'd warned me that he lied, but not that he lied about everything.

The easy thing to have done would be to tip Inspector Renton off immediately, but if the police raided the warehouse and found the guns everything would point to a communist-Jewish conspiracy and Thring's plot would succeed. Yes, I could blurt out what I thought I knew about Plan Red, and wave a crumpled photographic print, but my evidence was wafer-thin. Thring was far too good an accountant to leave a trail pointing his way. Renton might not even believe what he was being told, or Baxter might have deliberately given me the wrong address. I still had time to do a little stage management of my own.

It would have been good to implicate Parker in all this, but I needed someone who would help me without question. Julian had no idea how I was about to betray his trust. At a nod, he came over, shrugging off his father's attempt to stop him. 'Julian, be a chum and round up as many men as you can find. I need them in Wapping as soon as you can to put a guard on a warehouse. Levi and Company; Baxter's got the address. I should be on the spot already and be able to give you the score when you arrive. We may have to go in with knuckles flying.'

'Do we need weapons?'

'Only what you can grab quickly. I'm packing Sissy off home then going straight down there. See you soon.' I glared at Baxter. 'You coming?'

'I can't get involved.'

'What? This is your bloody mess!'

'Sir!' The club porter rebuked me.

I lowered my voice and cut out the expletives. 'You're saying it's up to me to save your bacon?'

Baxter shrugged his ill-fitted jacket shoulders.

I had no intention of saving Baxter's bacon. It would be fried to a crisp and served on Inspector Renton's morning rolls. I rushed outside to where Sissy had claimed a cab, plans still forming. I'd get to the warehouse sometime before Julian and his squad. If all was quiet, I'd bluff or bribe my way past that guard, identify the crates then wait for Julian. Once Blackshirts were swarming all over the scene, I'd slip away and telephone Scotland Yard. Hanrahan's double-cross would fail. Better still, Thring's Plan Red would also fail.

* * *

Julian Thring watched his friend leave, ignored his father's summons, and asked the Porter for a telephone. Baxter came over and stayed his hand as he was about to lift the receiver. 'This can wait until the morning.'

'But Hugh–'

'Chasing his tail.'

'But if he really knows something about–'

'About?' Baxter came closer. 'We need to be very careful what we know about.' His gaze was deep and long, and his face was creased by the bitter practice of survival. 'I want to stay alive and free. I don't know anything of what Clifton is chasing, and nor does your father and nor do you.'

'No,' said Julian. 'I truly don't.'

'What about that girl, Sissy?'

'I'm sure she knows nothing either.' Sissy had to be shielded from whatever Hugh had dragged her into. 'She... she's not very bright,' he added.

'No, and she keeps unfortunate company,' Baxter's mood lifted. 'I'd like to invite you in for a drink, Julian. I'm not one for clubs, but this one suits as good as any. They're used to my ways here. Moore will take your coat.'

Julian gave a glance towards the door. It was closed, in every sense.

'The taxi will have gone already, young man. Isn't that what people criticize your movement for—young men in a hurry? Come and have a drink with your father.'

Chapter Fifty-Four

I instructed the cabbie to drive directly to the end of the mews beside Havelock Mansions where the Alvis was garaged, batting down all Sissy's questions along the way. As soon as I got out of the taxi, I asked the driver to take Sissy home, but before I finished the instruction she'd also stepped out and pushed money past my shoulder.

'What are you doing?'

'Coming with you.'

'This will be dangerous. Remember how you don't like fighting. I don't want you hurt.'

The cab moved away.

'Oh for God's sake. We've got the vote, and you bloody well taught me to shoot a pistol so don't rattle out more of that...that Victorian *women's place is in the home* claptrap.'

I leaned forward and kissed her forehead. 'A friend once told me to make sure I had a guardian angel. Or a man who I thought was a friend. Remember the Irishman I told you about, Pat? He's one of the men I have to stop.' I unlocked the garage doors and pulled them open. 'Somehow he knows your Verity too. He's working with her.'

'Verity's alive?'

'Indeed, although everyone is supposed to think she's dead. And don't trust her if you ever meet again. She's not really called Verity and she made friends with Julian so she could spy on the Party. Someone tried to kill her when she grew too close to the truth.'

'About?'

'I'll tell you on the way. Shut the doors after I've driven out, would you, then climb in.'

'Shall I lock them?'

'Don't bother.'

Once the Alvis had been retrieved and Sissy was by my side, I drove around in front of Havelock Mansions and asked her to wait for a moment.

'You come straight back, no slipping off without me,' she warned.

I pulled off my bowtie as I thundered up the stairs. It took just two minutes to retrieve both pistols and a box of bullets. There was no time to don the shoulder holster or swap my overcoat for that fascists-mean-business leather coat either.

Bending to get into Alvis once more I deposited guns and ammunition in Sissy's lap. 'Here, you know how to load them.'

Even in the dark, I could see how wide-eyed she was.

I drove east to Wapping past the Tower of London and across Tower Bridge. Both starkly symbolized this country I was risking my life for, and now was also risking Sissy's life for. Once on the South Bank, we stopped to ask a policeman for directions. Sissy asked the questions from the passenger window.

'You don't want to go down there, Madam, this time of night.'

'Oh, sick member of the family. *His* side. We won't stay long.'

Close to the river ran a street of high walls, warehouse facades, and locked gates. I drove straight past Levi & Co, International Shipping, then parked on the opposite side of the road, fifty yards further along and well away from a lonely streetlamp.

Most of the buildings were many-storied warehouses, but Levi and Co were located in what looked like an older building that had been part-demolished then rebuilt with its windows bricked up and a low-pitched roof replacing its upper storeys.

'Get into my seat, I've left the keys in,' I said. 'Keep your eyes peeled; you're watching my back but watch your own as well. That man Baxter's got these stalking skills, he can sneak up unnoticed and I have no idea whose side he is on. Drive off if you see someone coming, then find a phone box and ring this number.' I took a pencil and scribbled Renton's phone number on the back of a stray calling card. 'I have a whistle with me too.'

She grabbed my face suddenly and kissed me passionately. We lingered over the kiss. How could I leave her after that and venture into the night? For a moment I was tempted to throw it all in and drive off with her. She sank back into her seat. 'Be careful.'

Any idea of the two of us escaping now was pure fantasy. 'You be even more careful.'

* * *

Sissy wrapped her sweating palm around the butt of her pistol. Hugh had left her alone and darted across the street. Putting his back against the brickwork he worked his way along the high wall which was overtopped by a corrugated metal roof. A huge sign spanned the gate, barely illuminated by the streetlight across the road. She was entranced. With all the colour soaked away by the dark, she could be watching a film in black and white. The film of that wretched book, *Blackshirt Detective*.

He investigated the gate, pushed it open a little, then vanished from sight. She broke from the trance and checked behind, then down into the gutter to check that Baxter person was not creeping up on her.

Now her eyes were adjusting to the dark she noticed another car, parked down a short road beside the warehouse that could lead nowhere but to some dock or cutting. On instinct, she ducked down in the seat. She pushed the door open and awkwardly wormed out onto the pavement. So what if her coat would be ruined? She wished she was wearing sensible shoes though—Hugh could have warned her that all this was going down. Cautiously she came into a crouch then edged to the back of the Alvis.

Yes, there was a man in that car. He was watching and waiting too.

She shuffled along to the front of the Alvis, looking around the headlamps. Two more people were hurrying to the gate, one taller than the other, both in working men's flat caps and calf-length coats. The taller man went inside, but the other looked about then crossed the road and went out of sight.

For a quiet backstreet in the dead of night, this place was extraordinarily popular.

On the drive across town, Hugh had blurted some story of guns and plots and foreign agents, and in this new world of lies and fear, people could be watching the people that were watching. Perhaps they could see her right now, even if she could not see them. Julian should be here soon with his men and there would likely be fighting. The safe thing to do was simply wait.

That Walther was such a comfort. With her back against the car's cold metal, she felt the pistol's weight in one hand, then in two. What did Hugh once say about not carrying a gun unless she was prepared to use it? She was prepared, Sissy told herself. Her hands shook as she slipped off the safety catch. She was prepared.

* * *

It was clear that the gate below the huge sign was unlocked. Gingerly I pushed it open. Any guard had been sent away or lured away or quietly disposed of and the scene was set for those boxes of weapons to disappear. A parked lorry was probably one of those I'd seen at the dockside. To the left, crates that looked empty were piled higgledy-piggledy and beyond those were the warehouse door. I was able to reach the door with the aid of moonlight but to venture inside would require my torch. The padlock was in place, so no one was inside, but it hung loose, unlocked. It might not be long before company turned up. With luck, the reds would choose to come in the small hours when the city streets were at their quietest, so that would give Julian and the troops time to arrive first.

The facts had to be confirmed before I made that call to Special Branch—this was not a cliff I could jump back up if proved wrong. I also needed Julian's Squad on site so that Inspector Renton's men would find a weapons cache guarded by Blackshirts; Thring's plan would be sunk, and along with it all chance that the British Union would ever win a seat in an election again.

I drew my Walther and eased the door open.

Julian would be arrested when the police arrived. It was a low blow to frame a friend who right now was mobilizing forces to help me but warning Julian would be out of the question. Allowing a friendship to form had been stupid, if it had ever been more than a pretence. Julian Thring was a fascist, and the fascists had to be beaten.

I switched on my electric torch.

Sissy was a fascist too and guilty by association. I could take betrayal only so far and must get her away from here before the police arrived, even though she'd never talk to me again. Once my treachery was known amongst the Blackshirts, I'd need to disappear completely; change my name, emigrate even. If I was right about Pat Harahan, I'd be in danger from the left too. Just possibly the Security Service protected its agents, but in this twisted world Calhoun could just abandon me to the dogs.

It was not a powerful torch. A small spot of light flitted from this heap to that nook. Anything in the far corners had clearly been here a while and anything with dust on its tarpaulin could also be ignored. The building measured perhaps twenty yards wide but was much deeper than the beam would reach. Piles of furniture under covers were on the left, then some tea chests piled high on the right. Beyond these, not quite hidden, was a neatly stacked collection of crates mostly concealed under green tarpaulins. I popped the Walther into my pocket to free my hand and pulled away the cover.

Here was the prize. The tell-tale shape advertised that the longer crates must be the ones holding the rifles, with perhaps two dozen in each. Other shapes must contain the ammunition and pistols, whilst spurious labels told lies about the contents.

'Turn around Hugh, and don't even think of putting your hands near your pockets.'

'Pat.'

Hanrahan must have arrived only a few minutes behind me, and he'd waited until I put my pistol away before making his move. His own torch clicked on, shining straight into my eyes. 'Hands up is the customary way of showing you're unarmed.'

I complied.

'And drop the torch.'

It hit the ground with a crack and the beam died.

'Don't be a traitor Pat.'

'I'm not a traitor to my class. My comrades will be here soon to take away these gifts you brought to the revolution.'

'Special Branch are on their way.' Oh how I wished that was true.

'You're a poor liar, Hugh, you're in the wrong sport.'

I wouldn't mention Julian. Not yet.

'For sure I don't want to shoot you. I know you're not a real fascist, I know you were just put up to this. Like me.'

'Except you've gone native. You've really become a communist.'

'I was always native, from day one. This wasn't an act for me.'

'Were you working for Russia from day one too?'

'The world is heading for an inevitable war between the people and the fascists. We all have to take a side – there'll be no room in the centre.'

I nudged my head towards the crates. 'And the war starts here?'

'And the fascists were about to start it.'

'No, no, this is Plan Red, it's all a fake. They're Russian guns.'

'Plan Red – it just insults the imagination. Anyone can buy Russian guns, but they're our guns now. Our guns, Hugh. You can be on our side. You can help us beat Mosley.'

'I am helping to beat Mosley. When the police arrive, he'll be discredited, the fascists will be finished...'

'And Special Branch grows stronger and they crack down even harder on the left. The Establishment is who you are helping. The British Empire, the Bank of England and sickly King George. This decadent so-called democracy is doomed.'

'It's not so bad.'

'Don't let me take that answer as no.' Hanrahan's pistol had relaxed, but now it was threatening again.

'Did you and Verity go back and kill those men at the Wipers Club?'

'No. And that's the honest truth.'

'That means there's another actor. The party within a party. You've not found them, but I have.' Sow a bit of mystery and hold back some information and I might buy my way out of here.

'Really? Who is this *other actor*? I'm letting you live because my comrades want to have a talk, but it would be less painful if you told me everything now.'

Talking bought time for Julian to arrive. He must come soon.

'Raincoat Man, Monkey Man, the American. If it wasn't you, it was him that killed his own men in that cellar like he shot his own man in Kensington. He's not a communist. I've found out his name and who he's working for.'

'He's an *agent provocateur* working for the state,' Hanrahan stated as if the words came straight off a memorandum from Moscow. 'Fooling working men into stirring up trouble to give the police more excuse to crack down. It's why he hasn't killed you – you're on the same side.'

'I know he didn't kill Williams the taxi driver, so was that you?'

'Not me personally, but a bit of torture or a necessary killing is all in a day's work for some comrades.'

I imagined being hooded and dragged away, then strapped to a chair in some basement to await my interrogators. Ewan Williams had been tortured in ways Department Z could only fantasize about. It would be better to die here, taking a chance to snatch out my gun or dive away into the dark.

'I'm sorry it came to this Hugh, I don't want to see you hurt. You should never have let yourself be talked into getting involved. Calhoun doesn't care if you die. This world has no place for gentlemen or empty-headed rich girls.'

Just visible in the darkness off to the left and behind Hanrahan was a slight motion, a shadow amongst the shadows. Rich, but far from empty-headed, the young woman was moving with ballet dancer grace and utter silence.

'Pat, we were friends.' I said gently. 'You need to put the gun down, and then kick it away,'

'Huh?'

'I don't want to see you hurt either, we were colleagues, we were mates, we got out of some hairy scrapes, but I want to stop a war not start one. I didn't come alone, so let the gun drop, then raise your hands.'

Hanrahan glanced sideways, but not for long enough to risk my making a move.

'It's not that girl, is it?'

The next voice was Sissy's, and she sounded both scared and angry. '*That girl* has a gun pointing at your back.'

'Is that Sissy?' Hanrahan called back, risking a glance again into the darkness.

'I've been training her for this war of yours,' I said. 'She's a bloody good shot. You know the aristocracy; hunting and shooting is in the blood.'

'Two hands on the gun and I point at the middle of the target, right Hugh?'

'Sissy, we're going to talk about this,' Hanrahan said. 'Nobody needs to get hurt. Enough people have been hurt.'

'I squeeze the trigger slowly, then I shoot again to make sure.'

Each time she spoke, Sissy offered Hanrahan more information. By now he should be able to place her at five o clock relative to where he stood. His expression was almost readable, calculating the time needed to turn and shoot Sissy, then switch back before I launched my shoulders into him or pulled my Walther. It was vital that I held his focus, not giving the slightest suggestion that my concentration was wandering. Sissy was mostly concealed behind a dark mass of freight, so I could only just see her. Dark hair, dark eyes, dark coat, she'd be a tricky target against the blackness. Oh, Sissy.

The Irishman risked it and swept his gun arm around, I tensed to move, Hanrahan spotted my flinch, hesitated, then wasted the last moment of his life searching for that shadow in the dark. Sissy fired, then fired again.

I froze as the sound hit me and the report bounced around and around the shed. Hanrahan crumpled at my feet, his gun falling one way and his torch the other. Sissy stepped out from behind her cover, took two steps forward, and fired a third time into the face that stared up at her.

The torch stopped rolling and came to rest with its flickering beam throwing Pat Hanrahan's shattered features into eerie relief.

'Sissy!' I grabbed the fallen Russian pistol, backing off to keep it well out of Hanrahan's reach, but his people's war ended here; twitching, hands thrown wide to each side, chest heaving its last. He'd been shot through the heart, through the breastbone and through the left eye. Sissy's hands shook so violently she would stand no chance of hitting anything with a fourth shot.

'Darling.' I took the Walther from her, my mind still registering that I was alive.

'Hunting and shooting,' she said, staring at the body only half-illuminated by the fallen torch.

I hugged her tight. 'Well done, well done, perfectly done.'

She was trembling violently, panting in short breaths. 'I killed him.'

'I'm sorry I ever involved you—'

Sissy pulled away. 'I'm not sorry. I had to do it. I had to save you…and stop, all this.'

'That's the spirit. Now we need to get out of here. And he needs to come too.'

'Him. We can't.'

'We have to. We can't leave him for the police to find, or anyone to find. He needs to just vanish.'

'But what will we do with him?'

'Put him in the car, then I know people who will complete the rest of his story.'

'You know people, what kind of people? Who are you? Who are you working for?'

'You mean who are *we* working for? King and Country.'

From outside, two shots came in quick succession.

'Guardian Angel,' I hissed. 'I wondered where she was.'

'Who?'

There was no time to fill the blanks. 'That's the only way out. We've either got friends covering it, or two sets of enemies blocking the way. Have this back.' I passed her the Walther. 'Keep close and follow me.'

I edged to the door along the cover of freight and tarpaulin-shrouded mounds, with Sissy immediately behind. Another shot barked from the yard outside and struck something with a solid whump. I risked looking around the door.

The moon emerging from cloud cast sharp shadows. Crates, barrels, and equipment were scattered around the yard, and that lorry was parked perhaps twenty yards away. Its outline changed slightly.

'After me, quick as you can.' I grabbed Sissy's upper arm and led her sharply to the right into welcoming darkness behind the nearest crates. Another shot came from the dark, clanging into the shed where Sissy had just stood. We ducked into cover behind that row of crates, jagged as a battlement. I coughed with the exhilaration, tried hard to suppress it, then coughed again. A bullet split wood and sprayed splinters into Sissy's hair.

'Stop coughing, you'll get us killed!' Sissy hissed.

'Sorry.'

Further to the right, behind a taller group of crates, another shadow moved.

My pistol arm jerked up and aimed straight and steady. 'Don't move!' I commanded.

Sissy copied my action a heartbeat later.

'Hugh Clifton?' Came the foreign voice.

'Bruno, what the hell are you doing here? If you're armed, put your gun down.'

'You first.'

Another shot zipped from the direction of the lorry and hit nothing in particular.

'Tell your man to stop shooting.'

'Tell *your* man to stop shooting,' Bruno said.

'It's not my man.'

'I followed them here, the reds. Promise me you're not a red, Hugh.'

'No, I'm not. I've just killed one for that matter.'

Sissy touched me as she realized what I'd claimed. And so the lies continued.

'There are more reds coming, we don't have long. Are you on our side now Bruno? I know what you were up to with Thring and Baxter, but Plan Red has been exposed and we have to stop this madness.'

I couldn't see another friend die tonight, if Bruno was indeed a friend and not the next person planning to betray me. My plan could still work if Julian hurried up, but the last thing I needed was a Nazi agent complicating matters. 'You need to get away before the police arrive, they can't find you here.'

'Yes, yes, it has to end.'

'So we need to work together. Now is that time we are useful to each other. If I'm to trust you, come where I can see you, Bruno.'

'My gun is down.' The German edged along the line of crates. 'Ach, Miss Sissy too? I'd say good evening but it's not a good evening. They are between us and the gate.' The moon glinted on Bruno's pistol. He edged up behind one of the taller crates.

'How many did you see?'

'You, then a man, then a woman,' he said.

'Well, the man's inside and won't be troubling us anymore. And Sissy here is the woman.'

'Then someone came in after me, a very sneaky person. I hid, he hid.'

'Just the one?'

'Ja.'

'I can guess who's over there. And it's a she, not a he. She's trying to stall us while more reds come.'

'Verity?' Sissy guessed.

'I've no idea who she's working for, but she's a very dangerous woman.' I raised my voice to yell. 'Verity! We know it's you. Pat Hanrahan is dead and Blackshirts are on their way. You can get out of this, you can live. Come back to our side.'

By way of reply she fired and hit metal machinery beyond where we crouched. The ricochet bounced back and scuffed the yard. I moved to a position two crates closer to the gate and risked a glance around one of those battlements. Something moved. 'She's almost straight ahead of us,' I said quietly. 'She's using that parked lorry as cover. Spread out and we'll all fire at once; we won't hit anything, but it will make it seem like there's a lot of us and we mean business. Are you fine with that Sissy? Crawl back to the end, just put your gun hand up and fire. Don't show your head, don't give her a target.'

Bruno wriggled to his feet behind the tall crate, and I put Hanrahan's pistol into my left hand and drew the Walther with my right. 'Now.'

A fusillade cracked out into the dark. Sissy fired slowly, once, twice, certain to hit the sky. Bruno had an automatic pistol and one shot followed directly on the last, tracking along the lorry body as he fired. I fired my Walther and the Tokarev, right-left, right-left. With no better target than the lorry I fired at its cab, its hood, and its wheels. Counting three shots with each hand meant I'd have bullets remaining. Sissy jerked her hand down, Bruno pulled back behind the crate, and I ducked down and moved to the very end of the row, dropping to my knees to peer around at the lorry. It was no more than fifteen yards away from that point and the unmistakable tang of petrol betrayed that the fuel tank was punctured. One more shot could spark an inferno.

A shape broke from the dark silhouette and darted for the gate. I brought the Walther into play, but my chance of hitting would be small and it was not a night to shoot a woman in the back. Not a woman whose motives remained obscure.

'She got away,' Bruno said.

'Yes, but the fact she ran means she's alone. For now. I'm going for my car, I'll bring it over to the gate. You help Sissy pull Pat over.'

'Who's Pat?'

'Just get him.'

'My feet are bloody freezing,' Sissy protested. She had removed her heels to tiptoe in to save me.

It seemed to take hours, but the move was accomplished in perhaps three minutes. Nobody looked back at the dark smear on the flags of the warehouse floor. Blood was going to ruin the upholstery, but we bundled the man who had gone by the name of Pat Hanrahan into the rear seat of the

Alvis. My grey overcoat was already doused in blood, so I slipped out of it and tossed it in to cover the body. A police whistle was blowing somewhere, then another more distant. There was no sign of Julian or any Blackshirts.

'So you're not a spy, Bruno,' I said.

'No I'm not a spy; *Führer's* orders.'

'In that case, you need to drop that pistol down a drain, then get out of the neighbourhood as fast as you can, else someone will blame all this on Germany. The last thing we want is a war.'

'We don't want a war,' Bruno echoed.

Sissy leaned into the car and tugged the coat to fully cover Hanrahan's face. 'Go on, Bruno,' she said.

'I will go. My car is close.' Shoulders hunched, the German who was not a spy walked away.

We also made our getaway. 'Were there guns in those crates?' Sissy asked as I drove.

'Yes, Russian rifles. Enough to disrupt the election if not to start a civil war.'

'And we stopped it,' she breathed, then let out a laugh which was close to hysterical. 'Oh God, fancy that. We went out for dinner and quite accidentally stopped a bloody revolution. We'll get medals for this; you'll get a knighthood.'

I doubted that the world of the spy worked like that.

After two minutes of driving, a police car tore past with its bells clanging. If it found the right location for the shots it would perhaps meet a crowd of communists about to start loading crates. Goodness knows what had happened to Julian, but I had run out of time to dress the scene with Blackshirts. Special Branch must get to that warehouse before the local bobbies discovered the haul or Verity's friends carted it away. If I gave Inspector Renton the glory, he might just believe my tale.

I pulled up beside a public telephone box. 'I need to make two calls.'

'Don't tell the police I shot that man Pat.'

'Pat wasn't even his real name, and you did exactly what you needed to do. I don't want the police finding his body, and there are people who can make sure they won't, so that will be my second call. You need to close your ears to that one.'

Once I was out on the pavement, Sissy came round to me. I wasn't sure who needed the hug the most.

'You're shaking.'

'You should be thankful I'm not a quivering lump of blancmange, weeping everywhere.' Her voice wavered, belying her words. 'Aren't you glad now you chose a true Blackshirt girl who can stand up for herself?'

'You're much more than that,' I said, kissing her on the forehead then releasing her. 'Thank you for saving me. Indeed, for saving the country.'

'Rot!' she said. 'And of course, you don't have any cigarettes, do you?'

'Breathe the air of freedom.'

'Go on, call your people, whoever they are. Let's get this horrid mess cleared up so we can go back to our normal lives.'

As I opened the door of the phone box, I doubted whether our lives would ever be normal again.

Chapter Fifty-Five

I parked the Alvis in the street in front of Havelock Mansions, such was my hurry to get Sissy safely inside. Of course, the wrong people knew where I lived and could come hunting, but with just a quarter of a tank of petrol, a car reeking of blood, and a few pounds in my wallet, past midnight in November was no time to be running anywhere. The street door was robust, as was the flat door once locked and bolted, and I pushed an armchair against it too for good measure. I had been surprised once that night, and it would not happen again.

Sissy collapsed on the sofa, throwing a forearm over her eyes. I pushed a glass of scotch into her eager hand, then reloaded both Walthers. Anyone still seeking trouble would reap it in spades.

The telephone rang. Calhoun rarely telephoned me directly. He wanted to know if I was back at the flat and that I was safe, and his concern sounded genuine. Two policemen would watch the main door until daylight. I moved aside a curtain and confirmed they had already arrived.

'Have a rest, and I'll come around about noon with Mrs Ainsworth and you can make a full report.'

'I can meet earlier.'

'Noon will be fine—we're having a busy night. Well done Clifton, get some sleep.'

'Goodnight sir.'

'Who was that?' Sissy asked. 'Oh, don't tell me, I'd be better off not knowing.'

I poured myself a scotch and refilled Sissy's with what remained in the bottle.

'It was a very small measure,' she said, accepting the glass with just a flicker of a smile.

'I'm proud of you.'

'I'm not,' she said. 'It wasn't a straw target I shot.'

'You did what had to be done.'

'Says who? Who did it have to be done for?'

'Britain.'

She looked away. 'I knew you were too good to be true. You're what, a spy?'

'Of a sort.'

'Working for?'

'The government.'

'And who was that man Pat working for?'

'Another government—Russia I guess.'

'And Verity too?'

'I don't know about Verity, and for all our sakes don't mention her to anyone. Certainly not Julian or anyone else in the Party. Let them continue to think she's dead.'

'So.' She sat upright. 'You became a Blackshirt just to spy on the Party, and you don't believe in Mosley or fascism or anything we're trying to do. It's all been a masquerade. Like pretending to love me.'

'That part isn't a masquerade.' I shuffled next to her and took her hand. 'I do care for you, and we're in this together now. That was my...boss I suppose you'd call him. When I meet him tomorrow, I'll leave you out of the conversation entirely. If he wants to know who shot Pat Hanrahan, it was me. I've got form, as the bookies say.'

'Will you be charged with murder?'

A good question. It depended whether anyone was needed to take the fall for what had happened. 'I don't know how they will play it. The fact that two men in a black van simply turned up and took the body away, no questions asked, suggests there's a procedure for this kind of thing. Hanrahan will just vanish, much as Verity vanished. With luck, I'll make my report, mission accomplished, then walk away. I don't have a rank or pension to worry about.'

'We can go abroad,' she said, with a touch of whimsy.

'Yes, we should; at least until this all cools down.'

'Somewhere warm – how about the Caribbean? That would be nice. First thing, we'll go to my flat and collect everything I'll need.'

'I need to stay here to meet my boss first,' I said. 'To make sure that we're safe.' I leaned forward and she allowed me to kiss her, but only briefly.

'Oh darling,' she said. 'This is going to be very complicated. And I can still smell…well right now, what I need is a bath.'

'If there's hot water this time of night, you're welcome.'

* * *

The phone jangled. It was a respectable 9am, precisely 9am as if the caller had politely waited for that moment. Sissy sat upright. Even with her hair ruffled and drowned by one of my pyjama tops in burgundy silk, she was the picture of loveliness. She'd never wear black again if I had my way.

I took up the phone and Lilley greeted me. 'There's a gentleman here wishing to speak to you by name of Baxter. Shall he come up, sir?'

'No, ask him to wait.' I laid down the phone and answered the question in Sissy's eyes. 'It's Baxter, he's downstairs. Get your gun, get dressed quick as you can but stay here. Lock the door and don't answer it until I give the safe knock.' I tapped out the signal on the bedside table; dum dididumdum, dum dum. 'Safety on for the moment but be ready to shoot anyone that isn't me. Anyone who breaks down the door won't have your welfare at heart so don't give them a moment's chance.'

'Two shots to make sure?' She smiled weakly.

'That's m'girl.' I put on a dressing-gown and slippers, taking the safety off my own Walther and slipping it into a pocket where my right hand would remain. The key scraped in the lock behind me the moment I closed the flat door, and the bolt slid across with a thump.

I must have looked the perfect picture of the eccentric Englishman with my royal blue slippers tap-tapping down those stairs and a tartan dressing gown flapping at the knees of my pyjamas.

'Good morning sir,' said Lilley, without a flicker of surprise at my appearance.

Dominating the centre of the lobby, Baxter waited with hands in each pocket of his raincoat, shoulders hunched, looking up from under the brim of his Panama hat. I paused on the bottom step to increase the morale advantage conveyed by height.

'Mr Clifton,' said the visitor.

'Lilley, you have a number, don't you?'

'I do sir.'

'Go and telephone that number.'

'No need for that, Lilley,' said Baxter. 'I just need a few moments with Mr Clifton.' His voice was all smooth and officer-class, with none of the colonial roughness he'd made use of at the Wipers Club.

'Wait on that call, Lilley.' I took that last step onto the mosaic floor but kept one hand in my housecoat pocket, gripping the Walther.

'Let's me and you just step out into the street for a moment.' Baxter turned about and left by the main door to wait on the pavement by the iron railings.

I caught Lilley's eye, made sure he was paying attention, then followed to the open door. Halting on the threshold gave me the option to dart back inside if things turned rough. The policemen had gone.

'I know a man here who works for the Secret Intelligence Service.' Baxter said, glancing up a few floors. 'But of course, they don't officially exist. There's a couple of Foreign Office chaps, an ambassador's wife... Ex-army porters, well vetted at the highest level, with a service revolver tucked under the desk.'

'Do you know that I Squad call you Monkey Man?'

'I've been called worse. We need to talk.'

'You shot at me,' I said.

'No, I did not shoot at *you*.'

'Fair enough, if you want to be pedantic. But you did murder two policemen.'

'Perhaps you refer to that unfortunate incident in Kensington where no witness could identify the killer. No *living* witness.' A threat lurked there.

'And you had a couple of goes at having me beaten up, then held me up at gunpoint and pushed me into a cellar where your men waited to finish me off.'

'But they didn't.'

'You went away to fetch a van, and then what was the plan? Take us out to the marshes where we'd never be found?'

'Did I fetch a van?'

'You planted bombs.'

'No bombs went off. No innocents were killed.' His tone was flippant.

'As if that absolves you? Was it you who stopped Julian Thring from sending reinforcements last night?'

'It would have complicated things to have a troop of Blackshirts running around when the police arrived, and you didn't need help in the end. You managed to beat the communists *all on your own*.' Baxter deliberately raised his eyes to the first-floor window. The curtain moved as if someone was watching.

I tensed, hand sweaty on that gun, conscious that the safety was off and the muzzle was pointing at my own knee.

'Look, Clifton, the world is a messy, violent, confusing place. I've crossed mountains, jungles, deserts. I've been bitten by snakes, a wild cat, and a shark. Shot by a poisoned arrow and stabbed with a sword. I've been cheated, back-stabbed, double-crossed, and triple-crossed so I'm not demanding a neat ending to all this. Because there isn't one.'

'So what do you want? Why are you even here talking to me?'

'I'm one of the few people still alive who understands what happened last night, and one of even fewer who knows you were involved. And how *deeply* you were involved. Howard Thring thinks you're just a remarkably resourceful member of Department Z. We should keep it that way. And you, of course, are one of a very select few who has any idea of my involvement.'

'In Plan Red?'

He gave a dismissive chuckle. 'Plan Red, ha. We have a lot in common,

Clifton, and we have a mutual interest in discretion. I know you have a pistol in the pocket of that faintly ridiculous garment, and you believe you won't hesitate to use it. And you're probably trying to work out whether my pistol is in my right pocket or my left. I'm a deadly shot with either, as you might guess. I've killed more men than I can count, and I have no need to add more to my tally. I have powerful friends. And…' He indicated the building with a flick of his head, '…you have powerful friends. So, no matter who pulls the trigger first, neither of us will win.'

'Whose side are you on?'

'Oh, we're beyond picking sides. Good against evil, black against white. Did you know that British agents are helping Germany's Gestapo to round up communists? Difficult times make for odd bedfellows, and nineteen thirty-six will be all about survival. You never know, we might be on the same side one day.'

'I doubt it.'

'The world is a strange place and getting stranger. I'm going to go now and allow you to dress like a gentleman. Don't look for me, I'll be abroad for a while. Take care, Hugh Clifton.' His eyes went back to that first-floor window. 'And give my regards to the lady.'

Monkey Man Baxter waited for me to step back inside the door before he turned and walked away.

Chapter Fifty-Six

Inspector Renton gave a brief statement to the gentlemen of the press later that day. A daring operation by Special Branch had foiled the communist plot to smuggle Russian weapons into Britain and disrupt the election. My call to him had been brief and the newspapers made no mention of where the 'tip off' came from. Heroic detectives and red factions falling out over the haul all featured in stories of the mysterious gun battle fought out in Wapping.

The Security Service was not disposed to spoil a good story.

It would of course have been noble to walk into the office of *The Times* and spill the whole plot. Perhaps I would be believed, and perhaps they would even print my version of events as 'allegations from an anonymous source'. Certainly, powerful people would not take it well. I was a disgraced former officer with no public credibility and a string of violent deaths demanded suspects be identified or scapegoats to be framed, not to mention a street robbery and a string of other offences to be taken into consideration. Worst of all, Sissy could still be hauled up for killing Hanrahan. Talking to the press could only end badly.

As far as the British Union was concerned, no Blackshirts had been involved in the incident at the warehouse, and the few who knew otherwise kept silent. Lucy did not even create a file.

Documents proved that the conspiracy had been funded by a network of companies receiving money from Jewish-owned banks, exposing the left and undermining the government just one week before British voters filed into the polling booths. A choice between the discredited National

Government and a Labour movement in the pay of Moscow split traditional loyalties wide open. The British Union won twenty seats in Parliament, a few less than the Liberals. Elected the Honourable Member for Evesham, Sir Oswald Mosley once more had a platform to speak to the nation, and to speak for the nation.

* * *

Calhoun folded his copy of the *Daily Mail* and set it between us on the park bench. It was a bitterly cold November morning, and we were alone apart from a few pigeons hopeful for crumbs. He pretended to watch the scraggy birds as I vented my disillusionment, frustration, and anger. My energy to continue ranting eventually faded. '…six months of lurking and lying and making friends I was going to betray. You sent me on a fool's errand and like a chump, I carried it out.'

At last, he gave me attention. 'And you succeeded beyond anyone's wildest dreams.'

'Success? How is this success?' I jabbed at the *Daily Mail* headline.

'First, the dramatic way you won the trust of the BUF with your front-page heroics. More importantly, breaking up the communist gun-running plot. Quite a feat in only a few months—it's a pity we don't hand out medals.'

'Or plaques to grieving relatives of the fallen. When did you know Hanrahan had gone native?'

'Only when he failed the test. He claimed to be a lapsed communist when we recruited him, and he played his part so well it was hard to spot where the act ended. Those guns were just too good a carrot for him to ignore. In the end, you saved us an unpleasant job—I assume it was you who shot him?'

'I'm not going to boast about it.' I had learned to lie without lying. 'You haven't been straight with me about Verity Laytham—whoever she really was. Did I inherit her mission after she was killed?'

Calhoun did not respond. If he wasn't going to correct my assertion that she was dead, I was certainly not going to tell him what I'd learned.

'Have it your own way, but it would have helped me enormously if you'd been honest about her. After she found out about Union Jack, someone ordered her killed. Was that you or the Blackshirts, or the Russians. Who?'

No answers came, and I would not believe what I heard even then.

'Then after I made a horrific mess of my car clearing Hanrahan's body from the scene, your men took it straight back to the warehouse for the police to find.'

'Hanrahan was a well-known communist agitator, and we have lists of all his contacts. Arrests are being made. Renton is hauling in people he's wanted to see inside for a long time.'

'So even dead, Hanrahan is still working for you. How have you explained the Wipers Club?'

'Special Branch believe it was an amateur terrorist organization set up by a few ex-servicemen down on their luck, encouraged and organized from within the Communist Party.'

'Except it wasn't. The whole thing was a charade cooked up to make it look like there was a genuine communist menace. Mrs Symes was never in danger, the bombs never went off and those guns were never going to end up in anyone's hands other than the police. Are the arrests just piggy-backing on events, or was Plan Red yours all along?'

'I wish I could claim the credit,' Calhoun stated. 'But Thring's plan very nearly backfired. Hanrahan would have dispersed those weapons and his comrades would have waited for the order from Moscow to use them – perhaps during the next general strike or naval mutiny. We could have seen armed uprisings in twenty towns, and attacks on armouries to gain more weapons. Trust me, this is a success by any measure.'

A chill wind stirred a pile of leaves and rustled the bare treetops. The pigeons took fright and scattered.

'But once I gave you all the information on what Plan Red really was, why wrap it up in a way that helped the fascists get into Westminster? Sorry, the British Union who honest cross-my-heart aren't really fascists anymore. MI5 has helped Union Jack succeed. We had the opportunity to destroy Mosley, but instead, you've allowed Thring to stage-manage events to bring him out of the wilderness. What's next, put him in power?'

'You're going to make a good thriller writer. Or you would if we didn't still need you.'

'You don't need me, I'm done, I'm going to...' At that moment I had no idea. For the past nine months, I'd found a purpose, and even enjoyed the thrill of it all. Suddenly my future was as blank as the heap of paper beside my typewriter.

'We need you more than ever,' Calhoun said. 'Mosley's had his success, let him savour it. The important thing all along has been to defeat the communists, they are the real threat to British democracy, not your bumbling National Socialists. And looking into the future, the fact the British Union has enjoyed modest gains won't do you any harm. You're the shining black knight of Department Z now, and everyone believes you're a dedicated fascist, from Mosley downwards. I think we ought to keep it that way. Loyalty will be rewarded.'

'And disloyalty?'

'Pah! You're a smart man Clifton, even if you pretend otherwise, like that girl Sissy you chase after. Not so dumb as she acts.'

'Nobody must hurt Sissy.'

We could copy Verity, change our identities and hide, but even though we had enough money to live in exile, it would always be with targets on our backs and never with anyone to trust. One day we would simply vanish. Quite possibly it would be that very afternoon.

'Don't worry about Sissy, she'll be fine. I know you'll keep her safe by doing the right thing.' Calhoun was not even trying to be subtle.

'The right thing? I'm not sure what that is anymore.'

'Wear your black shirt with pride and strive to build a better Britain.'

'But you know I don't give a fig for Mosley and the fascist dream.'

'I do. And it will stay our little secret.'

Author's Note

I've taken historical events as they unfolded up to early 1935 as the starting point of this novel. At that time the horrors that fascism would bring to the world lay in the future and recruits to the British Union of Fascists would be unaware of the evils to come. The BUF was a chaotic fringe political party, with a disproportionately large number of officials and many different factions with varying levels of commitment. Barely keeping an eye on it, the British Security Service was thinly manned, poorly resourced and surprisingly amateur. It had little idea what the BUF was up to, and indeed had a relationship with the party that is unclear to this day. All this fluidity and ambiguity made possible the creation of characters who move amongst real-life BUF or Security Service officers, and it allowed me to play with historical facts.

We now know that Oswald Mosley failed to gain power and his party was in too much of a mess to even contest the 1935 elections, so the BUF is consigned to being little more than a footnote to British inter-war history. In this novel Plan Blue corrects the weaknesses in the fascist movement that historically condemned it to failure, and Plan White is based on reforms actually made to the BUF in 1936. With Plan Red creating the air of crisis Mosley had been waiting for, the possibility is created for history to take a different course. In *Blackshirt Conspiracy* Hugh and Sissy's involvement with Department Z will deepen as the threat of a fascist-dominated Britain increases.

In writing this book my thanks go first to Dea Parkin who encouraged me to venture into historical thrillers and for her comments and those of her colleagues at Fiction Feedback on the early drafts. Many friends in the Crime Writers' Association continue to be supportive of my move into the genre. I must also thank the Dames of Detection, in particular Verena Main Rose and Shawn Reilly Simmons, for bringing this book to completion.

About the Author

Jason Monaghan trained as an archaeologist, but his career has taken unexpected twists including spells working on Roman pottery, on shipwrecks, in museums, in offshore banking, and becoming an anti-money laundering specialist. All this has provided plenty of inspiration for writing historical thrillers and mysteries set in the world of archaeology. Now a full-time writer he has returned to live in his native Yorkshire but travels as often and as far as he can.

Social Media Handles:
Website, Blog and Newsletter: www.monaghanfoss.com
Facebook: Jason Monaghan Author
Twitter: @Jasonthriller
Pinterest: Jason Monaghan
Youtube: Jason Monaghan (Studio Monaghan)
Instagram: docmonaghan

If you enjoyed this book please post a review or rating on Amazon, Goodreads, or follow Jason Monaghan on Bookbub.

Also by Jason Monaghan

Jeffrey Flint Archaeology Mystery Series

Darkness Rises

Byron's Shadow

Shadesmoor

Lady in the Lake

Blood and Sandals

Historical Novel

Glint of Light on Broken Glass

Historical Short Stories

Islands That Never Were